Selim Özdoğan was born in Germany in 1971 and has been publishing books since 1995. Apart from writing he likes being on stage, practicing yoga and drinking coffee, and is constantly trying to find ways to express the life within him.

Ayça Türkoğlu is a literary translator from German and Turkish. Her work has been shortlisted for the Helen & Kurt Wolff Translator's Prize. She lives in North London.

Katy Derbyshire translates contemporary German writers including Olga Grjasnowa, Clemens Meyer and Heike Geissler. She teaches literary translation and also heads the V&Q Books imprint.

A Light Still Burns

Selim Ozdoğan

Translated by Ayça Türkoğlu and Katy Derbyshire

 The translation of this work was supported by a grant from the Goethe-Institut.

V&Q Books, Berlin 2023
An imprint of Verlag Voland & Quist GmbH
First published in the German language as *Wo noch Licht brennt*
by Selim Ozdoğan
© Selim Ozdoğan and Haymon Verlag Ges.m.b.H., 2017

Translation © Ayça Türkoğlu and Katy Derbyshire
Editing: Isabel Adey
Copy editing: Angela Hirons
Cover photo: Unsplash
Cover design: pingundpong
Typesetting: Fred Uhde
Printing and binding: PBtisk, Příbram, Czech Republic

ISBN: 978-3-86391-366-3

www.vq-books.eu

I

Light glimmers under the door. Gül stops and listens. In the night's silence, she thinks she can hear someone smoking, and she opens the door without pausing to knock. Ceyda is sitting at the table, and her cigarette snaps in the ashtray as she hurries to stub it out. Gül looks at the clock on the wall. Half three.

'What are you doing up?'

'I couldn't sleep.'

'Sleeplessness is worse than longing.'

'Really?'

'Longing disappears when you sleep, or at least it subsides. But when you can't sleep, everything chases after you and there's nowhere to catch your breath. When you don't sleep at night, your worries grow so big that there's no space for them in the day.'

Gül has been here for a week now. She doesn't need to ask how her daughter is doing; she's had enough time to see for herself.

'Sorry for waking you up. I was trying to be quiet,' Ceyda says.

'I got up to go to the toilet and saw the light on.'

'Go back to bed. No point in you losing sleep too.'

Gül shakes her head and sits down. She hopes it makes a difference. She's been sleeping badly too, ever since she came back to Germany, but she hasn't said anything to her daughter. If sleep could be shared, she'd give all of hers to Ceyda.

When Gül came to this country for the first time, over twenty years ago, she only knew a couple of words of German; she felt helpless, lost in another world. The people, the language, the food, the rhythm of daily life were all alien to her. She had come from a small Turkish town and kept getting lost on the way to work. When Fuat was on nights, she used to sit in their tiny kitchen, her heart bleeding for the two little daughters she'd left behind in Turkey.

Now, having returned to Germany after almost eight years in Turkey, she has a much better idea of what to expect. She doesn't have to bear that same pain of separation, and yet she sleeps worse than she did back then – much worse. She reaches for the pack of cigarettes and holds it out to Ceyda.

'I can't.'

'You're a grown woman with two children; you can smoke in front of your mum if you want to. Look, I'll have one myself. Let's smoke one together and then get to bed.'

Ceyda gives her mother a light first, then sees to her own.

'Do you remember the time,' says Gül, 'when your dad found your cigarettes and put them on the table without saying a thing?'

'Of course I do. He didn't say a single word. Not even later. I went hot all over. I had no idea what to do; I didn't know if all hell was about to break loose. I was so frightened that I didn't smoke for three weeks.'

Fuat still likes telling the story now, to show how easy parenting is. 'You just need to know when to keep your mouth shut,' he says. Fuat, who likes to talk tough. Fuat, who loves to boast. The same man who, for months now, has failed to find a flat big enough for the two of them in Bremen. Fuat, who now lives in a flat that's even smaller than the one-bedroom flat Gül found herself in when she first arrived in Germany. Fuat, who for years has been putting her off every time she's asked him when he'll be joining her in Turkey, and who doesn't seem pleased that Ceyda has helped her mum come back to Germany now. Gül was a stranger the first time she moved to Germany, but she didn't feel unwanted, and she didn't sleep on a sofa bed in the living room; she slept in the same bed as her husband.

Gül hears a familiar scuttling sound coming from the hallway. It's the sound little Timur makes when he shuffles out of the bedroom in his baby sleeping bag at night. Ceyda gets up, and

Gül hopes her daughter will manage another couple of hours' sleep if she takes her son to bed with her.

Gül sits at the kitchen table and writes letters, like she did in her first days in Germany. Back then they didn't have a telephone, and when they got one later on, her father still didn't have one in Turkey. When the blacksmith finally got a telephone of his own, you had to register a long-distance call at the post office and wait for hours, which often led to groggy phone calls in the middle of the night.

Now she can just call him; she has the numbers for her father, her three sisters, her brother. It costs a fortune, but she could pick any one of the numbers and, with a few words, she'd be connected; she could bask in the sound of their voices, ease that sense of longing for a few moments, hear the melody that plays when they're together.

Ceren is the only one who doesn't have a number she can call. Ceren, who wasn't yet three when Gül left her with her mother-in-law; the same little girl who pulled her hair and scratched her face at the foot of the stairs when they said goodbye, as if she knew she wasn't going to see her mother for the next eighteen months. She's living in Erzurum now because her husband has to complete his first two-year teaching post in a province in the East.

Ceren had moved back to Turkey with her mother back then, and she'd struggled with her new surroundings for the first year. She's happy with Mecnun now though; at least one of the girls has found a good man, thanks be to God.

Gül is sitting at the kitchen table, but she doesn't know what to write. Worries, all that spring to mind are worries. The rift between her and Fuat, Ceyda's problems with her husband Adem, his indifference towards her. Gül's own fears for the future, her sorrow at having left Turkey again.

She wanted to return to Germany because she'd felt lost in her hometown when Ceren moved away and Fuat still hadn't come back to protect her from other men and their lewd remarks. She wanted to return to Germany so that she could live with Fuat and be there for Ceyda, but now she misses her father, misses her sister Sibel, misses the summer house, misses the distance from Germany. Ceren might feel bad about her own happiness if Gül were to write all this to her.

The pen in her hand has worries; the paper in front of her has worries; the envelope has worries; the stamps have worries. Nothing has that easiness, or so it seems to Gül; how is she supposed to write something for Ceren to carry with her, how is she supposed to find the words to forge a connection? Half an hour passes and she's barely finished the first paragraph, so she gives up, goes into the living room and turns on the television. On the German channel – they still can't get Turkish stations – there's an interview with a woman whose accent Gül recognises instantly. Tanja used to speak just like her. Tanja, the only German who lived on Factory Lane back then, who took on some of her neighbours' customs and was happy among all the foreigners. The old lady everyone knew as Auntie Tanja died shortly before Gül moved back to Turkey. Gül thinks about Factory Lane, where they lived for years before the wool factory closed and she and Fuat lost their jobs. That was before Fuat found a position at Mercedes in Bremen and Gül decided to move to Turkey, with Fuat planning to follow her a few years later. Ceyda was already married at the time and stayed in Germany; Ceren was still at school and moved back to Turkey with her mum.

They had troubles, even on Factory Lane, but looking back, Gül thinks, it seems they were happy there. When the children were too young to translate for her, she would often go to Auntie Tanja whenever she received official letters she didn't understand, and Tanja would patiently try to explain what the writing said. Tanja spoke differently to the other Germans, but Gül never wondered why that might be. Now she recognises the accent on TV and listens to this woman, who says she's glad to finally be allowed to travel, glad that those at the top are being made to pay for not taking their own people seriously.

Gül never asked Tanja where she came from. All she knew was that her marriage had been childless, and her husband had died before she moved into Factory Lane. She was amazed by how few Germans there were at Auntie Tanja's funeral; she thought it was because family was less important to the Germans, but now she thinks she understands better. All Tanja's loved ones had been left behind in the East.

Death is God's will; if only there were no separation. Gül murmurs these lines of Orhan Veli to herself. Separation finds people. It found her father, the blacksmith, when he was a young boy and his father died. Later, it found him again when it took his wife Fatma from him. It found Gül when she was almost six and her mother died.

But separation finds people without death, too. It found Gül when her husband was in the army, it found her two daughters when she moved to Germany without them, and it found all of Gül's siblings, who only see one another once or twice a year. Separation has followed Gül almost all her life. But it doesn't just follow those who lose their parents, and those who move away, it follows others too. It settled over all of Germany when the country was divided.

We are connected, Gül thinks. *The Lord's servants are all connected by separation, which follows us like a faithful friend. It's just the same for those who move away as for those who stay at home. And those who don't know it have drawn the lot of loneliness and are not to be envied either. Oh Lord, I shoulder the weight of separation a thousand times, and I thank you for my two healthy daughters, who can stand on their own two feet. Thank you for my hands, which can write letters, and for my eyes, which can still see.*

She turns off the television and goes back into the kitchen. She lights a cigarette and picks up the pen.

Her bookish son-in-law will like the quote too. 'Death is God's will; if only there were no separation,' the poem says. *But separation is life*, she writes. If you're no longer separated from anyone, you're dead.

Another poem springs to mind: a poem about wishing for an end to all the fighting, the hunger, the weariness, the needs of the body, the pain; a poem in which the person is basically wishing for death. *It's only separation*, she writes, *and it doesn't last forever. God loves his creations, and even if he has them endure separation, only after death does it last forever.*

Gül writes a letter full of melancholy and heavy thoughts, but not sorrows; she writes a letter in which there is a place for love amid the melancholy, a letter to warm a heart in springtime after a harsh Erzurum winter.

Fuat was already limping when he picked Gül up from the airport; he'd bumped his knee, he said. That was almost three weeks ago now. Three weeks in which Gül has been staying with Ceyda in a Hamburg suburb and only seeing her husband on the weekends because he lives and works in Bremen. Three weeks in which Fuat's limp has got worse and worse. Now, he calls to tell his wife he's in hospital and they're keeping him in. He's got an abscess on his knee that has needed surgery.

'He's never taken care of you, but still you want to rush straight over the moment he calls?'

'He's my husband.'

Ceyda looks at her mother. *Her husband.* The man Ceyda calls Dad, the man she and her mother often had to carry in from the car at night so that the next morning, their neighbours on Factory Lane wouldn't see that he'd been too drunk to make it inside.

'Fine,' she says. 'If you want to, we'll go. We'll take the car and leave the kids with Adem's mum.'

It's the first time Gül has seen Ceyda drive, and she's pleased for her daughter. She wanted her children to get a better education than she did, wanted them to be independent. She always admired her friend Saniye, who did a lot of the driving when their two families made the long trip to Turkey together. To Gül, driving seems like freedom, but even in the passenger's seat she's scared; she can't imagine ever having the courage to drive herself.

The first half hour passes in silence. Ceyda has never been much of a talker, and most of the time Gül doesn't know what's going on in her daughter's head. She doesn't know why she decided to train as a hairdresser after school, why she married Adem, or whether she still resents her mother for leaving her behind in Turkey as a child.

It's unusual for Gül to be quiet for so long, but she enjoys the first part of the trip. She enjoys it because the car is a private space, a space with only the two of them in it – no phone to ring, no one there to open the door unexpectedly, no children clamouring for attention. In the car with her daughter, Gül feels less troubled than she does in the kitchen at night.

'I didn't mean to be a burden. Maybe I can stay in the flat in Bremen while your dad's in the hospital.'

'You're not a burden, Mum. The kids are happy, and I haven't cooked a meal since you've been here, thanks be to your hands. And you know what Dad's like: he puts things off, but he'll find a nice flat for you both, maybe even from his hospital bed. He just needs a bit of a nudge. I'll take care of that. You probably won't be staying with us for much longer anyway, so I want us to enjoy the time we've got together.'

'Do you think Adem minds?'

Ceyda hesitates; lights a cigarette. In front of her mother. Gives a tortured smile.

'Honestly? To be honest, I don't know. I'd tell you if it annoyed him, I'd tell you and I'd be glad I could. I'd be glad of any sign of emotion. Sometimes he gets annoyed with the kids, but other than that he's the most apathetic person you can imagine. You've seen him, haven't you? All these years we've been married, and he's still a mystery to me. I didn't want a man like Dad; I didn't want a man who drinks, and now I've got one like the men Dad used to complain about, a man who lives like a plant. He doesn't hit me, he doesn't swear, doesn't gamble, doesn't overeat; he doesn't take pleasure in anything, doesn't help with the housework, doesn't care how I am, and he can't remember a thing I tell him. It wouldn't bother him if I upped and left. It's enough to drive me mad. Every time he comes home and the curtains are closed, he asks: *Why did you close the curtains? It's the middle of the day*. Every single time. And once I've answered, he opens them and says to me: *What am I supposed to do in the dark?* But he never loses his temper. Never.'

Ceyda looks at her mother. 'I don't think you being here bothers him. I think it bothers him more when the batteries run out in the remote control.'

What is Gül supposed to say? *I'm your mother, you can count on me. Do what you think is right – you're a new generation, you'll spend your whole life here in Germany, I'll stand by you and support every choice you make.* But would she really stand by her daughter? Wouldn't she voice her motherly concerns? Gül only has a sofa to sleep on; she doesn't earn a penny, and she couldn't get her husband to find a flat big enough for the two of them in time. But she found her place in Germany once before, and she vows she'll find it this time too. She'll stand upright so Ceyda has someone to lean on. She will. Eventually.

When Ceyda has found out which ward her father is on, they take the lift from reception to the fourth floor. As the two of them are leaving the lift, Gül notices a woman closing the door to a room and walking towards them. It's not until the woman has gone past and they're approaching Fuat's door that Gül realises the woman has just left his room.

Fuat is lying on his bed with the TV on and has a slight grin on his face as he sits up. He's been using a sunbed in winter for a few years, and now he looks a picture of health against the white hospital sheets. The young man in the next bed, a redhead, is reading a tabloid newspaper. Gül knows the Germans don't have words for this situation. They don't just walk into a hospital room and say *get well soon*. Ceren had to stay in hospital for a few days as a child after an accident, and that was where she met her friend Gesine; Gül spent a lot of time on the ward back then.

'May it pass,' she says.

'Thank you, thank you.'

'What exactly happened?'

'I just scraped my knee on the corner of my locker at work, I told you, remember? I thought it'd get better on its own, but it kept getting worse, and yesterday on my shift I couldn't put any weight on it, let alone work. They had to open up my knee to get all the pus out. I could have ended up with blood poisoning, the doctor said. It beggars belief, and of course it had to happen right when production's at full stretch. The amount of overtime I'm missing out on just because I have to stay in here.'

'How long are they keeping you in? Did they tell you anything?'

'A week. A week; it's almost like waiting for death.'

'Now that doesn't sound like you,' says Ceyda. 'You're hardly the type to lie around for a week, are you Dad? I bet you get all sorts of things done while you're here.'

'My daughter knows me well,' says Fuat, flattered.

There are all sorts of things you can say about him, but he's not lazy, and it's important to him to be seen as the crafty kind.

'I bet you'll even manage to find a flat for you and Mum from in here. It wouldn't surprise me.'

'We'll see, we'll see. It's not easy to find a cheap flat in this town. And I can't exactly go and look at anywhere in this state, can I? I can hardly make it to the smoking room with my leg in this state.'

'Do you want to give me the keys for your flat? Then Ceyda won't have to keep driving me back and forth.'

'What would you do all on your own in the flat? You don't know anyone in Bremen. Will you just sit in that tiny room twiddling your thumbs the whole time? Or worse still: spend all day here in the hospital? This is no place for healthy people. I'll be fine in here, just fine. Wouldn't you be better off with your daughter? First you want to come to Germany, then you can't think of anything better to do than keep going back and forth between a flat and a hospital? Get yourself a job if you've got that much time on your hands.'

Gül doesn't know why Fuat is so worked up about it. Her old friend Saniye lives in Bremen, though they haven't seen each other since Gül moved back to Turkey; they've only written letters and talked on the phone three or four times. She was going to mention Saniye, but after Fuat's outburst, she doesn't know whether the feeling in her stomach will want out in the form of tears, so she holds her tongue instead.

Get yourself a job. All the times she heard that same thing when she lived in Germany before. It wasn't her fault they closed the wool factory down, and it wasn't her fault the employment market was so tough. They were lucky enough that Fuat managed to find a new job. Fuat kept complaining about having to feed three mouths on one wage; he'd never be able to secure a future for them in Turkey. Money, money was what they needed to secure a future for themselves. The repatriation money was 10,500 marks for Gül and 1500 marks for Ceren. Who could have known, back then, that Fuat would keep putting off his own return again and again, or that Ceren would marry and move to Erzurum? Who could have known that Ceyda would move heaven and earth to help her mother get back to Germany? And who can know, now, that Ceren will live in Germany again one day, too?

Get yourself a job. It's like when he used to say he preferred slim women. It hurts. It dampens the light inside her. One time she retorted that she preferred men with hair on their heads, and he hasn't said a word about her figure since. *Get yourself a job.* There's nothing she can say in response. *Get yourself a job* – as if it were as easy as that.

'She's been here less than a month; you haven't even got a flat together yet. We'll find something, don't you worry,' says Ceyda.

Gül is surprised by her daughter's sharp tone. She's no longer the girl who could hardly tell left from right when there was a pack of cigarettes on the table.

'I can't wait to see how that turns out,' Fuat answers. 'A job doesn't mean sitting by a nice warm stove and getting 400 marks a month in the bank, not having to pay rent, and wasting the whole day on gossip and women's nonsense.'

'We came here to visit you and wish you a speedy recovery,' Ceyda says.

'Well, you've done that now. Thanks be to your feet.'

Gül sees Ceyda's hands trembling when she presses the button in the lift. She knows how much self-control it takes her daughter not to burst into tears when she closes the car door behind her.

'Don't let it get to you. You know what he's like,' Gül says, wondering what on earth she's doing in Germany.

Gül is amazed by how much Saniye has aged over the past eight years; there are lines around her eyes, her red hair has lost its lustre. She's still as slim as when Gül first met her, though, and despite the shadows under her eyes she doesn't look exhausted – she's radiant as she hugs Gül.

'What luck,' she says. 'Life is bringing us back together. I didn't think we'd ever see each other again. Though the Lord has shown me often enough in my life that we always meet the ones we love, again and again.'

Saniye's feelings are like water, they always find a way; but they never get dammed up. Gül is amazed all over again, every time, by how happy this petite woman can be and how much space grief takes up inside her.

Gül's heart grows lighter when she sees her friend. It's as if they last saw each other yesterday and Saniye has aged overnight. Their connection is there, immediately. Gül remembers it wasn't like that with her sisters when she moved back to Turkey. Perhaps because she was almost a child when she married Fuat and moved out of the house, and because she was a young woman when she met Saniye.

Saniye will be nearby. Now that her father is so far away, now that she no longer has her sister Sibel nearby and can't sit snuggled up by the stove with Ceren, Saniye will be the one with whom she can share everything.

Gül's second visit to Fuat was calmer, although she was much more upset. But she was more careful, too, because she wanted to get out of the hospital without hearing hurtful words. And because, after the visit with Ceyda, she was looking forward to going to see Saniye, who lives on a high-rise estate and is working at a bakery these days. She's had so many different jobs over the years that Gül can barely remember them all. Saniye doesn't mind stopping somewhere and starting all over again somewhere else. She gets used to new things quickly.

When Gül first came to Germany, she worked in a chicken slaughterhouse, sewed bras in a factory, and worked in an industrial bakery, albeit only briefly and without a permit. Her first proper job was at the wool factory, where she stayed until she was let go.

In Saniye's living room, there is a large bookcase full of Turkish books and another unit, almost as big, full of records and CDs. It's the first time Gül has seen a CD. The television is enormous. Fuat would be overjoyed to have such a huge TV, but it would hardly fit into his flat, and even if the flat were bigger, he probably wouldn't buy it. There are huge, expensive-looking speakers, and on the wall is a picture filled with everyday objects in strange, flowing shapes. But there's a blue eye hanging over the door, to keep away the evil eye, as well as a samovar, tulip-shaped glasses, little crocheted coverlets – all familiar sights to Gül.

Saniye's husband, Yılmaz, didn't come to Germany for work; he came after being kicked out of university for his political activities. *That explains all the books*, Gül thinks, but she doesn't know why anyone who reads so much would need such a big TV.

Gül stirs two sugars into her tea and is tempted to explain her anguish, but then thinks better of it. Ceyda has already gone home, and it's just her and Saniye now, but why drape a blanket of grief over their happy reunion? Why think back to those sad melodies? The two women light their cigarettes. That late afternoon, in a living room full of books and records and CDs, it all blends together: the sweet tea, the words, the stories from the past, the early days they shared in Germany, Saniye's silvery laugh, Gül's contented sighs – it all creates a bubble, lifting them both out of their everyday lives. They simply share what's moved them in recent years, who's had children, who's died, who's out of a job, and who fate has treated with particular kindness or cruelty.

Gül has already drunk six whole glasses of tea by the time she hears the key in the door. The sound pulls her back; there's still a world outside, and from it, Yılmaz appears. Once he's said a hearty welcome to Gül, he glances at his wife with a question in his eyes. She shakes her head gently. The smile disappears from his lips, and Gül feels out of place.

'We've run out of butter,' says Saniye. 'Could you pop back out to the supermarket for some?'

Yılmaz nods. Their daughter, Sevgi, arrives home while he's out.

'You remember who this is, don't you?' says Saniye.

'How could I ever forget Auntie Gül?' says the girl. 'I always loved visiting you on Factory Lane, even though Ceyda and Ceren were so much older than me.'

Gül has tears in her eyes. Sevgi must have been about five when they last saw each other. Without hesitation, the girl walks up to Gül, hugs her, gives her a kiss and lays her head on Gül's shoulder.

'That scent,' she says. 'You don't smell the same any more.'

'Sevgi—' says Saniye with a note of caution in her voice as they hear the key in the door again.

The smell will come back, Gül thinks, *I'll make a home for myself again, one where everyone will feel good again, one we'll remember, just like Factory Lane.* If only our good dreams could come true and the bad ones be forgotten.

Yılmaz comes back in, and his eyes are shining; he smiles.

'That scent lives with you now,' says Gül.

Saniye looks at Gül as if her comment were innuendo rather than a compliment, though Gül has no idea what she might mean.

Gül sleeps on another sofa that night, she sleeps as if sleep were the stuff of courage and not something you wake from to find your daughter smoking in the kitchen.

Gül is afraid of getting lost, she's afraid of finding herself in a situation she doesn't have the German for, she's afraid of words that wound, she's afraid of landing herself in unfamiliar situations – but she's not afraid of work. No matter how high the mountain in front of her, she won't hesitate to start climbing. Her father used to hammer away in the blazing heat of the fire. Gül remembers the sound of his sweat dripping onto hot iron. He never complained about his work, but he often griped about his itchy calves. Gül is not afraid of work; she and Fuat are alike in this regard. That said, Fuat is a keen skiver – not because he's lazy, but because he feels smart when he does less than he's supposed to without suffering any consequences.

Gül isn't afraid of work, and as far as she knows, her daughter is the same. So when Ceyda calls in sick to the salon one morning, Gül is surprised. Ceyda notices the astonishment on her mother's face and says: 'They know I have to call in sick now and then.'

'Sick? You look perfectly healthy to me.'

'I'm already getting little spots in the corners of my eyes, like the colours are running and turning spiky. And my fingers are numb. It won't be long before the headache comes on.'

Gül still can't believe it. Her daughter, calling in sick because of a headache? She looks more than able to turn up for work. Ceyda draws the curtains, and Gül thinks back, trying to remember if her daughter ever complained of headaches when she still lived at home.

'So how long have you been getting these headaches?'

'They started about a year after Duygu was born.'

'What did the doctor say about it?'

'They're migraines, there's not much you can do.'

'Why didn't you tell me about it when they started?'

'Oh, Mum, what difference would it have made?'

Ceyda has turned pale in the past few minutes, even in the half-light of the drawn curtains it was clear to see. Now she gets up and goes to the toilet, where she throws up. Gül still doesn't know what's in store for Ceyda today. Soon after she's been sick, Ceyda slumps onto the sofa and can't bring herself to do much more than lie there. She asks her mother to tread quietly, though the carpet is thick and swallows every sound. Ceyda turns down the offer of aspirin, saying they don't do any good; she won't take a coffee with lemon juice or a cold compress either.

Gül watches helplessly as her daughter writhes about on the sofa – only slowly, because moving hurts. She hears Ceyda whimpering and can see the agony in her face. If she stares at her for long enough, she gets an idea of how a migraine must feel: a hammering pain from inside, pressing against one side of your skull and one side of your eye, your stomach feeling like it wants to travel all the way up to your mouth, every move your body makes echoing with pain that resounds long afterwards. Gül wishes she could take Ceyda in her arms and comfort her, caress and support her, but Ceyda can't bear the slightest touch. She doesn't even want to hear her mother's voice.

'Mum, please don't say anything else. There's nothing anyone can do. Just be quiet, and with a little luck I'll be back on my feet by the time the kids get home.'

As usual, the children are with their cousins at their other grandmother's house. Their grandfather died before he got the chance to meet a single one of them, and his wife, now a widow, runs a strict but loving regime for the little hooligans, as she calls them. 'I raised seven children,' she says, 'I'm more than a match for these four.' But in two years' time, she'll feel too old for it all and will want her peace.

Gül goes into the kitchen to cook; she has to distract herself somehow.

'Mum,' Ceyda cries, and her voice sounds desperate, weak, broken. A little like it sounded all those summers ago, when she saw her mother again after eighteen months apart. *Mum*, those three letters form a sound that holds such pain, blame, despair, powerlessness and longing all at once.

Gül ventures into the living room as quietly as she can.

'Mum, please don't cook. I can't abide the smell.'

A few hours later, Adem arrives home from his early shift at the glass factory.

'Why have you closed the curtains?' he asks. 'It's the middle of the day.'

'I've got a migraine, Adem.'

'Don't you want to go to bed? I'd like to watch the telly.'

Gül struggles to keep a lid on her anger.

'I'm grateful, to be honest,' Ceyda says later. 'At one time he would've just picked up the remote and turned on the TV. *It's not like there's anything I can do to help*, he'd say, and as far as he was concerned, that was that.'

With those dark eyes, those bushy eyebrows and that head of hers – long despite her chubby cheeks – baby Fatma resembles her father in every way. Gül sits in Ceyda's kitchen with the photo of her granddaughter and can feel the force that connects her to the child, named after Gül's beloved mother. She only knows Ceren's daughter from this photo taken three months ago. Fatma is seven months old now and much bigger than in the picture; she's starting to crawl. Mecnun had to go into town to get the film developed, but the streets were snowed under for weeks. The temperature dropped to minus thirty over the winter, Ceren writes; she can count on one hand how many times she left the house in the first few months after Fatma was born. What would she do outside anyway? Mecnun didn't work for three weeks because there wasn't enough wood to heat the classroom.

So much time has passed since Gül's childhood. There's a telephone in every post office, though not in every house yet; people have their own cameras, and technology is making progress in every area of their lives. Gül wonders if all those things – telephones, televisions, cameras – came about out of longing: were they all invented because one person wanted to feel closer to another? Is longing the force behind it all? So much has changed since her childhood, but schools in Turkey still close for want of heating fuel. She used to shiver at school, Ceren shivered, and perhaps Fatma will shiver too one day. There is no way Gül could know that Fatma will go to school in the south of the country, where the winters are milder.

It's springtime now, Ceren is doing well, the school holidays are coming up for Mecnun, and in the summer they'll be heading to Gül's hometown, where they'll all be reunited for a while. Gül's sisters and brother will come with their children, Ceyda will be there, and the blacksmith will sit smiling again, his eyes welling with joy. Gül remembers how much she always used to enjoy the summers, how much life there was in those six weeks of holidays, how she blossomed, how those summers filled her up, how long they nourished her.

When Ceren told her she was pregnant, Gül was happy. Only a mother knows how a mother feels, she said. A person who doesn't have children can't understand what it's like to have them. People who've read and heard about it, studied and understood it, they don't know what it's like; only those who've lived it can know. Gül was happy. *I've set these girls on their paths, and now they're standing on their own two feet, having children of their own. I could die in peace, even though I'm only forty*, she thought. And yet she knew then that Ceyda was having problems in her marriage, and she wanted to make sure she was still around for her daughters.

Gül would like a photo of herself and her brother and sisters standing under the big mulberry tree in the garden as children. A photo that was never taken. A photo like a door to another world, which will always look beautiful because it's in the past, and because you can never be driven out of your own memories. A photo that reminds you that you felt whole, safe and sound. A note in a melody you heard every day. The melody they're all a part of, no matter where they are right now; a tune sung over and over, on and on, the melody to which every new child in the family adds a new note.

Photos can quench the longing of our eyes, a telephone can quench the longing of our ears, but it's letters that quench the longings of the heart. Reading the words over and over again, we come closer to something, as the words come from one heart, traveling through hands onto paper, and stream into our hearts through our eyes. They flow through hands and arms, which are extensions of the heart because the heart is nourished by touch, by fingers stroking cheeks, by hands transferring warmth, by arms laid around others, by shoulders leaning on other shoulders.

Letters quench the longing of the heart, but only for a while; longing can only be stopped if the skin's thirst is quenched too.

Fuat has had a fall and has broken his heel.

'You'd think everything would be done properly in a country like this,' he complains. 'I'd have taken the bleeding lift instead of the stairs with my bad knee, but one of them was out of order, the other one was reserved for porters, and I could have had a smoke in the time I spent waiting for the third one. It beggars belief – this is a hospital, but they practically force you to take the stairs. That Marlboro cost me a lot, I can tell you – now I can't even move without a wheelchair. All the overtime I'm missing out on, the muck they call food here, the life you're expected to live here, like you're not even an animal, just a weed by the side of the road. Smoking has its price – those non-smokers tell you how much a pack costs and how that adds up over the years – but do they want me to do my sums right here? What's the point in me giving up smoking now? The overtime's gone and I'm still stuck here.'

'How long?'

'At least another week, the doctor says, but I still won't be able to walk after that.'

'You need clean clothes,' Gül says.

'No… it's just a week… What I've got here's still clean. What do you think I get up to here? And I don't spill my food; I'm not an old man.'

'It's not right,' says Gül. 'Don't worry, we'll go and pick up a few clean things for you.' Gül doesn't have any ulterior motive when she says this. Or at least, that's what she thinks afterwards, that there was no motive behind it. But was there a force driving her that was stronger than her mind?

The flat's not as far from the hospital as she thought; it's only a walk away really. Gül unlocks the door, walks into Fuat's little bachelor flat and sees a pack of Lord cigarettes on the kitchen worktop.

The heat seems to be coming from two directions. As if someone were pouring boiling water over her, and at the same time, molten lava were shooting out of the roots of her hair.

'I'll just have a drink of water – you have a look in the wardrobe for some clothes,' she says to Ceyda, who's come in behind her.

She's amazed you can't hear the heat in her voice. She pockets the cigarettes; the ashtray next to them has been emptied. Once she's taken a glass out of the cupboard she bends down, looks in the bin under the sink, and finds what she suspected. She gets even hotter. It's only when she straightens up that she spots the postcard leaning against the microwave. *Welcome*, it says, under a picture of a house that looks like it was drawn for children. As she runs the tap, she turns over the card, reads the first two words. Her mouth is dry; she'd like to gulp down the glass of water, but she feels like her throat has closed up. With an effort, she forces two mouthfuls down.

'What's the matter?' Ceyda asks.

'I don't know, I just got really hot,' Gül says. 'Maybe it's the menopause already.'

'Do you want to have a sit down?'

'No, no, I'm alright.'

Her brain feels numb, like it's been rubbed with ice. Her ears don't seem to be hearing properly and the picture around her is starting to go blurry, but there are scraps in her mind's eye, coming together. As if she'd known it all along but had run away from that knowledge. As though she'd only ever looked into the light so as not to see anything around it. Now she'll have to get used to the dark.

But perhaps she wasn't running away at all; perhaps she was heading straight towards it, her eyes shut tight.

We all need someone to talk to. When you don't want to tell anyone how you feel, that's when you need someone to talk to most of all.

She holds it in on the drive back to the hospital, when she sees Fuat, on the drive home, over dinner, while she loads the dishwasher and watches TV. She holds it all in until she's lying on the couch with the light off. How can she let go when all that will come is tears? She can't get up, go into the kitchen and smoke, smoke all night long until her heart can no longer feel through all the fumes in her lungs. She can't smoke until everything's fogged up. She can't even keep the light off and just take solace in the dark – what would she say if the door opened and Ceyda wanted to know what she was doing?

She lies awake, thinking the same thoughts over and over again. *Why would he do this?* She asked him once – when he was plastered after they got home from Ceren's wedding, she said: 'We married young, we weren't much more than children. Lots of things can happen in this world. Is there something you want to tell me?' She gathered up her courage and asked him plainly. And he said no.

Is this why he kept putting off joining her in Turkey? How could he do something like this to her? Do his friends know? Who knows about it? What did she do to deserve it? Didn't she do everything to make a home for him? And with a *German*! The woman who came out of his hospital room looked like a German. What's he doing with a German woman? Isn't it enough, all the separation and longing this country has brought her? Does it have to take her husband away from her as well? Has Ceyda guessed? Why doesn't he make more of an effort to hide it? Does he think she's stupid? How does he imagine things are going to go from here? How could he betray her like this? How could he abuse her trust like this? Why does it hurt so much? Why did she shut her eyes to it for so long?

She keeps seeing the woman in the hospital corridor, and she goes over the same thoughts and questions again and again, turning round and round in circles. But that's not all. The thoughts stay the same, but the feelings change as the night wears on. The questions change colour. At first there's only black, a liquid black that threatens to drown her, but soon the black is joined by violet. Violet like the rings under Gül's mother's eyes before she died. The violet gradually turns to red, and new thoughts appear. *It was important for me to come here.* This is where she belongs. *What is he thinking? Why should that numbskull get to be so free? Where's his honour, his decency?* As morning comes, her thoughts are tinged red; as morning comes, she feels like getting up, going to the hospital and giving that man a piece of her mind. As morning comes, the fire of rage burns so brightly inside her that she feels she could walk all the way to Bremen, never fearing she might lose her way. If only she knew how to get there. As morning comes, she gets up and reads the postcard again in the first light of the day. *Sweetie pie*, it says, *welcome home. I'm so glad you're back on your feet. Karen – Kiss, kiss, kiss.*

Gül feels like ripping the card into a thousand pieces, but she's not that stupid. After reading it another ten times over, she goes outside to smoke two or three cigarettes without anyone disturbing her. Agitated, she takes puff after puff and feels the fresh air cool her wrath a little.

'I hope you're up early for a good reason,' says Ceyda.

'Like I said, I think it's the menopause; it brings all sorts of changes,' Gül answers.

She smiles. She knows the smile is fragile. She knows her thoughts will take on many different colours yet, before they fade. But she feels a force, a strength. Perhaps it's the same one that brought her back to Germany. A force that doesn't come from inside of her, but that belongs to everyone: the force that is passed on in our blood, the strength of our ancestors.

II

It's hot inside the flat, and Gül often stands by the open window, looking down onto the street. The attic flat in Bremen is her seventh home. First she lived with her parents, in the village and then in town, and later she moved into her in-laws' house; then she moved to Germany, where she lived in a little flat with Fuat before they moved to Factory Lane, an unpaved street, home mainly to other Turks. Happy days on Factory Lane were followed by years in her own house in Turkey, and now, after weeks on Ceyda's couch, she finds herself in a flat in an old building from before the war. Out the window, she can see a street with lots of shops, takeaways and restaurants, young people with brightly coloured hair, students, homeless people, and people who seem absent, moving a little too slowly, seemingly unaware of where they're going. She sees and hears Germans, Turks, Kurds, Italians, and she notices there aren't any children playing in the street here.

An old German couple who don't say hello live below them, and she still hasn't seen anyone in the flat two floors down. The first person she gets to know here is Herr Bender, who owns the bookshop on the ground floor. He's about fifty, with silver-grey hair – he wears dark-coloured shirts, and his blue eyes seem to smile kindly behind his glasses. He always acknowledges Gül and speaks to her a few times too. These are the first conversations Gül's had in German since she's been back. She's heard lots of German in the last few weeks and has been getting used to the language again, but when she starts to speak, she realises she exhausts her limits quicker than before. It makes her uncomfortable, but she smiles because she doesn't want to discourage Herr Bender. She explains, as best she can, that she lived nearby for many years, that she's spent a few years in Turkey, that she's now moved to Germany for a second time, that she has two married daughters, and that she's unemployed for the time being. Herr Bender is currently looking for a new cleaning lady. Gül has been living in the attic flat for two weeks when she starts work cleaning the bookshop after closing time.

If Fuat knew about this, he might be pleased to know his wife is so shrewd. But when he gets home after his shift, he picks up his dinner without saying a word, pours himself a whiskey and Coke, and plonks himself down in front of the TV. He watches German quiz shows, American action series, the news; he'll watch anything, but he seems grateful that there's more choice now and he can switch between channels at his leisure. But still, when a quiz contestant wins the jackpot, Fuat will open his mouth and say, 'It beggars belief.'

If it's a lot of money, he'll go one step further: 'All that moolah for twenty minutes' work – the only thing quicker is filling out a lottery ticket. Probably doesn't even need the money, just look at him. What a life – only the rich ever win. If only we could put that kind of money away without having to bow and scrape and sweat for it. That's clean money, crisp notes that've never seen the muck of the factory floor. Just look at it; every penny we've put aside stinks of sweat and hard work. Every single penny.'

Gül doesn't react. This is the second time she's spent the summer in Germany instead of going to Turkey; it's hot up on the top floor, she has no one to talk to, and when she takes the stairs up to the flat, she's out of breath and drenched with sweat by the time she's made it half way. She wonders if the stairs would be easier if she lost weight. She wonders if she should go to Turkey alone, if her daughters know what's going on. She wonders where they go from here. She wonders, every day.

Gül dreams she's in her father's summer house and everyone's together again. She dreams herself there without thinking of recent events; she dreams up that togetherness that they've only ever been able to enjoy for weeks at a time; she dreams herself to her daughters, who are spending the summer with their grandfather – she can call them now, because her father has a telephone at home. She regularly goes and stands in the stuffy phone booth over the road and calls them up. Some of the money she earns working for Herr Bender she collects in five-mark pieces, and she takes a handful of them in her bag when she goes over to make a call. They don't have a telephone at home, but even if they did, she wouldn't make calls from it; she wouldn't know how much she was spending, and this way, at least she can slot one coin after another into the machine and Fuat is none the wiser.

Fatma has said her first words; Ceyda hasn't had any migraines on holiday and has been staying in town with her children Duygu and Timur, while her husband Adem is off visiting his grandparents in their village. Gül's brother, Emin, has given up his job as a teacher and is moving to Istanbul, where Nalan, the youngest of his four sisters, has lived for years. Melike, the second-eldest, doesn't seem very happy about this for some reason. But of all the things Gül hears from her hometown that summer, what concerns her most is the news of Mecnun's constant stomach pains. He can hardly eat a thing and has already lost nine kilos while they've been on holiday. *Nine kilos?* He was no fatter than Gül's little finger to start with – he must be little more than skin and bone now. If only she could give him a few of the kilos she has to spare.

Gül can often be found standing in the stuffy little booth. She knows she mustn't take it for granted that she can hear her daughters' voices, and she knows she mustn't take it for granted that, in those short phone calls, no one seems to notice that she tells them less than she used to.

It's her second summer in Germany, a summer when Fuat comes home and can hardly wait for kick-off. When Gül sees the joy he takes in following the game, she boils with rage. How can he? His envy of other people's money, his belief that happiness is all down to your bank balance has hardly bothered her before, but now she finds herself wondering how he can be so detached. Gül's anger doesn't escape Fuat's notice, even though she bites her tongue. He says: 'Surely you can't begrudge me this game? I'm home on the dot every day, I don't drink with my friends, I don't gamble, I don't do anything anymore; I just go to work and come straight home. I'm like a prisoner here, you could—'

'Shut your mouth,' says Gül, 'or who knows what will happen. Just shut your bloody mouth.'

Fuat is so shocked, he falls silent.

Gül stands at the window, smoking and looking down at the street as it empties before the football starts. She looks down at the street and thinks every day about the words she's heard so often: *Leave home, no returning; come home, forever yearning.*

So say the ancestors.

Perhaps the world was different then, Gül thinks. *Perhaps it didn't turn as quickly. In those days you could still go back, but that's not possible now.* She knows she hasn't seen much of Germany – far less than she's seen of Turkey, and she hardly knows Turkey either. Her friend Aysel in Turkey told her she used to work in German vineyards. Gül can't imagine vineyards in Germany; she hardly knows this country, but the little she does know has changed. In the old days, you couldn't get peppers or aubergines, watermelons or lamb. Now, out of her window, she sees a kebab shop across the road selling döner and lahmacun, which everyone here just calls 'Turkish pizza'.

Germany has changed. She didn't notice it while she was living on Factory Lane, she was too close up; but now she sees that the country she originally came to no longer exists. Just as Turkey is not the same country she once left. Those who leave can never return, because the places they knew disappear.

What on earth brought her to Germany, why did she marry a man who followed the call of money, why did God give Fuat eyes that could only ever see the riches on the horizon but not the worries on his wife and daughters' minds?

And yet she's back here now, and there may be no returning, but there are reunions with the people she loves. You'll always see people again, as long as you're still on this side of life.

You have to stay together, she thinks, *you have to stay together, even if it means you have less than you once did.* There's no going back, and you can't just up and leave and find a new homeland because you weren't happy with the old one. The same way you can't just go looking for a new woman because you've sent your wife ahead on her own, only to never follow her. Staying together takes willpower. And loyalty. Being loyal means not constantly looking out for something better and trying to gain an advantage.

Gül never chose for her mother to die so young; she never chose to be the oldest of five and to have to look after the others. But she did choose Fuat, and after several others had asked for her hand. She was young back then, and there are days when she can barely remember why she said yes to him, but she's never turned away from him like this before.

What did that man ever learn, what does he know about loyalty and sticking together? He's betrayed her. Betrayed her for what? What did he get out of it? What did all those years alone far from home give him? Fuat doesn't know much – definitely less than her. He doesn't know there can be no going back; he wasn't the one who lived in Turkey for eight years. He doesn't know what it is to hold fast, to have faith, to be sincere.

He must be lonely, Gül will think three months later, when the late-summer light is the right colour at dusk, when it's cooled down inside the flat, when she's been down to the phone booth, when she's received a letter from Ceren, when she's met up with her friend Saniye. In three months' time there will be moments when she's not filled with grudges and grief, when she thinks Fuat is lonely, and when she almost feels sorry for him. But those moments will pass quickly.

Gül stands at the window thinking of how she used to see Germans standing alone by their windows, looking out onto the street. She used to wonder whether those people had no one to talk to. Now she's standing there herself, and she knows what it's like to have no company and nothing to do. The Germans sometimes jot down the number plates of cars parked in the wrong place or threaten to call the police on people cycling on the pavement. Gül's grudges aren't towards the outside world.

Over the weeks in which Gül stands at the window looking down at the street, smoking, cursing Fuat, bemoaning her fate and feeling sorry for herself, she works out a lot of what goes on down there. The young man who wears the same dirty off-white jeans every day and spends most of the time standing in a doorway near the kebab shop – he's selling something tiny. People come to him, talk to him, give him money and get something in return, something he often produces from his mouth. It takes Gül a long time to realise that it must be something illegal, something he'd quickly gulp down if the police showed up. Occasionally, she spots him fetching more supplies from a letterbox a few doors down.

Gül recognises the punters; some of them stop by every day, some more than once. People who seem to be in a hurry, sweating, often stride purposefully towards the man in the off-white jeans. Gül sees them sneezing, trembling, sees how miserable they sometimes look and how bad they obviously feel.

She remembers a conversation she once overheard years ago, on a tram. Two Turkish men were talking about all the money to be made out of drugs. The young man on the street below clearly doesn't make much, though.

Gül wonders whether Fuat knows what goes on here, right outside the front door of the flat he found, through another Turkish man he often went for cigarette breaks with at work. Briefly, just for a second, she thinks well of Fuat. Not because of the flat, but because he'd never sell drugs, despite all his other flaws.

From up there, she sees other obviously illicit business going on. People glance around to make sure they're not being watched, inconspicuously checking left and right and behind them, but never looking up. *The police could just rent a top-floor flat and catch them all*, Gül thinks.

She sees car radios being sold on the street, watches, coats, CDs. All in broad daylight. *In a swamp of nightlife:* that's something people often say when they're talking about her sister Nalan, who married a nightclub-owner in Istanbul. Gül wonders whether Nalan lives in a neighbourhood like this, and whether what makes a swamp has less to do with the time of day than the people living all around you.

Nalan is divorced now, and she always plays the sophisticated Istanbul lady when she comes home to the Anatolian provinces, but everyone badmouths her because they don't know how she earns her living. She claims to run a bar in Istanbul, but no one quite believes her. Does she sell drugs too? Gül can't imagine she would. Nalan's daughter is old enough to leave school; does she know what her mother does? If you're constantly surrounded by criminality and drugs and nightlife, do you outgrow your surroundings or will you always be tangled up in that kind of thing?

In the old days, Gül knew the world she sees down there only by hearsay; now, she recognises the faces on the street from a distance.

Mecnun weighs just 55 kilos now. He can hardly keep anything down; every bite he swallows soon gives him stomach cramps, and there's blood in his stool. He doesn't sleep much, but has been taking lots of painkillers, though he's never been one to complain before. The doctors don't know what's wrong with him. They want to send him for tests in Ankara, but Mecnun feels too weak for the six-hour bus journey.

'We can't go back to Erzurum with him like this,' says Ceren.

'It's still two weeks until the end of the holidays,' says Gül. 'A lot can happen in two weeks. Take heart, my treasure.'

'I will,' she says, 'I will, but whatever it is, he's going to need time to recover. I suppose it doesn't really matter though; we're in no rush to get back to the village. Fatma loves playing with her Auntie Sibel, and I get to see Dede every day. I do like being here.'

'And may God let this sickness pass,' says Gül.

'Teyze!' a young man calls out to Gül as she steps out of the phone booth. 'Auntie! I've seen you using this phone box a lot. Who've you been calling? Folks in Turkey?'

'Yes,' says Gül, hesitating. The boy seems familiar, probably because she's spent so much time staring out of the window onto the street, but she can't place him.

'Expensive, isn't it?' he says. 'How many five-mark pieces have you put in there? Seven, eight? Look, I've got some phone cards here. Just stick one in and you can make a 25-mark call. I'll give you one for five marks.'

Gül looks at the boy; he's muscular, dressed in a white vest with his hair gelled back. She guesses he's fifteen, maybe sixteen at most.

'Here, I'll show you if you don't believe me. Don't look like that, do you really think I'd trick a lady like you? You're a mother, anyone can see that. Your heart beats for your children and your family, your loved ones in Turkey. The separation's hard to take, all those miles between us. Hearing the voice of someone you love is like drinking water fresh from the spring when your lips are dry with thirst. Don't look so wary, now, I'm just trying to do you a favour. I've got a mother too, and family and friends in Turkey – a few photos and a couple of lines in a letter won't cut it, I know that much. Go on, I'll give you two cards for eight marks, now that's a bargain.'

'But where did you get the cards, son?'

'Does it matter? Will your family's voices sound any different? Stop fretting. Life's hard enough as it is – look at all you've been through already.'

Gül feels herself softening as the youngster speaks to her this way, as if he knows her, as if he really sees her, as if he can see all the way to her heart. It's like he's looking at her through clear water, though dark thoughts have swept back and forth in her mind on each of these sunny days, until she can hardly bear them any more. She softens, but she doesn't budge. And the boy seems to sense that too.

'There's this friend of mine,' he says. 'It's a long story, but he bought the cards to stock up and now he urgently needs the cash. And since I'm a bit better with words than he is, he asked me to sell them for him. He's a good guy, he's just in a bit of a tight spot.'

'No, thank you,' says Gül. 'But thanks all the same. I hope for your friend's sake you find someone else.'

'If you change your mind, just ask for me at the travel agent's over there. My name's Can. They know me.'

From that day on, Gül sees Can almost daily when she stands looking out of the window. His hair is always neatly gelled back; he never wears the same clothes from one day to the next, and he often wanders into the travel agency and stays there for a while. He speaks to people on their way in or out of the phone box and sells them phone cards. Gül can't hear what he says, but even from all the way up in the attic flat you can see his charm, his talent for coaxing and cajoling people and winning them over. Gül feels proud she didn't succumb to it. But like every good feeling that summer, it soon evaporates.

It's the third day since they got a telephone installed at home, and their third phone call comes when Gül is standing back at the window, staring out again. The first was from Saniye, and the second time it was Ceyda. Gül turns around and looks at the green phone. It's got buttons, this one. Buttons; Fuat was determined to have buttons, even if it cost a little more.

'Buttons,' he'd said, 'God bless progress. Remember how we use to dial our fingers raw with the other one?'

Gül stares at the phone. Mid-morning, half ten: Saniye's at work, and so are Fuat and Ceyda. After this call, Gül will come to fear that the phone ringing might herald bad news.

'Yes?'

'Oh, is this a bad time?'

'No,' says Gül, 'no, Sibel, not at all. You just caught me off guard. Is everything alright? Has something happened?'

'All well here,' she replies, a little hesitant.

'Why are you calling? Good news, I hope.'

'Gül, I need to talk to you. I don't know why you didn't come this summer, but it'd be good if you could find a way to come now. Someone has to talk to Ceren.'

'What about?'

'About Mecnun. He's not well. He's not well at all.'

'Yes, I know that.'

'No,' says Sibel, and Gül hears the tears in her sister's voice. 'No, I don't think you know how sick he really is. Oh, Gül, this bloody phone, you can't—'

The call is cut off. Gül could try to call Sibel back straight away, but then she'd have to explain the phone bill to Fuat, and she doesn't want to speak to him. Not one word. She doesn't want to have to explain herself. And she won't.

She could just go down to the phone box, but she doesn't have enough cash to hand, only a few small coins. She could ask Herr Bender for an advance; she could explain she needs to make an urgent phone call. But she's already told him they have a phone at home now; he wouldn't understand why she wanted to use the phone box.

What is it that Sibel wants to tell her? Why does she need to go to Turkey? How would she even get there? And how's she supposed to afford it? She's sweating. Her heart seems to be beating on both sides of her throat, as if it's been split in two. Maybe she's going to need money for more than just the phone call.

Gül imagines herself putting her shoes on and going downstairs. She wonders what's on the other side of our hearts, the part that no one sees. She imagines herself slowing down as she approaches the travel agency, her breath short, her pulse quick. She thinks of it like smoking. It's not the first cigarette that gets you addicted; you can always stop after the first one. It's all the other cigarettes that are the problem. The cigarettes you smoke after that first one will send you knocking on an enemy's door to ask for a light. She imagines herself walking into the travel agency and asking for Can, then she shakes her head, picks up the new phone's receiver and says, out loud: 'It doesn't matter. It doesn't matter what it costs, and it doesn't matter if I have to speak to Fuat – this is the right thing to do.'

The line is dead. She presses the cradle a couple of times, but there's no dialling tone. *So that's why it didn't ring again*, she thinks. *Sibel must be trying to get through right now. Bloody Fuat and his beloved technology – three calls and the phone's already broken.* She tries again and again, but no sound comes from the receiver.

She's sweating and she wishes she could just cry. She pulls herself together and puts her shoes on. There's nothing else for it. Just this one time.

'What's happened to you, then?' Can asks as she walks into the travel agency. 'Can I get you a glass of water?'

He's sitting in front of an untidy desk, drinking Coke out of a can. Gül is relieved he's there and she doesn't have to ask for him. She tries to take deep breaths. She's a grown woman walking into a travel agency. There's no reason why her knees should be wobbling, her hands trembling.

Behind the desk sits a fat, grumpy-looking man with a bushy moustache. Gül sometimes sees him standing outside his shop with a beer in the evenings, and she wonders who on Earth would want to buy a holiday from a man like that. He rarely shaves, he looks unkempt, and his greasy shirt is stretched taut over his belly.

'Yes, please,' says Gül, 'A glass of water would be lovely.'

She drinks the water and can't quite find the words to explain her situation.

'Teyze, this is Sezai, he's a good friend. But perhaps we should step outside, he was just about to make a phone call.'

Sezai reaches for the receiver and dials a number as Can heads outside with Gül.

'There's no need to be shy around Sezai,' says Can. 'He's family. You can always turn to him if you need anything. He'll find a way.'

Gül nods.

'How many?'

Gül looks at Can.

'How many phone cards? Don't look at me like that. I know a thing or two about people. You need to make a phone call. An urgent one.'

'Just one,' says Gül. 'But I've only got 3 marks 90. I can give you the rest when—'

'It's fine,' Can interrupts her. 'No problem. Let's not bother about a bit of small change. Here, take two cards.'

'I only need one.'

'And I'm only selling you one. The other one's a gift. You're not about to turn down a gift, are you?'

Gül's breathing is calmer now. She's crossed the line, she's on the other side. She looks Can in the eye.

'What do your parents do, by the way?'

There's something in Can's gaze, just for a second, and afterwards Gül will wonder whether she really saw it, or just imagined it.

'My dad's on leave,' he says, reluctantly, 'and my mum's a cleaner in a hotel. Why?'

'No reason.'

She walks over to the phone box and pushes the card into the slot.

Twenty-five marks in credit. She dials Sibel's number.

'You have to tell him,' says Ceyda.

'No,' says Gül.

'You've got to.'

'I'm not going to tell him.'

'Why not?'

'We're not talking to each other.'

'Why not?'

'We're not talking.'

'I'll tell him, then.'

'If that's what you want. Have you got the money for me?'

'Yes. How long do you think you'll need to stay?'

'I don't know.'

Ceyda nods. 'Fly over,' she says. 'Find out what's going on, and I'll call you. If you need me, I'll take unpaid leave and come and join you… He really hasn't cottoned on?'

'No.'

'What are you planning to say about why you're going?'

'Nothing.'

'You have to tell him.'

Gül shakes her head.

'What's happened?'

Gül shakes her head again, quicker and more determined this time.

'I'll talk to him. He'll be livid, you know that.'

Gül thinks. She doubts he'll get as angry as she is. Perhaps he'll abuse his freedom while she's away, though. And then what? Tears prick her eyes. She's tempted to tell Ceyda what happened, but then she swallows it all down and lights a cigarette, for a little comfort. The only comfort she has left.

The trees are bare, and school started back weeks ago, but some may still have a lingering taste of the days spent sitting and talking on the steps outside the summer houses, nibbling sunflower seeds; of the evenings when kids played dodge ball on the street, and everything was full of life, laughter and voices. Now the summer houses are abandoned, the streets covered in leaves, and the windows shuttered. Everyone has returned to town, and life no longer happens out on the street.

Gül can still taste those summer days, just as she can still taste the days she spent at her window, when she silently learned things about Germany and about her anger, about loneliness and betrayal. Days she thought were difficult enough.

'You have to talk to her,' says Sibel. 'There's no point in him going to Ankara now. It's clear where things are heading.'

'Yes,' says Gül. 'It's clear.'

'I wanted to do it, but I couldn't. She's still so young.'

Gül doesn't know whether her sister is talking about Ceren or Ceren's daughter, Fatma, but it makes no difference. Ceren has been happy with her husband. It was the way things can be between man and wife, so it seems. The way things must have been between Gül's own father and mother. Something she has never experienced firsthand or seen in others. A young woman and a young man – who'd have thought they'd have so little time together? Not even three years. Gül wonders whether this sickness is a punishment. And if so, for what? And for whom? What did Mecnun do wrong? What did Ceren, or Fatma, or she herself do to deserve this?

Mecnun is so thin, Gül has only seen the like in pictures before. He's taking morphine for his pain, and Ceren barely leaves his side. She doesn't leave the house; the only other person she has eyes for is her daughter. Ceren's mother-in-law, visibly worried about her son, often takes care of Fatma for her.

'You're going to get better,' Ceren tells Mecnun as she sits by his bed, holding his hand. 'You're going to see Fatma walking, running, jumping and laughing and rolling around; you'll see her singing and reading and writing.'

You're going to get better. It sounds like she really believes it, and Mecnun, hardly able to speak, gives a tired smile and a nod.

Gül wonders whether she was the same. Did she simply refuse to acknowledge that Fuat was cheating on her, even though it was plain to see? And would it have made a difference if someone had told her she had to look his betrayal in the eye?

Sometimes there's no way out; sometimes you have to push through, through the pain, the darkness, through the hours at the window, through the time when there seems to be nothing left to hold onto.

Sibel has no memory of her mother because she was so young when she died. It will be the same for Fatma later on, except she'll have more photos of her father than Gül, Melike and Sibel have of their mother. The wish for a child to grow up with a mother and father, a wish people make when a child is born – perhaps it's just a superficial phrase. When Gül told Ceren and Mecnun she hoped Fatma would grow up with a mother and father, she wished it from her heart – those weren't just empty words. And yet now her words are empty because they've found no echo, taken on no weight, led to nothing. And now there must be more words, other words.

'Let's take a drive to the river, to that place where we had a picnic two years ago.'

'Mum, it's autumn; it's too cold for picnics. What would we do there?'

Gül looks at her. She told Ceren she wanted to come to Turkey for another visit before she started work. She said she wanted to see Fatma, and that she needed the summer to get the new flat set up. Ceren didn't ask questions.

'That picnic was so lovely. I'd just like to see the river again before the long winter starts in Germany. Come on, do me this one favour.'

'I don't want to leave Mecnun alone for too long.'

'I understand. Come on, we'll borrow Aziz's car, just a couple of hours. It won't be long. We'll be back before you know it.'

Gül lights a cigarette and feels tears prick her eyes. Ceren looks at her mother.

'Here, why don't you have a smoke as well? It's lovely here, isn't it?'

'A bit cold, but yes, it's beautiful.'

'Look, I've brought us some tea, a blanket and some baklava. Let's have a little sit down.'

Gül talks about the baklava that tastes of nothing in Germany, about how she meant to lose weight over the summer, about how she gets out of breath when she climbs the stairs to the flat, about the boy she's met called Can, who's charming and has a way with words, about how she made friends with their Spanish neighbours' young son when she first moved to Germany. She just chats away, but she doesn't get the impression Ceren is listening.

'It's really lovely here,' says Ceren. 'We should come back next summer. Bring four or five cars, all of us together. Mecnun likes sitting by the water and drinking tea. Or rakı. Yes, shall we do that?'

Gül takes a breath. Her mouth is dry. She has another sip of tea, but it doesn't help.

'Ceren, my love, my heart, my one and only…' Her voice seeps away like water in sand. Ceren looks at her mother, who breathes in again now.

'Ceren, Mecnun is very sick.'

Ceren nods.

'He won't be here next summer.'

Ceren looks down.

'Did you hear what I said?'

No reaction.

'Ceren, you have to prepare yourself. It's going to be hard, but you can't run away from reality.'

Ceren talks without looking up. Quietly. 'Do you think I'm stupid? Of course he's going to die. He probably won't even survive the winter. Of course he'll die. Of course I'm lying to myself. But what else can I do? Tell me. What else can I do? Until he dies, I'm going to keep smiling and laughing and making plans for the future. For as long as it takes, I'm going to try to be happy, and when it's all over, that's when I'll cry.'

It's not that she has any special skills, but Gül is always conscientious when it comes to work. She doesn't skimp, she never thinks, *Oh, that'll do*; she doesn't tell herself they can't expect better than what they pay for; she doesn't hope that no-one'll spot what a superficial job she's done; and she never says it's no concern of hers at the end of the day because she's only there to earn money.

Herr Bender has recommended Gül to some people he knows, and she's got another two shops and a flat to clean now, but she'd like a permanent job, and Sezai has found her one – Sezai whose agency she bought her plane tickets in, even though she doesn't like him. He came up to her in the street when she got back from Turkey, said he'd seen her cleaning Herr Bender's place and heard she was meticulous. A friend of his had a cleaning company, he said, and was looking for staff. 'No, thank you,' Gül told him, but then later on, Can brought up the subject again. Gül and Can talk regularly when they spot one another on the street, and Can swears the cleaning company is all above board. He says there's nothing dodgy about it; the boss is German, and she'd get a contract, insurance, the lot – she could get a lawyer to have a look at if she had any qualms.

'I'll be honest with you,' he said. 'I know you don't want anything to do with my business. I respect that. You've got your life and I've got mine – I really never should have sold you those phone cards. You're an honest person; you're not the sort to only do the right thing because you're scared. And this is honest work, I promise. I swear on my mum's life.'

Herr Budnikowski is in his early thirties, and he greets Gül in Turkish. *He works with lots of Turks*, she thinks. *He must've learnt a few words.* But then he explains to Gül, in Turkish, that he founded the company, that it's still relatively new but has lots of big clients, that it's usually night shifts and they pay time-and-a-half, and that she comes highly recommended. He makes little mistakes here and there, but his Turkish is fluent, and his accent is barely noticeable.

It's the first time Gül has heard a foreigner speaking Turkish. When Mr Budnikowski finishes speaking and asks if she has any questions, she says: 'Where did you learn such good Turkish?'

'Is that all you want to know about your new job? Why the boss's Turkish is so good?' He laughs. 'I grew up around Turks. My parents both worked, and I was always round at my friend Zafer's. That's how I learnt Turkish. I thought Sezai would have told you.'

'No, he didn't.'

'I go by Orhan,' Mr Budnikowski says. 'My name's Jochen, but most Turks find that hard to pronounce, so everyone here calls me Orhan.'

Gül looks at him and smiles. She trusts him. It's not just the language; there's something in his eyes: sincerity, curiosity. But perhaps it is the language after all. Here's a German who speaks Turkish much better than she speaks German. Gül is touched. It's as if he's given her a gift.

When she leaves his office, she's got a contract in her pocket and she's happy; she's happy and she feels light, even as she's climbing the stairs up to the flat. But once she's home, she ends up going through Fuat's pockets, in case he's hiding anything suspicious. She searched the whole flat when she got back from Turkey, but found nothing.

In those first few months, she'll find herself thinking about Fuat's infidelity even when she's at work. She'll feel pain and fury, but either pain and fury become friends you always carry with you, friends you hardly notice after a while, or time settles on them like a blanket, letting them sleep soundly.

Gül works at night, while the city sleeps, in huge office buildings, under neon lights. While the city sleeps and Gül works, she doesn't know what Fuat's up to; she doesn't stop going through his pockets, just in case. He fancies himself pretty smart, but he's not that clever; Gül doesn't think he'd be up to hiding an affair. She runs the vacuum down corridors, hoovering the corners of the office, surprised that the other cleaners always neglect to clean the skirting boards, wondering all the while whether she'd notice if Fuat were visiting a prostitute. She's not sure. She can't even really picture a prostitute. A figure on the side of the road, yes, but not the person behind it. How can someone do such a thing? For money? What sort of person would you have to be? *I could never do that*, she thinks, *no matter how much money I might make, no matter how desperate I was.*

Gül works at night and remembers the times when Fuat used to do night shifts at the wool factory; he was glad of the extra fee, boasting that it made no difference to him, nor the job at hand, whether the sun shone or not. But it did make a difference to his pay packet. Fuat worked nights while the children were still small, and Gül was constantly warning the girls to be quiet when Fuat was asleep.

These days, she and Fuat only talk to discuss the absolute essentials, but he doesn't want Gül on the streets alone at night, so she gets a lift with Songül, who spends almost every evening telling her that she's fed up of her job and doesn't want to do it anymore. There's also Nurcan, who lives in the same district as Gül, and who she thinks capable of all kinds of nastiness, and Sabine, a pinched-looking German with tattoos, who knows a few scraps of Turkish and always acts like she doesn't care. Gül doesn't know why Sabine works as a cleaner; she's one of the few Germans on the payroll – surely she could find a better job.

Gül catches a lift at half past ten and comes home around five. Before she goes to bed, she looks through her husband's pockets and sniffs his shirts. She looks for stray hairs, for little presents from German women, an unfamiliar lighter or a key, but she doesn't find a thing. Her life ought to be brighter now, if only a bit: she's making money; Fuat's not deceiving her anymore; she has something to do, a distraction. But Mecnun's days are numbered, and she knows that when the time comes, she'll be of no help to Ceren. Gül calls her daughter regularly, still using the phone box to keep an eye on the cost.

Every day or two, she sticks a couple of five-mark pieces in the machine for a quick chat. She puts on an act on the phone. She acts like it's too dark to really see. She acts like it's too bright, like she could laugh. 'I'm not going to cry while he's still living,' Ceren said, 'I'm going to try to be happy.'

How Gül would have loved to stay in Turkey, but what could she have done there, except wait for death? And leave Fuat unsupervised for even longer.

Fuat doesn't seem moved by Mecnun's illness, but Gül hears him swearing now and then, something he never usually does. *It beggars belief*: these are the words he reaches for where others might swear. *It beggars belief, how stupid; it beggars belief, how sick, how shameless*, but never *ox*, *donkey*, *bloody*, *shit*, or insults levelled at mothers and sisters and whole tribes. But now, every once in a while, she hears him muttering, 'That godawful bloody disease.' And sometimes he says, 'It's so unfair, it beggars belief.'

After dinner one evening, when he's only had a little to drink, he asks: 'What on Earth is God punishing him for?'

Gül doesn't react. It's an opportunity to reach out; they could come together in their pain, but Gül refuses.

'Punishment, nothing but punishment,' he says, 'whichever way you turn.'

Gül has to keep her anger under control. She must keep her lips tightly sealed and act as if she hasn't understood his accusation.

Fuat has been eating more of late. He almost always has seconds at dinner, then later he snacks away on nuts, roasted chickpeas, and sometimes crisps or chocolate that he buys after work. He eats more and drinks more whiskey and Coke, and one evening, as he's sitting there chewing and drinking, with the light from the television reflecting on his face, when Gül's already got her coat on ready to head downstairs, she suddenly sees how scared Fuat is. He's not scared for his daughter, for his son-in-law or his granddaughter – no, he's afraid for himself. He sees the injustice of it all and he knows that, going by certain rules, his number should be up way ahead of Mecnun's. He knows that he's never taken care of his health, that he drinks and smokes a lot, that he often gets worked up and sends his blood pressure soaring; he knows that he doesn't get enough sleep, that the night shifts take their toll, and that the gambling has cost him not just money but his nerves, too. He knows that it could get him too, even though he's not old yet, and he's scared.

Suddenly, like jigsaw pieces slotting together, Gül can see his fear. She stands in the doorway a little too long, feeling sorry for Fuat, just for a moment or two, then he looks up at her, and she sees him pull himself together, tuck his fear away again, safely hidden; she sees how he turns hard again because the fear is clotting. And Gül feels sorrier still. But then he looks up at the clock on the wall and says: 'Shouldn't you be heading out?'

Every time she clutches her five-mark piece in the phone box, Gül takes a deep breath and prays the time hasn't yet come. As if the end could be deferred, paid in instalments. As if she didn't know that one of her five-mark pieces will be the one to bring her the news. She will put one of these coins in the slot, only to hear that it could be over any day now. One of these coins will announce that the time for crying will soon begin. She will have worked three quarters of an hour for that news: forty-five minutes of hoovering, dusting, wiping, emptying bins, cleaning toilets, polishing mirrors. Three quarters of an hour, only to hear by her daughter's breath alone, probably, that this chapter is ending and no one knows how the next will begin.

I have to work, she thinks, *I have to work to support my daughter. She'll be alone soon.*

'Can we bring her back over to Germany?' Gül asks. Ceyda stops rolling vine leaves, and at first Gül thinks she's considering it, but then she's not sure whether her daughter has understood her question.

'Ceyda?'

'Yes?'

'Can we bring Ceren to Germany?'

Ceyda looks at the vine leaf in her hand and says nothing. Gül doesn't know whether she's just lost in thought or close to tears. But when her daughter looks up, Gül sees that her eyes are glazed. When was the last time she saw Ceyda crying? She doesn't know.

'Mum, we could get you back to Germany because Dad was still here. And because I'm here and I said I'd take care of you. I'm your sponsor, that's what they call it. But Ceren's my sister, and you can't sponsor your sister; she's grown up, she hasn't learned a trade. I'd try anything, Mum, but I don't think…'

Without finishing her sentence, Ceyda gets back to her vine leaf. Gül keeps adding the filling, cursing the sin of avarice as she does. If only the Germans hadn't offered the repatriation funding, if only Fuat wasn't always so obsessed with money, if only one person didn't always have more than the next, if only our eyes weren't always bigger than our wallets. What in God's name is she doing here? What does she care that half of Adem's relatives are coming to visit later, what does she care what they eat? What does she care about anything? Death is knocking at the door; how can they be rolling vine leaves?

She pulls herself together, but later on she barely even knows how the evening went, what they talked about, or what she had to add to the conversation. *Perhaps that's how drugs work*, she thinks. *You only notice half of what's going on, and that makes life seem more bearable.* Gül feels like she's not really there. She's living her life like someone waiting at a bus stop for things to start moving at last. Every day that passes makes it harder for her to care about anything, and she notices she's distancing herself from everything, even from herself. It feels like she's not really there, even when she's asleep at night.

'We don't die with the dying,' Saniye says, hugging Gül to her. Gül controls herself for a moment, and then for another and another, but when the two women part, she starts to cry. It's as if two layers of her were sliding over each other, and now, when they finally fit together, the tears begin to flow.

Saniye gives a sad smile and hugs her again. Saniye, the same woman who lost her husband, her father and her son in one day; a woman who will let nothing get her down.

'It's going to be hard,' she says, 'let's not pretend otherwise. It'll be tough for you and even tougher for Ceren. But these things don't kill us. And they won't break us. When these things happen, we walk with a stoop for a while. We curse life, the lot that we've drawn, we curse that bitch fate and wonder what we've done to deserve it; we think we might die before the wound heals, die of agony and grief. Dark times are coming for you and Ceren, let's face it. It'll feel like all of life has burned up and you're left sitting among the ashes, wondering whether your bones will ever be warm again, whether they'll ever fill up with life again. No one can spare you both that. But I'm here and I'll be here then, too, so you'll see you can stay standing and keep a straight back. Gül, if I survived it, you'll survive it too, and Ceren is strong, she'll survive. Look, I had nobody, I came to this country all alone. Go ahead and cry, cry now, because soon Ceren will need you with dry eyes.'

Gül has prepared herself. How many times has she imagined how Ceren's breathing will sound, what her words will be? She's pictured herself going into the travel agent's and booking the flight, calm and controlled. She's been through everything in her mind, every day. She thinks she's ready.

She hears from Ceren's *Hello* that something is different, but she can tell it's not to do with Mecnun. A *Hello*, a single *Hello* is enough to know that something has happened, but she has no idea what it might be.

'What is it?'

'Dede's come off his moped.'

It's happened a couple of times in the last few years. He's getting older, more distracted, weaker, slower, his eyesight's getting worse. He's often come home with his jacket dirty and his trousers torn, claiming that nothing happened; just a damn mutt that ran in front of him, a new pothole, a watermelon that fell off a lorry.

'Is he hurt?'

'He had an accident, he's unconscious – they don't know if he's got internal injuries, and they think he might have hit his head. And his hand's broken. The driver didn't stop at the red light. Dede flew over the top of the car; they're thinking of transferring him to the hospital in Kayseri. I don't know…'

Ceren bursts into tears. Gül feels a coldness creeping inside her. And something flowing out of her at the same time.

She books the next flight; it doesn't leave for another fifteen hours. She gets picked up for work, but it's like someone else is inhabiting her body, trying their best to make her look human: talking, eating, drinking, cleaning, sneezing and thinking. But Gül herself is not there at all.

The next morning, she boards the plane to Ankara. At the other end, she takes a taxi to the coach station and the next coach to her hometown. On the six-hour ride, she tries to work out how much time has passed since the accident, but she can't figure it out. She thinks about the traffic light, the only one in the town. The last time she was there, the light was just being installed on the main road. How long has it been up and running? Gül doesn't know.

She prays to God, she prays she'll be allowed to see her father alive again, alive and conscious. *Oh Lord, please don't take my father from me, not now; please give me a chance to say goodbye. Let me see the light in his eyes one more time. Please, Lord.*

None of us knows which wishes will come true and which won't, which prayers will be heard and which won't, and which will only look like they've been heard. None of us knows what's in the diary of the future.

No one could guess, now, that the traffic light will be switched off in a few months' time because all the drivers simply ignore the signal. Or that it will be back in operation four years later. Life doesn't write stories, it always leaves the ending open; there's never a point that might be the last. Some lives are written as sad, and then happy again, some are crossed out of the book of life, others are written in, but the pages of the book are infinite.

Gül doesn't know where to go when she gets off the coach. It's early evening – she hasn't eaten since breakfast, her mouth is dry, her knees are weak, she feels heavy. She stands there at the coach station, her bag next to her; the place smells of urine and vomit. If she doesn't move, perhaps time will stand still.

'Sister, do you need a taxi?' a man asks. 'Do you want me to take you somewhere?'

Gül thinks for a moment.

'To the hospital.'

As the driver approaches the junction with the traffic light he slows down, looks left, looks right and then drives straight through the red light. Gül takes a breath but keeps quiet.

When the taxi pulls up, Gül pays the price the driver tells her, even though she knows it's too high. She asks for Timur the blacksmith at reception. The woman flicks through a list, frowns, and says: 'He's not here any more.'

'Where… where is he?'

'He's… he might have been transferred… I can't tell from this.'

Please, Gül thinks, *please let him be alive*. She registers someone pushing a chair under her, and only then does she realise how weak her legs are. They give her a drink and a squirt of lemon cologne on her palms to freshen up. The sharp smell of the alcohol makes her even dizzier.

She sees a man in a white coat coming towards her; she presses her hands against the plastic chair, notices her legs can barely hold her, and stands up nonetheless.

'Are you the blacksmith's daughter?' the man asks. 'My name's Zekeriya, I'm the consultant here. Have you come far? Your father's as stubborn as a mule – he discharged himself when he woke up early this morning. You go home to him; maybe you can talk some sense into him. It would be better if he came back and we could keep him under observation. He might have injuries we can't see – he might take a sudden turn for the worse.'

'He's at home?'

'Yes, he got up and left.'

'He…'

Gül doesn't finish her sentence. She doesn't even know what she wanted to say. She sits back down.

'You're the daughter from Germany?'

Gül nods. Eight years she lived in this town again until recently, but she'll always be the daughter from Germany.

'Bring her a tea and a glass of ayran,' says the doctor. 'Make the tea sweet and the ayran salty. You have a little rest here,' he says to Gül, 'and then try and convince your father to come back again. Even if he is as hard as nails. Have a little rest, go home, kiss your father. Celebrate seeing him again. Recover from the journey. May it pass.'

'You gave me a fright,' says Timur. 'I thought I'd broken my hand and cracked my head open too. I thought I was seeing the things I longed for, floating on top of what was really there. *Now every day my broken head's going to break my heart in two*, I thought, *It must be a mirage*. Gül, if I knew it was so easy to get you back here, I'd come off my moped every day.'

'God forbid! I prayed the whole way here that I'd see you alive again. You can't ride that moped any more.'

'Don't start! You sound just like your mother. It wasn't even my fault. You should be telling the owner of that car not to drive again. Can't tell red from green, but still has his driving licence! It's like a shepherd not knowing a goat from a cow. Are there shepherds like that? It's supposed to be my fault, is it?'

Gül says nothing. And she is glad. She's glad her father is well, and they can sit together like this. She's glad he's back to full strength.

That night, Mecnun dies. As if all he'd been waiting for was for his mother-in-law to get there to look after her daughter.

Gül stays for a week. It's a week full of tears, full of grief; a week where the days seem to shuffle along wearily, stopping to rest on the mourners' chests. When the sun sinks and the night clings to them, they can't quite tell which way is up. At night, Ceren wishes Mecnun were alive again, returned safe and sound from the world of the dead; at night, her whole being yearns so deeply for this one thing, and she finds herself amazed that reality can withstand the power of her yearning. Mecnun remains dead. Night after night. Night after night. Night after night.

Sibel is there, her grandfather is there, her grandmother is there, her mother is there, Fatma is there, but Mecnun is still dead. For Ceren, it surpasses all understanding that Mecnun will now remain dead, every night for the rest of her life. It is beyond the power of her imagination to understand how she might find the strength to do anything ever again. The only thing that gets her moving is her daughter. Fatma has to eat, drink and sleep; someone needs to look after her. Ceren has to talk to her and play with her, even if she'd rather just stare at the wall. She sees Mecnun's features as soon as she looks at Fatma, and she can't fight back the tears, even though she doesn't want Fatma to see her crying all the time. She can't get a grip on herself; even her love for her daughter isn't enough to help her keep it together for a few moments. She falls apart, falls into pieces of grief held together by the wish that Mecnun might return.

Ceren laughed, for as long as she had to. But now is a different time. This is how things are when Gül leaves her daughter behind and flies back to Germany.

'Come in,' says Yılmaz. 'Saniye's not here, I don't know where she is. She went shopping with Sevgi – she ought to be back by now.'

Gül is surprised that Yılmaz is home. She and Saniye wanted it to be just the two of them – that's what they agreed – but still she takes off her shoes and walks inside.

Within a few minutes, the conversation grinds to a halt and Gül finds herself remembering one New Year's Eve on Factory Lane, probably the last time she and Yılmaz were in a room alone together. It was just before midnight; the others had gone outside, and Yılmaz was so drunk he could hardly stand. That was the night Saniye told her he was actually drunk all the time.

Now Gül realises she hasn't seen Yılmaz drunk in a long while.

'How's Ceren doing, really?' he asks.

'It's early days,' Gül replies. 'I thought she was losing her mind at first. Perhaps she would have done if it wasn't for Fatma. She barely left the house for a year – a whole year. You couldn't even have a proper chat with her on the phone, she'd be so sharp. I don't think she spoke so much as a thousand words in that whole year.'

'But Fatma's speaking now, isn't she? At least that's what Saniye said. She must have learnt from someone.'

Gül nods.

'True,' she says. 'Maybe she's been talking to Fatma a lot. Who knows all the dark thoughts that child might have heard before she even spoke her first words.'

'Oh, Gül,' says Yılmaz. 'We all grew up hearing these laments full of longing and pain – it's what we come from. Melancholy's written in our genes; that pessimism, that grief. What other language would give you a word that describes both a lover and a singer of sad songs? Gül, that melancholy inoculated us; we drank it in with our mother's milk. You can't escape it. Is Ceren any different to you or me? What does one person ever have over another? It's not something we can shake off, Gül. The wood we're carved from is soaked with tears.'

Gül always feels inferior to Yılmaz. He went to university and, to her, everything he says almost always sounds clever and well thought-out.

'Now, Fuat,' Yılmaz says. 'Fuat's different. Many of us who came here are different, but you, Saniye and I, we'll always carry those tears in our hearts. People like Fuat can simply shake the Anatolian blues right out of their bones.'

There's something like admiration in his voice, and Gül is surprised. Fuat. Her husband. The drinker and gambler, the money-grabbing man who fancies himself so smart, the man who betrayed her. Does he have some quality she's somehow failed to notice?

'What is it Fuat has that you don't?'

'Courage.'

'The courage to turn his back on his family and fritter away his money?'

'No, the courage to come here. Saniye didn't come here because she was brave; she came because she was desperate. I came because Turkey didn't want me, and you came because your husband came. But Fuat? He could have stayed back home and worked as a barber.'

'Some might say he came out of greed.'

'Some might also say he came because he wanted a better future. Gül, whatever flaws he has, it takes courage to leave everything behind and move to a new place without so much as an inkling of what awaits you when you get there. You have to trust yourself; you have to talk to strangers in a language you don't understand; you have to be prepared to let go; you have to be a bit curious about the world. You can't do too well, it's true, but you still need that courage, that desire for action, for adventure. You've got to be savvy and have the gift of the gab. Even if you're thinking, *This is just for two years, and then I'm going home.* Even then, you've got to have some faith in yourself. Who'd go to prison for two years just for the money?

'Look, you and me, we're both shy. Saniye's not like that – she has that curiosity. But people like us, we just don't feel at ease everywhere; we need a little longer to warm up. We don't really belong here. Look at me, I've been in this country over twenty years, and I'll never feel quite right. And look at Fuat, he's creative, there are no limits to what he thinks is possible, he finds solutions. He got that 6000-mark bonus just because he came up with an idea for making production more efficient. He doesn't just accept things, he changes them. He has the courage and shrewdness of a peasant. And now he's proud. It's the second time he's been smarter than an engineer and been rewarded for it. But he's not smart enough to see that they're exploiting him. Ten thousand marks over three years. He thinks that's a lot of money because he's not reckoning on the profit the company's making from his ideas. It's much more than 10,000. Much, much more. More like a million, probably. And who do they have to thank for it? A barber from Anatolia. Not someone who studied here.'

The money was a blessing. Fuat was in a good mood for weeks. He bragged about what a sly fox he was and scoffed at the German engineers, who didn't have two brain cells to rub together.

Gül doesn't understand exactly what Fuat's improved at work, even though he's patiently explained it to her more than once. 'It doesn't matter,' he ended up saying, generously. 'I don't understand anything about women's stuff either. But if I did, I'm sure you could give me a few tips on how to get my hair to grow.'

Fuat was in a good mood – they spoke to each other over dinner, they watched TV together, they didn't moan when the other changed the channel. They made each other feel that their presence wasn't an unbearable imposition.

Should I maybe try to look at Fuat through Yılmaz' eyes? Gül asks herself now. There's another lull in the conversation.

'What will Ceren do now?' Yılmaz asks then. 'Does she want to remarry?'

Gül sighs and shakes her head. 'No,' she says, 'She can't bring herself to think about marrying again. But she can't sit at home forever either, and the pension she gets isn't enough to live on. Now she's got it into her head that she's going to study German and become a teacher. Like her poor husband.'

Part of Fuat's bonus will go towards helping Ceren to study, though he's not too pleased with the idea.

'I'm not cashing in my bonus just so my daughter can study something she already knows,' he said. 'You spend years dreaming of hitting the jackpot, and when the time finally comes, all you get is a few measly marks. You can't go spending it on some language that no-one speaks except for the Germans. It's like throwing money out the window.'

'She's your daughter,' Gül said. 'We owe her this.'

'Yeah,' he said. 'And I suppose I don't deserve to be rewarded for my efforts.'

'You could always take the money and go,' Gül replied. 'You've already done everything in your power to split this family up. So why not take your money and go, and be happy with it?'

Fuat went on griping, but Gül stopped responding.

'A German teacher?' Yılmaz says now. 'We're never done here – everyone's trying to finish everyone else's work. That's what people are like: we can never just stop, even the laziest among us. We keep going. Fuat's father drank, but he didn't manage to drink himself to death, so now his son's giving it a go, though his heart's not quite in it.'

'But you stopped drinking,' says Gül. Yılmaz smiles. He looks pained.

'Yes,' he says. 'Sometimes it looks like you're taking a different track. Like going to Germany, for instance, but most of us can hardly get over the starting line, even if we think we're going to run God knows how far. Even courage doesn't help. Fuat's father was a coachman, and now Fuat works at Benz. Nothing changes.'

Gül frowns. Smart as she thinks Yılmaz is, what he's saying makes no sense to her.

'You stopped drinking and became a communist. What kind of Turkish man is a communist and doesn't drink?'

'But Gül, I'm not actually a communist. People just say that because I argue for workers' rights and because I understand how this system is exploiting us. Our people think anyone's a communist if they've read a few books, if they listen to Ruhi Su and watch Yılmaz Güney films. Perhaps you're right, perhaps I did things differently, but it just led to me having to leave the country. But look at me, my father was a sad man who didn't have many friends, maybe none at all. He always sat outside the front door on his own with a cigarette in his hand, staring into space. We can't end all that, the grief, the wars, the beatings, the greed; we'll see all that we've witnessed over and over again, even if we believe that we've left it behind us. But teaching German's nothing to be sniffed at, Gül – it's a decent job and it's funny too, if you feel up to laughing about it. I hope you two aren't having money problems because of it.'

'No,' says Gül. 'No, no.'

They've got their savings. Over the years, not everything has fallen victim to Fuat's tendency to squander and gamble money away. A few months ago, Gül was promoted to forewoman at the company. She's still working for Herr Bender at the bookshop, too, and then there's Fuat's bonus; life in Turkey isn't expensive, they're not going to struggle for money.

When Gül hears the key turn in the lock she feels uneasy for a moment, like she's been caught doing something forbidden, even though it's just Saniye turning up late.

Saniye eyes Yılmaz briefly – searching, perhaps even disapproving – before she hugs Gül. The look only lasts for a moment, but it tells Gül that the two of them have a secret. Has Yılmaz been straying too? Maybe he's been chasing other women. Maybe there's a side to him that Gül can't see. A dark side. A side she can't imagine him having.

Gül still often stands at the window, keeping watch over the street. She knows who sells drugs, who deals in stolen goods, who's harmless, who often flips out, what the punks do with the money they beg for, who's in touch with whom, where there's bad blood, and which groups ignore each other. She knows the street, if only from above.

She doesn't know exactly how long it's been since she saw Can. Five months, six, maybe seven? She keeps an eye out for him every day, wondering where he might be. She doesn't want to go into the travel agent's to ask. She doesn't like the place, or Sezai. That was where she bought the ticket that took her to her healthy father and her dying son-in-law. Sezai looks worse from one day to the next, ever more scruffy and grumpy, but also sickly. A new travel agency has opened up further down the street, run by a young man in a suit.

When Gül spots Can down on the street, she's shocked. Perhaps because she's been waiting so long to see him. She feels like running down and giving him a hug, asking him where he's been. She steps back from the window, even though she knows no one ever looks up, and wonders whether to put her shoes on and go out. Just to the phone box, perhaps, where she hasn't been for a long time now. Or out shopping. She can pretend to run into him on the street by chance.

But can she really? Would she manage to conceal her joy? Could she feign surprise? It's worth a try.

'Can, my son, how lovely to see you,' she says, not troubling to act surprised. 'You haven't been around here for ages.'

'Oh, Auntie Gül, what a delight,' says Can. 'Seeing you here first thing in the morning – my luck's in today.'

'What happened to you?'

'Oh, nothing,' Can says.

'What, nothing?'

'I got in a punch-up, it's not as bad as it looks, really it's not. It'll all be forgotten in a few days' time. How are you? What's Ceren up to?'

'I'm fine, thanks be to God. Ceren's got a place at university to study German, at the end of summer.'

'That's nice, then she can take care of herself and her daughter. That's good. She's lucky to have you and your family to support her. If I'd had a mother like you, who knows what would've become of me. Maybe I'd be a German teacher.' He shakes his head.

'Where have you been all this time, that's what I meant. Anyone can see you've been in a fight. But a punch-up doesn't last months on end.'

He looks at the ground. Then back up at her. 'Auntie Gül, do you know the café inside Karstadt? Let's meet there. In half an hour. Is that alright? We can talk in peace there. It might not be good for you to be seen with me here. We haven't talked for a long time – shall we have a coffee there?'

She can't invite him up to her flat; someone might see them, and then what would they say? There's plenty of time before Fuat gets back from work, and she'd like to talk to Can, but she'd be keeping a secret and that would be a betrayal. Or would it? What does she owe her husband? She notices rage simmering inside her because she can't just say yes. All the things he's allowed himself and all the things she doesn't allow herself, just because it's not proper to have a coffee in public with a man who's young enough to be her son.

'No one will find out,' Can says, quietly. 'In half an hour. I'll be there. It's no problem if you don't come. May your day be blessed.'

Gül nods. Her heart's thudding. *It's not forbidden*, she tells herself.

Her fear feels petty, later, when they're sitting in the café inside the department store and Can tells her he was in prison for eight months. At the same time, she thinks she might get even more scared. She's having coffee with a criminal. But what did she think? That selling phone cards was Can's only income, that he did something like that just out of youthful recklessness? But what do you have to do to get an eight-month sentence?

Can trusts Gül, like many people do, though Gül will never understand why that is. He trusts her, and he was the one who wanted to have coffee with her, but he still doesn't tell her what happened, even though he doesn't seem embarrassed.

'It wasn't long,' he says. 'It wasn't even half of what they could have given me. And what am I supposed to have done? It was all about money. It's only ever money. If I hadn't forked out for my lawyer to have dinner with the prosecutor, I'd have been inside all winter and another summer on top.'

'What do you mean, it wasn't long? Your mother's heart will have been bleeding. Look, even I'm getting sad just thinking about it, but your poor mother…'

'Yes, my poor mother,' says Can. 'That poor woman slaved away her whole life, cleaning Germans' shit off their toilets because people who stay in hotels never use a toilet brush; my mother who slogged away to get us a bit of money, slogged away on Saturdays and Sundays but never earned enough on one weekend to stay even half a night in that hotel. I already felt sorry for my mother. What did she work so hard for, Auntie Gül? For money? How much money has she got now? Barely enough. And she never saw us kids either.'

'Look, I learned to earn my living with an honest day's work. We slaved away here too, but we put money aside even though Fuat drinks and gambles. You can make it doing honest work, too.'

'Yes, but make it where? Make it as what, Auntie Gül? Forewoman of a cleaning crew? Don't take it the wrong way, but we'll always be stuck down here. It's all about money in this world, that's just the way it is. Everyone's chasing after cash. If you're like me, you take risks. That's how it is. You pay your dues, and you learn to minimise the risk.'

'If you don't earn your living on the righteous path, you lose it all again.'

'That's not true,' Can says. 'That's just some old saying. Look, you tried the righteous path, and it lost you a year and a half of your daughters' childhoods. You tried the righteous path and that hurt too. I've got goals, Auntie Gül; I'm going to get rich, you'll see.'

'Good God, you're talking like a man who's going to rack and ruin, my son. If you won't do it for your parents or yourself, do it for me: Take the righteous path while there's still time to turn back.'

'Auntie Gül, I just want to have a coffee with you and talk. I don't want to argue. I don't want to upset you; I like you. But it's my life to live, you know?'

Just like the Germans, Gül thinks. *That's why people here are so lonely. They want to have their own lives just for themselves, without any consideration for others.* But she says no more about it, and before long they're talking about Gül's grandchildren, Can's new girlfriend, his mother, the promise he made to her never to go to prison again. They talk, and at some point Gül realises she has to dash off because she needs to make dinner before Fuat gets home. She feels guilty as she unlocks the front door, knowing she can't tell anyone. She feels guilty, but in the coming weeks and months she'll often go to that department store café to meet Can; she'll feel guilty each time she meets him, and she'll wonder why she keeps going and what it is she likes so much about the boy.

Something that felt for years like firm ground has suddenly become soft earth, and Gül is trying not to lose her footing.

'I never really liked cutting hair, to tell the truth,' says Ceyda.

Gül remembers encouraging her daughter to stay on at school, and how astonished she'd been when Ceyda told her she'd rather be a hairdresser.

'You said you'd thought it over back then.'

'I had. I wanted to get out of school and learn a trade, one that meant I'd never have to work in a factory. And now this suits me better. I come home in the mornings, so I can make breakfast and wake the kids, get Duygu off to school and take Timur to kindergarten. Then I can lie down and sleep. When you've got children, it's better to work nights.'

That's not what Fuat used to say.

'But you don't get enough sleep,' says Gül.

'Oh, I don't mind that.'

Ceyda seems happy in her new job at the post depot, Gül thinks. *We're both working nights and we don't see our husbands much, but we see how the world changes after dark instead.*

Ceyda lives in a slightly posher neighbourhood than her mother, and she doesn't get home until morning, when it's already light. It's still night-time when Gül gets home. The takeaway across from her house is open all hours; some of the people who go in are boisterous or vacant, others stare blankly while they place their order, and then there are those who come out of the shop, unwrap their kebabs and throw them away as soon as they're out of view, before disappearing into the gloom still clutching the foil.

At night, Gül sees things she can't explain, and when she gets out of the car she often thinks of Nalan, who probably works nights too but never talks about it. *Yes, we work nights*, she says to herself then, *but we make an honest living. I do what I learnt from my mother and father; I earn my money by the sweat of my brow, even though the world of night shifts isn't really for me.*

She likes these last few steps, when she's out of the car, before she's shut her front door; these last few steps, in which she's delivered into the night, the satisfaction of a job well done, the pleasant heavy feeling in her limbs – these moments of quiet and calm. For a few weeks, these moments will be tainted by something she can't quite put her finger on at first. She gets out of the car, and the feeling seems to use the cover of darkness to cast a shadow over her; a vague sense of unease. She simply ignores it the first three or four times, but one morning at half four, while she's climbing the stairs of the old apartment building, she suddenly realises that Ceyda is scared. She senses it, needing no skill or talent to do so; feelings and connection are gifts from God. She feels her daughter's fear; even though she doesn't know the cause, she feels the fear and wants to help her.

Two days later, the men are watching football, the children are in their room, and Ceyda and Gül are in the kitchen with the door closed. Gül doesn't know how to lay the ground before she asks her daughter how she's really feeling, when Ceyda asks her out of the blue: 'Are there any illnesses in the family, things I don't know about?'

She's been working at the post office for almost nine months now, and she's looking more and more tired.

'You mean migraines?' Gül says. 'Are you asking if migraines run in the family?'

'No,' says Ceyda, 'it's not the migraines. I don't get as many migraines now. Instead... I hear voices. Before the kids get home, I'll be sitting in the living room, and I'll hear voices from the kitchen. I hear them arguing but I don't understand the words. I know they're speaking Turkish – they sound aggressive; I even hear them throwing plates and mugs at the wall, I hear crockery smashing, I hear a woman crying. It all sounds so real, but as soon as I lean forward to look through the kitchen door and see if anyone's there, everything goes quiet. And then it starts up again the minute I lean back.'

Ceyda speaks quickly; Gül can sense how hard it is for her to talk about it.

'Did anyone in our family go mad, maybe? Was it really typhoid that killed Nene, like you always say it was? Mum, do you think I might be going mad? It's not like the migraines, it's not something you can just deal with. Hearing voices is a sign of schizophrenia, isn't it?'

'Why would I have lied to you about that? I saw for myself how sick my mother was – I remember the exact colour of the circles under her eyes. No, Ceyda, my darling, you're not going mad. You've turned your whole life upside down. You work nights and sleep during the day. You're not getting enough sleep, you never get enough sleep – it's perfectly normal for your head to get left behind. I used to hear voices when I started cleaning at night, but they weren't arguing. You just need to sleep to give your head a rest. You're not ill.'

Gül genuinely believes that sleep will help. And she knows that Ceyda isn't losing her mind; she knows it the same way she knew that her daughter was scared. But the thing about hearing voices herself in the past – that's a lie. Gül knows Ceyda isn't going mad, but she's still afraid for her daughter, still fears for her. Perhaps because she's always been afraid. It's a fear that has been with Gül ever since her mother died.

Perhaps it was her fear that helped Gül to sense something wasn't right with Ceyda. Perhaps the fear creates a tie between them – a connection that knows no longing and no distance, no day and no night, no hunger or thirst.

That fear's not a bad thing, Gül thinks. *Without it, I might not feel so connected to my daughter.*

We're always afraid of losing – losing someone we love, our honour, our pride, our money, friends, a father, a mother, brothers and sisters, our home – but we're never afraid of losing our longing, our grief, those lamentations and that rage. Gül listens to her feelings. No, she wouldn't want to lose the anger she feels towards Fuat. *That rage helps me to stay true to myself*, she thinks. *It helps me to keep my back straight.*

My fear is a bridge to my children. And my grief, perhaps that's my connection to other people. I can make a connection to anyone who's felt that grief. That's why I get on so well with Saniye. That's why I like talking to Yılmaz, even though he's so much better educated than I am. Perhaps it's the same with Can – perhaps he's sad too and just hides it better than others. He's sad that his mother was there to clean up the Germans' mess, but she wasn't there for him. And perhaps people trust me because I've been to the bottom of the well from which grief is drawn. She smiles at herself. But if anyone's been at the bottom of that well, it's Saniye, not her. People aren't as quick to trust Saniye, though. *I could spend another forty years thinking about it all, but I'd never work out this life.*

'Mum?'

Gül jumps.

'You were away with the fairies,' Ceyda says.

'I'll take a couple of days off,' Gül says. 'I'll come to stay, and you'll see – those voices will be gone as soon as you've had two or three good nights' sleep.'

Who knows whether the voices stop because Ceyda gets more sleep or because Gül is there. The sound of smashing crockery might never go away entirely, the same way Gül still remembers the sound of the spoon her father flung at the wall when he learned that his wife had died. Gül was just a child then, but that sound echoes through her whole life. Perhaps the sound of phantom crockery will go on echoing through Ceyda's life as well.

But Ceyda's fear of losing her mind wanes, even though the voices return once her mother has gone. She explains them away as a symptom of sleeplessness, and just keeps going. She even works more, leaving Duygu and Timur with her mother-in-law on the weekends so she can pick strawberries. On bad days, her back aches and she hardly earns a thing, but on good days she just comes home tired with a blue hundred-mark note – an eagle, as they call it. That's always the day's goal, to come home with an eagle.

The money adds up: a savings account here, a bank book there, and like her parents and many others, she also puts some of it into the Turkish central bank, which gives eight per cent interest. Perhaps Ceyda will buy a house in Turkey one day, like her parents did. But she definitely wants one in Germany, so her children don't have to share a bedroom, so they have somewhere no one can take away from them. She realises the two of them will probably stay in Germany all their lives.

Even as a child she was used to people saving, investing, calculating, comparing prices and cutting back. The rules only changed when the summer holidays were approaching. Then they'd buy presents for their relatives – they'd get proper Nutella instead of the cheap version; the chocolate that went in their suitcases would be Ritter Sport or Milka; and they'd have Maggi brand chicken stock. When the holidays came around, there'd be no more saving – they bought as many fancy things as their bank accounts allowed, to impress the family back in Turkey with their gifts.

In the past, the blacksmith's children would all get together every summer. For six weeks, they were one big family, a choir of many voices, all with different interpretations of the same song. They felt the power of their ancestors, the power that had brought them together; they could sense the same blood in their veins, blood that carried joy and light. Gül was the reason they only spent six weeks together; she was the one who didn't have more time. The others were all together before she got there, and they stayed together once she'd left. During the years Gül spent living in Turkey later on, she saw how difficult it was to bear the end of summer when she didn't leave but was left behind. But the summers have changed now, and the blacksmith's grandchildren are no longer those same kids who spent weeks playing together in their parents' hometown. Some of them are married, and one is widowed. Nalan's daughter is the youngest at fifteen, but she never comes any more; she stays in Istanbul with friends instead, prompting much chatter. Should a young woman – and one who, to top it all off, has got it into her head that she's going to be an actress when she's older – be allowed to stay in the big city unsupervised? That place is bound to turn you into some kind of floozy – doesn't that Nalan have any sense of responsibility?

Gül's brother, Emin, also lives in Istanbul now, where he's borrowed money to start a car hire business. Emin was always more ambitious than his sisters and has given up his safe job as a teacher in a bid to get rich. He can never take much leave – work's always calling – but his wife and his two unmarried sons spend the summer with the family in his hometown while Emin stays in Istanbul and apparently checks in on Nalan's daughter regularly. Melike's son, İsmail, has been a professional basketball player with Galatasaray for a year now and hardly ever visits, and recently Melike has been prioritising spending a couple of weeks on the Aegean in the summer, instead of with her family. Sibel, whose marriage has remained childless, is the only one of the siblings who still lives in their hometown.

Gül often longs for the old days, the flavour of those times. She's glad she can see her father, and she's happy to see Ceren, but she thinks the summers were better in the past. *Perhaps I'm just getting old*, she thinks. *Perhaps I'm becoming like those people who think everything was better in the old days.*

One day she's taking watermelon rinds into the stable to feed to the cows when, beyond the stable in the big orchard, she sees the outline of a figure leaning against an apple tree, sitting on the ground. She can't tell if it's her father. He looks like Timur, but the blacksmith wouldn't be sitting around at this time of day; he'd be working or stopping briefly to take off his cap and wipe his brow. She takes a few steps forwards, realises it is him, and quickens her pace. *He's just sitting down*, she thinks. *He's still sitting upright, it's not like he's fallen over.* She might not call out, she might not be running, but still, the sweat swiftly comes rising out of her pores.

The blacksmith turns his head, looks at his daughter and smiles. Gül slows down, her pulse steadies, but something inside her tightens. Her stomach, her heart, her throat. She can't be sure. Perhaps it's all of them at once. The blacksmith's smile broadens now and the grip on Gül's insides loosens a little, but it doesn't let go. The blacksmith's cap is by his side, and he picks it up and pats the ground, gesturing for Gül to sit next to him.

'Why are you crying?'

Timur looks at his daughter.

'How many children have I got?'

'Five.'

'How many of them are living and in good health?'

'Five.'

'How many grandchildren do I have?'

'Eight.'

'How many of them are in good health?'

'Eight.'

'How many great-grandchildren?'

'Three, and all three of them are healthy.'

'And are any of these people going hungry?'

'No, none of them.'

'I'm a lucky man,' says Timur. 'Each of us has their worries, but I'm a lucky man. All my children are living, all of them come to visit me, I've no bad blood with any of them. I'm a lucky man.'

Gül lays her head on her father's shoulder and breathes in the sour scent of his sweat, which mixes with the smell of the soil. The smoke of the forge would linger on him in the past, but it has since given way to the scent of age. But Gül also catches a hint of the strength and the gentle sorrow that his happy tears have lent his breath.

They sit there like this for a few moments, in the low late-afternoon sun, and perhaps the blacksmith notices his daughter's soft, sumptuous, motherly smell; a hardness has crept into it in recent years, something woody and rough, something you wouldn't expect to find in her.

Gül is still savouring this moment of calm with her father, when he turns to her and, without stopping to clear his throat or taking a breath, says: 'You're going to fall out.'

The brief silence after he says this is filled with grief.

'Who?'

'You children. You'll fall out when I'm dead.'

Gül shifts back a little and looks at him.

'Why would we do that?'

'You're my children, I know you. I know you better than your mothers know you. Knew you. You're going to fight, and one day you'll remember what I've said.'

'No, we won't. I'll make sure everything—'

'Shh,' Timur interrupts her. 'Don't make promises you can't keep. Let's be glad. I'm a lucky man.'

He leans over and kisses her forehead. Then he gets up, puts his cap on and says: 'I wanted to weed that patch up behind the swimming pool. Would you bring me over a tea?'

Gül nods. She hasn't gained weight in recent years, but she still finds it harder and harder to get up off the ground when she's been sitting down. She watches the blacksmith's broad back as he leaves.

In the kitchen, Sibel has just finished brewing the tea. Gül pours a glass for her father, adds lemon juice and three sugars, and goes out to take it to him. When she gets back, she sits down for a moment, then she gets up again and goes to the fridge, takes out a rice pudding and eats it standing up.

'Everything alright?' Sibel asks.

Gül nods and looks at her sister, who was just a baby when their mother died. *How could I fall out with her, with Sibel who used to draw little pictures along the edges of the newspaper?* Sibel now has so many pictures that she keeps them in the stable behind her house. Oil paintings, watercolours, chalk and charcoal. Gül can't understand why Sibel doesn't want to show off her paintings, but how could she ever fight with her?

Melike comes in.

'Is there anything else that needs doing before dinner?' she asks. 'If not, I'm going to head over to Yasemin's.'

Melike is already out the door before Sibel has finished shaking her head.

I've often argued with Melike, Gül thinks, *but she's still my sister. I'd always forgive her. I'd always do whatever it took to make it up.*

She takes out another rice pudding and thinks about Nalan, whose life Gül knows so little about since she moved to Istanbul, and who always acts like she's better than the others. Nalan was always different to the blacksmith's other children: she was a cheeky little girl, she feels comfortable wherever she goes, and she's never lost for words. Gül thinks about what Yılmaz said. If it's always the brave ones who leave, then Nalan would have moved away to some foreign land long ago. But Istanbul is foreign in its own way, a huge city where Gül always feels lost. She thinks about how her father's friend tried to console her when she boarded the train to Germany for the first time: *The whole world is a foreign land we will leave some day.*

I might fall out with Nalan, she thinks. *My connection to Nalan isn't as deep, but at the same time, it's not deep enough to ever break.*

It's not as deep, but that has nothing to do with blood or the fact that they have the same father but different mothers. Nalan has moved away from her siblings, from her past, from this town. Nalan considers herself an Istanbulite.

Gül feels close to her brother Emin – the youngest, the ambitious one, the boy she changed and fed, the handsome man with blue-green eyes, tall and strong like his father. She tried to be a mother to Emin, just as she did for Melike and Sibel, even if she never really understood why.

Gül goes into the kitchen, where her stepmother Arzu is busy preparing dinner. Arzu was a young woman when she married the blacksmith and suddenly had to care for three half-orphaned girls. She wasn't loving to Gül, Melike and Sibel, the children who weren't hers. She never kissed or cuddled them, or called them little pet names, and she rarely praised them. But she was just the same with Nalan and Emin, her own children. Gül learnt everything she knows about mothering in the first five years of her life, and she tried to pass that knowledge onto her siblings. As best she could. And her efforts were probably most successful with Emin, because she was bigger and stronger by then. *I was half a mother to him*, she thinks. *How could we ever fall out?*

'I'll take Baba another tea before dinner,' she says. 'He always has at least two at this time of day.'

Every summer, Fuat puts on a bit of weight, and he can't seem to shift it. He hasn't dropped the pounds he put on before Mecnun's death either, and this summer it's not just his waistband that's tight – it's his shirt too, gaping between the lower buttons. *Everyone gets a bit bigger as they get older*, he thinks, and he remembers the days when he used to go on a sun bed. Now his skin is soft and white, and he's surprised to find himself craving the food of his childhood and youth. In his early days in Germany, he missed aubergines, garlic, peppers, bread and lamb. Now he misses the grape juice dried with starch he ate with walnuts as a child, and hakırdak, cubed and fried fatty lamb's tail. Every summer he feasts on them, not caring that he'll be belching the strong smell of his breakfast lamb fat all afternoon. Later in the day he drinks rakı instead of whiskey and Coke, because it reminds him of his youth. He eats white cheese with honeydew melon and complains about the flavourless packaged butter in Germany.

'I don't understand how Germans ever get fat,' he says. 'How can anyone put on weight from that food? It's so bland – they only ever use two spices; salt and pepper. No red pepper paste, no cumin, no fenugreek, no coriander, no chillies. When it comes to technology, they're one of the most progressive countries in the world, but the place is a developing country for food. You might think it's because of all the pork; it fills them up and makes up for everything else. But I'm a curious person, I've sinned and tried pork, and let me tell you: it doesn't taste great. Maybe they'll find out one day that it destroys your taste buds – I wouldn't be surprised. But the Germans get so fat, it beggars belief. I bet it's all that beer.'

He performs this monologue a few times, and Gül wonders whether he's really tried pork or if it's just an empty boast. Maybe he's tried it at the canteen at work. Or with Karen, more likely. *Pork*. As if that were his biggest sin. Sometimes Gül prods at that wound, just for a moment when she has it under control, or for longer when she can't stop thinking about it, and her anger only serves to make her feel sorry for herself – and makes her think she could never be as guilty as her husband.

One evening, Fuat is sitting on the bed in the summer house. He looks down at his belly and says: 'Your sister's wise to go to the seaside every year. Sea air and exercise are good for you. I love my hakırdak, I love my köfter, but this little town is getting too small for me. Let's go to the coast next year, too.'

It's getting too small for you because your belly's getting too big, Gül thinks, but instead of saying anything, she just nods.

The next year, they spend a fortnight by the sea. Not just Gül, Fuat, Ceren and Fatma – Nalan, Sibel and her husband Aziz go with them. Afraid of missing out, Melike comes to join them with her husband from their holiday resort on the Aegean, and even Emin takes four days off to spend time with his sisters. The blacksmith jumps at the chance; only his wife Arzu says: 'You go. What would I do by the sea? I can't swim, and someone has to look after the cows here. There's nothing to do there – it's a place for young people.'

'Just right for me, then,' Timur laughs.

And so they arrive in four cars at a village on the south coast, not far from Mersin, an area not known to many tourists yet. They rent three houses from villagers, who simply move onto their flat roofs as long as they have paying guests downstairs. Up there, they sleep on mattresses with sunshades for the day and mosquito nets for night-time. They use two Primus stoves for cooking and don't seem the least bit bothered about having no privacy.

The days Gül spends by the sea are full of surprises. She's amazed by how little she knows, even though she's a grandmother now, though she's met so many people and heard so many secrets. She's surprised by all the things she hasn't seen before, even though they're not secrets.

Cheekier in her younger days, Nalan became more subdued when her breasts grew so big that men began to ogle her. She started sloping her shoulders forward and curving her back, as if that might hide her shape. It wasn't until she moved to Istanbul that she started walking tall again. Everyone in their hometown talked about her low-cut dresses without ever having seen them, but now Gül notices Nalan is still hiding her body, slouching as soon as she leaves the water, wrapping a towel around herself as fast as she can, often lying on her front. Nalan spends a lot of time in the water; Gül doesn't know where she learned, but she's a faster, more untiring and elegant swimmer than Ceren, who had swimming lessons at school. She's also a better swimmer than Melike, who learned from her husband and has always been sporty. Nalan doesn't swim like someone who grew up in a small town without a lake or a river, and who was twenty the first time she saw the sea.

'Who taught you to swim?' Melike asks on the second day, annoyed after losing a race by two lengths of her body.

'I'm an Aquarius,' Nalan says. 'Water is my element. And maybe living in Istanbul for so long has rubbed off on me – a city right on the water.'

'I live in Izmir, isn't that by the sea?' Melike retorts, and hardly says a word for the rest of the day.

Melike usually shows off about how much energy she has and how young she feels, saying she doesn't even notice her age, but now she just comes across to Gül as immature and childish. Melike will practise doggedly over the next few days, but she'll still finish second in the last race at the end of the holiday.

Gül is surprised by how chatty Sibel is; she's usually so quiet and reserved. She's surprised, too, by her beautiful singing voice. Aziz has his guitar with him, and the two of them often sing harmonies together in the evenings, songs they grew up with, by Aşık Veysel, Davut Suları, by Ruhi Su, Barış Manço or Sezen Aksu. Sibel sings with her eyes closed, apparently blocking out her listeners; she doesn't sing for attention, and she doesn't like them to applaud. Gül can't remember ever hearing her sister sing before. She sings the same way she paints, without pride, without any need for acknowledgement. Aziz is different; you can tell he loves having an audience. *They're my brothers and sisters*, Gül thinks, *but I know so little about them. I was fifteen when I left home; perhaps it's just that we were parted too soon. But I only left so they'd have it better, so there'd be one less mouth to feed.*

Gül knew her father could swim, but she's never seen him swimming. She's heard all the stories about him spending days and days alone in Istanbul or Ankara in his youth, listening to beautiful singers and drinking rakı. She remembers hearing him talk of staring at the ceiling in cheap hotel rooms with a smile on his face, how far away all his cares were, how calm his breathing, how the air tasted of honey, how life lost all its weight. He'd spoken of going to Ankara and Istanbul, even after he married Fatma – he watched Beşiktaş play in the stadium instead of listening to the match on the radio. Gül knows her father savoured those days and nights in the big cities, but she's never seen him anywhere other than home. She thought he'd be different in unfamiliar surroundings, a little like her: cautious, distrustful, fearful. But now she watches the blacksmith striding around the village like he's spent half his life in the place. He's as happy on the beach in his trunks, as he is chatting to the villagers in the tea house. He's the only one of them who navigates the village on his own. People treat him with respect, and by the third day, the brothers and sisters are already known around the village as the blacksmith's children.

Gül is surprised by how brave the villagers are, letting their children play tag on their flat roofs with low ledges. *All you need is courage*, she thinks. The Lord rewards the courageous, not the fearful. *I would die every day, I'd die and come back to life, if I ever saw my children or grandchildren playing like that. But look, nothing ever happens.* Maybe that's what Yılmaz means when he says: Who dares, wins. You have to take a risk. But not as much as Can. You mustn't put your freedom at stake. There are some things you do have to be scared of. Scared of the law. Scared of having no decency. Scared of losing yourself to the lie.

Is my life a bad life because I've been so scared? No, she thinks. *No matter how great fear is, it never takes any space away from love.*

They don't hear or see anything unusual as the owners sit upstairs in the light of the pneumatic lamp, while they're downstairs with electric light and ice cubes from the freezer compartment.

They've been staying in the house for a week now, and Fuat has taken to sitting in the same spot on the little balcony with his shirt off, boasting that mosquitos don't like him because they're only after the sugary blood of women and children who eat too many sweets. His belly doesn't come from chocolate and baklava; his belly is made of traditional fat and grape juice, of white cheese and rakı. He drinks, he smokes, he boasts – he's feeling fine.

There's a knock at the door, even though it's ajar.

'It's the owner,' Gül calls over to the balcony when she sees the man at the door, hat in hand. Fuat gets up.

'Sir,' the man says, still on the threshold. 'Sir, my son's fallen off the roof, his head's bleeding, we think his foot might be broken… Sir, you've got a car, do you think you could take him to hospital?'

'Yes, of course,' says Fuat. 'Let me just put a shirt on.'

It's almost one in the morning by the time they get back. The boy has had stitches on his head, his ankle is sprained, and his ligaments are torn; nothing that won't be forgotten in a few weeks' time.

The following evening, the other children go back to playing tag on the roof.

One lunchtime, as the sisters are walking back from the beach to their holiday home, one of the village women starts up: 'Just who do you think you are?'

'What a cheap slut,' she continues. 'You can't just go walking around our village like that with a tiny scrap of fabric between your legs. Don't you have any decency, you hussy? You think you can come here with all your money and rent our houses and drive our men wild with your easy pussy. You wouldn't walk about like that at home – what makes you think you can do it here? Are we worth less than you? Do you think we've no morals here? This isn't the beach, though our husbands go down there often enough. This is our street– never mind that it's not paved like the ones you live on. There are people living here. Isn't it enough that we rent out our homes to you? Do you want us to give you our men too? Even women who work down the knocking shop wouldn't parade about the street in an outfit like that. Where've you come from then, you tart? What does your father think about you running around in little more than a hankie? At least they shut the doors in brothels – you're walking about the place as if the whole village were your bathroom.'

'You don't mind taking our money though, do you?' Nalan retorts. 'No one forced you to rent out your houses to strangers. If you don't want the money, all you have to do is say.'

Gül looks at Nalan, who's busy trying to cover her chest but raises her voice like she's got nothing to lose. Gül feels hot, hotter than the midday heat could ever be.

Melike says: 'Sister, what makes you think you can speak to me like that? That's how a decent woman speaks, is it? Couldn't you just ask me to throw on a dress when I come back from the beach? And anyway, do you think my dress would save you and your men? Do you think you can just hide from the modern world here? Do you really think you can keep being so backwards for decades to come? Is that what you think? You won't be seeing me out on your streets in my bikini any more, even though I don't believe in being dictated to – not by you, or my father, or anyone else. But you'll remember what I've said today. These streets will be flooded with women in bikinis soon enough, and you'll be wishing for the days when you could still badmouth me in the street.'

Gül is speechless. She was speechless the moment the woman started attacking Melike. Then she was speechless because it was Nalan rushing to defend Melike, even though it should have been her. She's the eldest; she should have defended Melike, even though she agrees with the woman. But she was speechless.

And she's completely taken aback when she hears Melike's reply. What chutzpah! How's she supposed to protect someone like that? Gül is glad it's hot, so hot she can barely breathe – she feels like the air is slipping into her lungs in big gulps, but she can't get any oxygen. Gül is glad it's hot; she's glad she's sunburnt and that she's feeling faint and can blame the heat. Gül is glad that no one can read her thoughts. She's glad that feelings are invisible.

They talk about it all the way home. Gül hardly understands what they're saying; she hopes no one notices she's not joining in the conversation. They cook lunch together, then the subject is dropped when the men arrive, and after their midday nap it seems to have been forgotten.

Gül keeps the woman from earlier in her mind's eye. After Melike's retort, the woman spat, turned her back on them and walked off. For some reason, it reminded Gül of the blacksmith.

People in the South may well be different – they might eat goat meat, they might be able to swim, they might know about banana plants, they might never have seen snow – but they still know how to gossip. If Gül has learned anything about her homeland while she's been in Germany, it's that everyone's a gossip. Gossip, rumours, hearsay, chitchat and tittle-tattle are everywhere.

Gül seems to be the only one who's worried that all the chitchat might lead to news of the incident reaching their husbands' ears, or their father's. She's practically waiting for it. When nothing happens, she realises it can only mean the woman didn't tell anyone.

The day before they're due to go home, Gül feigns a headache so as not to have to go to the beach. When the others have gone out, she leaves the house and heads to the village square, where she asks after the woman with the birthmark over her eyebrow. Gül didn't know what to do when the woman was haranguing Melike, but now she does. She thanks the Lord that he didn't give her any words then when she had nothing to say.

Now she's standing in front of the woman; her heart is pounding, but she can sense this is the right thing to do.

'Thank you,' she says, 'Thank you for not gossiping, thank you for not badmouthing my sister to all and sundry. You were brave and frank and told her what you thought, but you didn't talk about us behind our backs. May the Lord thank you.'

'Come here,' says the woman, pulling Gül into a hug. 'Even in the street I could tell you were a decent woman, one with a heart. Hearts find each other, all over the world. Bless you. Get going, we don't want anyone seeing us together and starting rumours.'

Feelings are like light, Gül thinks as she lights a cigarette. She can hardly see the flame in the glaring sunlight. They don't take anything away. There can always be more light. Or less. Shadows and shade can overlap; the light of the day can blend with firelight, the glow of a lightbulb or a pneumatic lamp. There is a bright joy inside Gül. She'd like to run back and give the woman another hug; she doesn't think she'll ever see her again.

If she looks carefully, there's also a feeling of guilt inside her. She's betrayed her sisters.

And yet, these days by the sea will become happy memories for Gül. In a way, these days have tasted like the summers they spent together when the children were small. Despite the sea air and the heat, which doesn't even let up at night, and despite Fuat's tan, which reminds her of different times. They've tasted like those summers, though the blacksmith has often been elsewhere, separate from the others. They've tasted like happiness, like rest, like family. In these days by the sea, she's been able to hear the song that holds them all together playing loudly once more, the song in which she can hear the strength rushing through their veins.

Perhaps it was because we were all together in an unfamiliar setting, she thinks. *Perhaps it gave our energy space to flow.* Perhaps people who live by the water always see life differently. She thinks of her friend Saniye, who didn't want to live in Hamburg because of her fear of the water.

But perhaps it's just that we hear each other better when we pay no heed to the gossip and chitchat that usually surrounds us, because we're freer than we could be at home. Perhaps that's why people go on holiday – because they're freer there. But of course, not everyone's like us; not everyone uses their time off to make up for that separation. People also travel to places they don't know at all.

She hopes the song will resonate inside her for some time to come. How is she to know that this is the last time she and her siblings with come together so peacefully in one place?

Gül saw the man with fine blond hair speaking to the young woman with the pageboy haircut. She saw them go into a café together, then kissing in a doorway a few days after that, and she heard them, weeks later, having a slanging match about deposit bottles, but she didn't understand what exactly it was about, or who was accusing whom, of what. *Maybe I heard wrong*, she thought. *Maybe it's not about bottles. They're too angry for that. My German's probably not good enough, or the words didn't make it all the way up here.*

Now she sees the man crossing the street as soon as he spots the woman. She thinks back to what it was like sitting on the steps outside the summer house, on those early summer evenings. She was outside there, and now she's watching from above. She wonders what the difference is between sitting in front of the TV and sitting here at her window. In both cases, she sees worlds she's not part of.

The TV is on most of the time since Fuat got a satellite dish.

'It beggars belief,' Fuat said while he was installing it. 'Look at what's going on up there in space. You turn the dish a centimetre too far to the left and suddenly they're all speaking Arabic, a centimetre to the right and it's all in Russian. May these Germans, Japanese and Americans never have to suffer. They're not changing the world; they're changing outer space. TV, telephones, satellite dishes, planes – the world gets smaller and richer every day.'

Gül doesn't sit down to watch programmes very often, but she has them on while she's doing the housework, while she's at the window, while she's knitting, and she keeps track of shows where people fall in love, are drunk with happiness, pale with envy, eaten up by jealousy and resentment. She sees fears, cares, hardships, quarrels, fights, she sees what has always fascinated people – someone getting into difficulties and then finding their way back out. Or finding happiness – and losing it again.

Window or TV, there's no great difference except that she knows a few people here and there, out on the street. She thinks back to the times when *Nachbarn in Europa* was the only Turkish programme on TV, for twenty minutes every Saturday. Now she has eight Turkish channels to choose from, and she doesn't even know what's on German TV these days. They used to watch German programmes and learn German, whether they wanted to or not. Then came video recorders, and anyone who had once quenched their thirst for new things with American movies started quenching their thirst for home with Turkish films. And now TV has slaked all that thirst, has become a window for looking into the lives of strangers.

'People's heads are empty,' Yılmaz says. 'Take a look around you – is there a single Turkish video shop left? No. Because we've all got satellite TV. Like a soap opera's the same as a film, like you could compare those models reeling off their lines, with proper actors. All anyone wants is a moving image. They're addicted to distraction from their own emptiness. Look, the Germans are more cultured than us, there's a video shop on every corner – they don't just watch TV. I have to watch Turkish films dubbed into German because our heads are all empty.'

I can see from my window who goes in the video shop, Gül thinks. *They don't look all that cultured.* But she says nothing, and wonders whether her head is empty too.

She watches life on the street, and she listens to life in the shows, but she doesn't talk much herself. She talks to the young women in the car on the way to work, a few words of German with Herr Bender, and she talks to Saniye and Yılmaz and their daughter Sevgi, who wears make-up these days. The girl always has a subtle scent of expensive perfume and has started talking back to adults, much to her father's delight. Gül talks to Ceyda. She meets up with Can in the department store café every two or three weeks. She talks to Ceren on the phone. It seems like a lot to her when she counts it all up, but it's not much.

Back on Factory Lane, Gül knew all her neighbours. All she had to do was leave the house if she fancied a chat. Now she has more free time, but less contact with people. *Perhaps it's because I'm getting old*, she thinks. *I can't make friends as quickly. These days I know people's flaws and lies, their dreams, hopes and disappointments, almost as well as I know my own hands and feet, and I'm not as curious any more. I've seen the same things again and again, over the years – they haven't changed, but my eye for them is sharper now.*

Sometimes she talks to Saniye about the shows they watch, and Gül wonders whether it has to do with more than just their feelings of emptiness. They're only made-up characters, but the two women think about them a lot: Sonay shouldn't have kept her cleaning job a secret. Yes, but she only wanted to help her nephew get his operation. But her husband would never have let her do it. Too right – a primary teacher's wife going cleaning, with his permission, what would people think? But that's the reality over there, he just doesn't earn enough – everyone knows that – and then when a wife takes a cleaning job, they start bad-mouthing her.

'She shouldn't have let herself get caught,' Gül says.

She's amazed to hear words like that coming from her own mouth. She's amazed that she means it, too. *She shouldn't have let herself get caught. Her husband would never have found out how the money for the operation was raised. She shouldn't have got caught.* That's not emptiness. The show brings something out from inside of Gül.

'Look,' says Can, proudly, putting a passport down on the table.

'What is it?'

'A passport.'

'Did you steal it?'

'Auntie Gül, what do you take me for? Take a look inside.'

'Oh. Is it a forgery?'

'Auntie Gül.'

'Did you have to give up your Turkish passport to get it?'

'Yes, but I'll get myself a new one. You just have to apply.'

'Is that allowed?'

'How will the Germans ever find out?'

'Why did you do it? Your father's Turkish, your mother's Turkish – why have you got yourself a German passport?'

'So they can't deport me.'

'Deport you?'

'You know how I do business. If they've had enough of it, they'll just deport me. It doesn't matter that I was born here and never spent more than six weeks in a row in Turkey – they don't want us here, no matter what. But if you've got a German passport, they can't touch you – it's your right to stay, Turk or not. They have to accept us. We're everywhere now and they can't get rid of us. They'll have to live with it. You said Ceren can't come to Germany. If she had a German passport, they couldn't stop her. You can't always let your feelings decide things. The world's all about paper, not about people's hearts. *What grades did you get at school, what qualifications do you have, how much do you make a month, what kind of passport have you got, what about your criminal record?* Everything's on paper here. It's the paper that says how much you're worth.'

He moves his finger and thumb like he's counting money.

'What good will a Turkish passport do me if I have to go abroad in a rush? My parents come from a village near Zonguldak. The place is half-empty and falling down because everyone's moved here for work. What would I want there? I work here.'

'You call that work?'

'Auntie Gül, I want to get rich. Show me a man who's earned his fortune by the sweat of his brow. Just one. People get rich by making other people work for them, not by working themselves. The only way to make money is by exploiting other people. I exploit people. Just a bit differently.'

'Your path will lead you to ruin. To darkness.'

'I know,' he sniggers, 'dark blue, like a hundred-mark note. Dark brown like a five hundred. Dark is good! I want the dark notes, not those pale tens and twenties.'

Gül looks at their empty coffee cups and is glad she paid the bill. She told Can she'd stop meeting up with him if he insisted on paying. They argued over it for a long time, and it hurts his sense of honour, but something about their meetings is obviously important to him and eventually he agreed through gritted teeth.

Only four days after their conversation, Ceyda says to her mother: 'Mum, I've been thinking it over, and I think we should apply for German citizenship. Who knows what will happen here. Look, we're separated from Ceren. Refugee hostels are burning, people are dying. A German passport won't necessarily keep us safe, but we'd have a stable footing here. Once we've got German passports we can just apply for new Turkish ones.'

Gül eyes her daughter. Is she afraid of being deported too?

'Think about it,' Ceyda says. 'Think of all that time we've spent in offices and consulates just because of our Turkish passports, all the problems we've had, how much time it's cost us.'

Gül thinks about it. Residence permits, work permits, visas for the children's school trip to Denmark, taking their official address registration slips every time they need a membership card somewhere. Policemen who want to see their passports because that's the only correct identity document and who get annoyed when they don't have them to hand. The queue they always have to join to get into Turkey while the German tourists get waved through, all the hours on hard wooden chairs in the corridors of the foreigners' registration office.

'Maybe you're right,' she says.

Ceyda is surprised that her mother doesn't contradict her.

And Gül is surprised that Fuat doesn't object. On the contrary – he thinks it's a clever idea.

Maybe I'm the only one in this family who still feels anything about the paper my passport's printed on, she thinks. Not enough to take a stand, though. Still, she's relieved when she finds out Saniye and Yılmaz have already applied for German citizenship. *If Yılmaz is doing it, it can't be wrong*, she thinks. And yet it feels strange, in her case. Yılmaz has a good few German friends; people who think it's important to be friends with Turks, especially political refugees. Since Ceyda's been working at the post office, she's had German friends she meets for coffee, and she's friends with the parents from Duygu's and Timur's classes. Can has German, Tunisian, Lebanese, Albanian, Italian, Serbian, Bosnian, and Russian friends – it doesn't make any difference to him as long as they're people who move in his circles, even though he talks about the rivalries between them.

'I haven't got any German friends,' she says to Ceyda a few days later. 'Wouldn't it be strange for me to have a German passport?'

'A passport has nothing to do with friendship,' Ceyda says. 'It's just a piece of paper. It doesn't say anything about you as a person. Anyway, who's stopping you making friends with Germans?'

'There are hardly any at work,' says Gül. 'And even if there were, I don't speak their language well enough.'

'You were friends with Auntie Tanja, in a way.'

'She was the only German on Factory Lane.'

'Mum, we live here, we can live our lives freely. The doors aren't locked. We're residents of this country. We don't live on Factory Lane any more.'

Even though Can has completely different values to everyone else Gül knows, he used the same arguments as her daughter, just for different reasons.

Gül sinks into the sagging sofa, clutching her new passport. She won't be able to get back up without some effort. How many times has she tried to convince Fuat to buy a new sofa? He's always coming up with new excuses – most recently he claimed it would be impossible to get the kind she wanted up the wooden stairs in their building. But yesterday he finally agreed, perhaps because he's been finding himself creaking and groaning whenever he tries to get off the couch.

Gül sits there, passport in hand. She doesn't switch on the TV, and she has no desire to look out of the window. She thinks about what her father once said: 'What difference is there between Germany and the Beyond? From here, both of them seem just as unlikely. You disappeared to a country where I don't know the smells, where I can't imagine the streets, full of people I've never seen.'

Now she's officially a citizen of this country, and she remembers how she'd been planning to bring her father over to Germany, so that he could see the difference between Germany and the Beyond, so that he could get a sense of the place where his daughter lives, so that he could picture her surroundings and feel close to her.

'I've changed my mind,' she says to Fuat that evening. 'The sofa can wait. Let's bring my dad over for two or three weeks instead.'

'To this tiny flat? That poor old man who's never flown before in his life? What's got into you? What's he supposed to do with himself here with no garden, no stable, no friends, no cows, no moped? Do you want the man to die of boredom? Is that what you want?'

Gül frowns at him.

'May God bless your parents,' she says. 'They never had the chance to come here and see how we live. They never had the chance because we never thought to make it happen. It's a chance for us to be close to each other. And my father and I are going to take it.'

Fuat breathes in, ready to reply, but then he just exhales loudly, as if he's decided his wife is a lost cause. Then he takes another breath and starts talking about money, about the steep staircase up to the flat, about unfeeling Germans, the pain of seeing and knowing that your child lives in a foreign place, knowing that your own flesh and blood is looked down upon elsewhere. He talks about burning asylum hostels, racism, the bread that Timur will miss, the orderly traffic and all the cars that'll confuse him, the flight that'll be too much for him; he talks about Timur's health and his age and his moped accidents, how he'll struggle to adapt, he talks and talks and talks, and Gül lets him.

'I'm getting old,' says the blacksmith. 'The plane didn't really take it out of me, but the bus ride to Istanbul went on forever – my knees were stiff, my arse was aching, my hips were cracking. If you could fly to Istanbul and change there, the journey would be no trouble at all. And as for the four flights of stairs Fuat was trying to scare me with, well, they're child's play.'

'We'd like to move,' says Gül, 'to somewhere with a lift.' She senses Fuat is about to pipe up, but she throws him a look that stops him in his tracks.

'I expect it's rude to ask, but does the bread always taste like this here?' the blacksmith asks at dinner.

'I told you so.' Fuat can't resist.

'Yes,' says Gül. 'The bread always tastes like that.'

'So it's true, then. Germany's not a good country for bread. But the streets are clean, the traffic's under control, everyone sticks to the rules and no one's too loud. It's like the whole country's been freshly washed and ironed.'

It's not until this moment that Gül wonders if she made the right decision. How much will her father understand of the life outside her window, and what will he think? Won't he be sad, won't it break his heart? Won't he feel that it would've been better to know his daughter was in a distant village in eastern Turkey rather than in Germany, this place of legend with its bad bread, its squeaky floorboards, its young men running dodgy deals, with its scruffy homeless people and sickly junkies, its punks with dyed hair, and its women, who wear skirts that stop just beneath their petticoats and heels that go practically all the way up to the hem of their skirts? What will he think when he sees all the tattoos, the graffiti? Why hadn't Gül thought about all this beforehand? Why did she spend weeks ignoring the obvious? Why did her excitement leave her so short-sighted?

Gül feels bad that she's brought him to this part of town, and she consoles herself with the thought that he'll also be spending a few days at Ceyda's. Ceyda lives in a house now and it'll be paid off in fifteen years' time.

Strange, she thinks. *When we were in Turkey, we were always trying to get people to do away with the image of Germany as some kind of paradise. But now that my father's here, I'd much rather show him that dreamland, where places like this don't exist.*

It's the blacksmith's first evening in Germany. Fuat's in the bathroom and Gül has a little time before she has to leave for work, when the blacksmith sits down on the sofa and cries. He's not crying like he did under the tree that day; his cheeks are hardly moist, his nose isn't running, and his eyes aren't red. He cries just two tears. Two. One for joy, one for gratitude, he says.

Gül always lets each tear she encounters into her heart.

Now Songül is downstairs, beeping her horn. Gül is running late, for the first time ever. When she gets in the car, Songül asks what took her so long.

'I was making my father another tea with lemon juice,' says Gül.

On the drive to the airline company's offices, Nurcan and Songül talk about what it would be like if their grandfathers came over to Germany, but Gül's not listening. She looks at the tram lights, the neon signs, the car headlights, the streetlights, and she wonders whether man-made lights could cause a person as much fear as the darkness. She doesn't understand where this question comes from – she doesn't even know if she's happy or scared herself.

Gül works half the night, and her father is used to getting up early. For the first three days, she gets up at the same time as him, but on the fourth, she oversleeps. When she gets up, the blacksmith isn't there. *He's gone out*, she tells herself. *He probably got bored – it's not like he's been kidnapped. Of course he's bored, it's normal for him to want to get out and about – that's what he must have done.* But when did he leave? Why didn't she hear him go? What if he gets lost? How long should she wait? Half an hour passes and she's already getting restless. She starts pacing. She can hardly go out now – what if he came back and was left standing outside the front door while she's gone? She has to wait. This is Germany, it's broad daylight – what's the worst that could happen? Still, he doesn't know a word of German. She's never written down her address for him. There are plenty of people in the area who speak Turkish. But what if he's gone further afield? Gül stands there, smoking a cigarette by the window. Which side will her father appear from? Down below, she sees Can go up to a woman and speak to her briefly. She slips him a few notes and he continues on his way.

Just one more day until the weekend, then they'll go to Ceyda's and stay with her. Gül's time off starts on Monday. Ceyda lives in a quiet area, where everything is much calmer and more orderly. A place where, for a long time, Adem didn't leave the house without taking his air gun with him, because there were skinheads on the hunt for Turks. A place where Ceyda was afraid she might lose her mind. But that all seems to be forgotten now; no one talks about it any more.

The later it gets, the more Gül fears losing her wits. It's midday; her father has been out for at least two and a half hours; he has no money, no key, and he doesn't know the area. He might get lost, he might end up on the motorway because he thinks it's the shortest route back, he might get run over, he might be attacked and beaten up, he might have a fall, he might get picked up by the police without his passport. *What will I tell my siblings if he's deported or doesn't turn up? How could I ever forgive myself?* And all because sleep was sweeter than love.

She gives a start when the doorbell rings, as if she hadn't been waiting for it all along. It must be him. Who else would ring the doorbell at this time? She must have missed him coming because she couldn't bear to stay by the window and kept pacing the room.

She's never run down the stairs so fast in her life.

'Thank the Lord.'

The blacksmith spots what's happened and pulls his daughter into his arms.

'Sorry about that, I got carried away chatting.'

'Chatting?'

'Yes, I got talking to the owner of the garage.'

'Which garage?'

'If you take a right at the front door and then a left at the bakery, you come to a football pitch, and behind it there are these big concourses, then behind them there's a junction. You take a left there and there's a garage, behind the field. The owner's a mechanic, from Sivas. He doesn't know Fuat or you, but he's a decent chap; a village man, but educated. His father was a blacksmith – we had lots to talk about. He was keen for me to stay for lunch, but I told him I had to get home.'

When will Gül learn that not all people are like her? She knows the football pitch – it's twenty minutes away at least – but she doesn't know the junction her father mentions. She would never have dared venture so far.

She's only ever seen her father in her hometown, and once in the village by the sea. He moves around in Germany as freely as he did in those places. *Where did I get this fear from, this distrust? Is it just because my mother died so young, or would I have been like this anyway?*

'I'm the blacksmith's daughter,' she'll say, several weeks later, just as she so often did when she was little, and the mechanic will be glad to see her. The blacksmith has made the city into a place where people recognise her. Timur hasn't just built a picture of Germany for himself, something to distinguish it from the Beyond and the darkness; he's changed Germany for Gül, too. Its streets are now streets he has walked down; the mechanic who now gives Fuat generous discounts is a man who knows her father.

'People are talking about you.'

She doesn't know why she says it. She's been all muddled since she said goodbye to her father at the airport yesterday.

'What are they saying?'

'You know what.'

'No, I don't.'

'Yes, you do. Your life is your business, but do you really have to pull others into it? What have those poor creatures done?'

'Nothing. You know what they say. We all have to live with our own sins.'

'You earn money by making others do…' She grasps for the word. '…you-know-what.'

'Auntie Gül, that's how the system works. Orhan earns money by getting you to work for him. And it's not what you think, anyway.'

'I earn my money by the sweat of my brow. Yılmaz talks a lot about exploitation, but it's still a job with honour to it. I'd rather be cleaning strangers' muck off toilets than… And you…'

'It's not what you think,' Can repeats.

Gül doesn't know why she's pushing the issue; she appeals to his conscience less and less these days. On the contrary, she likes listening to him talk about how easy it is to steal a safe and how difficult it is to get it open without damaging the contents. You have to know what's inside before you do it – banknotes, jewels, or watches. Can doesn't sound like a criminal when he talks about this; he sounds like a young man who thinks long and hard about his work. Work that happens to not be legal. Perhaps that's why she's disappointed.

'How are things, then?' she asks.

'Business isn't great at the moment. I just know these women – we move in the same circles. Sometimes I chat to them, and if they've got something left over, they pass it on to me. That doesn't make me a pimp though.'

'How can you take that money? It's tainted… tainted with those poor women's souls.'

'What do you know about those women, Auntie Gül? Maybe they don't want what you call honest work. Maybe they'd rather earn 200 marks an hour. Orhan's slowly sucking your soul out too, but it takes longer, and you get less money for it. The world's split into rich and poor, Auntie Gül. Either you…'

He breaks off.

'I'm sorry, but it's true. Either you… or you get… Look, when you go overdrawn or take out a loan, then the bank's got you by the— by the scruff. But when you owe the bank two or three million, then you can sleep peacefully. They'll be nice to you then, because they know they've got to be nice to you if they ever want to see their money again. If you've got debts, you want a rich man's debts, not a poor man's. Act like a rich man and you get treated like a rich man. Look, if I slap someone, I'm treating him like a woman. A slap is an insult. If I punch him, it shows that I see him as my equal. You can't punch the bank, that wouldn't work; you've got to beat it. After all, who was it who got rich off all the people who left Turkey to work here? They all wanted to save some money – almost all of them have a house back home, but what price did they have to pay? Night shifts, overtime, time-and-a-half on weekends. My mother didn't get to see me grow up. She didn't notice that I was skipping school, she didn't notice I was stealing from supermarkets – she was always at work. She's got a house, but she's not rich. Vural Öger is rich, just look at his big travel agency. You get rich when you make others work for you. Think about it: what sort of bonus did your husband get? Ten thousand marks. What will the company earn from the improvements he made? Millions probably, over the years. Don't you feel sorry for your husband? Poor bloke. Racks his brains and then he's sent home with a bit of pocket money just because he happens to take his breaks in the canteen, not the executive lounge. That's how the world works, Auntie Gül. And those women aren't working for me, they just give me a little cash because we know each other and we're friends.'

Gül is amazed at how both Can and Yılmaz have argued the same thing, even though they're so different. Maybe there's something in what they say.

Gül feels guilty about these meetings at the cafe. She tries to convince herself that she's not doing anything wrong. She's not going behind anyone's back, she's not tricking or deceiving anyone, but she knows that's a lie. She can't tell anyone about her chats with Can. Not Fuat, not Ceyda, not Ceren, not Saniye, not Yılmaz, and not her sisters. She's been meeting up with a criminal, and she has to keep it a secret. The things we can't share are what make us lonely. And they lead to lies, because you're hiding part of yourself, because you're lying about it when it feels like you need to.

Gül meeting up with Can is like her smoking. She knows it's not a good idea, but she can't stop.

Perhaps it's because he's so different to me, she thinks sometimes. *He's more different than the Germans, but he speaks my language.* He's not a bad person, even if he lies and steals and tricks, even if he makes money pimping, even if he rejects everything that Gül believes. Something about this young man endears him to her. Endeared him to her. The matter of the young women troubles her, though.

In Turkish, pimp is an insult full of contempt; it's the lowest rung of criminality. Pimps come below thieves, conmen, drug dealers, even murderers.

After this, Gül won't meet up with Can for a whole year. She'll come up with excuses and she'll lie, but she won't feel bad about it, because she only lies so as not to hurt his feelings.

She looks out of the window, listening to her show on TV, and she thinks about prostitution. She tries to grasp how a person could sell their body. They're called hayat kadınları, life women, in Turkish, or call girls, because all you have to do is call them up. Whores, hookers, streetwalkers, hustlers, ladies of the night. There are always lot of words for things that are important. Like sex. Like the money that these women earn: dough, dosh, bunce, moolah, brass, squids. Is the body the most important part of a woman? Perhaps it is for men. After all, in the old days, Fuat didn't care who she was or what she felt when he used to drunkenly shake her awake at night. It could have been any woman lying in his bed, he probably wouldn't have known the difference. Do these women feel any different to how she did? They pick up men who've got enough cash, and who probably reek of booze as badly as Fuat did back then, but at the end of the night they go home alone with money in their pockets, and they don't have to answer to anyone. They don't have to tolerate the men in their lives for long. But their mothers' and fathers' hearts blacken when they find out what their daughter is doing. Their fingers drip with grief. Briefly, just briefly, like touching a ring on the hob to check if it's hot, Gül imagines what it would be like if one of her daughters…

Picturing this seems less painful to her than knowing Ceren is widowed and a single mum to her daughter in Adana. The pain can't be compared – there's a difference, she can feel it, but she doesn't want to find out what it is. There is no hob she could burn herself on and that's enough for her.

Perhaps Can is wrong to say the world is split into rich and poor; perhaps Can and Yılmaz are both wrong because they don't want to see that the world is divided into women and men. And men decide that the world has to be split between rich and poor. Men want money, and so they leave their country, their parents, their children, their home, their language behind and put up with lives full of hardship. Perhaps that's why she likes Can so much, because she sees a longing in him that he himself can't quite name. He thinks he wants money. But he's not like Fuat, who's also after a quick buck. Can wants money the way he wants a coat to keep him warm, to caress his skin and keep his back straight. He doesn't want money because he thinks it'll make him happier; he wants it because he thinks if he gets it, he'll be worthy of the love and care he needs.

They're back at the seaside, but this time they're on the Aegean because Melike has rented a house at a good price through an acquaintance, only an hour away from Izmir. Melike, her husband Mesut, Gül, Fuat, Ceren and Fatma are staying in a two-bedroom bungalow, while Melike's son, İsmail, is at training camp. Melike never tires of singing the Aegean's praises: the tourism infrastructure, the modern attitude to life, all the local villas owned by celebrities, which singer has been spotted on what beach and which actor in what bar, how that TV presenter was at the next table when she had the best ice-cream in town. She also keeps mentioning her retirement next year.

'I've only just got the hang of my job, and now my working life's coming to an end already,' she says. 'I used to be an impatient teacher, impatient and inexperienced. Getting older has brought me patience, and experience gave me a routine, which means I don't need as long to respond to students' questions these days. I hardly need to prepare my lessons either. I've reached my most productive, and now the state's going and putting me out to pasture.'

It sounds like she regrets it, but she's looking forward to leaving the school and giving private tuition to rich people's children instead, making more money than before.

At this point in time, women in Turkey have to work twenty years before they can retire; for men it's twenty-five. Twenty years – that doesn't seem long to Gül any more.

She still has more than ten years to go, and she started work much younger than Melike, who went to college. She's not envious of her sister, and she's not afraid of hard work, but she wonders what Can and Yılmaz would say about people in Turkey having to work so few years to get a pension, albeit one they can't live on, forcing them to go out and look for work again.

Gül and Melike wash the dishes and make dinner while the others take an afternoon nap. Melike talks about the new car she wants to buy, then she says: 'Emin's business in Istanbul's getting bigger and bigger – he sells motorbikes now. He's turned into a real city boy. And Nalan's an Istanbulite anyway. Sibel's so happy in her little house on the edge of our town, you'll be staying in Germany a while yet, and I'll soon be retiring… May God grant him a late death, but Baba will die one day and pass on the summer house for us children and Arzu to share. I've already spoken to Sibel; she's not interested in the house. I'll talk to Emin and Nalan; I reckon they'll say the same thing. But you, I bet you'll always want to go back to the house from your childhood, won't you?'

Gül has never thought about what might become of the summer house. 'Yes,' she says.

And with that answer, it suddenly feels as if her childhood is not just in her head, but also in that house. It's almost like the house has its own memory, which it passes on to Gül, a memory that imposes itself on hers and tells her things she'd forgotten long ago. Gül feels dizzy; perhaps it's the heat. The world seems to shift – she grips the table for support and needs to sit down.

For a few moments, everything blurs together and Gül sees her childhood not in events and distinct recollections, but in patterns and colours, intertwining. She feels lost, like she did as a child – she has that sensation of how vulnerable she was, how unprotected. She looks at Melike, and in that moment she realises that part of her sister's childhood felt exactly the same. She realises that part of every childhood probably feels that way. That every child feels lost and helpless; at the mercy of the adults' world and the vastness of the cosmos.

'Gül? Gül? Are you alright? Do you need a glass of water? Gül, what's the matter?'

'I'm fine. I was just… a bit dizzy.'

She shakes her head; the world seems to straighten up again, and then she says something she regrets even before she's finished speaking.

'Have you got enough money?'

'Yes,' Melike says. 'İsmail earns good money. Half the world's population chases after balls, and even if he just sits on the reserve bench, he makes more in a month than I do all year.'

Gül holds her tongue, but the words her father once said to her pop into her head: *There are two things that darken a person's heart: speaking when you ought to be silent, and being silent when you ought to speak.* Now she's guilty of both. *Why are you relying on your son's money?* she wanted to ask, but she swallowed the words.

'You mean the two of us should buy the house off the others?'

'Well, that's your suggestion, but I'll have a word with Emin and Nalan.'

Gül nods. And doesn't ask: *What about Arzu?*

Over the next few days, she gathers up her memories of the summer house. She sits on the beach, looks out at the sea, and slips back into her childhood. *I was lucky*, she thinks. *I had more time with our mother than my sisters did. I ought to be grateful.* She sees Fatma on the beach and knows the little girl will never remember her father. *She should have a place too*, Gül thinks, *somewhere we all belong, a place that gives us strength*. Over these few days, the summer house becomes a place Gül loves to daydream about. She sees Fatma and Ceren playing in the sand and imagines her daughter and granddaughter picking and eating mulberries in the summer house garden.

Ceren is happy studying German, even though almost all the other students are younger and have very different lives to her. No one at her lectures has any children; they can lead student lives, leave their dorms at night until curfew, go to the cinema or out for a beer. They can make spontaneous decisions, while Ceren's routine revolves around picking Fatma up from nursery.

On top of her widow's pension, Ceren gets 200 deutschmarks a month from her parents, and the rent from the house back in their town, where she's no longer living. When she's paid her rent, the nursery fees, the phone, gas and electricity bills, and once she's bought food and books for school, she has enough left over to go to the cinema twice a month, but not enough to pay a babysitter. She lives in a flat of her own, so she doesn't have to slip past a porter to get back into a dorm, but she never has a chance to get home late.

Ceren tells Gül about how all the students meet up at her place, how they do their assignments together, how she serves them tea and pastries, how much her friends like playing with Fatma, how helpful they are, how friendly and obliging. She tells her about one friend who can forge her signature perfectly and signs the attendance list for Ceren if she has to stay at home because Fatma is ill – or if she simply skips a class because it's all too much for her. She doesn't mention that part, though.

Gül is glad her daughter has found her feet; after Mecnun's death, she spent so much time staring at the wall, sinking deeper and deeper into something, never hitting the ground. 'It's like the dreams from my childhood,' she lamented at the time.

'I'm falling and falling, and I never get to the bottom. But it's different to then, because I can't wake up – I'm trapped in a bad dream that won't ever stop, not until the end of my life.'

Now, two years into university, Gül sees that Ceren is a good student, a cheerful and attentive hostess, a loving mother. *And in all that time she was still my child*, Gül thinks. *She's still my child, no matter where the light comes from, no matter how dark it is, no matter how little I can help her or how often I have to leave her on her own.* Gül wonders whether Ceren has it harder than Ceyda. From Turkey to Germany and then back to Turkey, confronted with death and loss so early on in life. But Ceren doesn't have migraines, she isn't scared of losing her mind, and she doesn't have a husband who's not interested in her. A husband who lives like grass, as Fuat would say.

For a while, Gül thought she'd set her daughters on their paths and they could walk them alone, not stumbling or staggering along the way. But did she herself walk without getting out of step? Did she walk without her back ever bending, her legs ever growing heavy? Life is hard, hard for all of us, but perhaps our breath always has the same weight. Perhaps ultimately, we all bear the same burden of lives on loan.

Then she looks at Fuat. His worries these days are all about money, about getting indigestion from alcohol. She looks at Fuat, who may well have suffered from her having denied him any intimacy since his betrayal. She looks at him and wonders whether he bears as heavy a load as the others. She doesn't know whether his conscience scratches his skin from the inside. She looks at her tanned husband, then turns her gaze to the water, the rays of evening sun playing off the waves. She goes back to thinking of the summer house, turns the thought over in her mind, looks at it from this direction and that.

It's always dark in your head; the light doesn't shine in from outside, not even through your eyes, she thinks. *The light only ever comes from inside, from your thoughts and from inside your heart.* The thought of the summer house brightens her mind, and she finds herself wondering how much light might weigh.

At first, Gül thinks there's been a mix-up. The man looks like Serter, but he seems older and is much better dressed than the Serter she knew. His suit is made of wool, his shirt spotless and freshly ironed, his black leather shoes shining. He looks a little out of place in the Turkish supermarket, but he's turning the tin round and round in his hand, just like Serter would, as if to work out if its contents are poisoned.

The man notices Gül looking, turns to her and looks her in the eye without moving, until Gül murmurs: 'I'm sorry, I didn't mean to disturb you – you just look like someone I used to know.'

'Really, Gül? You still don't recognise me? Not even now?' the man says. 'What did I do wrong? You were always different from the others – have you gone and switched sides?'

'No, Serter, no I haven't. Sorry. It's been so many years… I couldn't be sure it was you.'

'Yep, my hair's grey now, it's all the years I've spent watching my back. But as you can see, they didn't get me. I'm in rude health.'

'The suit looks good on you.'

'Thanks.'

'Perhaps that's what threw me a bit. The Serter I knew never wore suits like that.'

'Gül, I've got God on my side. How could my enemies ever triumph? I'm still here, and with different clothes to boot.'

'He still speaks to you?'

Serter looks around, then nods. Gül smiles. Not to be patronising, or from pity. She smiles out of love for this man, who she feels must be lonely, even if he does hear the voice of God. Back in Gül's Factory Lane days, Serter split up with his wife because – as far as he was concerned – she was bent on nothing less than his demise, because she had poisoned his food and was out for his blood. Serter saw every person as a threat, but he did his work and wasn't a danger to anyone. Everyone made jokes about him and talked about him behind his back; no one took him seriously, but Gül has always found him genuine. She felt proud, even, that he would eat her food when all he ever usually ate were pre-packaged meals for fear of being poisoned.

Serter sighs. 'It's rare He does now,' he says. 'He speaks to me less and less, but often enough for me not to feel completely abandoned. Sometimes I think He made me this different to other people so that I wouldn't lose myself in them and move away from Him. But enough about me. What are you doing in Germany? I thought you moved back to Turkey years ago. Are you here visiting friends? No, you wouldn't be at the supermarket on your own if you were. What are you doing here, Gül?'

The happiness he felt at seeing Gül disappears from his eyes.

'You've moved back,' he says, before she has a chance to answer. 'This country's a magnet – you can't turn your back on it and leave. It pulls you back. The problem is, they don't want us here. Haven't you heard about how the asylum hostels burned down, haven't you heard about the skinheads? But that's just the beginning, it's only going to get worse. This country is like a scab; we can't help but keep picking at it and reopening the wound. And as for me, it's even worse than that – they want me dead! But I know how to look after myself, even if everybody thinks I can't. Oh Gül, it's only those of us with wounds who get the urge to pick at them. Couldn't you have stayed over there?'

Gül takes a breath, but in the end she says nothing. How can she tell him how lonely she felt in her hometown, about Fuat's dalliances, about Ceyda's offer to help bring her over to Germany? How is she supposed to stand here in the supermarket and explain that her husband might have left her if she hadn't come back?

'No,' she says. 'No, I couldn't have stayed.'

'Brace yourself,' says Serter, 'you can't defend yourself against a magnet or a storm, but if you steel yourself, you can survive it at least. Look at me, I've always been careful, and now here I am, standing right in front of you, chatting away.'

He's aged considerably, but the years of loneliness haven't broken him, Gül thinks. *Maybe he's doing something right.*

'That suit really looks good on you.'

'Yes, I think so too. I've got a whole wardrobe full.'

'Have you landed on your feet?' Gül asks.

'Yes, thanks be to God. I won the lottery and now I'm rich. One less thing to worry about.'

'Congratulations. The lottery, you say?'

'Yep. I only played it three times and I won on the third go.'

'On the third go? It beggars belief! How many years is it I've been playing the lottery? Is there no justice at all in this world? What could that loon even want with all that money? Last time I saw him, he was going around asking for donations for terrorist organisations. I suppose he can give them plenty of support now,' says Fuat. 'I've heard nothing of him in ages. I thought he'd been sectioned. He shouldn't be allowed to walk the streets – he's a threat to public safety. He shouldn't even be allowed to use a pen to fill out a lottery slip. Can't they declare him mentally underage and take the money back? Money's not enough to cure him, that's for sure. What justice is there in this world, honestly, when a man like him gets rich – a laughingstock who trusts no one? He doesn't deserve a penny.'

'Would you deserve it if you won?'

'Of course I would! Just look how many years I've been playing the lottery. I haven't been lucky once. Fate fobs us off with a couple of coins, but Serter's pockets are stuffed with cash. What's the bloke even doing with the money?'

'Well, what would you do?'

Fuat's really on his soapbox now. He can't even tell that Gül isn't taking him seriously.

'I'd buy myself a Mercedes S-Class, a brand new one, with all the latest tech, in black. I've had one parked outside my dreamhouse for a while now. And I'd buy suits in a silk-wool blend, shoes with leather soles, a massive TV. I'd quit work on the spot – half my life's been spent on the factory floor. I'd buy expensive whiskey for 120 marks a pop, whiskey as mild as a spring day, so smooth it'd never give you heartburn. And I'd get us out of this flat, buy us a sofa, we'd only ever fly first class… when you've got money, you've got plenty to keep you entertained. I wouldn't be short of ideas.'

What about your daughter in Adana? Does she matter less than a good whiskey? Gül thinks, but she doesn't say it out loud.

'Serter's bought himself some suits,' she says. 'Really smart ones.'

'It's strange that I haven't heard about it,' says Fuat. 'There's usually a fair bit of gossip about when someone like that wins the lottery.'

The next night, Fuat comes home with three bottles of beer. Gül looks at him, baffled.

'I haven't had a drop for weeks,' he says. 'It's no life. I thought at least beer won't give me heartburn.'

He turns out to be right, and Fuat takes to drinking beer regularly, with peanuts and salty snacks on the side.

'This is what it does to you, living in a different country,' he says. 'Now I'm drinking beer like a German.'

It's Friday evening and Fuat has lugged a whole crate of beer up the stairs; he's unusually taciturn and sullen. After his fourth bottle that night, he says: 'Ungrateful bastards, that's what they are.'

Gül does him the favour of asking who.

'Those snobs, the managers. When I optimised their production process they gave me a bonus, but now none of them are asking: *What has Fuat done for us? What do we owe him?* Now all I get is: *You can go now. We don't care that you've worked your fingers to the bone for us for years.* It's not that the place is closing down like the wool factory, no – Mercedes is still going strong, they'll be making plenty of money – it's just us they don't want any more. It doesn't matter what we've done for them.'

'Last time you were only unemployed for a day before you found a new job,' Gül reminds him.

'I'm tired,' Fuat says. 'Nothing but ingratitude, wherever you look.'

'It's not ingratitude,' says Yılmaz. 'It's the law of money. First they brought cheap workers into the country, and now they've worked out it's cheaper to outsource the whole production line. They don't have to pay national insurance for the workers abroad, the wages are low, and no one gets unemployment benefits over there. Gratitude, ingratitude – those are human values. They don't count; business is all about numbers. Just think of the poor buggers who'll work for them now – what would they say to all this?'

'I don't know of any jobs, but there's a flat to let here on the estate,' Saniye says. 'You could move here. I bet you've had about enough of your neighbourhood and all those stairs by now. It's nice and green round here – you can just go outside and sit on a bench, and we'd see more of each other. There are lifts, too.'

'How are we supposed to move if I don't have a job?' Fuat says, suppressing his rage.

'Something's bound to turn up. There's no rush, you've still got six months or more.'

'And who'll give Gül a lift to work? She can hardly take the bus at that time of the morning. No one will want to come all this way to pick her up. Do you want her to learn to drive like you?'

'Why not, though, Uncle Fuat?' says Sevgi. 'What's wrong with women driving?'

'Nothing,' Fuat says. 'There's nothing wrong with it. But you ask Gül if she's got the guts, go on. You need guts for everything. My wife's so jumpy, even in the passenger's seat. You could give her a heart attack by so much as bursting a paper bag.' He looks over at Gül and says: 'Go ahead and tell me I'm wrong.'

'He's right,' says Gül. 'I haven't got what it takes.'

'Anyone can drive a car,' says Sevgi. 'You just have to give it a go, Auntie Gül. Look at all the other things you can do. It's hard for me too. I've had twenty-four driving lessons already, and my instructor says I'll need a few more yet. But I'm going to learn.'

'But even if she could drive, what am I supposed to do?' Fuat asks. 'Buy a second car?'

'It's not just up to you – you both earn money. The days when husbands had the say are over, now we have equal—'

'Didn't you have homework to be doing?' Saniye interrupts.

'Yes,' Sevgi says. 'Of course, I forgot. Excuse me.'

She gets up, and if she's angry she doesn't show it. In the doorway, she turns back towards them.

'I'm sorry,' she says. 'I didn't mean to interfere. It's none of my business.' She sounds genuine.

'Perhaps she gets her sense of justice from me,' Yılmaz says once Sevgi's closed the door to her bedroom. 'And she's starting to want to join in with the adults,' he adds. You can hear the pride in his voice.

'He thinks he's something special,' Fuat complains. 'Just because he went to university. Look at him, though – no proper work for years, calls himself assistant director in some Turkish theatre that only ever Germans go to. Sits at home watching films, reading books and listening to music. I bet all he does in that theatre is make coffee. But when it comes to handing out advice, he's always first in line. *Don't put your money in those new banks, Fuat. It's not safe. They'll all go bust if there's a crash tomorrow.* They're not corner shops, they're banks. Twelve percent on every deutschmark. What idiot would miss out on a chance like that? Only clever dicks like Yılmaz who don't have anything put aside, eaten up by jealousy. Scaredy-cat clever dicks who never take a risk but have a fancy stereo. He lets his wife go out to work for him, and he opens his mouth so wide a fully-loaded camel could walk right in. Have you ever heard of a bank going bust? There's no need to be scared of things just because they're new. Think of all the new TV channels there are – has any one of them shut down again? Yılmaz might know about football, I'll give him that, but other than that he talks too much. There's no need to be scared of people who talk too much; it's the ones who actually do things you have to watch out for.'

'Maybe Yılmaz has a point,' Gül answers. 'Maybe we shouldn't just put all our money in. Maybe we should keep some of it in the central bank to be on the safe side.'

'Maybe, maybe… No one ever gets rich from work alone. You've got to have a bit of good luck in the game or let your money do the work for you. Take a good look at the people who are giving you advice. No one would take diet tips from me, would they?' He grabs his belly with both hands, and Gül remembers the days when he used to make hurtful remarks about her figure.

The lift stops between floors. Either you press five and walk down half a flight of stairs, or you press four and walk up. In their first few weeks there Gül always walked the whole way, thinking the exercise was good for her; it's an effort Fuat never makes. But when they get back from work early in the morning, Gül is tired and her legs are heavy and since Fuat never takes the stairs if he can help it, she gets used to taking the lift with him. Only in the morning to begin with, but then she starts making more and more exceptions, and soon the two of them always squeeze into the little lift together.

Back when they worked in the wool factory, Gül and Fuat weren't just in different departments; they also worked different shifts because of the children. Now, even though they usually work on different corridors, Gül can see that Fuat works in the same way as the colleagues she doesn't understand. 'Oh, that doesn't matter, no one'll notice, it's not like anyone's going to check I've dusted under the telephone. Who's going to see if there's dust on the top of the doorframe, who can prove that scratch wasn't there before?...' At least she doesn't hear Fuat saying the other things she's all too familiar with. 'Cleaning cloths, no one counts them. It's only cleaning fluid, it'd get used up anyway if I sprayed a bit more of it about. Just five hundred sheets of photocopy paper, just toilet rolls, just three rolls of Sellotape...' People steal without the slightest sense of injustice, and there are times when Gül doesn't know how much of a difference there is between her workmates and a man like Can. Can seems almost more sincere to her; at least he doesn't pretend to be honest.

In the first few weeks, she occasionally reminds Fuat to be more thorough because that's what they're paid for, not to sniff around for ways to shirk without getting caught.

'Good grief,' he says then. 'Good grief, woman, we're working in the middle of the night to clean things that are already clean. There's not as much to do here as you think. You've got to be a bit savvy – what do you think I got those bonuses for at Mercedes? For sticking to the rulebook? No, because I found out how to get the same results with less work. You've ended up like the Germans – they always want to do everything by the book.'

Gül shakes her head. *I've always been like this*, she could say. *I've never had an ear to the ground for the best ways to cut corners. I was this way before I even knew Germany existed.*

Not long after Fuat started working with Gül for the office cleaning company, not long before they moved to Saniye's neighbourhood, Songül handed in her notice. Having talked about it for years, she finally gave up cleaning at night, and now she works the early shift at a baker's shop. Nurcan takes the train to work, and Gül and Fuat go together in Fuat's A-Class Mercedes. They talk about their workmates on the way, or sometimes they don't talk at all. When there's no talking on the way back, Gül often falls asleep, much to Fuat's annoyance. 'It beggars belief! You get a nice gentle ride to slumberland, and I get to be your chauffeur.'

Gül never used to fall asleep when she got a lift with the younger women; she'd listen to their conversations the same way she watches her soaps, often gazing out of the window. She rarely joined in.

Gül and Fuat get three or four hours' sleep before they go to work, and then three or four hours when they come home from work. They have the same rhythm now and it's harder to avoid each other. During the day, Fuat sometimes goes to the tea house to play a round or two of rummy or backgammon, chat to other men and watch TV. Gül reads more books now than she did in the attic flat, which feels strange to her. She didn't read all that much in the days when she saw Herr Bender every day; she had the window to look out of then. Now she sometimes misses her hours at the window; they have a little balcony with a view of a patch of grass, and with the satellite dish attached to the wall. Sometimes Gül sits out there, but hardly anyone walks past.

She meets up with Can less often. He has a mobile phone now, which she sometimes calls from the phone box to arrange to meet him at Karstadt. A few weeks before they moved, he had to go back behind bars for ten months, which didn't seem to bother him because it was day-release. 'It's not that bad,' he said. 'Look, we can still see each other, I just have to stick to a few rules. And as soon as I get out of here, I'm going to set up as self-employed. I've got loads of legal business ideas.'

Fuat and Gül spend more time together than they ever have done before, and Gül often catches herself being kind and friendly towards him. A few years ago, she could never have imagined she might be like that with him one day. When it feels like she's being too nice, she thinks of the hurt, holds it close long enough to make the pain flare up again.

What I want is peace and harmony, she thinks. *It's in my nature to be nice. It takes a lot of energy to go against my nature.*

There are afternoons when they sit in front of the TV and Gül sneaks glances at Fuat. Then she realises she never knows what's going on inside his mind. Not because he's a man, but because he never gives anything away. *Maybe that's where Ceyda gets it from*, she thinks. *We'll never break off this tie we have through the children; we'll be tied to each other forever, whether we like it or not. I love my daughters, and even if he never really took care of them, part of him lives on in them. I love them, and so in a roundabout way, I love him too. If you like apples, you have to like light, earth and water.*

But perhaps it is partly to do with him being a man. They're all that way, even if they don't appear to be. Mecnun, Can, Emin, Yılmaz: all the men she knows seem to have a corner inside themselves that they can't look into; they seem to lack the light for feelings. Perhaps they just lack the courage or the right door, but it seems there's something inside of them that's locked away and out of their reach. It *is* there, Gül is sure of that.

Maybe I'd understand better if I had a son, she thinks.

Now and then, Fuat launches into one of his monologues, praising or condemning this or that, talking himself into a flow, making comparisons and getting carried along by the subject and the sound of his own words. He's clearly glad it's Gül listening to him. But on other days he gets exasperated with his wife. 'You women,' he says, 'it takes you hours and hours to get ready when you want to leave the house. Just putting on a coat and shoes and going out would be too easy. The only reason God made women was to show men how complicated you can make life. If women were in charge, there wouldn't be a straight road in the world; they'd all snake around because you women can never decide on anything.'

If you're so great at making decisions, why have you lost so much money on the cards? Gül doesn't say. Fuat, on the other hand, says: 'Why are you tidying up again, just sit down, can't you? There's no one coming to visit, no one will mind that there's a blanket on the sofa and the newspapers aren't put away. Stop bustling around all the time.'

Why do you wash your car every Saturday? Gül doesn't say. But then sometimes she does. They don't shout and yell at each other – they spend more time together now than ever before. And even though Gül thinks of their daughters, even though she's friendly and there's peace and harmony between them, she doesn't delude herself about the wall between her and Fuat. She doesn't even know if she'd like to tear down that wall. When she looks around, she sees that wall almost everywhere, between most people; sometimes it's thick and grey and heavy, sometimes it's made of paper and the light shines through, sometimes it's so thin that the other person's song rings through effortlessly, but sometimes you have to shout to be heard on the other side. And sometimes people don't bother to shout. They accept the wall and lean up against it. When Gül looks around, she's no worse off than most other people.

'Sevgi knows what her father's up to,' Saniye complains, 'and now I'm scared it's going to cause problems. I'm not worried about Yılmaz, but Sevgi… It's illegal, and who knows what else she's been happy to try thanks to the example he's setting. I just feel desperate, I don't know…'

Saniye notices the way Gül is looking at her.

'We've never talked about it, but you know, don't you? What Yılmaz does?'

Gül knows he listens to music and watches films, but that can't be what Saniye means.

'So Fuat doesn't know, either? Maybe some people don't know. Oh Gül, we never talk about it but it's so obvious, I assume everyone knows Yılmaz has been smoking pot for years.'

It's like something solid inside Gül falls apart and sinks to the ground, but there's no ground for it to fall on. Or like a picture with a puzzle hidden in it – suddenly the pieces come together, and she realises she's been taken in by an illusion.

She remembers how often Yılmaz used to be drunk and how, at some point, he started turning down drinks; she remembers the glint in his eye, the peace, how uneasy he looked when someone turned up to visit unannounced. But more distant memories flash up, too: the gossip about Nalan, the swamp of nightlife, Can telling her about the junkies who buy their döner at night, just so they can use the foil to smoke heroin in dark corners. The sniffling, sneezing figures she has so often seen on the street, who could hardly keep their eyes open at times and fumbled with the cigarettes they tried to smoke. She's surprised, appalled, confused, and the longer she says nothing, the more uneasy she feels because she knows it's getting more uncomfortable for Saniye with every second that passes. She has to say something, react. Words fail when the world falls apart and becomes impossible to grasp.

'I'm sorry,' says Saniye, 'I thought you knew. You've lived in that bit of town, you've seen so much going on there. I thought you knew, and you were just being discreet. You... I'm sorry.'

Gül gets up and puts her arms around her.

'It's alright,' she says. 'You've no need to apologise for my ignorance. I'm sorry you've had to go so long without being able to talk about it. All these years we've known each other, and you kept it to yourself, you thought I wouldn't want to talk about it. All these years...'

Her voice breaks and she has to hold back her tears. She finds it easier when Saniye starts to cry. Each secret is a chord in life's lonely song.

'I know someone who smokes pot,' says Gül.

'Really?' Can looks at her curiously.

'I'm sure you'd know more about that kind of thing than someone like me.'

'Are you asking me to get him some? And pass it onto you? I'd never do that. Someone who doesn't know where they're getting their next bag shouldn't be smoking it in the first place, simple as that.'

'No, I just want to know how dangerous it is. And be honest.'

'Hash? Just hash and weed, yeah? Depends. It's not dangerous for most. But some people can't hack it.'

'He's got a wife and a daughter.'

'Does he drink?'

'Practically never.'

'He won't hit his wife because he's stoned, he won't hit his daughter, and he'll always remember what he did the next day. There shouldn't be a problem as long as he's just smoking what he buys and not mixing it with anything else.'

'Really?'

She doesn't quite know why she asked. His truths and hers are poles apart; the world looks so different for Can to how it looks to her. The word 'spicy' means something different for a person who eats chillies every day to someone who avoids hot foods.

'Yes, Auntie Gül, really. He's better off staying away from the rest – no cocaine, heroin, or pills, and no Valium or rohypnol either. As long as he sticks with pot, he should be fine.'

'What if the police find out?'

'The police won't be interested in the likes of him. They don't care if you smoke a joint here and there. Almost everyone in this part of town between the ages of thirteen and thirty smokes, but the police are more interested in people like me.'

'How can you say that? Fuat has to pay a fine when he runs a red light or parks in the wrong place. There are laws in this country – the police don't just let you off.'

'Auntie Gül, don't let them suck you in – the police in this country let people off too. People are the same everywhere.

When you run a red light, there's no getting out of it, but crime's different. And even when you do run a red, you pay your fine and you're on your way. There's no need to be scared of uniforms, or the law. You can't go letting them make you feel small. Fuck their fines. They got us over to this country like we were beggars, but you've got to take what you want; no one gives you anything for free, nobody owes you anything.'

Gül smiles. She's never taken anything. You can't take a person's heart, you have to win it. *He's a man*, she thinks. *Men know less about hearts and minds.* They think hearts have to be conquered, but it doesn't work that way. Men don't ride the tides of their feelings; they want to stand on firm ground. Still, she's relieved to hear Can say that Yılmaz isn't in danger. *I'm so easily led*, she thinks on the way home. *I hear what I want to hear and I'm glad of it. This life will make you believe anything. I always thought I could never break the law, but then I bought one of those phone cards from Can. I thought drugs were a sure-fire route to destruction, but now I know that's not true either.*

Lord, let me grow older, she prays on the way home. *Let me get so old that every belief I once held falls away, until I see things as they are and stop letting myself be blinded or tricked by the shadows that I and other people cast on things. Lord, let me live long enough to see everything in the same light, without picking a side. Lord, let me see everything in your light.*

Gül does a lot of thinking over the next few weeks. She talks to Saniye, watches Yılmaz, remembers her conversations with him, rearranges her images of the past and comes to the conclusion that smoking hashish can't be all that bad. And it must have been a help for someone like Yılmaz – even if it is against the law. Even if she wouldn't want Fuat to do it, or her daughters or grandchildren. Fuat used to do a lot of drunk driving – that was against the law too – and she and Ceyda would carry him into the house at night. If he'd only smoked hash, he'd have managed the stairs on his own and he wouldn't have smelled so bad. He'd have made a fool of himself less often, he might have lost less money, and he wouldn't have been hungover and irritable, but still Gül's glad that he only drank. What kind of people would he have been dealing with, who would he have bought it from?

My eyes are getting worse and worse, but there are some things I see more clearly now, she thinks. She's had reading glasses for a few years, but recently she's started feeling like everything's misting over. The first two or three times, she was afraid it might be the beginning of a migraine, but no headache ever came; nothing ever happened. Still, she gets the feeling her vision hasn't cleared up since. The mist isn't always the same; it gets thicker or sometimes she doesn't even notice it, but it never quite goes away. She knows her work takes her longer because she's not sure sometimes if she's missed any dust or smears.

'No, you don't need glasses,' the doctor says. 'You've got cataracts. You're not that old – we should operate.'

'Operate? Hospital?'

'Yes, it's a relatively straight-forward procedure.'

Gül nods; her heart beats faster. *Operation, hospital.* Every part of her tenses up – she feels dizzy and the mist before her eyes grows heavier, but she nods.

'If we don't operate there's a risk you might go blind,' the doctor says. 'No need to worry. We'll refer you and then you can make an appointment there. The wait will be about six weeks.'

Gül nods again. Her life in Germany is swathed in mist; she doesn't understand all the words – at times she can only make out the contours of the sentences, she's never sure she's got everything right. In the doctor's surgery, she wishes she had more ears: two for listening, and two to memorise everything – that way, she could reel it off word for word later on, and Ceyda could translate it for her, so that no doubts remain. As it is, she asks again and again, overcoming her embarrassment, but the doctor says 'operation' every time.

He says 'go blind' every time. And there was she, thinking a pair of glasses would solve the problem.

The day before the operation, Sibel calls. Gül has been nervous about the appointment for days. Her stomach seems so tiny she's surprised she can get any food down, but when she hears her sister's voice, all of her insides seem to sink like a stone to her bowels. Sibel never usually calls. None of her sisters do; it's too expensive.

'I hope it's good news – why are you calling?'

'It's Baba… We found him in the stable, he must have collapsed while he was mucking out. They say he's had a stroke. He asked for you. I wanted…' Sibel suppresses a sob.

'How is he?'

'Oh, Gül, how are we to know? I'm not a doctor. The doctor says he might recover. But then again…'

Gül steadies herself. She steadies herself like she did the time she flew to Turkey because he'd had a moped accident. Back then, all the fuss was for nothing. Maybe it'll be the same this time. A stroke. Lots of people live for years after having a stroke.

'Have you called the others?'

'Yes.'

'Why didn't you call me first? I'm the oldest.' She hears how harsh she sounds, even though she didn't mean to.

'You're the furthest away and I didn't want to worry you for no good reason.'

'What are the others doing?'

'Emin says he has to work, but he'll make sure he gets two or three days off. Nalan's coming. Melike's not sure yet. But Baba asked for you, especially.'

It's as if something has settled on her chest; she tries to take a breath, a deep one, but her ribs simply won't rise. *If tears could heal my eyes*, Gül thinks, *then I'd cry, I'd cry for days on end.*

'I'm having an operation tomorrow,' she says. A moment ago she was surprised by how harsh she sounded, and now she's shocked at how her voice is almost smothered. She forces herself. She forces herself to breathe in.

'Tomorrow at noon,' she says. 'I'll call you from the hospital at noon tomorrow and then you can tell me how he's doing.'

'Alright, that's what we'll do.'

Gül struggles to sleep; she dozes, sees her father's eyes before her, sees herself lying on an operating table. She sees the stable where the cows are kept, the other stable where Sibel keeps her paintings. She remembers the blind people she knew when she was little, sees herself on a train the first time she came to Germany. She sees Ceren in hospital when she was hit by the car, the hospital where her daughter met Gesine. She hears Fuat snoring next to her; for a moment she thinks it's her father, and joy shakes her awake, but then she realises her father is far away – miles and miles away, and seriously ill. She wishes she could doze off again, even though that sleep is restless, muddled and hard. Reality is worse than feeling like this. She remembers a sheep her father slaughtered for Kurban Bayram, its eyes dulled and empty, its head so alone in the blood-soaked grass.

That night, it feels like her whole life is mixed up, a stream of chaos she'll never escape. As morning approaches, she half-sleeps her way through dreams in which she misses trains and aeroplanes, gets lost in factories and cities, watches her daughter drown. As she dreams, she remembers dreams that connected her to her daughter – she remembers these dreams, but while she's sleeping she can't tell whether it's the past or the future she's remembering. Tonight, she wouldn't be surprised if her bed disappeared, or her name vanished from the world altogether.

It might all be different, she thinks. *I might have been dreaming all along and be waking to a reality where no one knows me, a reality where I don't have an operation in the morning.*

When her alarm clock finally declares it time to get up, she feels weak, as if she hasn't had the night off but has spent the wee hours cleaning the whole building all by herself instead.

Lord, give me strength, she prays, before she sets her feet on the floor. *Give me strength*. He's never forsaken her. She's had her doubts, she's foundered and at times she's thought she might fall apart, but He has always given her the strength to keep her back straight. He's never asked for more than she can bear.

She sits up. Her palms are moist, and she feels something pulling in the soles of her feet. In the name of the Lord, she stands up; and there it is, the thought that she's going to see her father well again once she's had the operation, once the mist has cleared.

Fuat drives her to the hospital and, for once, Gül pays no attention to the traffic.

Before she knows it, she's slipping under – it all happens so fast that she can barely appreciate those few moments where everything falls away. When she comes to, the panic sets in: she feels sick, she doesn't know where she is; she thinks she's late, she thinks she's missed something but can't remember what. She remembers the first dead person she saw and her father telling her it was customary to tie a cloth under the person's chin, so that their mouth wouldn't hang open. 'You'll do it for me too,' he'd said. 'It's the path we all take.'

She remembers this, but it takes her twenty minutes to get her bearings. Realising she has to call Sibel, she suddenly feels hot all over. It's taken her all this time to remember her sick father. She's not pleased to have had these brief moments of respite – how could she be? All it does is make her feel guilty.

'Call Sibel,' she says to Ceyda, who's sitting by her bed. 'We have to call Sibel.'

Together, they go downstairs to the payphone; making a phone call from the hospital room is too expensive. Gül thought anaesthesia would feel like a deep sleep, but instead she feels battered and beaten. She feels as if she's not quite back in her body, in her surroundings, in her mind, in her heart. *Perhaps I've woken up in another world*, she thinks. *Perhaps everything's a little bit different, a little bit mad.*

When she hears Sibel saying the blacksmith is doing slightly better, it doesn't help her find her way back. The news seems slightly unreal, just like everything around her.

Ceyda hugs her mother and says: 'Try not to worry – everything will follow its own path. You can't bend it to your own will.'

Oh, this head of mine, every thought in it twisting and turning, looking at every fear from all sides. It wants to find a home for every hope, it wants to soothe all fears and find solace for suffering. My heart doesn't seem to have been made for separation.

'Would you have a look for flights?' Gül asks her daughter, 'I want to fly out. I've got a bad feeling.'

'When?'

'Tomorrow.'

'Alright. I'll sort it. And try to relax, Mum. You've just had an operation.'

Ceyda stays with her mother for some time, telling her about the children, their school, about work and how much post gets stolen, about kitchen appliances and picking strawberries, about her savings, and about her mother-in-law, who's not doing too well. Gül's astonished at how much her daughter can talk when she wants to. She tries to listen, she even manages it, though the whole time she feels as if there's a hand poised over her neck, waiting to grab her and hurl her into the darkness.

At the airport in Ankara, Gül notices how many more people have mobile phones than in Germany. There aren't more rich people or businesspeople in Turkey. *Perhaps that's the sort of people we are*, Gül thinks. *Perhaps longing has taken root so deep within us that we want to make sure we can always hear the voices of our loved ones.*

She wonders about calling from a payphone to hear how her father's doing, but when she doesn't find one straight away, she decides not to lose any time and takes a taxi straight to the coach station. *Imagine that, a phone you can just carry around in your coat pocket. Wouldn't that make life easier?* But the only person she knows with a mobile phone is Can, and his life certainly isn't easy.

She falls asleep just before the coach reaches Bolu. When she wakes up, she can't remember where she is. She looks out of the window and sees mist; she remembers her eye operation and worries that it hasn't worked, but she's glad to see the scenery, which reminds her of Turkey, and in the next few seconds she's back to reality. Everything's in its place. She realises that there really is mist outside and that fear, anguish, intuition and worry can move about freely in the emptiness inside of her.

She doesn't know that her father was already dead when she stepped off the plane. That all his other children were by his side and that his last word was her name. She doesn't know she's too late as she gets out of the taxi and sees Sibel waiting at the front door. Gül's knees go soft; for a moment she wonders if she ought to sit back down in the seat of the car. She sees Sibel running over to her, and she grips the roof of the taxi to steady herself; the image blurs, as if the whole world is falling away. She sees herself from above, dropping to her knees– she hears a cry from her throat, but it sounds strange to her. That's not her voice, that's not her sister, huddled on the floor with her arms around her, that's not her body, cold and numb all at once.

It can't be her, singing suddenly in tongues. She never sings, certainly not on the street. She heard someone singing in tongues once, over forty years ago now. It's strange, it's not common in this region, and it can't be her, sitting there singing and wailing. Gül sees the pain – she feels it too – but it doesn't seem to belong to her.

In the next few nights, Gül and the pain grow closer and closer. *Soon I will be nothing more than this loss*, Gül thinks one night. *I won't exist any more. I'll lose myself and I won't be able to find myself again – everywhere I look will be loss and grief.* She wishes she could vanish; time and again, she wishes she could just disappear to a place of sanctuary and solace.

It's good that the siblings are all together, it's the only comfort that remains for Gül, but she wonders if their father's death is hitting her the hardest. *Perhaps it's because I was so far away. Perhaps it's because I was too late. Perhaps I'd feel better if I'd sat by his bedside in his final hours and said goodbye to him, like the others. Perhaps it's just that I was closer to him than the others were when we were children.*

Her siblings are her anchor, but Gül still feels she's on her own. The night after the burial, she wakes up and can't get back to sleep. She goes out into the yard for a smoke.

She's just brought her lighter up to her mouth when she senses her father. He's right next to her, over her, behind her, in front of her, inside of her, as if his spirit has settled over hers. He seems so close that Gül takes the cigarette out of her mouth and whispers, 'Baba?' The feeling intensifies and her hands drop to her sides. Her father's never seen her smoke before. Slowly, she sits down on the stool that Arzu uses when she splits apricots to dry in the sun. Gül wraps her cardigan tighter across her chest and sends a thought to her father.

I'm sorry I didn't make it in time.

It feels like the blacksmith smiles and strokes her hair. He won't answer. Gül won't hear his voice, but she's sure he's quite close and he understands her. She knows this is their last moment of contact.

Thank you for coming to see me. Thank you for being there for me.

The night, the stars, the air, the moon, the stool she's sitting on, the ground, the house, the old acacia tree, all of it feels like her father is smiling, a smile that spans the world. He shuts his eyes and he's gone. He goes in peace.

We all go back into the light.

Gül sits there until the muezzin calls the morning ezan. She sits and gives thanks; she sits and remembers. She sits and mourns. She sits and feels joyful peace. She sits there and feels safe in the night and the universe. She feels the stars watching her, a fellow part of creation and splendour. She sits and feels the stars watching her, as though she might be alone forever. But even then, she can still sense a light. She floats through feelings and memories, forgetting to move, forgetting to smoke, forgetting to breathe – at least that's how it seems to her.

When she goes inside, she notices there are tears in her eyes. There are tears, but they won't taste salty or bitter; they'll taste sweet. Her body relaxes beneath the heavy woollen blanket – she feels warm, though she hadn't felt cold before, and she flows gently into a sleep that feels full of reconciliation and solace, peace and colour.

In the nights that follow, her sleep is nothing like those two or three hours in the grey dawn light. In the nights that follow, she wakes outs of dreams gasping for breath, with strands of hair clinging to her forehead, her pillow damp as if it were midsummer, her heart racing. She remembers how, as a child, she was afraid to go back to sleep after a nightmare. But she can't remember ever having dreamed like this before. At night, she finds herself in warzones, trenches, field hospitals. She hears bombs, gunfire, shelling; she sees severed limbs and open wounds. She sees weeping mothers and wives buckled with grief; she sees blind children, little more than skin and bone. She sees galleys full of convicts, caravans of slaves; she suffers drought, hunger, thirst; and she wanders endlessly. She sees every kind of torment from the moment she begins to dream.

She wonders where these images come from – she's never experienced war, slavery or forced migration, and she doesn't watch films or read books about them. *Perhaps these are memories of an old life*, she tells herself. *Perhaps something's jostling about inside my head because I'm the next in line to die – perhaps something's shifted.*

The day Gül's due to leave, Melike whispers to her: 'Now would be a good time to set about doing what we spoke about before.'

Gül looks at her, tries not to give anything away, and feels lonelier than ever.

For weeks she finds herself caught between nightmares and dreams, the pain of her father's loss, working, cooking, sleeping, phone calls and crying; for weeks she feels herself growing heavier with each passing day, even though she's lost weight for the first time in years. She notices her strength waning – at work, she sits down to take a break and can hardly get back up again. She can't make herself listen when people tell her things; sometimes she feels that other people are empty husks with no-one living inside. She feels cut off from everyone. She can't even connect with Saniye. The feeling only abates when she's with Ceyda and her grandchildren.

She wonders if anyone can spot the thick pane of glass that stands between her and the rest of the world. She wonders if this is how Ceren felt after Mecnun's death. But her daughter had a small child; she can't have seen Fatma as an empty husk.

It's life that binds us to life. And it's life that gradually teaches us to breathe differently, to smile, to trust; it's life that brings us back to life. Death dies, and in the spring, months after her father's death, Gül feels something rising, stirring inside her again for the first time.

'Maybe you ought to try hash like Yılmaz,' Saniye says. 'Maybe it would help.'

Gül shakes her head. 'Have you ever tried it?'

'No,' Saniye answers. 'No, I'm too scared, but if I understand Yılmaz rightly, it makes you dream less. It would help with the dreams, at least.'

'They're terrible,' says Gül. 'But it feels like they're tidying up, somehow. I don't think it would help if they went away. Anyway, I'm not having them as often now. I'm starting to feel like myself again.'

'You weren't yourself at all, but who can blame you? There's nothing that can't be eased with enough tears. But these things never heal. Our wounds stay with us, and the scars are bound to itch now and again. We're human, even if sometimes we feel more like vessels with suffering poured inside. Separations and wounds are written in the books of all our lives. Let's be thankful that we have each other.'

Gül smiles, and she senses it's the first smile that she's smiled with a little warmth.

By the time the trees begin to bud, Gül realises how well the operation has gone. The winter seemed grey, as if someone had turned the colours down; in winter, her eyes didn't see much better, or perhaps it was just her grief veiling everything, like mist. Now Gül is glad to see the green of the grass, the strips of light across the floor through the balcony door; even the façades of the buildings seem brighter.

I'd like to die in the autumn, like my father, or at the end of the summer, she thinks.

It's only in springtime that Gül remembers her grandmother, whose eyes got worse and worse as she got older, until she went blind. *Perhaps she had the same illness*, Gül thinks. Her grandmother's hearing improved back then, though; she could tell by Gül's footsteps that she'd put on weight. She could even tell the new bank notes apart, despite never having seen them. Gül remembers her sitting on a cushion on the floor, a second cushion behind her back. She used to lend money to the neighbours; people trusted her, and she knew a lot because everyone told her things.

Life came to her through her ears, thinks Gül. *Perhaps life always needs things that come in pairs. Two eyes, two ears, two lungs, two extensions of the heart. To take on life, you always need two of everything. Two, to reach the wealth that life strives for, two to find a centre.*

Two. She thinks of the marriages she knows. Marriage isn't like the photo love-stories of her youth; it's not like back when she was in love with a boy named Recep. It's not like in the

American films, where there's always a happy ending, but it's not like in the Turkish ones either, the ones that end with banishment, pain, blood and death. She thinks of the show *Marriages in the Dock*, which she used to watch in her first years in Germany because there was nothing else on. She always thought that programme was odd: how could anyone want to destroy a home? Ceyda and Mecnun were the only happy couple Gül ever knew. Yılmaz and Saniye come to mind, too; then again, the two of them may not argue but they spend a lot of time avoiding each other.

'I've got a new girlfriend and I'd like you to meet her,' Can says.

'Why would I want to meet her?'

'We've known each other so long, Auntie Gül, I trust you. You can't trust anyone when you're as big a fish as I am in this town. No one knows about our meetings – it's not just you who's careful to avoid gossip; I am too. The bigger you get, the more envy, the more attention, the more enemies you have.'

'Big?' says Gül. 'What are you on about, big? Will you never learn? Don't you want to grow up one day?'

'Yes, I do – that's why I want to introduce you to my girlfriend. Elena.'

'A German?'

'Yes, she's a German.'

'Well, then I won't even be able to have a proper conversation with her.'

'You don't have to say anything. I'll bring her along; all you have to do is take a look at her.' Can leans forward and lowers his voice. 'I'm not selling drugs any more, no breaking and entering, no more funny business for me. I'm opening a locksmith's – well, I'm not doing it, someone else will do it, but I'll run the business. I've got someone at the post office, I've got someone who's a plumber, and someone who installs satellite dishes.'

Gül looks at him, confused.

'I'm not working any more myself. I'm getting other people to work for me.'

'I still don't understand.'

'Anyone who goes inside people's homes can collect information there. I'm not dealing in goods any more; I'm selling information. They can't impound it and use it as evidence in court. I've grown up, in business and in person. I have more experience and more expertise now. Soon all my business will be legitimate, but you can't just switch over from one day to the next. I was five years old the first time I nicked something from the supermarket, that's more than twenty-three years on the wrong side of the law; I can't just switch over from one day to the next. But I'm going to change everything, you'll see.'

Gül has heard him say this plenty of times, and though she doesn't believe it, she's still glad to hear it.

'There's no way but the honest path,' she says. 'I've always told you that. You'll see: you'll start sleeping better once you've left it all behind you. You'll sleep better, you'll feel lighter, you'll be happier.'

'So?'

'What should I say?'

'Whatever comes into your head.'

'Does she not speak any Turkish at all?'

'Not a word.'

Gül looks at Elena, who simply smiles, sitting on her hands, leaning forwards slightly. She doesn't seem nervous. Her blonde hair is chin-length, her face rounded but not full, she's wearing jeans and a white T-shirt. Gül puts her in her mid-twenties but there's something girlish about her – you could take her for ten years younger at first glance. She doesn't seem at all bothered by Gül and Can talking Turkish, possibly about her.

She told Gül earlier that she works for a customer-service phoneline and has heard a lot about her. She said something about a cat that Gül didn't really understand, something about a bookshop and a concert.

Gül has noticed the way Elena looks at Can. *Anyone with eyes in their head would notice that*, she thinks. *It doesn't mean anything, though.*

'Oh, I don't know,' Gül says. 'I've told you about Ceyda and her husband. If I was any good at this, I'd have seen where it would lead. If I was any good, I'd have spared my own daughter her misery. And Adem and I speak the same language, and if—'

'Auntie Gül,' Can interrupts. 'Look, we're sitting here together because—'

'I know. She's completely besotted with you. I've never seen so much warmth in such pale eyes. If she goes on looking at you like that for a few more years, something might come of it. But I don't know how long she sticks at the things she's started. I don't know what it means to her to build a home. Take no notice of what I say, apart from this: there's no way but the honest path.'

'If she looks at me that way for a few more years…' says Can. 'First we'll have to see how she looks at me in nine months, when I get back out.'

It feels like someone's dipped Gül in boiling water. She looks at Can and feels her tears, but she holds them back, sensing her rage and disappointment.

'It'll be different after that,' Can says. 'I've already told you that.'

'You've said that plenty of times before.'

'You can talk! Have you ever given up smoking?'

'May the Lord give your mother patience; patience and strength.'

'Amen,' says Can. 'Amen. I really appreciate the love you've shown me, Auntie Gül, for no reason at all. I appreciate my mother's love, which she showed so rarely. I want to be a different part of life. I want to stop leaving this trail of violence behind me. I want to have a woman by my side. I want…'

He looks down at the table as Elena looks at him, hearing the emotion in his voice.

'...I don't know if there's a word for it. I don't want to be afraid all the time, at least not on my own.'

'A home,' Gül says. 'A proper home.'

'Yes, maybe. I don't know. I want somewhere to rest, catch my breath.'

'But why a German woman?' Gül asks.

'Why not?'

'The Germans,' she starts, and then she stops. 'A Turkish woman,' she says, 'a Turkish woman knows much better what you want and need, and what you expect.'

'How do you mean?' he asks. There's an uncertainty in his voice that Gül's never heard before.

'A Turkish woman knows our customs. No matter how often you say you grew up on the street, the fact is you had a Turkish mother and a Turkish father. The Germans see a home as something different.'

'A home, I don't give a... What kind of home did they offer me, eh? My mother was never around, and my father was in and out of jail like he got a bargain deal on a revolving door.'

'But why a German?' Gül asks again. This time, though, it sounds different. Now she's thinking of Fuat. Can hears her interest, though he can't understand where it comes from.

'She's not a real German,' he says. 'Her great-grandparents came from Riga, Latvia. Something to do with the Hanseatic League.'

'Hanseatic?'

'Yeah, Bremen and Riga were both Hanseatic cities. They were merchants. All these rich merchants.'

'I see.'

'But she doesn't speak Latvian or Russian.' Can pauses, seems to be thinking.

'Turkish women might make you a glass of tea when you get home – they'll keep the place tidy, they'll make you feel like you're in charge and try to control everything in the background and do your thinking for you; they're prepared to make sacrifices, but they're… Do you know any Turkish women who are interested in football? Or gambling? Who smoke the odd joint now and then? I bet you don't. I know what Turkish women are like. They're all good for nothing; they're stuck in the mud. Women from here are different: a German woman is interested in what her man's interested in, too. She goes to watch football with him or smokes a joint with him or goes to the porn cinema with him, but that doesn't mean she's a slut. A German woman goes out with you, and a Turkish woman waits at home for you.'

Can turns his head and looks at Elena. Gül has known him long enough to see that the warmth in his eyes won't burn out overnight.

'Well, you have my blessing,' she says. 'May the two of you not suffer pain.'

On her way home, Gül is full of emotion for Can, for his mother, his new girlfriend, full of emotion for everything, as if she could see love in all suffering. Later, she'll remember the people on the tram and how, when she looked at each one of them, she could understand that the Lord is either everywhere or nowhere. She'll remember thinking that every dawn is a gift and, at the same time, a thief with a light in his hand; every dawn gives us a new day and immediately starts carrying it away again.

Our hearts have touched. They were always close in an intricate way, but they have touched, creating a spark that has brightened this day.

She'll be grateful for this day, once its magic has become nothing but memory. And she won't look for days like this again; she'll look for touches like the ones she had on that day.

I don't need roses, she thinks. *The thorns are enough for me. I don't need light; the warmth is enough for me. I don't need an ocean, because a drop is enough to see the whole ocean.*

The next day, that feeling has gone, perhaps swept away by her thoughts of Fuat and his lover. What did that woman give him? How long was he with her? Did she go out playing cards with him? Did she watch football with him? Did they go to a porn cinema? Could she satisfy one of his needs better than her? Did she understand him better in some way? Did she drink with him? Did she like whiskey? Did he lie in bed naked with her afterwards? Could he, even? Would he want that? Has he been missing something all these years? Or was it just because the German woman was slim?

The thoughts and questions are no longer as painful for Gül; it's easier for her to think about them now. So many years have passed, and maybe she'll feel like talking to Fuat about it all one day. But she suspects she wouldn't get a word out of him, not a peep.

I can't understand that man, she thinks, *because he's not honest and he never talks. There must have been something he wanted and never found, that's for sure. But another thing's for sure, and that's that he never said it out loud; all he ever did was drink or complain, or both at once.*

'She could have done fine art or film, for all I care. Or not studied at all,' Yılmaz says. 'I wanted her to be free to choose.'

'Now don't make out like you were so relaxed,' says Saniye. 'You had a problem with her moving to Göttingen.'

'I know, that was the first time I wished we'd had a son instead of a daughter. If we'd had a boy, I'd have let him go anywhere to study, and I wouldn't have noticed how little freedom these old beliefs really give me, and how difficult it is to shake off my childhood and this bloody country.'

Gül thinks for a moment. If her daughters had wanted to study, would she have let them move to another city? Would Fuat have allowed it? Gül would have trusted her own daughters, even when they were still young. But Sevgi, on the other hand… She's always dolled up, squeezing herself into short, tight dresses, wearing high heels. Her eyebrows are plucked, she's strikingly pretty and petite; men's eyes follow her along the street. She has her mother's freckles, but her father's dark hair; her lips seem almost too full for her doll-like face, and she smiles as if it's always raining rose petals.

'People are proud to have a son who beds anything that moves – their little heartbreaker – but if a daughter does the same, they'll call her a slut. Perhaps it's all just in our upbringing. My father always said: a key that opens many doors is a good key, but a door that opens with any key is a bad door. For years that made sense to me, but then at some point I asked myself: why do we assume the door is the woman? Asking these questions and letting go of their hold over you are two different things, though. Sevgi has my blessing, I hope she'll be happy in Göttingen, that's the only thing that matters.'

'Perhaps German fathers are the same,' says Saniye. 'They're just not as willing to admit it.'

'It's how they were brought up too,' says Yılmaz. 'Sometimes I wish we could stick our heads out and see past our upbringings, to see what's really going on out there.'

He takes a drag on his joint. Since he found out that Gül is in the picture, he's started smoking in front of her.

'Medicine,' he says. 'Medicine and law. That's every Turkish parent's wet dream if they want a respectable job for their children. We've never dreamed of that sort of thing, or even spoken about it. Sevgi was good at art and music, always straight As; she can draw, she can sing, but she's now got it into her head that she wants to be a paediatrician. And it has nothing to do with how I brought her up. I want her to be happy and live like a human being, that's all.'

Gül wanted this for her daughters too. But she'd never have imagined either of them becoming a doctor or a lawyer. She wanted a better life for them than she had; she wanted them to have an education, but she never would have dared to dream so big. Yılmaz is right – you can't shake off everything you learned as a child. No matter which way she turns, her shadow will always fall on her daughters and keep them from seeing all the paths that are open to them. Her shadow, and Fuat's shadow too.

Saniye has tried to give Sevgi the love she couldn't give her son; she has loved her daughter as if she were two children, and

Yılmaz has passed on his knowledge and his mellow ways. Sevgi has been given everything, but in the past few years her Turkish has increasingly deteriorated – because almost all her friends are German, because she never watches Turkish TV, because she spent last summer with friends in Spain instead of going to Turkey with her parents. Spain is a good deal further away than Göttingen. Gül wonders if Sevgi can still feel the strength of those that came before her, if she can hear the song she carries with her, if she can recognise the melody in her blood.

A single word is enough to make the fear and horror rise in Gül's throat. One word, and it's as if fog has settled over her ears. She sits down. One word. *Hello.* One word, which tells her Melike is on the other end of the line.

'I hope it's good news. Why are you ringing?'

'I wanted to hear your voice.'

'Has someone died?'

'No, no. Can't I just give my sister a ring every once in a while?'

Like you've ever rung before, Gül thinks.

'Of course,' she says, 'of course you can, anytime. How are you? How is everyone?'

'We're well, we're in Istanbul. İsmail has a huge flat in Erenköy now. It's his phone I'm calling on, so we won't be disturbed – a call to Germany like this is hardly worth mentioning to him.'

Melike talks about Istanbul as if she has all the time in the world. She talks about İsmail's twice-daily training sessions, six days a week, not forgetting the games themselves. She talks about how she has more time now she's retired, how she'd like to use the time to get to know her country better, and how she's going on a trip to the Black Sea coast.

Gül relaxes a little, but she knows her sister; she knows she hasn't called to chat. It's a good ten minutes before Melike says: 'You haven't mentioned it, but do you think I should see if the others want to sell their shares of the summer house?'

'There's no hurry, is there?' Gül replies. 'I'll be there in three months' time. We can speak then.'

'Who knows if we'll all be together then? I also did a bit of research; the house was originally in our mother's name. So, if you look at it that way, Arzu, Emin and Nalan don't have a claim to any inheritance – it's just the three of us. Maybe I should hire a lawyer before the summer to find out if we would even have to pay off the other three, or…'

'No,' says Gül, 'no, we're siblings; we've all got the same father. Don't bring our mother's blood into this – let her rest in peace.'

'I'm not talking about blood and feelings, I'm talking about legal regulations.'

'No,' says Gül, 'I won't hear another word of it.'

'As you wish. You're the eldest, but maybe have another think about it. Perhaps we should keep this option open, to make it easier for all of us.'

'Let's talk in the summer.'

Melike is crafty, Gül thinks. She's selfish and calculating, but Nalan and Sibel could do with the money, and someone ought to have the house to avoid everything ending in chaos. The thought that it could belong just to her enters her mind, and she can't fight it off. And once it's there, she watches it.

I looked after Melike and Sibel when we were half-orphaned. I tried to be a mother to them when I was still just a child myself. I tried to salvage what was left and pass on what I could. It's not like I asked to be born before the others. I was lucky, I got to know my mother better than my sisters ever did. We always shared everything, even when it wasn't technically fair. We belong together. It doesn't matter that we've spent all these years apart. My door would always be open to any of them.

Then she pushes the thought away.

'I've spoken to a lawyer,' says Melike that summer, in Turkey.

'I don't want to hear about it,' says Gül.

'But we've got to talk about money. The value of the house and the plot of land is about twenty-three billion lira. Split six ways, because there are six shares. Times two, because each of us will have to pay two of the others off – you Arzu and Sibel, me Nalan and Emin. Or however we split it. That's about 11,000 marks. Do you have that kind of money?'

Gül knows how much Fuat invested at the new bank and it's much more than that. She nods and she can see her sister suppressing a smile.

'I'll talk to Emin and Nalan,' says Melike.

Emin has given up the hire car business because it caused too many problems, and he has since taken on a shop selling dairy products. He has no time to visit his hometown this year. Nalan doesn't want to come home either, not now their father's dead.

'I called Emin and Nalan. Have you spoken to Sibel yet?' asks Melike a few days later.

'Yes. She's got nothing against selling her share, but she wants to know that whatever happens, she'll always be welcome there. And Arzu says she'll take her cues from us children.'

'We could do it up. But you know what'd be nicer? We could build a new little house where the stable is. With a toilet, a patio, a balcony, a new kitchen, all the mod cons. Then we wouldn't need to renovate the house we all remember. And the summer house isn't really enough for all of us now anyway. We'll keep the old one and build a new one, then in the summer we can live next door to each other for weeks on end and spend the whole day together without anyone putting anyone else out. What do you reckon?'

'I don't know if that's a bit beyond our means.'

'Oh, it wouldn't be that expensive. There's a different problem though: Emin doesn't want to sell his share. You know what he's like – he's never liked sharing. But he has that new shop and he's got debts, so maybe that could work in our favour. I'll see what I can do.'

'Why doesn't he want to sell?' Gül asks.

'It belongs to all of us, he says, *and that's how it should stay*. I told him somebody has to take responsibility for everything, for the renovations, the plumbing, the land tax – who stays there when and for how long. Too many cooks spoil the broth. It's not as if the others are cut out, but you need someone to make the decisions – that's how any democracy works. Everyone has a voice, but only one person has the final say. Otherwise, all you get is chaos. I'll talk to him again. But we could always—'

She doesn't finish the sentence, and Gül doesn't react.

'I've met a man,' says Ceren, who is always open about these things. Gül knew this would happen sooner or later – she's thought about it often since Mecnun died – but still she's surprised, and she's also afraid. Though she trusts her daughter, though no one knows the family in her town, though she's only met Ceren's friends, neighbours and acquaintances briefly, Gül freezes up at the thought of what they might say about her daughter. Her stomach and heart react instantly, but she's barely caught her breath when Ceren tries to calm her.

'Don't worry. There's no gossip and there won't be any either. Hardly anyone's noticed. When I was first with Mecnun, I learned how careful you have to be.'

By now, she can say Mecnun's name without grief casting its shadow over her voice.

'Who is he?'

'He's called Ferdi. He's a student on my course. He grew up in Karlsruhe but came to Turkey when he was nine. His parents are from the Black Sea, Bayburt.'

Gül smiles. Ceren's first husband studied German, this man is studying German and he grew up in Germany. This Germany has become a mark none of them can get rid of. A scent they can't wash off, that doesn't evaporate even after decades of absence; a scent anyone picks up if they've lived in the country themselves, perhaps as strong a tie as the brown earth of home.

'Is it serious?' Gül asks, though she knows the answer.

Ceren nods.

'What are we going to tell your father?'

'I don't know, Mum. I'm over thirty, can't I just say I met him at uni?'

'You could; I'm not sure.'

'Dad would like him.'

Gül's body leaps into alarm mode.

'What do you mean?'

'Why do you always think the worst? He's a good man, Mum. He's a smoker like me – but he doesn't drink, doesn't gamble, and he's got a smart head on his shoulders. He's good with people, better than Dad; he likes talking a lot; he's always got his finger in lots of pies; he's clever and resourceful. I wouldn't have made it through my course without him. He's the one I get to forge my signature, not a girlfriend. He's always taken care of everything when I didn't know how to manage. He knows all the tricks; sometimes he doesn't take the straightest road, but he's a decent man.'

'How long has it been going on?'

Ceren looks at the floor. 'Since my first year here.'

Silence. She looks up.

'At that time I didn't know... I didn't even like him that much because he was always talking. And then I didn't know if I'd ever... marry again. I thought it was better not to tell you before I was sure myself. I didn't want you to worry for no reason.'

There's a pain that Gül tries to subdue. Since her first year at college. Such a long time without telling her a thing about it. It feels like betrayal. Like disregard.

Ceren lives her own life; she's not accountable to me, she can stand on her own two feet. No, she can't. We've been supporting her all this time; she owes us... she really should have... Gül pushes the pain into a remote corner of her body, or perhaps entirely out of it; she doesn't know.

'We have to find a way to introduce him to your father.'

'It'll be tricky. Ferdi always spends the summer holidays with his parents in their village. What if you came back in winter? Around Christmas?'

'And then what?'

'His parents are coming too. Then they'll ask for my hand, officially.'

'How old is he?'

'Five years younger than me.'

'Oh. But unmarried men your age are hard to come by. Don't his parents mind?'

'Of course they mind; they don't want a wife for their son who's five years older, a widow with a child.'

'Ceren, have you really thought this through?'

'I have – you don't want to know how many sleepless nights it's caused me.'

'And his parents would still ask for your hand?'

'Yes, they wouldn't refuse him what he wants.'

'It'll be hard for you both if you don't have their blessing.'

'You can't blame them for wanting something different for him.'

'Oh, dear me,' says Gül. 'Is there nothing we're spared? It's a tough life; the longer you live, the more tribulations come along to stop you from getting bored, to stop you from leaning back and thinking you've got the wind in your sails.'

Sie looks at Ceren, who gives a sad smile.

'Alright,' says Gül. 'We'll walk through this fire too without burning. We'll climb this mountain without losing our nerve. Come here, come into my arms – I'm glad you've found a man.'

The cows were sold after the blacksmith died, and the stable, which was already in a bad state, is now visibly falling apart. Gül likes Melike's idea of building a small house in its place. She keeps imagining herself sitting on the terrace of the little house, with a view of the apple trees and a glass of tea in front of her after finishing her work. The memories open up – her childhood settles in over the scent of the garden, and the green and the earth reach into her mind. These images let light into Gül's autumn and winter.

These days, she sometimes feels tired at work and can't resist the temptation to sit down in a swivel chair. In these moments she thinks of Arzu, who used to complain that the housework was too hard and say she needed to sit down for a rest. Gül always thought Arzu was exaggerating or lazy, but now she's started to notice her own energy dwindling with age, and she, too, has to sit down to rest now and then. But every time Gül takes a seat on an office chair, she sees the summer house before her, and it seems to give her the strength she needs. She gazes blankly out of the office windows at the city lights; she breathes in sunshine, peace, hears birdsong, and has the scent of damp earth and cow manure in her nostrils.

It won't be long now until she retires. Then she'll be able to spend months at a time in Turkey. That's always her last thought before she gets up to carry on with her work.

Unlike Ferdi, who will simply have a conversation with himself if need be, Ferdi's father is a quiet man. It's hard to keep a conversation with him going, even if it's about football or politics. Ferdi's mother, on the other hand, talks more and is surprisingly open.

'We're not happy with our son's choice,' says Hazer. 'It has nothing to do with your daughter. Every mother wants a nice young woman for her son, one who doesn't already have a child. But then again, every mother wants her child to be happy too. Times have changed. Young people today are making decisions for themselves, when we wouldn't have dared to have opinions of our own. Love is like rain; you can't choose where the raindrops will fall.'

Hazer speaks in the dialect of the Black Sea, her pitch-black locks peeking out from under her headscarf. She's thin, despite her full cheeks, and Gül spots the glint of her gold teeth every time she laughs.

It's like light is pouring out of her mouth when she speaks, Gül thinks. There's something light about her, though it's clear she's spent many years working in the fields; though she has farmer's hands, stubby-fingered; though she's raised four children, one of whom is already dead; though her life must have been so heavy that many shoulders couldn't have carried its weight.

If Ferdi has so much as a pinch of that lightness, everything's going to work out, Gül thinks. She finds herself feeling glad that this marriage will connect her to this woman, too.

It's winter still, and they've just returned from their short trip to Adana, when Gül discovers she can no longer bask in fantasies about the summer house. They get so many Turkish channels now that Gül doesn't know where to start, and she limits herself to two soaps. But suddenly, the same programme is showing on almost every channel and Gül can't understand it and she doesn't want to believe it. Fuat understands almost as little as she does about what's happened, but he doesn't let on.

'"What's happened? *What's happened?*" Can't you tell?' he shouts. 'The lira's dropped forty per cent in the space of three hours. Everything's all over the place: the stock market, the banks… The inflation rate's taken to its heels and run off, companies are going bust, the default rate on loans is exploding – it's absolute chaos. Bastards, those bloody bastards are ruining the country.'

'Who?' Gül asks.

'Who do you think? Politicians, banks, the rich and powerful.'

'But rich people's money will be worth less now too, won't it?'

'They'll come out without so much as a scratch; the rich always do. Whenever something happens, it's us who bear the brunt. The poor.'

'So what's going on?'

'How should I know? But we'll be the ones footing the bill, that's for sure. We'll be the ones bleeding for their mistakes.'

'What'll happen to the money you invested?'

'How do you expect me to know? Do I look like I've been snacking on a psychic's turds? It's all descending into chaos – the whole country's going under, and all this woman cares about is our money! What good will your money be when they sell Turkey to the Americans? What will you do with your measly deutschmarks when the IMF turns up and bombs us back into the Third World with its restrictions?'

'The IMF?'

'Be quiet, for God's sake,' Fuat bellows, red in the face. 'You haven't got a clue, have you? It's not just that they don't want us in Europe; they want us to be like Mali or Somalia or Ethiopia or one of those countries. They want Turkish kids running around with bloated bellies and the whole country to sink into destitution.'

'What about our money?'

'Bloody hell, how am I supposed to know? It looks like it's gone.'

'*Gone?* Gone how? And what do you mean, "measly deutschmarks"? I earned that money by the sweat of my brow. I made every bit of it through honest work – there's nothing measly about it! My sweat, my blood, the work of my hands, and my ambition all went into that money. It can't just disappear. It's you! It's all your fault – you don't know the value of money. *Measly marks*! I told you not to put it all in those new banks. Yılmaz said it was a bad idea, everyone did. It's not the rich who've driven us to rack and ruin, it's you and your greed.'

'Oh, yes, of course. You haven't the foggiest what's going on, but you've still managed to find the guilty party. Congratulations!'

'Yes, I have. He's standing right in front of me. Burns our money just so his wallet doesn't feel too full. As if I haven't known for decades! It's been like this since we've known each other, you're always splurging on something, you're always feeling generous – and then there's all the cash you pour down the drain gambling. And the next thing I know, you're handing it over to a bank, one I never trusted in the first place.'

'The money's gone!' Fuat bellows, 'If you'd ever played the game, you'd know that you've got to be able to lose, too. That's life. You can't always have your cake and eat it too.'

Gül sees the shower of spittle flying out of Fuat's mouth. She knows it hurts him to see the money disappearing, but he just can't admit it. And she knows she's in denial about it, too.

'It's my money,' she says, 'I never spent so much as a penny on cards or drink, never wasted a mark. I don't care how you do it – I want every penny back, every single one. You're going to work and get me my money back. I earned it, it can't be gone.'

She's not quite got a grip of her senses, but she's almost there. She notices that she's repeating herself, the same way Fuat does when he's drunk. She feels drunk. The loss has driven all reason from her mind – she can't think properly, can't speak properly, can't shout loud enough. She feels furious tears brimming behind her eyes. She gets up; her heart's beating too fast, but it feels weak at the same time. Her legs are wobbly; she yells at Fuat without really knowing what it is she's saying, and at the same time, she thinks: *So this is what it's like to be drunk. When Fuat's drunk he can hardly stand either, and loses control. What am I supposed to do with a man who thinks that's a good way to be?*

She goes into the bedroom and sits on the bed. Her throat hurts. The room seems to spin – her thoughts are racing, she can't get a hold on them, can't follow them; they're just loose tatters now. And still, there's a hope that what she saw on TV is not reality, that perhaps that one bank will be spared. The feeling lasts until she's calmed down; she can't say how long it lasts. She turns the TV on, looks out at the patch of grass outside, and lights a cigarette.

A bank can't just go bust, she thinks. *There must be some kind of insurance, security, something.* Otherwise anyone could open a bank. *But this is Turkey*, she thinks then. *Anything's possible there. This would never have happened in Germany.*

Germany. All these years in Germany, and for what? Nothing. All this time in a foreign country, all the longing, all the separation, all the winters, all the long-distance phone calls, all the letters, all the long car journeys, the flights, the conversations with teachers where her daughters had to translate, the days in the chicken factory, at the bread factory, at the sewing machine, the shifts at the wool factory, the nights cleaning offices, all of it. It all seems to have been for nothing.

They wanted money so that one day they could have a life in Turkey, so they could put their feet up for once. They wanted to feel secure in something, and they only felt secure in their money. The money's become an anchor for them, tying them to the future, to security, to their house in Turkey, to the new summer house where the stable used to be – all their dreams were made of money. And now that money's gone, as if it were little more than a dream. The numbers in their savings books mean less than the images Gül sees in her dreams.

Gül barely sleeps in the nights that follow; she tosses and turns, and she can't believe how the man she calls her husband could so carelessly toss away the money they saved for all those years.

Is this what we came here for? Are we really going to go home empty-handed? Money – that was all we came here for. Money was all we lived and breathed. Money is always blind, mute, and homeless. A lack of money, even if it's just five pfennigs short of a packet of cigarettes. Money – they've all become slaves to it. It's money that's made them spend hours sitting in front of the TV, watching special broadcasts they don't understand. It's money that keeps them up at night; money decides everything, whether you've got it or not.

The bank where Fuat deposited the money has gone bust, and it's unlikely they'll be able to cover their customers' losses.

Gül can't relax and she sleeps badly, but on the third day of the financial crisis, she doesn't feel drunk anymore. *I always thought Fuat was the greedy one*, she thinks. *I always laughed at him doing his little sums, his card games, lottery tickets, his dreams of getting rich, the way he spent all his time counting and counting, how all he could focus on was cash.*

Money didn't matter all that much to her – at least that's what she'd always thought. But now she feels empty. Cheated. She feels as if her whole life's been stolen away, and she has to start again from scratch. Now, when she stops for a rest at work, she spends longer in the office chair, exhausted, spent. Now, she spends longer staring into the night, and she has no thoughts, no images that might lend her strength.

Life doesn't stop when someone dies or when the money runs out. Ceren has finished her degree and will soon be starting work as a primary teacher. That's not what she trained to do, but there's no call for high-school German teachers at the moment. Ceyda's daughter Duygu has got herself an apprenticeship as a legal assistant and her son Timur wants to train as a hotel clerk. *We came to this country as labourers*, Gül thinks, *and my granddaughter's future is here, where she can learn a decent trade, where she'll never work a night shift or go out cleaning or picking strawberries until her back aches. Maybe it was worth it for all that. We managed to pay for Ceren's degree. Our time abroad meant Duygu and Timur will never go hungry. But it also means they'll always be foreigners in Turkey.*

Ceren and Ferdi want to marry in the summer, in Adana where they met, though neither of them has family there. It's not far from Gül's hometown, but the Black Sea is in a whole different part of the country. They don't want the usual big wedding, though.

Fatma, now twelve, asks her mother: 'Will I have to call Ferdi Dad after the wedding?'

'No, you can still call him big brother – just keep on calling him Abi.'

'I haven't told anyone at school,' she says. 'It sounds funny to say: *My mum's getting married.*'

She doesn't resemble her father as much as she did in her early years, but her head is still the same shape as his, she still has those bushy eyebrows, and recently she's been asking lots of questions about him. *How did you two meet? How long did you see each other in secret? Did anybody notice? What was he like? Why did it take you so long to realise he had cancer? Do lots of people die of cancer so young? Did he love me? Did he cuddle me? Did he have pet names for me?* Ceren tries to give her daughter detailed answers, tries to explain everything, to make something come alive with words, and yet she knows she'll never fill that gap. Words can't fill the gap, but perhaps they can close it a little.

'Ferdi will always be a big brother for you. Us getting married has nothing to do with you or your father. I won't love your dad any less. But he's gone, and life's hard when you're all on your own. You and me, we're tied together by your father, so tight not even a hair could pass through. You'll always be my only daughter.'

She doesn't know that this truth will hold, even if she means it in a different way now.

They want a small wedding, but even a small wedding costs money, and Gül doesn't know how they'll manage it. She hasn't worked for Herr Bender for a few years now, but she decides to go back to their old neighbourhood and ask if he needs her to clean the bookshop again.

Herr Bender's eyes are as friendly as ever, but everything else has changed. His face looks like it's slipped, like it's listing; his hair is sparse and seems to be falling out in clumps. When he comes out from behind the cash desk to say hello to Gül, she sees how much weight he's lost.

'Frau Yolcu,' he says. 'Frau Yolcu, how nice to see you. How are you?'

'Fine,' says Gül. 'I'm fine, thank you. And…'

She breaks off. She can't ask how he is – she can see for herself. She doesn't know which words would be right. In Turkish, she'd say: *May the Lord give you strength.*

'I've been thinking of you over the past few weeks,' Herr Bender says. 'How nice that I get to see you again. I've always liked you, Frau Yolcu. You're a good woman, hard-working, a woman you can trust.'

Gül has to say something; she can't stand there speechless like this. Quick: something, anything.

'Cancer?' she asks.

No prior warning, no politeness, no decency. She's instantly overcome with shame, but she can't take the word back. One word, just one. Without a friendly comment first. She flushes.

Herr Bender nods.

'Yes,' he says. 'That's right, Frau Yolcu, I've got cancer. Most people don't know what to say, get all tongue-tied.'

'Get well soon,' says Gül, sensing that those aren't the right words. They can't be. She speaks because not speaking would be worse, but she gets the impression she's making everything worse with every word. She speaks enough German to go out to work, but not enough to talk to a sick man.

'It's not looking good, Frau Yolcu. The cancer keeps coming back. I haven't got much longer. It's nice to see you again. That's why I'm here in the shop. So I see the people again who are important to me.'

Gül smiles and tries to put all her feelings into her face. She knows she has to do something with her hands as well; a smile's not enough. She's too shy to hug strange men, let alone German men. They never hug properly anyway, their upper bodies never touch; at most, they pat each other on the back. Gül hesitates for a moment, and then she opens her arms and presses Herr Bender to her chest, hoping to make up for her unfortunate words. Herr Bender's arms dangle in mid-air for a good two seconds, but then he hugs her back.

'My son-in-law cancer, too,' says Gül. 'Stomach cancer, very young, twenty-seven. I tell you, my daughter cry very, very much. Cancer bad. You good man. I always like see you, I like work here.'

She talks, and she scolds herself for not learning enough German all these years.

But who would she have learned it from, she'll wonder on her way home. *Where were we together with Germans in sorrow, together in grief, together in need? The Germans were always work for us, authorities, papers, rules and regulations.* The first German she really met was Gesine, the friend Ceren made in hospital after an accident. The two of them were children, and Gesine soon started popping in and out of their house like one of their own. It was through her that Gül learned that most Germans don't eat a hot meal in the evening; that the Germans have a different relationship to their bodies and shame, and to hospitality and money. But it took a hospital to bring the two children together. And now, death approaching is what it takes for a hug.

We're connected to people in pain, in love, in friendship, in sickness. There are no ties to be had through money. What is money worth anyway? – it won't bring back Herr Bender's health. Money doesn't make you happy when you have it, it just makes you unhappy when you don't.

When Herr Bender and Gül let go of each other, she feels close to tears. Gül sees him tearing up as well, and with her next breath, she no longer holds back; two silent drops run down her cheeks as her chin remains soft, not seizing up as it often does when she cries. Her vision blurs and two more drops follow, but then she breathes her tears back in. Herr Bender takes off his glasses and dries his eyes on a handkerchief he takes out of his pocket.

'What brings you here, Frau Yolcu? Is there something I can help you with?'

'I just visit friend. Come and say hello to you,' Gül stammers.

She turns down his offer of a cup of coffee, and then she finds herself outside her old building, unsure which direction to take. *Home*, she thinks. *The only way is home*. But as she walks to the bus stop, she keeps her eyes open. As much as she wishes she could lie to herself, she knows exactly what coincidence she's hoping for. But how would Can help her? Get her another honest job like back then? The shop that used to be the travel agency sells phones now, and Gül has never seen the people behind the counter.

We'll just get a loan, she tells herself. *We'll borrow some money. What's the worst that could happen? Our lives have been work, and we've not shied away from it for a day.*

It's the first wedding for a while where Fuat isn't so drunk by the end that he can barely stand, but it's not good sense that has him laying off the booze; it's his stomach. The wedding hasn't ended up bigger than they originally planned; they've hired a restaurant instead of a hall, with room for all sixty guests. Sibel is there with her husband Aziz, Emin's come all the way from Istanbul, and Melike's there; Nalan is the only one missing. Many of the guests are Ceren and Ferdi's student friends, and nineteen of Ferdi's relatives have made the journey south all the way from the Black Sea.

The food's good and everyone gets on well – both Ceren and Fatma seem happy, Gül has plenty of chances to chat to Hazer, and Fuat doesn't get carried away – but Gül's memories of this evening won't all be happy. When most of the guests have left, she sits down at the end of one of the tables for a moment and enjoys just watching, without having to speak or listen. Melike sits down next to her. Her breath smells of rakı, *but it's no excuse*, Gül thinks. *Not for this.*

'The financial crisis must have hit you two, mustn't it? If I remember correctly, you were with one of those new banks. How much did you lose? Will you be able to buy the house?'

Gül is stunned for a second, but by the next she's furious.

'No,' she says. 'No, we won't be able to buy the house. When's your son going to get married, by the way? Can't he find anyone?'

She'll regret these words. And she'll find herself wishing she could be as angry as she was that evening, when the fury gave her words momentum, moving faster and faster, always in circles. Just pure rage, without the desperation and grief that will follow. Just the urge to protect herself, without the understanding that she has already been hurt.

Duygu still seems like a child to Gül, even though she's finished school and has started work now. What has she learnt so far, and what has she seen of life? What did the blacksmith think of Gül when she was the same age? She was already married and had moved out by then, and he would drop by to see her every morning. Perhaps that was just because she still seemed like a child to him.

Gül is sitting at the kitchen table with Ceyda, and she asks her granddaughter to make some tea. *She'll be interested in boys now*, Gül thinks. She's more than old enough. Even if she hides it, even if she thinks she's forced to go about it in secret, even if she's supposed to be scared. But she won't tremble, her knees won't go wobbly for fear of being found out. Her thoughts will revolve around a man, or they might be doing so already, and she'll suffer disappointment too, and separation and longing, and she'll find happiness, perhaps not with a man, but with the people she can tie her heart to.

'Oma,' Duygu calls her; she uses the German word. Other than this, she usually speaks Turkish with her grandmother, slipping in a word or two at most of German when she can't think of the Turkish, but she always says this one word in German. Duygu only speaks German with her brother Timur. *Perhaps that's why Timur's Turkish is worse than his sister's now*, Gül thinks. She gets the impression that the first children born to Turkish families in Germany usually speak very good Turkish, but the younger the siblings, the less capable they are of wielding their mother tongue.

'Oma,' says Duygu, 'I have to bring the water in the bottom of the samovar to the boil first, right?'

Gül looks at her.

'This can't be the first time you've made tea?'

'I drink coffee, Oma, you know that.'

'But… Come on, I'll show you how to make it.'

'I've *tried* to teach her how to make tea, Mum,' says Ceyda. 'And how to roll vine leaves, how to make aubergine salad. She's not really got the knack for cooking.'

'Every woman has the knack – one might be a bit better than the next, but anyone can learn. Even men. Just look at Yılmaz.'

'She's just not interested, Mum. It just doesn't suit her. I've tried everything. In fact, she only really helps when you're here, so that you won't notice. I try to hide how useless she is around the house. She's no problem with washing, ironing, cleaning, but she doesn't like cooking.'

'But what about in the future? I mean when she has a husband?'

Ceyda shrugs. 'Maybe she'll find one like Yılmaz. Maybe she'll find someone rich. Maybe she won't get married at all. I can't force her, Mum. I can't make her do anything – she's almost nineteen now.'

Gül nods. That's how it is, then. Her daughters are keeping secrets from her. One hid her boyfriend for years, the other's been hiding her daughter. She sees less and less of the world because she only wants to see the things she approves of.

'She's your daughter,' says Gül. 'You're old enough now. It's no business of mine. And why should she have as few freedoms as you or I did?'

She looks at the packet of cigarettes on the kitchen table. In her mind's eye, she lights one up. She sees herself taking a couple of drags, taking her time. She can feel the thought of smoking relaxing her.

'Look,' she says, 'I've come a long way, and I probably haven't always been fair to you. I've probably been too narrow-minded about things, and perhaps it hurt you when I left you girls behind in Turkey – but I've always loved you. I don't want you to have secrets from me, I don't want you to have to hide. Who knows how much longer I'll live? I want to be able to see everything. I don't want my daughters to dim the light when I'm around.'

Ceyda looks at the ground. Swallows, takes a breath, swallows again. Then she looks up.

'I want to get a divorce.'

Ceren laughs on the phone. What else can she do? The whole thing reminds her of her first basketball match back in school, when she got so excited seconds into the game that she dribbled the ball the wrong way down the pitch and scored two points for the other team. Everyone in the gym laughed at her and she wanted to give up basketball altogether. Back then, the feeling lasted until she found herself able to laugh at it.

She's laughing this afternoon because this morning her whole class laughed at her. Since starting at the school, she's been trying to teach the Year 3s from her own lesson plan.

She was so nervous in her first few days that come the evening, she could barely remember what she'd done or what she'd talked about, and she could hardly remember any of the pupils' names. It was two weeks before she'd got used to the situation and could walk into the classroom in the mornings without her palms all sweaty.

By her second Friday on the job, she's learned about half of the thirty-eight names by heart and recognises many of her pupils in the playground. She's able to do her job without feeling overwhelmed every second of the day. The second Friday after starting at the school, she opens the window because she thinks a little fresh air couldn't hurt. She opens the window and the whole class roars with laughter. Ceren looks around, confused, and tries to work out what she's done wrong. She feels hotter than she did before. But she doesn't know what's happened. She has to ask. What else can she do?

'What is it? Why are you laughing?'

Jülide, noticeably eager, gets up. 'Miss, they're laughing because you opened the window.'

'They are?' says Ceren. 'I've opened the window because I felt hot. What's there to laugh about?'

The pupils laugh again. Orhan in the back row has tears in his eyes.

Ceren looks at Jülide, who's still standing, biting the inside of her cheek to keep from grinning. 'The glass,' says Jülide, struggling not to explode.

'The glass?'

Jülide takes a deep breath and says, very quickly: 'There'snoglassinthewindows!'

Ceren looks at the windows. She feels hot.

'I'm new,' she says. 'You've all been here for three years already.'

When she gets home later, Fatma is at a friend's house and Ferdi isn't home yet. Ceren is desperate to tell someone about opening the window with no glass in it, so she calls her mother in Germany. Gül laughs. Ceren joins in.

When Ferdi gets home, she tells him the story, but this time she's laughing as she tells it.

'It does sound like you,' says Ferdi.

He's a teacher too, but he teaches German at a middle school because someone he knows got him in. He's not nervous when he walks into class, but he doesn't like his job.

'I'm worried I'm not suited to being a teacher,' he says, 'I'll have to keep my eyes open and see what happens. We can't be stagnating here, working as teachers.'

It doesn't seem like stagnation to Ceren, even though she never wanted to teach primary school children, even if she doesn't think she's got any skill as a teacher, even if the past fortnight has sapped her energy.

'Look,' she says to Ferdi, 'I'm thirty-four now. I've never earned my own money. First it was my parents' money, then Mecnun's, then my widow's pension, and when that wasn't enough, it was my parents' money again. Now, I'm earning my own money. That's a good thing. Who cares if I opened a window with no glass in it, who cares if I'm doing a job I'm not cut out for?'

Fuat gets out of breath climbing stairs, washing his car, getting dressed; he has to use both hands to get up off the sofa. His trousers haven't fit for a while now, and neither have his shirts. His belly looks like he's lugging a medicine ball around with him, but he moves like he's carrying three. Gül notices him cutting even more corners at work than usual, and she thinks of his hurtful words about her figure. More than once, it's on the tip of her tongue to say: *Now you know what it's like.*

That's life, she thinks instead. *Anything can happen to you. No one should point the finger at liars, cheats and thieves. No one should think themselves above men who sell women or beat them, above people who cut corners at work or only look out for themselves. Life can be long, and the only thing that befalls you is yourself, but you never know yourself well enough to be ready for the future. You have to embrace life*, she thinks more and more often now. *You can't separate it into right and wrong, good and evil; you and life are one and the same.*

She doesn't know how many judgements she will make in the future, nor how much anger awaits her, how much disappointment, alienation and sorrow.

Fuat comes home one day, takes several cans out of a bag and beams at Gül. 'Look,' he says. 'Lose weight without going hungry or harming your health. All the vitamins, minerals and nutrients the body needs are right here. Instead of lunch, you just make yourself a drink with this powder and it keeps you full till the evening. The pounds drop off without any of the pain. A light breakfast in the morning, fruit in the evening, and you lose up to three kilos a week. Science is a blessing. No counting calories, no sums, no guilty conscience – all humiliation is consigned to history with this drink. And if that doesn't help, there's these pills that swell up in your stomach and make you feel full. It can't go wrong. I'm starting tomorrow, just you watch.'

He's as happy as he'd be if he'd got a new TV or a car; he's happy that life has so many conveniences, innovations and improvements to offer.

'Did you get some for me?' Gül asks, although she knows the answer.

'No. Did you want some?'

'Go on then, if it's that easy.'

'We can get you a set as well. You get a discount for every new customer you recruit.'

'How much does a set cost?'

'159.'

'Deutschmarks?'

'Marks are history, have been for months now. Euros.'

'That's 320 marks!' Gül is horrified. 'Are you crazy?'

'It's enough for a month. That's thirty meals you're saving. How much does a meal cost? It might look more expensive at first, but it saves you money in the end. And time.'

'Time?'

'Because you don't have to cook.'

'My time, then,' says Gül.

So that's progress – you have to pay to lose weight, and you save your wife time while you're at it. I don't think it's for me.

After his first month, Fuat has lost almost seven kilos; his belly shrinks and he no longer gets so out of breath. He treats himself to two or three beers on the weekend with dry-roasted peanuts on the side – as a reward, he says – but during the week he sticks firmly to his diet. He only sits down for a moment for lunch, downs his drink and gets up from the table. Gül stays behind alone and can't get up. She finds it hard to get used to cooking less, and while he loses weight, she puts it on. She's annoyed and resentful; she doesn't want to admit that Fuat's success is winning her over.

Once she's held back for long enough, she says to herself: *Alright then, why not? Anything Fuat can do, I can do too. Why should he be the only one to spend so much money? Why should he be the only one to lose weight without trying? Why shouldn't he have got something right for once? Why should I deny myself a convenience out of stubbornness?* It's not easy for her, but she asks Fuat to buy her a month's worth.

'Oh yes,' he says, 'that's what they're all like. First they're sceptical, but when they see it working they want it too. This stuff's going to take off all over the world – it's the only healthy and easy way to lose weight. If you'd started at the same time as me, you'd have lost ten kilos by now. And I'd have already got a discount. Women – slow at getting dressed, slow at getting ready, slow at going out, losing weight, thinking for themselves.'

'You be quiet,' says Gül. 'Just do me a favour and stop talking. Buy the stuff – it makes the person not taking it even fatter. That's probably the whole trick to it. Oh, and women – you're always blathering on about women. But who is it round here that can't keep his trap shut and takes every opportunity to mouth off like a fishwife?'

She knows Fuat will reply, but she simply turns around, marches into the kitchen and shuts the door. There are a few leftovers from lunch. She might as well eat them if she's starting a diet soon. She has to eat to stop her from getting up in a rage and telling Fuat where to stick his powder.

The drink doesn't fill Gül up, at least not all day long. She eats crispbread with red pepper in the afternoon, ten, twelve, fourteen pieces. She loses weight, but it doesn't feel like an achievement. She doesn't cook, doesn't go shopping; she sits around the kitchen doing nothing, just smoking and thinking back to the days when she was a child and the whole family ate breakfast and dinner together. She thinks of the tin cup her father used to drink out of; she thinks of how Nalan didn't like cheese as a child, how Melike rubbed chilli peppers around the edge of the tea glasses. She thinks of Sibel drawing on the margins of the newspaper over breakfast; of Emin, who made her wonder where he put all the food he ate while he stayed as thin as a reed. He's fat now, though Gül almost never sees him eating; as if he's only now putting on the portions from back then. Gül thinks of her mother, who always knew exactly how much everyone had eaten and who never seemed to sit still. She thinks of the hours with her daughters in the kitchen on Factory Lane. Vine leaves, lahmacun, moussaka, imam bayıldı, kadayıf, yufka, içli köfte, sıgara böreği, okra, chickpeas, white beans, sıkma, mücver, all the food they cooked, all the hours they spent looking forward to eating, full of love and caring.

Gül does lose weight; but she also loses cooking, her satisfying pastime. There are days now when she feels she's barely alive. All she has left are memories of the kitchen, a place that no longer serves a purpose.

Until, that is, she comes up with the idea of cooking for Ceyda and her family: poğaça, pastries, kurabiye, cake, mercimek köftesi, anything that will keep for a few days and can be eaten cold. When she runs out of ideas, she starts watching cooking shows on TV for inspiration.

Almost every weekend for months, Gül takes plastic boxes of food to Ceyda or gives her some to take home when she comes to Bremen. Ceyda telling her not to bother doesn't stop her. But when Gül sees that both Ceyda and Duygu are putting on weight, she vows to cook less. Too much weight isn't good for anyone, she knows that. But she can't just stop cooking. It's like smoking. When she tries to cut down, it works fine for one, two, three weeks, but at some point Gül always gets back to her ten cigarettes a day.

Gül has lost twelve kilos when she finally starts cooking for herself again.

'Abla?'

She recognises Emin's voice, but this time fear doesn't immediately flood through her. She stops to think who might have died, though Emin's voice harbours neither death nor accident. Still, she says: 'Emin, yes, it's me. I hope you're calling with good news.'

'It's nothing special, I just wanted to hear how you're doing. While Baba was alive, he used to tell me how you and the family were. And now I don't know anything about you – it's like our ties have broken, even though we all have telephones and they don't cost a fortune any more.'

Gül calls her brother regularly, but not often. Something tells her there's another reason for this call. They talk for so long that Gül forgets all about that; she stays on the line until she tries to end the conversation two or three times, thinking it will get expensive for Emin. Eventually, her brother says: 'Listen, what with the crisis and the euro, I thought the two of you might use a bit of support. The crisis hit us too, of course, but we can take it. We're alright when it comes to money... So if you're interested in selling your share of the summer house, I'd be willing to pay for it.'

Gül is surprised, but it takes her less than a second to hide it. 'No,' she says. 'Thanks, but we're not interested. What good would our share do you?'

'Nothing. You can have it back when the situation settles down. I just thought, because you had money in the Turkish banks... And because it's still not clear... I'm fortunate that things are going well with the hospital supplies shop we opened up. We're brother and sister, you've helped me so often in the past. I thought this might be a chance to give something back, and I didn't want to just offer you money, so I thought a deal...'

'Thank you,' says Gül. 'Thank you. I'm grateful for your offer. But we're not doing too badly. We didn't work abroad for years for nothing.'

'I'm glad to hear it. If there's anything I can do to help, you just let me know.'

'I will.'

After hanging up, Gül feels the anger all the way to her fingernails, all the way to her eyelashes and the tips of her hair. She feels like she'd send out sparks if she clicked her fingers. What on earth is he thinking? His *generous help. No plans for her share.* He can tell that to an ice-cream cone, and even that wouldn't believe a word of it. Emin, the boy she fed, bathed, whose nappies she changed, the boy she cared for and consoled. Emin, who she was more of a mother to than a big sister, that same Emin calls her and wants her share of the summer house? And acts like it's all about brotherly love and family ties, too. He's forgotten who darned his socks, mended his pants, wiped his bum.

Money spoils a person's character, so they say, but Gül's never thought that's true. Money just brings their character to the forefront. What an ungrateful rascal – just because he has a few notes in his pocket these days, he thinks he can put on an act of generosity to his big sister. She'd never thought him so devious, but his money's betrayed him.

By the time she smokes her second cigarette on the balcony, she's calmed down a little. She feels the cold on her skin, a cold that can't get inside her because there's a furnace in her body, fuelled by rage.

She realises Melike must have put him up to it. Emin would never have an idea like this of his own accord. What's she playing at? Phone in hand, Gül has dialled the first two zeroes and the nine when she decides to hang up.

Not because it would be unwise to call, but because she doesn't know what to say. And because it would only be pouring oil on the fire anyway. Her words would hurt and echo for so long that they'd resonate for years to come, in her body. There's enough pain, enough anger, enough grief and sorrow. Why should she stand beneath dark clouds and beg them to rain down on her? What she and her brother and sisters need is a little warmth, a little light. And she's the oldest; it's her job to make sure there's light. There's another voice inside her, one that denounces Melike and Emin, their greed and dishonesty, curses them for being so two-faced. But she tries not to grant that voice any space to sound out. Why should she join in a dissonance, when she knows there's light enough to warm them all?

Gül stopped going through Fuat's pockets a while ago now, and she thinks nothing of it when he stays home alone one weekend to get the car fixed. Ceyda picks Gül up in her car, but when she goes to drop her back on Sunday morning, the engine won't start. After a few tries, Ceyda starts to get nervous, but Gül stays quite calm.

'What is it with our cars this weekend?' she says. 'Leave it for a minute, you've got it all worked up.'

They sit side by side in silence and look at the car parked in front of them.

'Have you thought any more about it?' Gül asks then.

'Yes,' says Ceyda, looking down, her hands in her lap. 'I have. I'm still waiting. Until both the kids can stand on their own two feet. Another couple of years won't make much difference.'

'Do you think anyone suspects anything?'

'No, I don't think so.'

'Don't slip up just because you know more than he does. And don't get careless. Make sure you don't put a foot wrong.'

Ceyda nods.

'I feel more relaxed now,' she says. 'Now that you've given me your blessing. It's a relief to know the end's in sight. Sometimes I've felt like I'm going downhill.'

'May your hands never tire, may your back never be crooked, may your legs never weaken, may the ground beneath your feet never be too hard or too rocky,' says Gül.

And may everyone be granted these same things, she thinks.

The car won't start. Adem's not home, and the neighbour can't help, so Ceyda takes her mother to Hamburg station. When they get there, she buys a ticket, drops Gül on the platform and says: 'It's very easy. You just need to get off at the next stop and you'll be at the station in Bremen – you know the way from there.'

Gül's scared of getting lost, of ending up God-knows-where in Germany and not being able to find her way home. Ceyda can tell that her mother is nervous and offers to go with her.

'No,' says Gül. 'No thanks, I can manage.'

'Are you sure? The kids are old enough, they'll be alright on their own. I'm not working tonight, I could just come with you.'

'No thanks, I'll manage,' says Gül, fending her off.

'Come on, Mum, I don't want you to have to worry.'

'Thank you, sweetheart. But I'm fine, really, all I need to do is get off at the next stop.'

When she's finally sitting on the train by herself, the tears come. She thinks of all the times she left Ceyda on her own. With her mother-in-law in Turkey, when she was still a little girl; at the airport in Istanbul, when her passport expired; in Germany, when she'd just got married. How often she left Ceyda behind, alone. Now she wants to be by her side when she gets divorced. Neighbours and friends will gossip, they'll badmouth her, she'll be the talk of the town.

But this is Germany, this country is freer. Ceyda lives here – why shouldn't she enjoy a bit of that freedom? Why should she continue to suffer with a husband like Adem?

Times are changing. Melike's son lives in Istanbul with his girlfriend, and they're not married. People will talk, of course, but behind closed doors. İsmail is a man, he makes good money, and it's Istanbul. Why shouldn't Ceyda be able to live freely too, now she's fulfilled all her obligations? These are new generations – the world seems to turn faster with each day that passes, and everything is changing.

I'll stand by her this time, Gül tells herself, *whatever happens.*

Twenty minutes before the train gets into Bremen, she's standing by the doors and wondering what she's supposed to do if she can't get them to open. She hopes other people will need to get off too, so someone will be able to help her. With each passing minute, her heart beats faster. She's thoroughly flustered by the time the train begins to slow. By now, a long queue has formed behind her. What will people think when they see she doesn't know how to open the doors? Just another Turkish country bumpkin, a peasant woman who's never taken the train, one who doesn't know how to navigate this modern world of ours. She turns around as the train begins to slow to a halt, but what excuse can she come up with to let someone else go in front?

Gül sees people on the platform in front of her, but while she's standing there, petrified, the doors open with a *hiss*. She's unsteady on her feet as she steps down from the carriage.

She's walked several feet along the platform and still doesn't feel quite herself, but then she spots Serter sitting on a bench from some way off. He's wearing an expensive suit, smoking, and he seems to have sunk into a melancholy quite unlike him.

'Hello, Serter,' she says, standing in front of him, but he simply stares into space and doesn't respond. For a brief moment, Gül's unsure whether it really is Serter after all, but then she gently puts a hand on his shoulder. He turns, looks at her blankly for a second, and then a smile of recognition beams across his face.

'Gül, how lovely to see you.' He stands up and shakes her hand. 'What are you doing here?'

'I'm just on my way back from Ceyda's. She lives in Hamburg and her car's broken down. What about you? Are you waiting for someone?'

There are no tears in Serter's eyes, but they're shining, reddening in an instant.

'No,' says Serter, 'I'm not waiting. Or perhaps I am. But you can't call it waiting when there's no end to it, can you? Come, Gül, let's sit and have a smoke. You still smoke, don't you?'

'Yes.'

'Sit yourself down. Here, have one of mine.'

'Thanks.'

They light up and Gül relaxes, but she gets the feeling something's not quite right with Serter. Something different from usual.

'Sorry to ask again, but what are you doing here if you're not waiting for someone? Are you going somewhere?'

'No, Gül.'

His voice is husky; he clears his throat.

'I often sit here. Quite often, anyway. I always sit here when I'm missing home. I feel closest to home here. I could get a train anytime and go south. I've never flown, you know. The train station's my last link to my homeland. You know, you've got it good: you're not scared someone's going to poison you, you can eat what you want. You buy pastırma at the supermarket and have village bread sent to you from Turkey. You can press a whole loaf of home to your chest and cut yourself a slice and spread it with longing. There's nothing left for me, everyone thinks I'm crazy, I've got no one I can go home to. I'm shut out of society because there are people who want to kill me. May the Lord never leave anyone without a home to go to. Just look at these people, running this way and that, racing after money, happiness, wealth, a home, fame, women, revenge. They work and graft and sleep – it's not their labour they're selling, it's hours of their lives. But I'm the mad one, they say. Gül, I sit here at the station because it's my only connection to a world that no longer exists.'

'That world doesn't exist for any of us, now,' says Gül. 'Turkey's not the same country we left. And perhaps all of us have gone a little mad here; we don't quite fit in over there any more.

People there remind us of the years we've missed, like holes in our hearts. They can tell straightaway that something's off. When I went back to live in Turkey, it took me three years before I began to feel like I belonged there again.'

'But they don't want us here either, Gül. And unlike me, you could still get away. The path's open to you, but I can't get further than this point. And you know what train stations mean in this country. After those plane attacks, they want to get all the Muslims out of the country, not just the Turks. They'll make all of us Muslims now, even the biggest unbelievers. They're out to kill me because I know they need enemies. They need them, to spread fear. Fear makes people small. Everyone always thinks I'm the one who's scared, but that's not true; I'm just cautious. How else would I have survived so long? I'm cautious, but I'm not afraid – if I was, they'd be able to control me in this kingdom of fear they've built. I've got this longing, though, a longing that even the voice of God can't quench.'

Gül looks at Serter. She has so often wondered if he's the loneliest person she knows. He's rich now. Money doesn't make your heart full; it just fills up your pockets. And what is it the ancestors say? It's not where you're born that counts, it's where you get your fill. No one gets their fill without money. And no one is happy with money alone. No one escapes loneliness without trust.

'I ran into Serter at the station,' Gül says.

'Ah, that reminds me – I heard something about him: he's living with a prostitute these days, a Turkish woman.'

'A prostitute?'

'Yes.'

'I don't believe a word.'

'It's true, I'm telling you. Dursun told me, he saw it for himself. Serter gives her money, so she doesn't have to work any more. If you've got the cash, there's nothing you can't buy. He can just spend all day... lying down and watching TV... and being waited on hand, foot and finger. That's the life.'

'Serter's lonely, very lonely. He misses Turkey.'

'What do you mean, lonely? If a man with that much money can't find any friends, he must be doing something wrong.'

'You can't buy friends.'

'Of course not. Just think of that woman. What am I saying? Finding friends! You can buy ways of meeting people, and if ninety-nine out of a hundred are only interested in your money, there's still always one who might be a friend. Rich people just have more opportunities; they get more attention. But you can't hide your money away, of course. You have to show it off, you have to spend it. If a man's lonely, even though he's got money and time, something's not right with him. Like with Serter. Who would he make friends with? People as crazy as him? People like you and me? That man's all tangled up in his complaints and his loneliness – he doesn't want to let go of his unhappiness. Think about it: he's got money now, he's got a... servant, but he just sits there and complains and moans and groans. That's how the Ottoman Empire fell; they just sat and watched other people working. How many years has he been in Germany? You'd think he might have learned something about hard work, about goals.'

As if you ever learned anything about that, Gül doesn't say. All these years she's been living with this man, and she still doesn't know him. Sometimes he reacts just the way she expects him to, but sometimes, like now, he surprises her. She looks at him and wonders whether, perhaps, he ever feels lonely too. He might have reason to, but somehow she doesn't think he's capable of the feeling. His world seems too small; a person can hardly feel alone in the kind of space he navigates – it only has a tiny window that he rarely looks out of, and when he does, it's only ever with one eye.

Fuat doesn't understand how people feel. He can't feel their fear, their loneliness, their worries and doubts. Perhaps because he doesn't find those feelings in himself. He can see people's greed and their good ideas; he recognises drunks; he can distinguish brands of cars and TVs, the different whiskies; but he doesn't know about types of longing. In the same way that Fuat can reel off car models, Gül can name the different types of separation. The separation that hurts immediately, the kind that doesn't hurt until weeks and months later, the separation you forget but that creeps up on you again, the separation that gets worse when you hear their voice, the separation that their voice soothes, the separation that tears you apart, and the kind that only ever pulls at you. The separation that sits on your shoulders when you write a letter, and the separation that washes your soul in warm water when you receive a few written lines. She knows about types of longing, doubt and fear; she knows about types of melancholy and homesickness; she knows all the ways of feeling out of place – and when she looks at Fuat, he seems like a child to her most of the time. Like a child no one can mother because he's lost all curiosity for his surroundings.

It might be true, the thing about the prostitute, she thinks. *But if it is true – doesn't Serter feel even lonelier with her than he would without her?*

It's not the same childish joy that shows on Fuat's face when he's bought something new, but his expression is similar. Even before he opens his mouth, Gül has a word for it: triumph. She doesn't begrudge him losing weight, but she begrudges him this triumph, or whatever might have caused it.

'They've confirmed,' he says. 'We won't get all the money back, but we'll get the full amount they insured.'

For a while it's looked like the damages might be covered, but there was still some uncertainty until now. Gül feels relief – but she tries not to let it show.

'I told you: fear doesn't get you anywhere. You have to take a few risks.'

'How much have we lost?'

'It's not worth mentioning.'

'How much?'

'Just under 5000 euros.'

'Not worth mentioning. Great.'

'If it wasn't for me, you'd never have seen a cent of our savings again.'

'If it wasn't for you, I wouldn't have lost the money.'

'If it wasn't for me, you'd never have saved that much in the first place.'

'Oh really?'

Gül hesitates for a moment. Only 5000 euros. How reckless he is with money.

'You're poor because you feel poor,' she says. 'And you'll always feel poor, no matter how much money you squirrel away.'

'Oh, will I?'

'Yes, you will. You know what they say: the Lord delights his poor creatures by letting them lose their donkey and find it again. It's always the poor who delight over things they thought were lost.'

'Women!' says Fuat. 'No clue about money, no clue about delight, no clue about being bold and taking risks, but they're always at the front of the queue when it comes to making clever quips. You should be pleased, for God's sake.'

'Pleased about what? About never forgetting how it feels to be penniless, even after decades of hard work?'

She goes out to the balcony to smoke. 5000 euros is a lot, but she senses something has softened the money's grip on her. The numbers on their bank statement give her a quiet sense of peace.

No matter how much money we've got, she thinks, *we come from poverty; in our minds, we'll always be poor.*

Sevgi's Turkish seems to have got even worse since she moved to Göttingen, but Saniye's daughter has grown into a confident young woman. When she finishes her degree and starts working in a group medical practice in Bremen, she thinks the world is her oyster. Sevgi Özcan, paediatrician: her name brings in Turkish parents, including many who don't speak particularly good German. Sevgi has always worked hard, and now she's started reading Turkish books, watching Turkish films and learning vocab to improve her Turkish.

'Auntie Gül,' she says, 'it's so wonderful to come back to the language. There are no barriers in Germany these days, we can move freely. Your generation were all workers when you came over, and look where your children are now: doctors, lawyers, politicians, actors, hairdressers, estate agents, filmmakers, telephone salespeople – we've spread out of the factories all around the country. No one talks about repatriation any more; we're here, we're part of society. All of us. And I mean *all* of us. Even the criminals and the ones who have to marry someone their parents bring over from Turkey, the ones who don't want to learn German and the ones who win big movie awards, go into politics or TV. It's not about good or bad foreigners now, about enrichment or burden… We've spread out across society; we've left the factories and the ghettos behind us.'

'How great it is to be young,' Yılmaz says when Sevgi goes out. 'She sees the whole world as if someone's sprinkled it with icing sugar. She thinks we're everywhere just because there's one filmmaker, one TV presenter, one politician, one writer and one who-knows-what. Only ever one. If you go out in the street we're everywhere, yes, but if you turn on German TV, we don't exist here. They always need a token Turk so nobody notices. We're totally underrepresented in the entire cultural sector – we don't appear in their films, their books, their songs. But Sevgi's young; I'm not going to rain on her parade.'

'Isn't it dangerous for a young woman to live in that neighbourhood?' Fuat asks.

Although Saniye and Yılmaz would have welcomed Sevgi back to live with them after her degree, she decided to rent a small flat in the town centre.

'You lived there too, though.'

'Yes, but a woman on her own, and one of us… a Turkish woman…'

'What's so Turkish about her? Didn't you hear how she talks? She's spent a total of six months of her life in Turkey if you add it all up, and that's fine. Take a good look at Turkey – the crisis was just the beginning; the country's going down the drain, slowly but surely.'

'I know why I don't like going over there,' Fuat complains on the way home. 'That man's a traitor to the fatherland, if ever there was one – he doesn't have a drop of pride in his homeland. Just because they wouldn't let the great Yılmaz finish university, the whole country must be bad. Maybe his daughter does only see icing sugar, but all he can see is dust and dirt, envy and betrayal. He acts all understanding and wise, but he's full of hate, full of anger at the whole world – nothing's ever right for him.'

He pauses and looks at Gül, expecting her to defend Yılmaz like she usually does, but Gül says nothing.

If he didn't smoke hashish, he might not be able to stand his life, she thinks. In silence, the two of them walk to the other end of the estate. When Fuat opens the front door downstairs, Gül asks: 'Remember when you used to drink so much? Were you full of rage at everything too, back then?'

Fuat turns around and looks at his wife. 'I'll never understand what goes on in your head. I used to drink because I enjoyed life, and I'd still be drinking if my stomach would let me. *Rage…*'

He shakes his head, takes off his shoes and goes inside the flat. 'Women! You can't expect logic from them.'

When he comes home the next day, Fuat's face is a picture of pride and joy. He looked like this when he bought his first big Nordmende TV, when he was the first person to own a video recorder on their street, when the satellite dish was installed; he looked like this when he came home with his first used Mercedes. He looked like this the first time he brought that expensive diet powder home with him, the one he still drinks twice a week. But today Fuat says nothing, and Gül doesn't ask questions, though she knows she'd be doing him a favour.

'Call this number here,' Fuat eventually says.

'Whose number is it?'

'Just call the number.'

'You call it.'

'Oh, woman, just dial the number will you? You can't always know everything in advance. It's a surprise.'

'Why should I call someone I don't know? What's this funny number anyway? Where's that code for?'

Fuat sighs, picks up the phone and dials. There's a ringing from inside his jacket pocket, and he takes out a mobile phone, beaming.

'Whose is that?'

He sighs again and sits down.

'Whose d'you think? Probably that woman who choked on her stepmother's poison apple. Or was it the seven dwarves with the fourteen arms? Mine. It's my phone.'

'What's it for?'

'Well, it's no good for shaving, so I thought I'd use it to make phone calls.'

'But we've got a phone.'

'Why do I bother trying to talk to you? This is the future! You can't even see it when it's right in front of your nose. Wait and see, in a couple of years you'll have one too. Haven't you noticed more and more people walking around with mobile phones? That's progress – you can put your phone in your pocket now and take it everywhere you go. We used to dial until our fingers got sore, and then they invented push-buttons. Then we used to trip over the cables until they got rid of the wires. The Germans, the Japanese, the Americans, they're changing the world, but my wife's fast asleep.'

'I bet it's expensive.'

'It makes your life easier – it's a kind of translator you can take along everywhere. And they're getting cheaper and cheaper.'

'But it's…'

…for businesspeople, she wanted to say, but she interrupts herself. *Or for criminals like Can.* Why would she need something like that?

'…nice that you've got something new,' she says.

She smiles. It's easiest to understand him when he's indulging his simple pleasures. But that won't stop her asking Ceyda how much these mobile phones cost.

In the weeks that follow, Gül sees three of her colleagues repeatedly standing by the office telephone and dialling a number. They try to hide what they're doing, but it doesn't escape Gül. They pick up the receiver and enter the number, but they never speak. Gül can't understand who they could be calling at this hour. She can't make head nor tail of it, but she doesn't mention it to anyone. She gave up criticising other people's work or pointing out their mistakes a long time ago. She's not a good supervisor – all she does is delegate jobs and try to keep an eye on things. Everyone has to bear their own misdeeds, and it's not for Gül to bother about whether people can keep their backs straight under the weight of it all. She tries to keep her breaks short, but when she sits down in an office chair, it's not the window or somewhere indoors that her eyes automatically wander to, it's the phone.

Who do you call in the middle of the night? And why wouldn't you say anything? Is there some kind of secret code where you communicate via the number of rings? Isn't it strange that you can type in a few numbers and reach anyone else who happens to have a telephone? One voice can nestle up close to another; in a person's voice you can hear the tiny details that are lost in the words in a letter. A short 'Yes?' can tell you exactly how the other person is feeling.

A few days ago, Gül heard joy in Ceren's voice; there was a little excitement, and fear too. Gül had already been wondering whether the day would come when she'd receive this news, but she had never spoken to Ceren about it.

'What is it?'

'I'm pregnant.'

'How lovely,' Gül said. And she hoped her worry wasn't immediately obvious in her voice. Would Fatma be jealous that her brother or sister, whichever God willed, would grow up with both a mother and father, something she was denied? Would Ferdi love his own child more than Fatma? Would the little family manage to stay together? Or would it break up over this child?

Once the child is here, we'll be able to delight in the wonder of it all – we'll marvel at it and be glad. And may the Lord have mercy for everything else.

Looking back, she thinks she managed to keep her fears out of her voice. It won't be easy, but every path looks rocky when you peer towards the horizon. But once you get there, you'll always find something to help you put one foot in front of the other.

One day, this child will have a telephone number of its own. Its voice will mingle with another person's voice, and it will share in joys and keep its fears to itself, Gül thinks, standing up to get back to work.

'May he grow up with both his mother and father,' says Gül, as they say for every birth. The words that leave her mouth are honest, but for a few seconds she feels paralysed. She sees Can beaming, and finally she gets up and wraps her arms around him. Then she cups his face in her hands and kisses him on the forehead.

'May he grow up with both his mother and father,' she says again. They sit back down, and Gül thinks for a moment, hesitates, wrangles with herself; she chews her words over, but doesn't swallow them down.

'Now you've got to leave that life behind you once and for all. Just look, you almost missed the birth because you were in prison again.'

'I know, Auntie Gül, I know. I can't get sent down again, this has to be the end of it. I want to be there for my son, I want to see him grow up. But I've changed everything, really I have. We've set up two companies in my wife's name.'

'What sort of companies?'

'We sell ringtones and greetings cards over the internet. And we've got a helpline for bus and train timetables.'

Gül is hearing more and more about the internet these days, but she doesn't know what it is exactly, except that it has something to do with computers, which she doesn't know anything about either. So she asks about the helpline; she wants to know how you can make money from that sort of thing.

'There's a fee to ring up,' says Can, 'nearly three euros a pop. If ten people call every hour on average, that's 30 euros. The directory's open 24 hours, so that's 720 euros a day. If we take off rent, employees, fees and taxes, we've got about 300 euros left over. Do that for thirty days and that's 9000 euros a month. It's not all that much, but it's clean money, it doesn't need laundering before you can use it.'

Gül looks at him, wide-eyed. 9000 euros, in one month. She'd have to work about six months to make that much.

'Why do people ring up if it's so expensive?'

'Advertising,' says Can. 'We run loads and loads of ads for the line.'

'So it doesn't actually cost much to run. You're tricking people instead of robbing them.'

'Auntie Gül, it's an officially registered company. They'd close us down if it was a scam. The whole system's based on lies anyway; if we're tricking anyone, then at least we're doing it on the right side of the law.'

Gül takes a sip of her coffee. The insight comes unexpectedly; she doesn't think about it, the understanding simply presents itself. She feels warm. She's not shrewd, she's not creative, she doesn't think like these people, and yet suddenly she understands how it all hangs together. She feels the weight of the words on her tongue, but they won't slip down her throat.

'Son,' she says, 'you're a father now. It's good that you're not getting mixed up with drugs and break-ins and thefts and… women any more, but you've got to take some responsibility. You've got to set an example for your child. You need to raise him to be a decent man. You're still not on the honest path. You're scamming people.'

'Auntie Gül, I'm not scamming anyone, I —'

'You're paying people to call the hotline from private numbers.'

Can doesn't feel he's been caught out. He leans back and smiles.

'No one could prove it,' he says.

'And you call that legal, do you?'

'It's a legal business, a taxed income, there's no risk of ending up in jail.'

'It's not honest work.'

'Auntie Gül, I have to make money somehow, and the stuff you call "honest work" hardly gets you rich. Not when you start out poor, like we have. The rich are the only ones who can make money from honest work. But they get to do it without breaking a sweat. How many years have you been slogging away here? And how much cash have you managed to put aside?'

'Not much, but enough,' she says. 'You could probably buy a small house in Turkey with it. And my conscience is clear.'

'So's mine.'

'But I don't have to worry about being found out.'

'Neither do I, not any more. Auntie Gül, you're happy with what you've got. And that's great. Maybe you learnt different things to me when you were young. I'm different. It's always the older generation who complain that there's no closeness anymore, no unity, no humanity. They say all anyone's after is money. But they want young people to act like the world hasn't changed. This is the world we're living in, and in this world, money counts. Name one single person who's got rich without tricks, or without their forefathers tricking anyone.'

'Serter won the lottery,' says Gül, because it's the only example she can call to mind fast enough.

'Serter? The mad bloke?'

'Yes. Do you know him?'

'The whole city knows him.'

Can leans back again. Now he seems to be the one who's weighing up whether some words might be best left unsaid.

'And those that don't will have heard at least one story about him,' he says then.

The lottery's not a real job, but at least it's honest. He got rich without having to scam anyone, Gül thinks. Can leans forward and rests his forearms on the table.

'Auntie Gül,' he says, lowering his voice. 'That might be what everyone believes, but I know the truth. Serter didn't win the lottery. But don't tell anyone.'

'What?'

'The lottery win's just a line. The rich always have an official story about where they got their riches. We even mocked up a lottery ticket – we bought it from a guy so there'd be some proof for the story. But Serter, how's he supposed to have won the lottery? He never even plays it.'

'So what did he do?'

'He took care of a few things for us.'

'A few things?'

'Yes.'

'What sort of things?'

'Things, you know.'

'Serter might be mad, but he's an honest soul. I can't imagine him doing anything like that.'

'You've got to understand people,' says Can, 'then you can get them to do what you want. It works for almost all of them. When I was younger, I let the store detective catch me nicking stuff at the shopping centre. I wasn't even fourteen and I knew nothing would happen to me. I told him my parents would beat me if I brought the police home, that I knew older kids who stole stuff too; I told him if he let me go, I'd let him know next time they were in there shoplifting. I told him I'd leave my jacket there as insurance, so he knew I'd really rat on the others. But the jacket was just one I'd nabbed off someone else. I managed to convince him, and he went along with it. Meanwhile, my brother had cleared out half the shop while the detective was busy with me.'

As is often the case, Gül doesn't know whether to be disgusted or impressed.

'What's that got to do with Serter?' she asks, though she suspects she's not going to get an answer.

'Serter feels like there's always someone after him, that's his weak spot. Just like the store detective has his weak spot. It's easy to manipulate people when you know these things.'

'I like Serter. I like him a lot. If I find out he's suffering because of you...'

She stops. What does she want to say? Does she intend to threaten him? Can doesn't react.

'I'm done with all that now,' he says. 'I'm not doing any dodgy stuff any more, and I'm not working with Serter. He's safe.'

'Is it true he lives with a prostitute?'

'Not any more, as far as I know. He was scared she might poison him.' He smiles. 'I like Serter too,' he says. 'Really I do. And I'm glad he's got no money troubles these days. You should be happy for him too.'

'I am.'

On the way home, Gül wonders if she would have saved as much money without Fuat. Or if she'd have saved more. He drank a lot and gambled it away, and he'd often be the one to get a round in, whereas she was always a thrifty saver. But he always kept an eye on where it was best to invest, the best terms, conditions and percentages. While she was trying to keep things together, he was always looking for ways to turn one mark into two. Without Fuat, she'd never have come to Germany; without Fuat, she might never have had the chance to save, because you needed money for that. Perhaps it took two people to put that money aside. Two people to achieve wealth. Even if their marriage has never been full of love. That drive requires two people. One person on their own is doomed to stagnation and solitude.

I can't handle these temperatures any more – I'm getting old, Gül thinks. They're staying by the sea with Ceren, Ferdi, Fatma and the eight-week-old Ersin; they'd hoped to escape the heat of Adana, but it's humid and the water is so warm it brings no refreshment. Gül is glad every time she gets to go shopping in Fuat's Mercedes, because then she can enjoy the air conditioning before the hot air envelops her again, as if to squeeze all the strength out of her.

Fatma wakes up every morning with her hair damp with sweat, and the first thing she wants to do is go to see Ersin. She spends a lot of time stroking her brother's head and telling him what's going on around them. Gül and Ceren are often beside them, and they exchange smiles, pleased by this warmth.

'It is, yes, it is,' says Fuat. 'I'm sure of it; this is the place where we came on holiday with your brother and sisters that time.'

'I don't recognise anything.'

'Me neither, but it's definitely the same place.'

'Where have the villagers' houses gone?'

'Torn down, probably.'

It's the place where her father made friends, and where someone shouted at Melike for walking around in a bikini. Gül keeps looking out for the woman with the mole above her eyebrow, though she's not sure she'd want to see her again. She has good memories of those days, despite that one incident. She's in the place where they were all together, although none of them would recognise it now. There are hotels all along the beachfront, restaurants, roads, and the new buildings have dripping air conditioners attached to their outside walls; not that the hotel they're staying in has one.

Gül's fat feels like it's storing the heat, and though she has no appetite, drinking a lot and eating little, she still doesn't seem to lose weight. Fuat, on the other hand, nibbles his way through every evening, eating so much grilled meat and so many oily pastries that she can practically see him putting on the pounds. He drinks beer, often tipping a shot into his glass. The rich food, combined with the hidden vodka, seems to outwit his stomach; it doesn't give him indigestion and he gets drunk every night.

Gül enjoys these days with Ceren's family, despite the heat. Back in her hometown, she wishes all she had to put up with was torrid heat and extra pounds, not her thoughts as well. She wishes Melike would suffer, pay a price for being the way she is. She wishes everyone who feels unfairly treated by Melike would join forces with her, Gül. When Melike was young, she was just selfish, only ever fighting for herself; she would lie and offload work and guilt on her brother and sisters if she had to. Her free time, her sports, her studies, her husband, her freedom – nothing else mattered. But at least she wasn't false; she wasn't two-faced then like she is now.

Getting out of the air-conditioned car and being smothered by the heat is easy. Getting out of the car and seeing that the summer house stable has been torn down and replaced by a ditch for a foundation – her knees go weak; fear and rage and bewilderment flood her body faster than the heat could ever grab it, and she doesn't know whether she's going to vomit or faint.

In the beginning you just lie there, but then you start crawling, pull yourself up on furniture, and eventually you learn to walk. In the beginning you often land on your bottom or stagger around like Fuat used to after a bottle of whiskey. But you get more and more sturdy on your feet – you trust yourself, and at some point, you barely struggle any more. At least, you don't struggle with balancing. Perhaps with your knees, those surplus pounds, your hip, the heat – but not with your balance.

Still, the ground Gül was just standing on seems to be dissolving, and the older she gets, the more it happens – at least that's how it feels. Firm ground dissolves, all the tree trunks you used to lean on for a rest simply disappear, and you find yourself in a treeless void with no stones, no ground and no sky; a dark void in which you fall – falling and falling and never landing. There's nothing you can rely on, nothing is solid – everything disappears from one moment to the next.

'But we agreed we wanted to build this house,' says Melike. 'I don't have to ask your permission first.'

'No, that's not what I meant; it's not about permission. We wanted to do it together. It belongs to all of us, you can't just start—'

She notices how her voice has risen and become shrill. She breaks off mid-sentence, but Melike seems perfectly relaxed, which makes Gül even angrier. She takes a breath, tries to calm down.

'It belongs to us all – we'll find a way to share it between us.'

'You did it in secret!' Gül shrieks. 'You could have said something. I was here the whole time. Who paid for it?'

'Emin and me. I don't understand what you're getting so het up about. You knew we'd be building, and we just put the money down up front.'

'Enough,' Gül shrieks. 'Enough! I'm your big sister, it's disrespectful. Don't act all innocent, it drives me round the bend. It wasn't right and you know it. Apologise, for God's sake! I want an apology.'

Her face is flushed – she's sweating, she's lost control, and the hint of a grin on Melike's face makes it impossible for her to get a grip on herself. Her anger takes over; the Gül she knows has vanished.

'You can't treat me like this.'

'And you can't treat *me* like this either,' Melike says. 'I'm not a five-year-old you can just scold. We can talk once you've calmed down.' She gets up, slams the door and leaves.

'Come back,' Gül yells. She runs to the door, opens it and yells: 'Come back right now and apologise!'

'You know what she's like,' says Sibel.

'Yes, but this time she's gone too far.'

'Maybe she has – I can't judge, I wasn't there.'

'You knew they'd started digging the foundations.'

'But we'd all agreed we wanted to build a modern house on the plot.'

'Oh, so you knew.'

'Yes, of course I knew. I live here.'

'Why didn't you tell me?'

'I thought you knew.'

'Who from?'

'Abla, what do I know? Are you accusing me, now? What have I done wrong? I've never hurt a fly. We have to calm down, all of us. These things aren't worth arguing over. All of us have enough to eat, all of us have a roof over our heads, all of you have healthy children.'

She pauses, and Gül realises she's touching a sore spot. All these years, Gül has seen Sibel and Aziz as happy; Sibel had her paintings, her husband had his music. They had books, they'd sing together instead of watching TV in the evening, and they seemed to be happy with what they had. They'd built a world for themselves in which their own song rang out, drowning out the noise from outside.

All at once, Gül now sees how inadequate Sibel has felt, how small, how inferior – because she was the only one who couldn't have children. It's as if someone has stopped a film and she can examine the image in detail. As if frozen light were suddenly liquid, opening up a view of the next layer.

Gül sees that there's more distance between her and Sibel than just a few countries and plane flights, and that her years in Turkey didn't close that gap. She suddenly understands why Sibel doesn't want to exhibit her pictures. She understands the pictures aren't just a result of her passion; they're also a chance to hide herself and her pain, to chop them into smaller pieces and store them in a stable.

Her anger, her fear, her worries – they fall from her all at once, and she feels the need to protect Sibel. Now that it's all fallen, what remains is love. And then doubts come rushing in. Has she made a mistake? Has she failed her sister? Should she have done more, should she have taken more time for her? Was she wrong to have let herself be fooled so easily? Perhaps she's failed Melike too? The thought of Melike brings her rage right back.

Sibel looks up at her sister.

'You're right,' Gül says. 'We all need to calm down.'

The light freezes again, and Gül wonders whether Sibel felt that it was liquid for a few short moments.

When her night shift is over, Ceyda drives to Bremen to go to the pensions office with her mother. She has coffee and cigarettes on her breath; her eyes are red, and she looks tired. But who else could Gül have asked? She didn't want to go on her own. She'd been to all sorts of places on her own before – the job centre, the immigration office, the residents' registration office, to the doctor's, to sign the children up for school; she'd often gone alone to places where her German failed her, but she'd always managed, somehow. Sometimes there'd be someone to translate for her, sometimes all it needed was a little patience and goodwill, and sometimes she'd come back clutching a slip of paper with everything she hadn't understood written on it.

She only has to go to the pensions office once, and she doesn't want to go alone. She's nervous. Perhaps it's because she knows her life is going to change when she stops working, perhaps it's because she's had to gather so many documents for her application. She has to verify everything, provide proof of her working life in Germany without any gaps, and prove that she was a housewife without an income when she lived in Turkey. She knows that she worked off the books at the chicken factory and for Herr Bender, she knows that the repatriation money was supposed to cancel out any claim she might have to a pension, and that she wasn't really supposed to come back to Germany.

Gül is nervous about this appointment; she struggles to sleep in the days leading up to it. She's even more tired than Ceyda, but at the same time, she feels restless – as if all her nerves were roaming aimlessly about her body, in search of a place to rest.

When they sit down in front of the white Formica desk, Ceyda takes over the speaking and Gül sits there, surprised. It's not the first time she's heard her daughter speaking German, of course. But usually all she hears her say is a sentence or two. Now Ceyda speaks for longer, much longer, and she seems to be answering questions in detail. Gül listens to her daughter with admiration. *Ceyda understands every word she's saying*, she thinks, awestruck.

One language, one person; two languages, two people: that's how the saying goes. Language multiplies a person – it makes them bigger, richer, fuller. It determines who they can connect to through the sounds of words, and who they can't. A person who can only speak one language remains trapped inside it forever.

Gül remembers this over a year later, when she's retired and she sees a poster advertising a German course in Turkish.

I've got time now, she thinks. *It's never too late. Ceyda's going to stay here, her children will stay here, and we might not go back either. I mightn't have a head for languages, but I'm a hard worker. I'm going to go right in now and sign up.*

There's no one who speaks Turkish inside, but Gül knows she has enough German to sign up for a language course. Her German's good enough and she wants to learn, but when she's filled out the form and the time comes to show her ID, the woman at the reception gapes at her and says: 'This is a German ID.'

'Yes.'

'The course is for foreigners.'

'But I not good German. I am like to learn. Good German.'

'Sorry Frau Yolcu,' says the woman. 'The course is exclusively for foreigners. I can't let you sign up.'

'At home also Turkish passport. I come back.'

The woman shakes her head.

'I'm sorry, but I couldn't accept that. I've already seen your German ID.'

'I am like learn German.'

'Then you'll have to go elsewhere. Our course is strictly for foreigners.'

'What are they, bloody guard dogs?' Fuat says that evening when Gül tells him what happened. 'Like their language is some kind of treasure they've got to protect. Let them cluck over their words – they'll soon see their language isn't wine but vinegar! It's like they think French and English and Spanish don't exist. They should be grateful that anyone wants to learn their ugly language. It's just German – not silk from Samarkand! Forget about it. You've managed well enough without it for forty years. Everything's about papers, here. Money, ID, certificates, sick notes, discharge papers, tax statements, pension statements. What do you want with a language that doesn't recognise the value of human beings? Money, money speaks the same language everywhere, no matter what's printed on it, no matter whose face is on it, no matter what name you give it. It's the language everyone understands. Forget about German; we've got euros now, who needs German?'

Gül doesn't understand what he's trying to say, but she's not sure he does either. He just likes to talk.

'We want to move to Germany,' says Ceren.

'What?'

'We've applied to go to Germany on behalf of the government, as teachers for Turkish children. Ferdi knows someone there, it should work out.'

Gül looks at her and doesn't know what to say. Germany?

'How long for?'

'It's limited to three years, but once we're there it could end up being more.'

'When would it start?'

'Probably not until the school year after next.'

'What about Fatma?'

'She'll be old enough by then – she'll stay here.'

'And Ersin?'

'He'd come with us of course, and he'd go to school in Germany.'

Gül thinks about the times when Ceren used to share everything with her. Now she's married to a man she hid for years and she's applying for a job that will change her life. This is Ceren, the woman who at one time would always ask her mother for help. *I'm losing her*, Gül thinks. *She's my daughter, she's over forty, she has two children and she's outlived one husband, but now I'm losing her.*

Just like I lost my mother, whispers a small voice that Gül recognises as her own. *I'm losing. I'm losing love, trust, closeness. I'm going to be on my own again. Maybe I wasn't a good mother to her, but that was only because I never had the chance to learn what a good mother is.*

People often push their happiness into the future. *I'll relax as soon as my shift's over, when the kids have gone to sleep, when the money's in my account; I'll breathe a sigh of relief when I see my father alive again, when I've got out of here – that's when life will start again.* Now, Gül pushes her tears there too: *I'll cry when I'm on my own.*

'Where in Germany?' she asks, hopeful. 'Somewhere near us?'

'We don't know yet.'

'Germany…'

'Mum, it sounds ludicrous when you say it like that. What are you doing there if it's so bad?'

'We're… stuck. Like flies on paper.'

'Mum, it's a much freer country, and you're trying to tell me you're trapped? I don't know why I want to go. I haven't been to Germany for over twenty years now. Maybe it's nostalgia; we both want to see the country where we were children again. Perhaps we feel like something's missing without it.'

'May it all go according to your wishes,' says Gül, 'May you be satisfied and happy, no matter where you are.'

When a person loses their homeland once, they'll never find it again. They'll find their inner peace and lose it again, time and again throughout their lives.

Later on, when she gets the urge to cry, she thinks: *I didn't ask my father for advice the second time I went to Germany, either.*

Fuat's knee hurts.

'It started when I got fat,' he claims. 'Being fat is a real ordeal; you can only understand it if you've been fat yourself. It's harder to get up, it's harder to lie down, sitting's harder, standing's harder, eating, driving… You don't fit into places any more, and to make matters worse, you damage your joints too. Only people who've been fat can ever really understand what it's like.'

Gül doesn't point out that he often used to bring up her weight without having a clue what it was like himself.

At first, Gül thinks Fuat is feigning a bad knee so he can retire earlier. He still has another two years to go, but he doesn't want to work any more. When Gül stopped working at the cleaning agency, he quit too and got himself a job working nights as a security guard. For some time now, they've been living much like they did when Gül first came to Germany. Fuat comes home in the morning, they have breakfast together, then he goes for a lie down and Gül has the day to herself until the afternoon. She often goes to see Ceyda. These days, her daughter can hardly stand to be in the same room as Adem.

Gül would like to meet up with her friend Saniye more often, but Saniye's retired too and spends most of her time in Turkey, whereas Gül can't decide whether it's a good idea to leave Fuat alone in Germany for more than a couple of weeks. Not because she's worried he'll have an affair – he seems too old for that – but because she can see that he struggles with daily life on his own. His limp is getting worse and worse, his knee is swollen; it's not an ulcer this time – the joint has worn out. Fuat goes on sick leave and stops going to work, until a year later when, after numerous visits to the doctor, they finally let him retire.

Fuat and Gül don't talk about what will happen when work no longer ties them to Germany.

III

'What am I supposed to do with it? I can't work it. I'm old, I can't learn how to use it. Look, in this country you work until you're old, and I'm retired now.'

'Mum, you said you wanted to learn German. You're not trying to tell me you can learn German, but you can't work a mobile phone?'

'Why would I even need it? We talk on the proper phone every other day.'

'You can call if you're running late for something. You can call if you've lost your way. You can call if you need someone to translate for you.'

Gül looks sceptical.

'If you won't do it for yourself, do it for me, so I can call you. All you have to do is pick up. Then I won't have to worry about you. Please, take it.'

Ceyda calls her mum twice on the mobile phone. The first time, she just wants to try it out, Gül thinks. She asks for a recipe she ought to know by heart. The second time, she just wants to say she'll be a bit late.

Now the handset is switched off and sitting in some drawer or other. Why would she need a German mobile phone in Turkey? To carry it around as a symbol of her longing? Everyone has a mobile here, even Sibel and Aziz, who never usually pay any attention to fashion and what everyone else does; people think they're strange because they don't have a TV. In Turkey, there's always a phone ringing somewhere and Gül hears snatches of strangers' conversations every day.

'We talk more than the Germans, so obviously we're going to have more mobile phones here than they do in Germany,' Fuat says.

'No,' says Gül, 'it's just because we like to show off. We love to brag – that's why mobile phones took off faster here than they did in Germany.'

'Bragging, bragging – everything's always about bragging for you. Driving a Mercedes, wearing a nice suit, putting on jewellery. Maybe we shouldn't have built this house, so people don't think we were trying to brag.'

The house is more than twenty years old now, and they've been letting it out since Ceren left. Gül and Fuat usually spend the holidays at the simmer house, but as they want to stay in Turkey for longer than six weeks this time and no one knows what's going to happen with the summer house, they've given the tenants their notice.

That summer, Fuat spends a lot of time with tradesmen. The bathroom and kitchen need doing up, four of the plug sockets are duds, the tiles in the living room have seen better days, the walls need a coat of paint. Gül would like to say they need new furniture as well, since they probably won't get rid of the musty smell of storage from the old sofas, but Fuat is never in the right mood for her to talk him into it.

Fuat loses his temper. He loses his temper with every single tradesman who comes to the house, and many of them only ever come once. Fuat is soon holding daily tirades, at every opportunity. The tradesmen don't turn up on time, they're trying to cheat him, they keep putting him off from one day to the next and lying to him, their work is shoddy, nothing but cowboys; the toilet still leaks even after the plumber's had two goes at mending it, the skirting board is wonky, the dishwasher has two centimetres to spare in the fitted kitchen, the gas pipe for the cooker has been installed on top of the worktop instead of under it.

'What kind of cowboys are these people? Do they have the faintest clue about the work they're doing? Don't they have any sense of pride – wouldn't they rather earn their money working properly instead of doing all these botch jobs? Can anyone who knows what end of the hammer to grab call himself a tradesman around here? Don't they have rulers and tape measures in this country? Is a grown man really telling me that not all the steps in a staircase can be the same height because the last one would never work out? I'm surrounded by imbeciles – ever since we started doing up this house, I've been surrounded by imbeciles. Is there no one who understands the slightest thing about what he does all day long around here? Amateurs, they're all amateurs. How's a country supposed to function right if there's not a single man who can fit a toilet, not one of them? In the space of eight weeks, I've cancelled umpteen builders and given the jobs to new people, but I've yet to see a single professional tradesman. They wouldn't even let them be apprentices in Germany, these cowboys with their two left hands and empty brains. The economy's looking up again but that must be a miracle, nothing short of a miracle. It's a miracle anyone lifts a finger around here. I'm amazed houses get built in the first place. Houses with floors and kitchens, power and water, tiled floors and walls. No one here wants to lift a finger, no one works for a living,' he bellows.

At the barbers, the bakers, the butchers, at the market, in the corner shop, when he's talking to his brothers or his nephews, Fuat has a one-track mind. He loses his temper every day and blames the builders for giving him indigestion again, saying he can't even drink beer with vodka without lying awake for hours on end. He doesn't notice his audience only half-heartedly agreeing with him; he doesn't understand that his standards don't count here, can't see how far away he's drifted from Turkey over the decades. He has no feeling for how insulted they are by his long lectures.

Gül has a head start; she lived in Turkey for several years, not just visiting in the holidays. But when she tries to explain to Fuat that this isn't Germany and he can't expect German workmanship, he gets even angrier.

'German workmanship, what's it got to do with German workmanship?' he yells. 'Is Germany the only country where the toilet bowls aren't surrounded by a puddle of water? Do only German builders know the rule of three? Is Germany the only place with common decency? It's nothing to do with Germany; it's a question of morals. All we get here is botch, botch, botch. They've no professional honour, they've no honour at all. It's got nothing to do with Germany.'

He's so preoccupied with his complaints that he doesn't notice the row smouldering between his wife's brother and sisters. *But even if he hadn't been so preoccupied, he couldn't have done anything to stop it*, Gül will think later. *Perhaps this is a curse we just can't escape.*

Gül says nothing. She says nothing when she sees the finished summer house standing in the place of the old stable. She says nothing about the living-room windows being lower than the kitchen windows, making it look as if a child drew the house. She says nothing about the toilet being fitted so high up that her feet barely touch the floor, she says nothing about the concrete veranda with a brick wall around it instead of a metal fence. She says nothing, but a lot of talking goes on. Gül learns that things are tense between Melike and Emin; they steer clear of each other in the few days when they're both in town. Over the autumn, she gets wind of some of the neighbours' chatter. She hears people taking sides, judging, criticising, maligning, slandering, vilifying. Melike and Emin argued over the construction, and then they each made the architects add to the original plans – hence the different window levels, the ugly stone wall, the toilet installed to suit Melike's height.

Gül says nothing, hoping if she keeps out of it then things will calm down. *If I tried to reconcile the two of them, I couldn't hold myself back; my anger would break through, and we'd end up further apart than before.* She says nothing and hopes it'll all blow over. And she trusts in the money they've got again now.

There are three ways to face life: put up with it, fight or flee. Gül's way is to put up with things; she didn't choose the way things are, but that doesn't change the fact that she cultivates resentment in a hidden corner of her heart, sometimes without even noticing herself.

She still has nice times with Sibel, still looks forward to being in town for the first time in ages without knowing what day they'll have to get in the car and drive back home. While Fuat goes on arguing with the builders, Gül takes the bus to Malatya to visit Saniye and Yılmaz, who are in a similar situation, only without any inheritance to divide up between siblings.

Yılmaz finds it hard to get by without his hashish and he rarely leaves the house, spending most of his time in front of the computer; every other day he quotes the satirist Aziz Nesin, who said sixty percent of Turks are stupid. Asked about it later, the writer said he hadn't had the guts to say eighty percent.

'We're messed up, those of us who've lived in Germany,' he says. 'We were there too long – we won't be able to integrate here now. Once you've seen more, you can't just close your eyes and forget everything. There are two big mistakes you can make in your life. The first one is leaving your country, and the second is going back.'

He laughs.

'Yearning,' says Gül. 'Our lives were made up of yearning. But the same goes for everyone. Look at all the things they've invented to soothe our yearning and lessen the distances between us; the post, telephones, cameras, aeroplanes.'

He laughs again.

'That's a lovely thought,' he says. 'But I'm going to have to disappoint you. Most of those things are military inventions. None of it was thought up to bring people closer together, only to put up higher walls between them. All those inventions came from fear, not yearning. They're for defence, not contact. We tend to see things emotionally. Look at me – I get this false nostalgia, I talk about things that never existed. The reason I left was because this country was no longer a home to me. I didn't feel safe here any more, and I couldn't fill my belly either.'

Gül wonders whether men perhaps find it more difficult to settle back into life in Turkey. Their world consists of tradesmen, work procedures, organisation, football. Their world is made up of authorities, traffic rules, politics and economy. Not conversations and smells, colours and light, not walnuts with dried grape juice, the taste of apples and apricots, not neighbourhood gossip, sunflower seeds nibbled on the steps outside the house, jam-making in a crowded kitchen.

Yılmaz may know more than Fuat, she thinks, *but it's no use to him. He's capable of understanding and describing his situation, but that doesn't change much.*

Saniye is glad to be back in the town that holds so many sad memories for her; where she lost her husband to death, her father to prison, and her son to her in-laws – her son Ufuk, who now runs a restaurant and has sons of his own, both of whom lead unmarried lives in Istanbul. Saniye spends a few hours a day in the restaurant; she likes helping there.

In the three weeks she spends at Saniye's place, Gül often goes with her to the restaurant. As the two women sit at a table between the cash desk and the kitchen, Gül enjoys the bustle and life, the conversations with her friend. She feels free in these surroundings; a place with no stories that tie her to it. For three weeks, she sees Saniye every day – in all their years in Germany, that never happened there. For three weeks, the women keep going back to the table in the restaurant, for three weeks Gül meets Saniye's friends and relatives, for three weeks she laughs and cries. In those three weeks, she grows milder and softer from one day to the next. Everyone assures Saniye she was lucky to find a friend like Gül in Germany, a friend with warmth dripping from her fingertips because she has too much to fit inside her.

Years later, the locals will still remember Gül in Malatya, and when they talk about her, she'll be a different person to the woman people talk about in her hometown.

It's November by the time Gül and Fuat finally fly to Germany. Three days before they leave, a neighbour tells Gül about the gossip that's been spreading behind her back. People are saying that Gül wanted to have the summer house and the stable and the garden all to herself, that she would have succeeded if the financial crisis hadn't scuppered her plan, that she's grown distant from her siblings since she's been living in Germany; they're saying she only invited her father to visit her there to coax him into making her his sole heir, that all the years in that country have turned her heart cold, that all she cares about is money, gold and property, that the Gül everyone remembers is long gone, no longer exists. They say she sulked about not being the first to be told about her father's death, because she already had an inkling that not everything would be left to her. They say she has nothing better to do than bitch about why Melike's son isn't married, they say she screams at her siblings, that she behaves like a grumpy little child.

Gül can't dismiss this as something the neighbour's made up, or as a mere rumour – there are too many details for that. There's no doubt about it: Gül knows at least one of her siblings must be badmouthing her behind her back. She wonders why; but she doesn't question why the neighbour has decided to tell her everything.

Gül has kept her opinions to herself, but the others have been talking. They've been talking about her behind her back. They've twisted everything. They've implied that she has the worst of intentions. Maybe they believe what they've been saying. Maybe they really do think she's a bad person.

Back in Germany, Gül keeps thinking about what the neighbour said. Every day. All winter. She lets her resentment grow quite openly now.

She makes lots of phone calls, but not on her new mobile phone. She calls Ceyda, and Ceren in Turkey, going over and over what she heard from the neighbour; she finds ever new motives for her siblings' envy and ill will, and in every conversation, she mentions that she tried to be a mother to her siblings. She's just like Fuat when he keeps repeating the same monologue in summertime, but she only has her daughters to listen to her. Fuat isn't home much; this winter he's taken to drinking coffee in the mornings with other pensioners at the bakery in the shopping centre. Saniye has stayed in Malatya, and Yılmaz came back to Germany in early October. She doesn't want to confide in him alone, and she has no real excuse to visit. He's her friend's husband; they can never get too close.

When Gül calls her siblings, she tries not to let on that anything's wrong. Perhaps it's the voice of reason she's listening to – a voice of blood, a voice of hope that tells her distance and time will solve everything. A voice that protects her from the worst, perhaps. She tries to convince herself of this.

She needs distracting, so she watches a lot of TV this winter; she watches shows full of intrigue, betrayal, disloyalty, full of conflict and doubt, full of disappointments, lies, false promises, full of schemes and nasty surprises. She sees Nalan's daughter in two of these series; she's an actress now, but Gül struggles to be pleased for her. The things she once saw as make-believe stories on TV now seem real to her. *This is what people are like*, she thinks. *They're only ever out for themselves, and there's nothing that ties them to each other.*

She regrets some of her words. She knows that her comment about İsmail failing to find a wife was inappropriate. She regrets getting carried away and saying things that could be used against her. She regrets shouting at Melike like that; she regrets it, but she thinks the others ought to have more regrets than she does.

Can invites Gül to his wedding party; he wants to celebrate it after the fact. He wants to have a party because he's been married for five years, his son's four years old now, and he's had not so much as a suspended sentence in three years.

'We want to celebrate now we've got it all together, now our days of dodgy dealings are behind us, now we're finally rich,' he says on the phone. 'I'd really love it if you could come.'

Of course, there's no mention of this on the invitation, which comes in the post the next day.

'Can? Which Can is that?' Fuat asks.

'One of my old colleagues' sons,' Gül replies.

She's surprised how easily the lie slips from her lips. *It's not just other people*, she thinks. *In a world where everyone taints themselves by cheating, by going behind others' backs, keeping secrets and disregarding the sound of truth, in a world like that it's impossible to stay clean. Anyone who lives among liars ends up lying too.*

But I haven't done anything wrong, she consoles herself. Can's mother died of cancer the last time he was on day-release, and Fuat doesn't tend to pay much attention to what's going on around him; Gül doesn't need to worry about him finding out. And even if he did ask, she'd say the woman only worked alongside them briefly before moving on to hotels, and that she hardly knows Can.

It's a Turkish wedding reception: the music, the food, the customs and many of the guests are Turkish, but there are more people than Gül's ever seen at a party before. More guests, more drink, more food, louder speakers, more musicians, but more dodgy characters too. There must be 2,000 people in the hall.

'Well, hats off,' says Fuat, 'look what they've pulled off here, it beggars belief! Why did he let his mum keep cleaning if he's got so much money?'

Gül hadn't reckoned on this. She's a bad liar, no match for Fuat.

'He didn't come into his money until after she died. He's got a phone company,' she says.

'A phone company? So he got rich off the backs of nattering old women? Crafty devil.'

And which one of us was the first to get a mobile phone? Gül might ask. But she feels hot, and she's worried her face might be flushed. She gets up to go to the toilet.

She feels out of place at this wedding. She came because it would make Can happy, but she feels bad about her lies, about all the years of secrecy, about all the people, the loud music, her siblings, Germany, Turkey, about the summer house, about the winter. She wishes she could just disappear.

On the way to the toilet she bumps into Serter, who greets her warmly, taking her face in his hands, kissing her left cheek and then her right, then wrapping her in a hug until she can hardly breathe. It seems genuine but over-the-top, and something about him seems odd to her. She thinks about what Can said and wonders if she ever really knew this man. She wonders if, like Melike, he might have two faces, or even three or four. If he might be madder than she thought. And perhaps less lonely than she'd feared.

'Gül, how lovely to see you here! An honest person among all these liars. Shall we head outside where we can smoke in peace? Go on, do it for me – we haven't seen each other in so long. You know I'm fond of you – I've always trusted you, I've always eaten your food, drunk your water, poured my heart out to you. You've never judged me and never badmouthed me behind my back, Gül. It's so good to bump into you. Come on, let's go for a smoke.'

Before Gül can agree, Serter is pushing her towards the exit. Gül lived in this part of town for long enough; she saw all kinds of people out her window, and she can tell from Serter's eyes that he must have taken something, but his pupils are huge, not tiny like the peoples' she often saw in the street.

She feels hot again; people on drugs are unpredictable. But what's he going to do to her, here, in front of all these guests? On the other hand, he's mad, and Gül doesn't know what to expect from a crazy man on drugs. She wonders what excuses she could use to get away from him, but nothing comes to mind as he gently leads her outside by the shoulders. Her knees seem to go soft, the music drones inside her head, and she wonders if the easiest thing wouldn't be to just faint now. But that would draw too much attention. The thought of coming round to the sight of people stood around her, their faces full of concern, sends the strength streaming back into Gül's legs.

'I'm a bit worn out today, let's not go too far,' she says to Serter as they reach the exit.

He smiles, takes out a packet of cigarettes and offers her one. He gives her a light, then takes one for himself. He beams at her.

'How are you, Gül?'

'Good,' she says. 'Thanks be to God. I'm retired now and we spent five months of this year in Turkey.'

'Ah, Turkey, the place we all long for. It's like we think that country could wash away our sins, as if happiness sits on its street corners there, just waiting for us. I've spent so many hours sitting at the train station feeding a longing that hollowed me out from the inside. I've nursed regret at my breast, Gül. I've made so many mistakes, enough for a whole city. Everything's gone the wrong way; you have to look inside if you want to find something, not outside. You have to look inside yourself, into your past. Look, I've always been scared of people, but I claimed I was being careful. I was scared of people, but not of you. I was afraid and I tried to seek sanctuary with God, but God isn't a hiding place, Gül. If you can't see God everywhere, you can't see him at all. He's everywhere. Not just with me. But my fear of people is greater than my fear of God. I'm talking too much, aren't I? Too many words, and they're all confused. Am I scaring you, Gül?'

'No.'

'I am, I can tell – I'm scaring you. Sincerity isn't as easy as it sounds, Gül.'

He lowers his voice.

'I'm a bit different from usual today because I… One of Can's friends gave me a pill and said it would make me feel good if I took it. I didn't believe him, of course; I thought he wanted to poison me, so the truth never came to light. But I felt so hollowed out by regret and longing that I was ready to die. I was ready to die, Gül, but then when I took it, it was my fear that died. You don't need to be afraid of me. Anyway, tell me, why's your heart so heavy?'

'I told you, I'm fine.'

Serter looks at her, smiles, shakes his head. 'Fear,' he says. 'It's the biggest obstacle in life. But I don't want to pester you. I'll just ask you one more time: what's making your heart so heavy? I can see it, Gül, I can see your heart.'

Gül believes him, but she just shakes her head.

'Let's make it a clean break, wipe the slate clean before we say goodbye?' says Serter, as people say when they take their leave of each other without knowing if they'll see one another alive again.

'Serter…'

'Please. A clean slate?'

'A clean slate,' says Gül, the customary reply. Serter hugs her, pressing her too close to him for a long while.

Gül wonders if it will really be the last time she sees him, if anyone will notice the way he's hugging her, if she needs to explain away the hug with the fact that he's so drunk, and if it might be a good opportunity to tell him about the argument over the summer house. Serter lets go, looks at her, and says: 'I was right about the Germans, though. We're right to be scared of them. They don't want us here.'

Gül places a hand on his shoulder and smiles.

Then she goes back inside.

It won't be until the following year that she learns that Serter was found slumped in the car park at the end of this night, and that he died on the way to the hospital. He was buried in Turkey, where he hadn't lived for forty-five years.

Ceyda bought the tickets for her, but Gül has to make the journey alone – including changing trains. She's scared of getting lost at a German station, not finding the right platform, missing her connection, boarding the wrong train, not speaking enough German to find her way to Ceren and Ferdi.

'You've got your mobile,' Ferdi says on the landline. 'If anything goes wrong, just call me and I'll come and pick you up in the car. It doesn't matter where in Germany you are. Don't worry about it.'

'I know – I won't get lost,' Gül says, but that doesn't make her any less afraid.

Up to now, all Gül has seen of the south of Germany is the autobahn on the long drive to Turkey. This is the first time she's seen the vineyards her friend Aysel in Turkey told her about.

The landscape outside the train window seems much more welcoming than the flat region where she lived for decades. *All the years I've spent in this country, and there's still so little I've seen of it*, she thinks. *At least I know Turkey from the stories my neighbours on Factory Lane used to tell. I've seen Istanbul for myself, and Ankara, Malatya, Adana, Mersin, Kayseri, but I've never been to Bonn or Berlin, Kassel, Hannover, Kiel or any of the cities here. I've spent so much of my life here, but I still only know less than a tenth of the country, much less than that. Perhaps my world is no bigger than Fuat's, after all. I went to work and sat in a room and looked out of the window; I didn't see much. But at least I tried to feel what other people were feeling.*

Mannheim – what a strange name for a town, she thinks later, when she gets off the train. *Man-home: do they only let men feel at home here?*

'Do you want me to have a word with Auntie Melike?' Ceren offers a few days later. 'You have to sort it out, you really do.'

'No, it's between the two of us.'

'Dede wouldn't have wanted you to row like this.'

'No, he wouldn't.' Gül chooses not to mention that the blacksmith saw it coming.

Ceren notices that her mother – even now, months later – can barely think of anything else, but she can't imagine the waters won't calm again. Though she never experienced strong family ties on her father's side, all the relatives on her mother's side were so close every summer, so warm and loving to each other, that she finds it hard to believe their connection might fall apart over a little house.

'Don't you think she shouldn't have talked? It's between us sisters and our brother. You can't go around telling outsiders.'

'You know how it is, Mum – if you don't want anyone to find out, you'd better not tell anyone. Not your sister, or your best friend, or your husband. There's only one way to keep a secret, and that makes you lonely.'

'You're not on her side, are you?'

'No, I'm not on anyone's side.'

She looks at her mother and corrects herself. 'Of course I'm on your side, I'm your daughter. That doesn't make me blind though. The people on the other side are people too. No one got up in the morning and thought: I want to cause Gül harm.'

'Maybe not. But it's enough to want everything for yourself. That causes harm. Melike's always been that way; she was only ever out for herself. She's never cared about anyone else.'

'Maybe that's why she was the only one of you girls who made it to uni. Nothing's ever just good or just bad.'

'Do you think I'm worth less than her because I only went to primary school?'

Ceren hugs her mother. 'Of course not. Everyone has their own talents, their own strengths and weaknesses. Everyone's born different. Look at me and Ceyda. Neither of us is worth more than the other, are we? We are different, though.'

'Can't anyone ever just say I'm right, for once? She shouldn't have gossiped.'

'She shouldn't have gossiped. But she did. We can't turn the clock back. We have to look ahead. You'll find a way together. You've always found a way together.'

Ceren sees that her mother's not quite herself. She asks only briefly how they feel here in Germany, and she doesn't listen properly when Ceren answers. Ceren can see her mother's suffering; she tries to distract her, she tries to weigh things up differently, to play them down, to offer different perspectives. And even though she sees it doesn't help, she believes the family will find a solution.

When they part ways a few days later, her mother perhaps believes the same.

'How long has it been since I last spent spring in this country?' Fuat says. 'Forty-two years. How much bad weather did we put up with, how many decades did we let that grey sky darken our moods? Spring, this is what spring should be like – the trees blossoming and the sun warming your face, you can smell the earth and your eyes get their fill of green. How long did that concrete jungle Germany lock us out of nature?'

He blusters and moans, but he's genuinely pleased about it, and Gül is surprised to see how content he is just to sit in the orchard. He drinks rakı every evening without getting stomach ache or indigestion, and Gül wonders when she last saw him so happy.

She, though, is jumpy and unsettled. Both she and Sibel try to cover it up, but it's clear they've grown cooler with each other. She talks less to her stepmother Arzu than usual. Melike isn't in town, but she's bound to come at some point over the summer. Every time Gül sees someone, she wonders if they know what people are saying; every smile makes her wonder if it's a mask, every hug she suspects of coming with a price tag.

Gül doesn't know who she can trust and who she can't, and she tries to watch every word she says. She spends time with her neighbour Bahar, who told her about the gossip last autumn. But she does her darndest to avoid finding out whether any new gossip came up over the winter. Instead, she tries to work out whether Bahar is on her side or not, which she finds difficult. Though Gül weighs up her every word, though she pays attention to her every step, one day she tells Bahar how old she was when her mother died, and how she tried afterwards to be a mother to her sisters, how she helped at home and didn't finish school, how she married young so there'd be one less mouth to feed at the table. It just comes gushing out of her, and later she consoles herself that at least she didn't talk about how difficult Melike was as a child, how she always shirked her chores, that Gül was the only child their father never hit. It's on the tip of her tongue, but she says nothing about Melike. She talks about herself, about the old days, and she lets herself get carried away by her own words; her eyes are wet when she says: 'I never cursed, I never lamented, I never said: May your house collapse, may your hands be crippled, may your eyes go blind and your feet lame – cruel mother fate! I don't expect thanks for any of it, but no reproach either.'

Afterwards, she scolds herself for her words, the words she used to try and win Bahar over; she scolds herself, but the words have been said. That spring, they take on a life of their own and leave Gül's mouth again and again, and every time she scolds herself a little less. *It's the truth, what I'm saying; it's nothing but the truth. Why shouldn't I give it a little space?*

She repeats the words, lets them form a story and lets the story become part of her. She clings to that part like driftwood on the course that the ancestors' blood takes through our bodies. She clings to that part as though it might help her survive, as though she'd never heard the melody that carries the whole family along.

One day when the summer houses all have people living in them, Gül is at Sibel's place, and although she's vowed not to talk about it, the words still come bursting out: 'People are talking about how I asked you why you didn't call me first to tell me about Baba's death.'

'I know,' says Sibel, not betraying the slightest emotion.

'You must have told them.'

'Yes, I did. Arzu asked how you reacted, and I told her.'

'But it's not like I asked because I wanted the summer house for myself. That doesn't make any sense.'

'I know,' says Sibel. 'But what I said was nothing but the truth. God is my witness. What would I get out of badmouthing you? I can't help what people add to my words. I live my life here and don't cause anyone harm. I've always tried to keep out of things, living here in my own world with a husband who wanted the same. But do you want to know the truth, Gül? It didn't work. There's always someone coming along from outside and trying to bring envy, hate, gossip and bad thoughts into this house. There's always someone coming along with accusations.'

'I didn't want… Forgive me… I only told you what I'd heard.'

Gül's eyes alight on a tin cup in the glass cabinet. The cup her father used to drink from, there's no doubt. Why does Sibel have it?

'Why should I care what you've heard? You know what, Aziz and I should have moved to a village with thirty or forty houses. But we wouldn't have found work there. We stayed in this town because of money, but money got us tangled up with the people here, with all their false words, their lies and hypocrisy and all their gossip. Maybe we should have gone to Germany, I don't know. We tried to find a quiet spot, but we didn't get far. I've never gossiped, Gül, never. I've got ears, I hear what people say, but I've never used my mouth to join in. You don't know me. If you knew me, you'd never have started talking to me about all this.'

'I just wanted… I just… I'm sorry… I didn't mean…'

'Gül, Abla, if you've something to say, just say it to yourself. I won't be your judge and jury. I'm trying to keep my heart pure. You should do the same.'

Rage surges. Great anger and rage. For three, four, five seconds, she thinks she's capable of suppressing it.

And then she yells: 'My heart is pure! What kind of accusation is that? I didn't come here to have you tell me there's something wrong with my heart.'

She gets up and leaves. She leaves because the story she's told so often that spring has become part of her, a part that she's beginning to take for the whole.

'You're not on your own, Mum. Just wait until we get there, and we'll find a solution. There's no point talking to Melike or Sibel or Nalan or Nene. You all need to sit down together, calmly, and talk it over. Ideally with someone who isn't part of the family.'

'Like who?'

'Maybe Uncle Tarık.'

'Who?'

'Tarık – his dad was Emin Effendi, you know, the prison guard.'

'Is he here then?'

'He worked in Istanbul for years but then he moved back. He's been living in his parents' summer house since they died. He's calm and level-headed, everyone respects him.'

'How do you know this?'

'People always talk, Mum.'

'I lived in this town for many years too, but I don't know this Tarık.'

'Yes, he was still in Istanbul back then. Find him and ask if he can help. But ask the others first. The most direct route is always the easiest.'

Gül relaxes a little after this phone call with Ceren. The situation seems solvable. They just need an outsider, someone who's not going to be led by their emotions. She invites her siblings and her stepmother to get together in the presence of someone who's not invested in the matter, to clarify the issue of the summer house and who it ought to belong to. To her surprise, they all accept.

She finds out where Tarık lives and, one afternoon, she and Fuat find themselves knocking on the wooden door of an old summer house. A lean, grey-haired man with friendly eyes opens the door in a vest, greets them and then looks at them both curiously. Gül waits a second or two for Fuat to begin speaking, but he says nothing.

'I'm Gül, the blacksmith's daughter.'

'The one who lives in Germany,' says Tarık.

Gül nods. 'I know this is a bit sudden, and I'm sure we're disturbing you—'

'Of course not. Not at all. Please, come on in.'

The floor is not stone but trodden-down earth, and the clay plaster on the walls is crumbling. The divan where Fuat and Gül take a seat was probably around when Tarık was just a child. Tarık has thrown on a threadbare shirt and buttoned it up wrong in the rush.

'I don't get a lot of guests,' he says. 'You'll have to forgive me. I know it might seem a bit odd in here, and I might look a bit odd, but when a person's in touch with themselves, they can sometimes seem strange to others. What brings you here? Is there something I can do for you?'

'We wanted to knock and say hello,' Gül stammers, surprised by his directness. 'We're all neighbours after all.'

'Sister,' says Tarık, 'leave the customs and pleasantries to one side – they're dry crusts and it's hard to see a person through them. Look, I'm asking you honestly and without suspicion: what brings you here? Answer from the heart; you've no need to hide.'

'How should I put this? It's to do with an inheritance.'

Gül throws Fuat a sideways glance. He doesn't react.

'We can't agree on what should happen to the summer house that my father left us,' she begins. 'A new house has been built where the stable used to be, but it's not clear who it belongs to. My sister and brother paid for the building works, but the plot itself belongs to all of us, and originally I was supposed to have a share in the house, but now everything's mixed up. We wanted to sit down together and talk about it and have someone neutral there. And I was told you'd be the person to come to. I'm sorry to heap all this on you.'

Tarık nods.

'A game of chess is better to watch than it is to play,' he says. 'I don't know if I can be of any real help, but I'd be very happy to try.'

'That's the bloke you're expecting to help?' says Fuat on the way home. 'If he wants to sort anything out, he could start with his own house, or his clothes, or his buttons. He looks like a tramp! You can hardly tell where his hair stops and his beard begins!'

'Did you see his heart shining?'

'What?'

'I'm old now and I might not have learnt much in all my years of life, but I can tell when people are genuine and good-hearted. I think we can trust that man.'

'Women! I wouldn't trust anyone who's that much of a stranger to a comb.'

Gül tells the others she's persuaded Tarık to come to their meeting.

'How can he be impartial if you know him better than we do?' Melike asks on the phone.

'But you said you were fine with the idea.'

'Yes, but then I thought it over and I don't like it. It's between the six of us, it's a family matter; it's not right to bring in a stranger – who knows what he might say about us afterwards.'

Gül takes a quiet, deep breath. She feels resentment rising to the surface, but she lets it flow through her instead of suppressing it. Then she says: 'Look, if there's no one there from outside, we'll probably end up arguing. I've got grievances, you might have grievances, Nalan might have some – everyone feels unfairly treated. I've been angry a lot, and you probably have too. If we want to find a solution that works for all of us, this might be the best way. And Tarık's not a gossip. I'd stake my life on that.'

'You're only two years older than me,' Melike says. 'That used to be a lot, you could put on all sorts of airs and graces. Now you're still my older sister, but it doesn't mean you know everything better. You've spent most of your life abroad, but now you're an expert on problem-solving in Turkey? Since when? And why does it have to be someone you'd stake your life on? Wouldn't it be better to find someone I trust?'

Gül thinks of Tarık, his warm eyes, his open nature; she thinks of the voice inside her that tells her he's the right person. She sees the light, the light she'd like to move closer to. She can't let the resentment flow through her any more; all she can do is try to look away.

'Melike,' she says, 'my sister, let's find a solution together. We're all one blood – do this favour for me. Let's try this out in memory of our mother. May the Lord strike me down if I have any ulterior motives.'

'I don't know if I even have time to come this summer,' says Melike.

Gül is glad to hear her sister say this, but she doesn't let on. She knows Melike; it's as good as a promise that she'll be there.

'How did it go?' Ceren greets her mother outside the house. But she needn't have asked; she can tell by her face.

Nalan didn't come to the meeting because she's spending the summer with her daughter in Bodrum. She gave Sibel the right to decide on her behalf. Gül puzzled for a long time over why she chose Sibel and not Emin, who lives in Istanbul like her, or Arzu, who's been trying all along to remain neutral. Gül listened out, cautiously; perhaps there was a rumour that explained why Nalan decided that way – but she couldn't find any explanation.

'It escalated,' Gül says, now. 'It blew right up. Everyone but Sibel was shouting and insulting the others.'

'But...'

Ceren hadn't thought that was possible.

'Come inside.'

'Is your father in?'

'No.'

'Good.'

Gül has a cigarette in her mouth before she's even taken her shoes off.

'Selfish – that's what Melike called me. She talked about blackmail. Emin said I ran away from the truth to Germany. He accused Sibel of retreating and egging on his own sister against him. Melike screamed and shouted that I had no honour, and a minute later, Sibel refused to vouch for me. Arzu told us to shut our traps, said even Baba wasn't as bad as us when he was angry. Melike called me a skinflint, and apparently Emin's taken out a loan.'

Gül's never been much good at telling stories; her listeners always have to pick up the thread themselves. Now Ceren asks: 'But what about Tarık? Wasn't he there?'

'He was, but he left.'

'Just upped and left?'

'He said there was no point if we weren't going to talk to each other like adults. He said we're children fighting over a piece of cake.'

'Did you scream and shout as well?'

'Yes, but only because Melike was so shameless. No matter what happens, I'm her older sister; she has to show me at least a shred of respect. That's just basic humanity.'

It takes Ceren over an hour to get a full picture of the family at the meeting; an hour in which she hears her mother crying, cursing, shouting, begging; an hour in which she sees her mother at her most distraught. She sees her turning red with anger, hears her uttering threats, making ultimatums, lamenting and moaning. Ceren sees her trembling hands, her rage and impotence; she sees her pain seeming to increase at every mention of an affront; she sees the cigarette butts in the ash tray; and though she's vowed to keep a clear head, at some point anger, love, pain and her own tears cloud her eyes. She doesn't understand. Her aunts and uncle. She doesn't understand.

At the meeting, Melike started saying the house originally belonged to her mother. Apparently, there was proof that it had only been put in their father's name after her death, and so Arzu, Nalan and Emin had no real right to the house. Emin replied that the legal situation was different now, they all had equal shares and claims like that had no bearing, and anyway Melike was only trying to sow discord. Melike accused him of being greedy, said everyone knew how much he earned in Istanbul and he didn't need the summer house at all. He was her brother; she'd never made a distinction between siblings and half-siblings. He was welcome at the summer house at any time, but there was no need for him to own it as well.

Tarık urged them to stick to the facts, saying that accusing someone of greed wasn't going to help matters. Melike responded that it wasn't an accusation, it was a well-known fact. He could never have become as wealthy as a teacher as he was now; he'd been driven by greed and ambition. It was obvious – why couldn't they just admit it?

Gül said she felt they'd gone behind her back by building the new house without her knowing. Melike hit back that that wasn't true; Gül had known about it – just not the date when the construction started. But everyone knew Gül had lost her money in the financial crisis.

Tarık agreed with Gül that they ought to have informed her, Melike accused Tarık of taking sides, Gül tried to defend Tarık, Melike took that as proof of her claim and said they'd never all agree and they should just auction off the summer house and divide up the money – every other solution left someone feeling hard-done-by. Tarık said that might be a possibility as long as they all agreed, but Gül replied that it wasn't about the money.

She said the summer house was all that was left of her mother, and it was about the memories attached to it; she said it would break her heart if the house were owned by strangers, begged all of them to look for another solution. She said she'd put so many hours of work and love into the house, and that if it belonged to someone else, it would be like ripping out a part of her body. Melike said she'd had just about enough of Gül's emotional blackmail and anyway, Gül was so fat, no one would notice if a bit of her body went missing. After that they lost all control, Tarık left, the rest of them yelled insults, accusations and grievances at each other – until Melike was the first to leave the room, slamming the door behind her.

'What's going on?' asks Fuat when he sees Gül and Ceren sitting on the sofa. 'Has someone died?'

'We argued about the summer house.'

'Dear oh dear, the blacksmith's children,' says Fuat. 'Your father will be turning in his grave... or maybe it's him you get it from.'

'What?' says Gül.

'The way none of you are ticking on the right track.'

'What?' Gül says, again, but before she's quite finished asking, she understands what Fuat means.

'Out!' she bellows. 'Get out, get out of my sight! I don't want to see you.'

Fuat nods as if to say *That's exactly what I mean*. He leaves. Gül lights another cigarette. The room is hazy with smoke now, despite the open window.

'You know,' says Ceren, 'when I think about my childhood, the first thing that comes to mind is the summer house. My most vivid memories are from those six weeks we'd spend here – not the ten-and-a-half months we'd spend in Germany the rest of the year. It would be a shame if it was put up for sale. I'm amazed how small the garden seems now, but when I sit under the mulberry tree, it's like a gateway to my childhood. It's the same when I'm down at the little swimming pond where I almost drowned. I can see Dede eating hakırdak, I can smell his sweat, see his rubber galoshes, the tin cup he always drank his water from, I see all my cousins, I remember all the ball games out in the street when Auntie Melike would join in and everyone wanted her on their team. I spent most of my childhood in Germany, but what I remember best is the holidays together in the summer house. Back then, we'd never have imagined it could all fall apart. I can't understand what's happened. I can't understand how those days don't hold true any more.'

Ceren notices that her mother seems calmer now; calmer and sadder. Something shifts in the room, as if some barrier has crumbled, as if light has pierced the space, as if for a moment they might forget all the bickering and envy, the strife and the slights, and picture something that goes far beyond themselves.

Gül remembers her father predicting they would argue. She thinks about how early her mother died. Her mother, who was an orphan too. She thinks about how she left Ceyda and Ceren behind in Turkey. How Ceren's daughter lost her father so early. How Ceyda's children have grown up with a father who never really seemed present. She thinks about the pain of separation, the loss of easy comfort, the lack of a foothold, and how these things run through the family; how variations on this wistful melody are woven through the song of her blood. Perhaps her father may well have known it too. But perhaps he might have seen it differently. Perhaps this melody is the reason for the fear, the envy, the feeling of being short-changed, of not getting enough love. Perhaps that's why the fear just binds it all together, into something she can't shake off. That's where the melancholy comes from, the sense of futility.

Silence expands in the room – the fury wanes, but the grief remains, as if it were water finding its way. No cigarettes, only sounds from outside, and silence that brings them together. For minutes on end.

Then Gül clears her throat, tentatively, but that one cough seems to judder through her whole body, as if she'd just been about to drop off to sleep. 'What are you thinking about?' she asks her daughter.

'You grew up without a mother, Ceyda and I stayed behind in Turkey on our own, Fatma has grown up without a father, Adem was never really there for his kids, and who can say if Ferdi and I will manage to bring Ersin up together? But you and your siblings… you're anticipating misery in places death and separation have yet to reach.'

Gül nods. She looks at the packet of cigarettes and decides against having another. She lowers her voice and, for the first time, explains how her father cried when he predicted that his children would fall out. 'He knew something,' she says. 'I should have asked him about it when there was still time.'

'Maybe Dad's got a point,' says Ceren. 'It's not that we're mad, though; we're just cursed, in a way. It sits on our souls.'

'Since when has your dad ever known anything about souls?'

'He knows something, even if he doesn't understand exactly what.'

A sense of peace settles on Gül all of a sudden, but she can't quite grasp it. Peace, as if they might find a solution to the problem with the summer house after all; a way for the siblings to cooperate, even after today, now that she has heard the sound of the blood beating briefly – amid the fear and the fury, the rage and the anguish – seen the light of the generations, felt the others' pain.

But perhaps it's just the desire for everything to work out for the best, which outshines everything else.

'We're going to have a lot of time on our hands,' says Fuat. 'Property prices are going to go up – I've been looking into it. We should get our own house by the sea.'

Gül looks at him. A couple of years ago, Melike's son İsmail bought his mother a house on the Aegean, a dream for many

Turks. For many people, in fact. A house by the sea. A place of tranquillity. A chance to see the blue of the ocean any time, to look out onto the horizon every day, to breathe in the salty sea air and adjust your pace of life to fit with nature. The sound of the waves. The dazzling midday sun. The peace of mind that comes from owning a place. A house by the sea.

It's not as if this yearning hasn't tugged at Gül too, but there are so many dreams and desires inside her, always so many voices; which ones should she listen to, and which should she ignore?

'We're Anatolians,' says Gül. 'We're used to water from a cup, as they say. We're bound to this earth, not to the sea.'

'Everyone is connected to the sea,' says Fuat. 'We're eighty percent water. All life comes from the sea. It was always so lovely when we had our holidays on the beach. Our grandchildren are reaching the age where they might have their own children. Everyone would love it, coming to us in the summer, sunbathing, swimming, grilling fish in the evenings.'

Gül looks at him, amazed. He's in a good mood, he seems to have prepared for this conversation; he's trying to win her over.

'How would we buy it?'

'With our savings.'

'The ones you almost flushed down the toilet, you mean? It's only down to luck that we've still got them. And depending on what happens with the summer house... No, that money's our last bit of security. If we lose it, all we'll have left is our pensions.'

'Property prices are going up, and that money's not going to bring in any meaningful interest. The smart thing is to invest in property now.'

'Since when have you been an expert in this sort of thing? Why should anyone trust you? You've already proven once before how good you are at investing.'

She expects him to get tetchy and answer back, for all his preparation to be of no use, and for this conversation to end in a fight.

'No one can predict an economic crisis,' he says, calmly. 'I got the tip about property prices off Emin, and he's got heaps of cash – you've seen it for yourself. And maybe you don't trust him either, but have a think about it anyway. It doesn't look like you're going to be able to agree on the inheritance. Life is a game you can't always win. And then we'd at least have a house by the sea, instead of one with an orchard.'

'You're underestimating us,' says Gül. 'The blacksmith's children have always stuck together in the end.'

Fuat simply nods and leaves the room.

A few days later, he comes home looking pleased with himself, like he's bought a TV, a video recorder, a Mercedes and a new mobile phone in one afternoon.

'Life in this country is such an ordeal,' he says. 'All the peddlers, the labourers, all the officials and all the traffic – nothing works the way it should.'

He pauses.

'And yet, this country brings me good luck. It beggars belief – I spent decades playing the lottery in Germany, decades! What did I ever win? 600, 700 marks at most? You're not even allowed to cross off your own numbers in this country, you have to buy a ready-made slip at the shop—'

'We won?' Gül interrupts him.

'*We?* Since when have you played the lottery? *I* won. I actually won, Gül. 80 billion lira!'

'What's that, 40,000 euros? All these zeros, why are you still attached to them? They crossed six of them off to make it easier, but everyone still talks in millions and billions. 4,000 you mean, surely? That's not to be sniffed at.'

Fuat shakes his head, grinning. '40,000,' he says. 'It must be a sign. Just last week we were talking about a house by the sea, and now the money falls into our lap! This country wants to indulge me, Gül. It's tormented me because it was so far away, tormented me with its chaos, tormented me with its corruption.

It's driven me mad with its incompetent cowboys and mindless citizens, but now it wants to show me it still cares, that it'll bring me luck and wrap me up in cash. Gül, how many years have I been playing the lottery? But I always knew it would pay off, one day it'd pay off. You've got to be prepared to invest. Come on, let's drive to the seaside and go house-hunting.'

'Now?'

'Yes, now.'

'Drive to the Aegean?'

'*The Aegean*? Woman, honestly. You and your ideas. Are we going to want to drive all the way to the Aegean every year? Of course not. To Mersin I mean, it's much closer. Come on, get ready. We'll take Ceren and Ferdi too, if they fancy it. I'll give them a call.'

'You don't even have the money yet. What if there's some kind of problem?'

'It's just a spot of window-shopping. Now, are you coming or not?'

On the way there, Fuat calls Emin. 'It's the best investment you can make at the moment,' he says. 'If I'd won, I'd do the same.'

Fuat races along the short stretch of motorway; the car pushes 160 km/h going downhill. Gül holds her breath and clings on to the handle above the window.

Soon after, once they're at the estate agent's, it no longer seems to be about a house, or peace, of the sea, or even fulfilling a dream; it's about money, numbers, square footage, distance from the beach, year of construction, fittings, neighbours, infrastructure. While the men chat, Gül goes outside with Ceren to smoke and wonders what she's doing here. It occurs to her that she hasn't thought about the summer house or her siblings for several hours. She smiles.

Later that afternoon, when they find themselves standing inside a show home, Gül feels completely dazed by the win, the speedy drive down, the hours out in the heat, the hustle and bustle and noise on the streets. Three small bedrooms, a small open-plan kitchen, and a living room with a balcony. It's a little way out of town, in a development consisting of six high-rise buildings arranged in a square with one side missing, two high-rises for each wall. There's a swimming pool in the middle. It's four minutes' walk to the sea and there's a supermarket downstairs in one of the high-rise blocks. The water is supplied through modern plastic pipes, Gül learns, and there are worktops of marble and artificial stone, abrasion-proof, waterproof tiles, parking facilities. Screens to keep out mosquitos. Caretakers, maintenance, modern air conditioning, peace, solitude, community, investments, rental fees, winter weather resistance. Gül's head is buzzing.

She thinks about the summer house, about the 40,000 euros and how many hours she would have had to work for that, and what she could have done with the time instead. She stands on the little balcony and looks down at the swimming pool. It has a lifeguard. Much safer than the open sea, the estate agent said. And cleaner, too.

The sun reflects on the surface of the pool, and Gül remembers the summer, years ago, when they were all here together. She remembers the sweltering heat, the light, her father, the boy who fell off the roof, and how, at midday, the flame from the lighter was hardly visible when she'd go to smoke a cigarette outdoors. She smiles.

'There's more of Adem's family than there are of us; maybe you should move out,' Gül says.

'And sell the house? No. Timur and Duygu are big now, but they still live at home. I don't want to uproot them. They're not stupid, they'll get the picture. I put up with that man for decades – a little bit of gossip's not going to break me. How long are they going to talk, how many are going to blank me? I've got enough German friends who don't care about all this. I've been preparing for years now; I'm not scared. If you walk towards a fire, you might as well take a pair of bellows. And I'm walking tall.'

Duygu is a legal assistant at a Hamburg solicitor's office, and she takes the train to work every day. She doesn't have a boyfriend and doesn't intend to marry, but that doesn't surprise either Ceyda or Gül. She stays over with friends at weekends; Ceyda knows they go out to clubs, often staying out until dawn. But she also knows her daughter doesn't drink, doesn't take drugs, always goes out in a group; she never worries about Duygu. The only thing she worries about is someone they know seeing her and then gossiping.

Before she talks to Adem, Ceyda wants to have a word with her children. She knocks at Duygu's door. Duygu is sitting at her desk, chatting online. Ceyda perches on her daughter's bed. Never usually quick to leave her computer, Duygu turns around in her chair and looks at her.

Ceyda doesn't take a deep breath; in a quiet voice, she just says: 'I'm going to leave your father.'

She can see that Duygu doesn't know how to react. Stand up, hug her mother, nod, smile, ask questions? What Ceyda can't see is how Duygu feels.

'Are you surprised?'

Her daughter looks up. 'No. And yes. How will you work it out?'

'I haven't spoken to him yet, but I'm going to ask him to move out. If he refuses, which I don't think he will, we'll look for a flat.'

Duygu nods.

'Either way, not much will change for you two. He was never… never really…'

Another nod.

Ceyda wonders whether her own mother often found it difficult to talk to her too, given that she usually kept her feelings to herself as a child. She gets up, goes over to her daughter, takes her hands and pulls her up from the chair for a hug.

'People will talk,' Ceyda says. 'They'll probably talk a lot. I don't want anyone to spot you out and about at night for the next few months. That would just make everything worse. Promise me you won't go out for a while.'

'But…'

'You have to promise me. There's no other way.'

Duygu lowers her head. 'What should I tell the others when they ask why I'm not allowed out?'

'I don't mind what you tell them. You can tell them the truth if you like. But you have to promise me, alright? I'm just trying to protect us.'

'How long for?'

'About three months, four, maybe five. We'll have to wait and see – it depends how much people talk, and how long it takes them to stop.'

'That long, really?'

'Yes.'

'But…'

'Promise?'

'Maybe I could…'

'Promise?'

Duygu sighs. 'I promise.'

Her next stop is Timur's bedroom. He's had a girlfriend for two years, a German girl he met at a club. Jennifer is always popping in and out; she even has her own key now. But Jennifer's mother won't have Timur in the house – she's against her daughter being with a Turk. Because she knows Turks, she says, because she deals with Turks every day. She checks their ID cards, tells them to get in the back of the car, and sometimes just telling them isn't enough so they have to wear handcuffs. One of them broke her colleague's nose. She's never seen an innocent Turk, not in all twelve years of her career, not one. Timur seems strangely unmoved by her views, while Ceyda can barely keep her anger in check when Jennifer talks about her mother.

'We're not like the Turks she knows; you tell your mother that,' she often urges Jennifer. 'Invite her round for dinner, she's welcome here any time. She doesn't even need to take her shoes off or anything. She's like a cobbler who thinks all shoes have broken heels. Does she think all people who drive cars cause accidents? Does she think all houses get broken into? Does a doctor think there are only sick people? What kind of world does she live in?'

'Relax,' Timur tells his mum in Turkish.

'I know, Ceyda,' Jennifer says. 'I've been trying to explain all that but it's not easy. I went to school with Turks, Serbs, Bosnians and Kosovars, but my mum only grew up around Germans; she doesn't understand.'

Jennifer's parents are separated; she's an only child and her mother is scared. Scared of something she doesn't know but thinks she does.

It's funny, Ceyda thinks when she's not angry. *People say German girls are freer and make their own decisions, but Jennifer kept Timur a secret for a whole year because she knew full well what her mother would say about him.*

Timur has finished his hospitality training but doesn't want to work in a hotel; he says he'd rather join the police. He seems serious about it, and of course Ceyda's said she'll support him. She tries to imagine him in uniform but can't quite picture it.

'Timur,' she says to him. 'Timur, I'm going to leave your dad.'

Timur's eyes well up. Ceyda tries to remember the last time she saw him cry. It was years ago. Many years. He seems young to her, but you can see the man in him, and sometimes he reminds her of her grandfather, who she named him after. He's tall, much taller than his father, and taller and stronger than the blacksmith. Since he started weight training at a fitness studio, his back has got broader, his chest has expanded, and he's been eating even more than before.

He turns his head to the window, and after a moment he looks back at his mother.

'Are we going to move out?'
'I assume he'll move out.'
'You haven't spoken to him yet?'
'No, I wanted to talk to you two first.'
'And Duygu knows already?'
'Yes.'

Timur nods. Ceyda regrets deciding not to tell them both at the same time. So many muscles, so vulnerable.

'You know,' Timur says, 'it was in Turkey, I was still a little boy, and Dad and I were throwing stones in the well at the back of Uncle Yücel's garden. It was a deep well – you couldn't see the water, and I was totally fascinated. We only ever heard the stones splashing into the water. I often think of us sitting on the edge of the well and the sounds of the stones in the water. I was scared of the well, but Dad was there with me.'

His voice has long since broken, but now it wobbles. He almost always speaks German with his mother, unlike Duygu, but that's not the reason why he can't find the words now. It's not a question of language; there are never enough words when you want to tell someone how you feel.

Ceyda's eyes well up too. She wonders whether at that moment by the well, Timur felt a connection to Adem that went beyond anything there ever was between her and him.

'He's your father,' she says, 'and he'll always be your father. No matter what happens between him and me.'

Saniye comes to Germany for just six weeks, to attend to a few formalities. Six weeks – the same amount of time they used to spend in Turkey each summer, back when the girls were small. Six weeks to see doctors, go to the bank, talk to the health insurance company; six weeks to spend with Yılmaz, who came back to Germany in the early autumn and doesn't want to leave again until the end of spring. Retirement has pulled the two of them apart.

When Gül looks at marriages, it's clear to her that none of them run smoothly. Everyone judders along on rocky, pot-holed roads, wheels squeaking, axles warped. Marriage doesn't mean sharing the load, it means adding others' problems to your own, so you can help carry them too. It's the price everyone pays so that the song of the ancestors can go on being sung.

Saniye and Yılmaz seemed to have had a lighter load to carry compared to others, but they see each other less and less now because he wants to stay in Germany with his hashish, his films, his intellectual theatre friends and his daughter, in a country which has accepted him, even if it's not quite home. Yılmaz lives his life in a world he has built for himself, while Saniye is living the life she might have wanted to end up living.

Gül can see that they can't find enough common ground to keep them under one roof. *Perhaps it's Germany's doing*, she thinks. *Perhaps Germany changes you in ways you can't predict. Just like alcohol. It has a different effect on everyone: some turn melancholy, some cheerful, some grow aggressive, and others just feel dizzy and sick. Some experience all of these things one after another, but you never know how much Germany is too much, just as some drinkers struggle to know their limits.*

Gül spends a lot of time sitting at home watching shows she's already seen in Turkey; she goes to the doctor; and sometimes she meets up with Saniye's daughter Sevgi, who's always glad when Gül helps her a little with Turkish idioms and proverbs.

Often she stays at Ceyda's for several nights in a row. Though she spends a lot of time in front of the television there too, she at least feels she's like she can make herself useful: she cooks, does the washing, cleans, hoovers, but she doesn't leave the house very much; she doesn't want to give the neighbours more reasons to talk.

Of course, there's been plenty of gossip and tattle, of course people have been saying Ceyda must be heartless, of course they're wondering why she had to go and break up a home for no good reason, of course they blame her for becoming too German, or they suspect her of having a lover. Of course they lament that this woman is tearing the kids away from their father, regardless of the fact that the children are grown up now. Of course they bitch that Gül is behind it all – she never did get on with her son-in-law, they say. Of course people talk, but the gossip, the rumours and the allegations aren't especially fierce. Ceyda finds she can bear it, Duygu hears what they say but pretends not to notice, and Timur says he and his friends don't even talk about it: they only ever talk about chest presses, cable pulldowns, training methods and protein shakes.

'It's just tittle-tattle,' he says, 'every Turkish woman's favourite. You're all addicted to gossip. And if there isn't any, you just make it up. German women manage to keep things to themselves, they're not addicted to criticising everyone else. You're always looking for someone to badmouth. Even if it's just someone who's made the mistake of slagging off someone else.'

'Yes,' says Ceyda, 'because German women never criticise anything. Jennifer's mum's got no problem at all with you going out with her daughter.'

'That's different,' says Timur.

Once he's left the room, Gül smiles and says: 'He's becoming a man.'

People are talking in their hometown – not about Ceyda's separation, but because everyone has something to say about who has what stake in the blacksmith's summer house and why, about who's in the right, who's lying, who's spreading falsehoods and who's scheming. Gül has vowed not to correct anything, to keep out of it; but the more she hears, the more she's dragged into a maelstrom, the more her head fills up with thoughts on the argument. And the more her head fills up with thoughts, the more she needs to talk.

After just two weeks back, she escapes to their flat by the sea, which is still unfurnished. Cupboards and shelves, chairs and a kitchen need to be picked out, ordered and paid for, as well as a TV, washing machine, beds, bedding, crockery and carpets. They buy a lot in instalments, and once again Gül furnishes a new home – but for the first time ever, only with new things bought here in Turkey.

When she first moved back to her hometown, she had all her furniture brought over from Germany on a truck; their things were held up at the border for months, and they had to bribe the customs officers who hinted for tips. There was less choice in Turkey back then, and the quality was worse. But these days the kitchen appliances have more functions than the ones in Germany – they're better adapted to the climate, the freezer compartments have a no-frost function, and the fridges have an extra drawer for breakfast bowls, and no butter dish.

Gül stows things away, sorts, cleans, imagines the place filling with life when her children and grandchildren come to stay. She meets the neighbours and often stands on the little balcony, smoking and looking down at the swimming pool, the water filthy because it's still spring and the pool isn't officially open yet.

She feels good as long as she can work away in the flat and daydream. She feels good because she's preparing the ground for other people's happiness, because she's free here and no one knows her, because she feels she can start over afresh in a light she knows neither from Germany nor from her hometown. She's grateful for this new beginning – one nothing like back then in Germany, when she had nothing in her pockets and less than five words to her name. She has a bit of money now and she can talk to anyone here, meet people everywhere.

She feels good, even though she often argues with Fuat.

'A dinner service for twelve people? Twelve? How are you going to get twelve people in this flat? How are you going to cook for so many? We're pensioners – there's only two of us, if you don't mind me reminding you.'

'We'll have visitors, and plenty of them. Plates will get broken, friends will come over, friends of friends… Timur will bring Jennifer along, maybe they'll have children, maybe even Jennifer's mother will come and visit.'

'Jennifer's mother? What planet are you on? Planet Daydream? Do you know what all this has cost so far, have you totted it all up? A fridge, a washing machine, a cooker, two sofa beds, two beds, two spare mattresses, four cupboards, a table and chairs – and you said that was all we'd need. And then came the mixer, the toaster, the iron, the hairdryer, the telephone, the lampshades, the tablecloths, the balcony chairs and table. Before long, all the stuff in here will have cost more than the flat itself.'

'Well, what would you like us to do? Bring along a hairdryer, a toaster and a mixer every time we come? This is just how you set up a home. If it was up to you, we'd be staring at bare walls with two chairs and a bed, like when I first moved to Germany.'

'All this pointless women's stuff makes me sick, it really does. In the old days we'd load up the car until it nearly scraped the ground, and now we're buying knick-knacks and bric-a-brac until the whole block comes tumbling down. Why do women have to overload everything? Can't life ever just be simple and clear? Why do we always have all these belongings weighing us down? The flat's getting smaller and smaller, and my wallet's getting lighter and lighter. We might as well just throw the cash out the window and into the pool. Skip the wife,' he says, 'that's my advice for any man looking to get rich.'

On her way home from buying the dinner service for twelve, Gül sees a woman walking into the next building along. She looks familiar; Gül's sure she's seen her face before, but how would she know anyone here? She won't go up to the woman; she thinks back to where she knows her face from and wonders whether it's just a similarity. But the woman has noticed Gül stopping in her tracks, looking like she's trying to remember something. She turns around and looks at Gül, perhaps for two seconds. Then she lets go of the door handle and makes her way over to her.

'It *is* you,' she says. 'Years ago, you were walking around here with your half-naked sister. Yes, it's you.'

Now Gül can see the mole above her eyebrow. She feels uncomfortable to be here again, and to have bought a flat, as if she'd helped destroy the village. As if she'd helped make people walking around half-naked an everyday phenomenon now. Her eyes fill with tears, and she doesn't know what to say.

'It is you, isn't it?'

Gül nods.

'Have you bought a flat here?'

Ashamed, Gül nods again.

'May you live there happily.'

'And you?' Gül asks. 'Do you have a flat here too?'

'Don't ask,' the woman says. 'Yes, I have. They pulled down the houses in the village and we got flats here instead. Actually, we had to pay but they gave us a special deal. The others sold theirs off again, long ago. I lived in my own house for decades, and now all of a sudden, I have to climb stairs because the lift's always broken. At least I get a view from above of how they've blighted the village. The young folks all moved to Istanbul. The old people moved in with relatives away from the coast. And I'm still here. Do you live in that one?'

She points at the block.

'Yes.'

'You're lucky – they didn't put any villagers in that one, and the lift's never broken down there either. In my block it only works a dozen days a month. I'm on the twelfth floor, so I always think twice about whether I want to go down in the first place. I get most things I need delivered from the shop.'

'And now, what did you need just now?'

'Now?' she says, looking at Gül as if her question was indecent. 'Now... Well, you know what? I just wanted to get out and stretch my bloody legs. I don't know how many days I've been up there.'

'Come,' says Gül, 'come up to my place, I'll make us some tea.'
'No thank you,' says the woman. 'I've just had a glass.'
'Come on, there's always room for one more tea.'
'Thank you, but no. I'm sure you must be busy.'
'Just for five minutes. Come on, be my guest. It'll bring me good luck.'
'Maybe another time.'
'You want to turn down one glass of tea?'
'I'm as happy as if I'd already drunk your tea. Thank you for inviting me.'
'What's your name?'
'Öykü.'
'My name's Gül. Öykü, do me this one favour, come up with me – we're neighbours. Just for five minutes; don't turn me down.'
Öykü looks around and then nods.
'But just for a few minutes.'

Gül is used to people trusting her easily, revealing their secrets and feeling safe with her. Öykü is cautious, almost wary of her; she's obviously weighing up what and how much to say. After this visit, Gül finds herself thinking back more often to the scene with Melike years ago, thinking about this determined woman with the powerful voice, giving her sister an earful. Or wanting to, at least. Gül wonders about everything that's happened since then. Why is Öykü less quick to have an opinion on the matter now? She doesn't seem tired or broken, sad or bitter, but something has changed. She hesitates to accept Gül's invitations each time, she doesn't speak openly, and she never invites Gül over to hers. Nevertheless, the two women get on well. Gül calls time and again through the spring, has the grocer say hello from her, seeks out Öykü's company. One day in summer, she summons the courage to simply knock on Öykü's door unannounced. It's a while before she opens it and, when she sees Gül, there's a look of alarm on her face before she smiles.

'Come in,' says Öykü, 'come in, how lovely of you to visit.'

It's the kind of flat Fuat would feel at home in: sparsely furnished, many of the walls bare. The one sofa in the room is old, its cover threadbare, and the table in front of it has rickety legs. Gül feels uncomfortable about having put Öykü in this position, but her host just smiles and says: 'I'll make us some tea.'

'It's not my fault,' she says, stirring sugar into her tea. It wasn't laziness that made me poor. Just look at my hands, I've worked my whole life but now I've ended up here. Maybe I brought my kids up wrong, maybe I wasn't a good mum, but I was never lazy. Tourism brought in big money, more than you could earn with your two hands and the sweat of your brow. Everyone's eyes were bigger than their wallets; greed ate them up, and those that weren't greedy went to the dogs. In the old days in the village, we used to pinch stuff off each other – there were spats and feuds, and the men would get into brawls – but we were a village. Like a family. But now, not only has the village broken up because everyone suddenly fancied the chance to swim and sunbathe and stuff themselves with grilled meat and fish; families have broken up too. No one cares about blood.'

Gül knows that Öykü's husband died nearly ten years ago, of lung cancer, and now that Öykü has stopped talking, Gül asks a question that seems obvious to her. 'Was there a fight over inheritance?'

Öykü laughs. 'No,' she says, 'it's not like it is for you, it's much worse. I've wished myself dead, as God is my witness. My daughter Necla, the eldest, she lives in Silifke. One day she came to me and said: "Mum, you've got all these bracelets at home, they're not safe there, let's put them in a deposit box at the bank." I had twelve gold bracelets – five from my wedding, and I saved up for the others in the years after that – plus there were six big gold coins, and seven small ones. I put them all in the deposit box. When I was setting up my flat here, I needed money and I wanted to take a couple of gold coins to the jewellers, but there weren't any there. There were no bracelets either. At first, I thought the bank had made a mistake, but they told me exactly when Necla had last been to the deposit box. I called her and said: "Necla, where are the gold coins? Where are my bracelets?" And she said she'd pawned them for cash so that she could set up a shop. A dressmaker's. As if she was any good with her hands! Or her head, for that matter. She wanted to pay me it all back, but the dressmaker's went bust and now my money is gone. My own daughter robbed me. My pension's hardly enough to live on. I don't take sugar in my tea when I'm on my own – this is the first packet I've bought. I'm poor, Gül – all I've got is this flat and I don't dare sell it. If I did, I wouldn't even have a roof over my head. Perhaps you're right, perhaps it is about inheritance. Necla won't get anything when I die, nothing at all. I'll make the flat over to social services instead. My own daughter stole from me.'

She looks up from the floor and peers into Gül's face.

'What can I be accused of? Raising a thief for a daughter? I've never stolen anything, Gül, as I sit here now. I tried to raise my children to be honest people. But I failed. And I'm poor. This is where I live now, and you're the first visitor I've had.'

Gül would like to get up and give Öykü a hug, but the woman's pride prevents it. She might be complaining, but she's standing there with her back straight, ready to take more blows. She's standing there with her shoulders back and proving she can carry the weight of it all, all by herself, with no one to share the load.

Do I have less strength than she does? Gül wonders. *Have I complained more? Am I less equipped to suffer the blows life brings? How many times now must I have told her about the summer house, about the fights, the injustices, the exclusion, even though I'm the eldest, and in all that time, Öykü didn't say a word.*

Perhaps the words turn hard inside her, Gül thinks. *Perhaps they're inside her but they've got hooks and barbs, edges and sharp corners, because she can't let them out, and they scratch at her from the inside, grating at her bones, her soul, ripping away her flesh in hidden places, weighing her down and pressing on her lungs and her liver.* But Gül knows that's not the case. The Lord gives each of us different natures, different strengths and different weaknesses. The children we have are not blank pages we can paint in our favourite colours. Children come into the world colourful, and we have to try to recognise their colours, and let none of them escape our love. But people make mistakes; we overlook things, we let ourselves be led by our desires. Or we leave our children alone. So that both carry a wound – our children and ourselves – a wound that will not heal for the length of our lives.

Gül isn't jealous of Öykü's strength, but she wishes she had a little more of it herself. It's Öykü's story that gives her a little of this strength. We're not alone. Our daughters might be stealing from us, or we might find ourselves drifting further from our siblings with each day, but we're not alone in our suffering.

That summer, Gül's stepmother stays in the old summer house, and Melike stays in the new one. Nalan and Emin stay the night with their mother when they come to visit, and Sibel visits Melike regularly. And Gül is here, by the sea – she doesn't belong back there any more.

'What's wrong?' Öykü asks.

'Oh,' says Gül, 'just lost in my thoughts.'

'Even when the worries disappear, the place they leave behind doesn't stay empty for long, Gül. You can't find reason in these waters. No matter how deep you dive, you'll never get anywhere. The people with no worries are all lying in the graveyard. Rust eats away at iron, just as worry eats at people. Your worries are no lighter than mine, and look at us: we're old but we're not in the ground yet – we're still standing, drinking tea, cursing that trollop we call fate, but what has she done to us? She dug deep into my pockets, stole your siblings and a house that reminded you of your childhood. You think she took your homeland because you've been away, but look at me: she took my home too, without me ever leaving. And yet we're still standing, Gül. Look how old we are now. It's not the concrete dust from the houses we live in that's turned our hair grey. Let's be grateful: those with worries find comfort in sleep, those who are hungry need only food. Let's be thankful for Fate, the old tart.'

It's Boxing Day. Gül, Fuat, Ceyda and her children, Ceren, Ferdi and Ersin are sitting around Ceyda's table eating dinner, when the phone rings. Ceren is closest, so she picks up.

'Yes?' she says.

She stands there saying nothing for such a long time that they all stare over, but she's got her back to the table.

'I will,' she says, 'I will. May the Lord give strength to the bereaved.'

She hangs up and turns around – only then does she notice everyone looking at her. She makes a helpless gesture with her hands and says: 'Nene's dead. Yesterday she felt dizzy and had a fall. She died an hour ago.'

'May the Lord bring peace to her soul,' Gül says. 'She'd always wished for a swift death without being bedridden, without being a burden on anyone. The Lord granted that wish.'

Her voice cracks but her eyes are clear.

Ceyda and Ceren look at their mother, searching for signs of grief. The children sit frozen to the spot, not knowing what to do. Their great-grandmother is someone they only ever saw for a few days a year. Fuat stares at his plate.

'May the Lord give the bereaved strength,' Ferdi says after a while; he's not usually short of a word or two. Ceren is about to sit back down but then changes her mind, stands behind her mother and puts her hands on her shoulders. Ceyda looks from her mother to her sister and back. The air seems dense, all their movements slowed down; everyone is waiting for a reaction from Gül, but she hasn't realised. She's pushed her plate away and is looking at her folded hands on the table.

In the end, she moves over to the sofa. There are tears in her eyes. Ceren goes after her and sits next to her. The children watch, unsettled, their only anchor the glances they exchange. They're not sad; they don't have to be, and they're not alone.

Timur picks up his fork and looks over at Ferdi, who closes his eyes briefly in approval.

'She tried hard,' Gül says. 'She tried, even though she wasn't our mother. I never felt close to her, never secure and protected. But she wasn't bad to us. She was a good person, but I never felt close to her,' she repeats, 'even though we spent so many years together. We're parting ways with no regrets.'

'Will you fly over for the funeral?' Ceyda asks.

'No,' says Gül. 'I wasn't at my father's funeral, so why should I go to hers?'

'So that people don't talk.'

'It's winter in Germany,' Gül says. 'I'm sick in bed, I can't travel.'

'But you're not sick,' says Ersin.

Gül smiles. 'May you grow up with your mother and your father,' she says. 'There's nothing more important for a child.'

'May your wish be fulfilled,' Ceren says. 'Fate isn't always as kind to everyone.'

Gül flushes, anxious for a moment because she doesn't know what Ceren means by that. Tears roll down her cheeks, but her voice is firm when she says: 'How good it is that we're all here together. If only Fatma could be with us too.'

'Don't cry, Mum,' Ceren says.

'Death comes without asking what your plans are,' says Gül. 'Who knows when we'll be together again like this, who knows whether we'll have another opportunity. If only Fatma could be here,' she sobs.

Ferdi looks at his watch and then says: 'I know it's bad timing, but I have to pop out, I'm sorry. I'll be back soon.'

'Where did Ferdi go?' Gül asks, three hours later.

'I don't know,' Ceren says. 'You know him, he's always doing deals on the internet, used cars, good-as-new electronic goods, computers – he makes a good bit of money on the side.'

'Couldn't it have waited?'

'We should get you a computer,' says Ceyda.

'What would I do with a computer? I can't work that kind of thing.'

'It's not that hard,' Duygu chips in.

'You can watch your shows on the internet if you miss an episode,' Ceyda says.

'Really?'

'Yes.'

'Oh, I don't understand all that.'

'And you can join Facebook,' Duygu says.

'What's that?'

'You can see what we're all up to.'

'And you can find old friends on it,' says Ceren.

'Have you got it too?' Gül asks her daughter.

'We've all got it, Mum. It keeps you in touch with everyone, all the time.'

'No,' says Gül. 'I'm too old for that kind of thing. I barely finished primary school – how am I supposed to work a computer? Not even your dad has one, and he's always the first to get every new thing that comes along.'

Her daughters know her well enough to hear the curiosity in her voice. Ceyda gives Duygu a look.

'It's really easy, Nene,' Duygu says. 'I'll teach you.'

'No, no, I'll only break it. I've never even used a typewriter. I can work a sewing machine and that's about all.'

'Timur has an old laptop he doesn't need any more. Nothing can go wrong. And you've got us. Come on, I'll set it up for you. It's easier than making a phone call.'

The doorbell rings; Ceren gets up to open it.

Ferdi comes into the kitchen.

'Phew, am I thirsty,' he says. He goes to the fridge and helps himself to a carton of orange juice.

Gül casts a quick glance at Ceren and then asks Ferdi: 'Where have you been all this time?'

'I had something to do, luckily.'

'Fuat's all on his own in the living room.'

'I know,' he says, grinning at Gül.

'Why are you grinning like that? Have you no shame? Not even on a day like this?'

'I do. But I've got a surprise for you. Come with me.'

He takes her hand and leads her into the hall. For a brief instant, Gül can't believe her eyes. Then everything seems to blur into one, wobbling in and out of focus. As if the world were falling apart and had to be put together again.

It's Fatma. She hugs her nene, who holds onto the doorframe for support, not breathing. Gül closes her eyes but it's as if someone had turned on a light. A light that flows out of her eyes as warm tears. She feels like her arms are big enough to press the whole world to her heart.

Finally she lets go of her granddaughter. 'My son,' she says, 'what did you do?'

'It's easy to make people happy,' Ferdi says.

'Did you know?' Gül asks Ceren as she hugs her.

'Of course,' she says.

'You all knew.'

'Dad didn't.'

'Why didn't you say anything?'

'Because then it wouldn't have been a surprise.'

Fuat is standing in the doorway now, and even before he greets his granddaughter, he asks: 'How did you get here?'

'On a plane.'

'Without a visa?'

'With a visa.'

'So it was all planned?'

'Yes, we've been planning it for ages.'

'How long are you staying?'

'A fortnight.'

'Come here, let your Dede kiss you.'

Their cheeks touch in the ritual way, but Gül can tell by Fuat's eyes that he's happy.

It's always dark in your head, Gül thinks later, lying in bed. *The light doesn't shine in through people's eyes; the light shines out from their hearts.*

The siblings sit down together with Tarık for a second time. This time, it's Nalan who has given Emin power to act on her behalf; the two of them have inherited their mother's share. Sibel says she'll agree to whatever they decide, but she doesn't want to have to be there and vote. Despite the accusations and blame that are dished up once again, none of them turns loud and abusive this time. In the end, against Gül's wishes, they agree to put the house up for auction, and the siblings pledge not to buy it themselves. Emin votes to sell, for Nalan too, and they cast their mother's vote as well, which makes three. Melike also votes to sell, and no matter how much Gül pleads and begs, no matter how hard she tries to convince the others that the house is more important than money, no matter how much she warns them that leaving the house in the hands of strangers will destroy all their memories, no matter how hard she tries to remind them that it's not about the money, it's all in vain.

After the meeting, she goes to Sibel's and asks her to take her side so that they can talk it over again.

'I love all of you,' says Sibel. 'I don't want to fall out with anyone. I'll support whatever the majority decides.'

'How did you come by that tin cup?' Gül asks now. 'It's a keepsake from Baba and I can't remember anyone promising it to you.'

'Accusations,' Sibel says. 'That's all anyone hears from you these days: accusations.'

Gül feels empty, but at the same time she's furious. *I won't speak to them any more*, she tells herself. *I won't speak to any of them. What kind of person wants to just flog off our memories of our father and our mother? What kind of people are they if they can't agree on anything? What sort of blood is ours if it can be traded for cash? What's wrong with the world? It wasn't all about money in the past. What's happened to people? What's happened to the paradise of my childhood? All the things I must have missed because I was in Germany. We thought people in Germany were cold to one another, we thought German families didn't stick together, we thought everyone there was at odds with everyone else. But we're like that too. Is it my fault? Did I get stuck somewhere while life just carried on?*

Her thoughts are going in circles again, looping around like ribbons with no beginning or end. These ribbons have a life of their own and have picked Gül's head to make their home. It doesn't matter whether she's cooking, washing up, shopping, asleep or awake – the resentment, the fury, the pain and the defiance are there, held together by the fear she might lose something important.

She tries to distract herself, but she can't concentrate on anything. She loses the thread when she's watching her soaps; she can't remember when Sevda cheated on Erci with Sinan, whether Nuran's lying to her sister, or why Vedat takes a bribe. She sits in front of the television and feels like she's missed a few episodes every time.

Maybe I'm losing my mind, she thinks, *first my body aged, and now it's my head's turn*. But something tells her that can't be right. And yet there's no room in her mind for anything but the dark ribbons, which seem to keep whirling even in her sleep.

Fuat pushes for them to drive down to the flat by the sea, and though Gül thinks a change could do her good, she feels as tied to her hometown as she does to the ribbons. She doesn't want to leave.

Gül is pleased when Saniye rings. She hasn't been in touch with her herself because she didn't want to tell her what has happened. Because there's shame mixed in with those dark ribbons, because it feels like she's failed, because she hasn't managed to keep the family together. She's happy that Saniye has called, but she's already cursing herself, knowing she's bound to start moaning about the summer house within a couple of sentences. It doesn't come to that, though. At first, Gül's too wrapped up in her own problems to notice that something's not right, but after the initial pleasantries she senses that Saniye has something on her mind. She pulls back and tries to give her friend space.

'You're on Facebook,' says Saniye. 'I sent you a friend request, but you didn't reply.'

'Yes,' says Gül, 'Duygu set it up for me, but I never actually turn the computer on.'

'Anyway, I haven't put it on Facebook,' says Saniye. 'Even though I'm on there a lot. Gül... Gül, I was at the doctor's because I found a lump in my breast. It's cancer. They say I've got to have an operation, and chemotherapy too.'

Oh God. That's terrible, she wants to say, but then she thinks for a moment.

'You're strong,' she says, 'I know you. There aren't many people I'd count on to beat cancer, but you're one of them. You've always found a way through. You won't let it break you.'

She hears Saniye crying quietly.

'No, I won't let it break me, but death is God's command — there's no getting away from it.'

'May it be a late death. You're still young, it's too early for you.'

Saniye says nothing, and Gül is sure the tears are running down her face in silence.

'What does Yılmaz think?'

'He says I should go to Germany because they have better doctors there.'

'He's right there, Saniye.'

'I don't want to go to Germany.'

'Why?'

'I just don't.'

'You know what the hospitals are like here. If you get sent to one of those, you're lost. Of course you should go to Germany.'

'No. No, Yılmaz should come here. Please, give him a call, talk to him. I don't want to go to Germany.'

'Why? You've got your health insurance there, and they've got the best care you could wish for. There's no reason to suffer in a Turkish hospital.'

'I just don't want to.'

Something in her voice stops Gül from pushing further. But even two hours later, once they've hung up, Gül still doesn't know why Saniye doesn't want to go to Germany. She calls Yılmaz.

'I don't understand it,' he says. 'She doesn't want to die, that's for sure, but I don't understand why she doesn't want to come to Germany.'

'Will you come here?'

'And support this stupid decision she's made? No.'

'But you should. I'm going to see her tomorrow.'

'Good, you should; I'm glad.'

'You're not dying yet.'

'It's cancer, Gül. They have to remove the whole breast, then send me for radiotherapy, chemotherapy, all of it. My neighbour's mum died during chemotherapy.'

'How old was she?'

'Gül, I'm nearly seventy. You've seen what women my age look like in this country.'

'You're sixty-five – you've a lifetime's worth more fire in your belly than any woman I know.'

'Yes, but I've also lost more than any woman you know.'
'Are you tired?'
'No, it's not that.'
'What is it, then? I don't understand.'

Saniye lights a cigarette. It occurs to Gül that she hasn't thought about the summer house for almost the whole day. *Please, Lord*, she prays, *let Saniye be well again*.

'I'm scared,' says Saniye.
'We all are.'
'No, I mean, perhaps I've always been scared. And what you all thought was fire, was just fear.'
'You can speak good German, you can drive, you've always pushed through, you've had all kinds of different jobs, and you've never hesitated to try something new.'
'Maybe because I was scared of old age. I learnt to drive because I was scared of being dependent on anyone. I wanted to prove that I could do everything, I was scared of failing.'
'Maybe it's the illness that's making you think this way. Maybe the fear is so great right now that you think it's always been that way.'

Gül's thoughts wander elsewhere for a moment. The anger, the greed, the self-righteousness, the conflict between the siblings – was that all there before the inheritance was even an issue?

'There's only one thing I'm more scared of than death.'
Gül listens carefully.
'I'm scared of dying in Germany. I want to take my last breath in this country, no matter what happens. Here, with the scent of the earth that I missed for so long. I want to die at home, Gül. It's better if I don't go back to Germany.'

Duygu set up her account, but it's Saniye who introduces Gül to Facebook. Gül brought her laptop with her to Turkey, but she hasn't switched it on once. She hasn't brought it along to Malatya either, even though Saniye told her she should. They have to call

Duygu to find out Gül's password for her Facebook account, and then Saniye logs in and adds Gül's maiden name – so that her teenage friends can find her more easily, she says.

'But Saniye, I got married when I was fifteen. And why would my school friends be on Facebook? They're the same age as me.'

'They're on Facebook, believe me. This is Turkey – no one's afraid of technology. You just have to spend a bit of time on here and you'll be amazed who you meet, people you've forgotten even existed. Do you have any old photos from school?'

'No. Melike and Sibel have photos from their final years at primary, middle and high school, but I didn't finish school.'

'Never mind. Come on, we'll write all the places you've worked, here. And where you've lived. I bet we find lots of people from Factory Lane. And here, look, Ali Pınar Primary School, your year. Aziza Gülen Keskin – do you know her?'

'Yes, she used to sit in front of me.'

'Come here, have a look at the picture.'

'Yes, that could be her. It is her. Her eyes haven't changed at all. She looks so elegant; she used to be all grubby and unkempt at school.'

'She's married to the old mayor of Silifke.'

'Silifke? That's not far from our summer apartment.'

'Send her a friend request. I bet she knows more people from your old class.'

'How do I do that?'

Every morning, the two of them sit at Saniye's laptop, and Gül gradually works out what this Facebook is for Saniye, and how she uses it. In the space of a week, Gül's Facebook friends go from six – her daughters and grandchildren and Ferdi – to forty-two. After breakfast, the two women sit down together and look at who's done what, who's shared and liked quotes, sayings, poems, short videos. They see photos of weddings, engagements, holidays, family get-togethers, new-born babies and toddlers. Gül writes to people she hasn't seen for decades; she knows where they are, what they've been up to since they joined Facebook, what their grandchildren are doing. Hesitantly, she starts to share photos and quotes herself, lines from Orhan Veli poems or lyrics by Aşık Veysel.

Three weeks later she shares a post saying she's going to the coast; this time she takes the computer with her. Duygu takes a photo of her on the balcony, from high up so that you can see the swimming pool in the background, and that becomes Gül's new profile picture. What her soaps didn't manage, the internet and Facebook do: she's distracted and starts focusing on other things.

'What do you do all day long in front of that computer, like a child? It beggars belief,' says Fuat. 'Are you using that laptop or is it using you?'

'What's your problem?' Gül says. 'Have I ever said anything about how much time you've spent on your car? All that washing and polishing, which kind of wax, which kind of wheel rims, and whatever else you do with it all the time. I'm sitting here to keep in touch with people.'

'Your keeping in touch costs money, you do know that? We need internet here and internet there, you'll probably want internet in Germany too. It's a great invention, your internet. You can't take it with you anywhere, you have to buy it all over again everywhere you go.'

'We've got three TVs as well. And three fridges.'

'Yes, but they're things you can touch. In theory, you could take them with you. But the internet doesn't weigh a thing and you still can't take it anywhere. It looks like a scam to me. And who falls for it? Women, of course.'

Gül looks at her screen. Aziza is in New York and has shared a photo with the Statue of Liberty in the background.

When she's not on the computer and they don't have visitors, she meets up with Öykü almost every day this year. They compare their childhoods in Turkey. Öykü never ate köfter, Gül never learned to swim. They both like nature; it means something different for each of them, but it has been taken away from them both. From Öykü because she lives in a concrete tower block now, and from Gül because the summer house and the orchard will soon belong to a stranger.

Gül still doesn't know why her neighbour Bahar tells her all the gossip. To win her confidence and draw her into something she doesn't want to be part of? To stir up trouble? Because she wants to take sides? Because she feels sorry for her?

Gül says hello to Bahar and chats to her, but she never really warms to the woman, who lost her husband young, comes from a rich family, goes to the hairdresser's once a week, and owns more shoes than Gül has probably worn in her life.

'Melike says you always got special treatment,' she says. 'You were your father's favourite and he never hit you, but she was often beaten. She says you never had to fight for anything and that's why you expected to get the summer house. She and Sibel were always in your shadow, she says, and you've never given Sibel a chance to develop on her own. You always try to make other people feel guilty. No one asked you to be a mother to them, she says. You can't demand love back, it's not a swap – that's what she says.'

'But why?' Gül asks.

'Why's love not a swap? I don't know.'

'No, why are you telling me all this?'

'That's how the world goes around. Every word that's spoken gets passed on. Everything that happens to thirty-two teeth spreads around thirty-two neighbourhoods. Every word makes a sound, and that sound doesn't disappear. Some sounds lead to love, others to strife. It's not down to me whether something leads to one or the other. I don't make the sound. I don't judge the ears that take it in. The spoken word belongs to all of us.'

Gül looks her in the eye. Bahar accepts her gaze. There's no shame there, no pride, no resentment or deviousness. Or at least, none that Gül can see.

Once the chatter has died down, once Ceyda realises she hasn't been ostracised and the butcher, the hairdresser, her workmates and neighbours are still speaking to her, she begins to relax a little. Perhaps everyone who knew her and her husband could always tell they didn't belong together.

Ceyda was ready for the worst, but now that the hardest part seems to be over, now that she's swapped the night shift for the day shift at the post office, and the children are more or less standing on their own two feet, now that she might finally be able to get some peace, she can hardly get up in the morning. Her alarm goes off over and over, every seven minutes, but she doesn't know how to find the strength to put her feet on the floor. She senses her legs will feel weak all day long and she'll only make it through work with an enormous effort, dragging her body from one hour to the next as she tries to act like a human being. She doesn't feel human, and no matter how much she sleeps – six, eight, ten, twelve hours – she can still barely get out of bed. She feels weak, exhausted. She's afraid of big parcels in the post office; she shirks work, goes to the toilet at every opportunity, and can hardly find the energy to smoke in her cigarette breaks. For weeks on end, she drags herself through her life and tries not to let it show. She drinks freshly squeezed orange juice, takes multivitamins, and buys mesir macunu – a herbal paste from Manisa that's said to have a vitalising effect on the whole body. She takes spirulina and enough iron supplements to give her constipation, but nothing seems to help. There are days at the weekend when she doesn't get up until eleven, despite going to sleep at nine the night before. And she only rouses herself then because she knows the kids will be awake soon, and she doesn't want to be getting up after them.

She's just tired, that's all it is – she's just low on energy. It seems a bit much to go to the doctor about it, but after almost three months she doesn't know what else to do. *He'll tell me to get more sleep*, she thinks. She doesn't expect anything from the doctor; in fact, she's scared he might tell her she's severely anaemic or even has cancer. Or, at best, that it's the menopause: just something every woman goes through, a passing phase that's no cause for concern.

She calls and makes an appointment because she can't think what else to do. One day later, her left ear suddenly goes almost deaf.

'Sudden hearing loss,' the doctor says. 'It'll sort itself out. But Mrs Demirtaş, I've known you for so long, even if you don't come in much. Along with your other symptoms, your body is sending you signals that you've been doing too much for too many years. What you need is a break: time to let other people take care of you, time to rest and recuperate. Away from home, with no obligations and no chores to do. I'm going to prescribe a rest cure for you. Six weeks.'

A rest cure is something Germans do, but that's not what bothers Ceyda.

'Six weeks – isn't that too long? Wouldn't three weeks do? Don't people usually get three?'

The doctor smiles. 'It's often three weeks, yes. But you need more time; six weeks is better in your case. You need to really recover. Forget everything that's keeping you here, let go. You're still young – listen to your body, make sure you have the best of it for a long time to come. Stop overdoing it like you have been. That's what I recommend. But it's up to you to decide, of course.'

Ceyda nods. The doctor's words sound like a sign of defeat.

'You should come and be with her in Turkey, you should stand by her,' Gül says.

'No, she should come here,' says Yılmaz on the other end of the line. 'You know she should. She and I talk on the phone every night, I've told her a thousand times over. She won't die here, I've promised her I'll fly back to Turkey with her if things aren't looking good. No one dies from one second to the next. Not with an illness like this, one that can be cured.'

'She's all on her own.'

'If I go over, she'll only feel vindicated, and she'll never come to Germany for treatment.'

'She's not going to go to Germany, whatever happens.'

'Maybe she will. She wants to live. We're all more attached to life than we'd like to admit. She'll come over eventually, but by then it might be too late. That's what I want to prevent. You have to fight cancer early on. Gül. If I give in and come over now, there's no way she'll come and get treatment here.'

'She's already made her decision, and you ought to support her, even if you don't like what she's decided.'

Yılmaz takes a drag on a cigarette or a joint. 'That's what Sevgi says too, but that way of thinking will only put her in her grave. We've got to force her to come to Germany.'

'No one can force her. What will it cost you? What will it cost you to get on a plane and spend a few days with her? She's your wife. You've spent half your lives together. In times like these, you get to see who's on your side, who you can lean on. Don't leave her on her own.'

Gül's surprised by her own clear words, and she wonders whether it's to do with Yılmaz's habits that she thinks she can adopt a stronger, more direct tone with him. He's never quite there; he swathes everything in smoke and fogs up his heart with the fumes in his lungs.

'It sends the wrong message,' he insists.

Gül looks at her left hand. She used to have a lot of respect for this man – because he was different, because he was gentler and seemed to treat his wife as someone with equal rights. Now she finds herself thinking he's just a man after all, a man who's shirking responsibility and finding rational-sounding reasons to hide his own fears. A man who can't make connections, a man whose heart goes untouched.

'It's your decision,' she says. 'I don't have a right to say anything at all. But Saniye is my friend – that's why I'm talking to you.'

Nine months after their conversation, Yılmaz flies to Malatya. It's his last chance to see his wife alive. Six months after her mastectomy they found cancer in her liver, spreading quickly.

Yılmaz cries a lot, mostly alone in a room, and Gül doesn't know if he regrets his decision to stay in Germany.

He flies back the day after the funeral, while Gül stays in Malatya and feels the pain echoing with Saniye's family and friends, grieves with her son, and reads the condolences on Facebook.

Yılmaz and Sevgi were the only ones who'd flown into the funeral from Germany, even though Saniye had a lot of friends from there. *But what would they have done here, anyway?* Gül thinks. *Most of them have never been here before; they wouldn't have known anyone, and they'd have felt out of place among all the mourners, among Saniye's friends and relatives. If any of them had come, it would probably have been their first time in Malatya. I'm so glad I came to see her here before. I'm so glad we could extend our ties from Germany all the way here.*

She cries a lot, perhaps because she senses it might soon be her turn.

Their few months in Germany are spent waiting for spring. Later, all the hours sitting in waiting rooms at the doctor's surgery are what Gül will remember most of all. Fuat has high cholesterol; there's a mention of early signs of coronary heart disease, and the cardiologist tells him to watch what he eats and to avoid animal fats.

'They want us to live like blades of grass!' is all he says. 'No alcohol, no fat, no going to bed late, and ideally no more gambling either. Apparently, you can grow older without these pleasures, but the question is, why would anyone want to?'

But after this visit to the cardiologist, Fuat simply stops smoking, and Gül is amazed by how easy he seems to find it. She's given up several times herself, but she's never managed more than six months without cigarettes. *He'll start again too, no doubt*, she thinks with a touch of relief.

Gül's hips are giving her grief and she has to go to the orthopaedist. Her left shoulder joint isn't right either – she can't stretch her arm straight up any more – but it doesn't bother her too much. *It's been a good while since I was at school*, she says. *I don't have much reason to put my hand up these days, and I've still got my right arm, so what's the problem?*

But her hips ache when she sits down, they ache when she stands up, they ache when she's lying in bed at night, and they ache on every flight and every long car journey. The doctor prescribes her physiotherapy, but it doesn't help much, and she neglects her exercises at home. She lives with the pain like a good friend she's known for many years, an old friend whose mistakes are ignored or have been long since forgiven.

Germany is for waiting. At one time they lived from summer to summer, waiting for their six weeks in Turkey, and though they spend eight months a year in Turkey now, the time in Germany still seems to drag.

'I'll come and drive you down,' says Ferdi one day. 'We can't have you travelling all on your own and having to change trains and whatnot. You can see Ceyda, stay the night at ours, and then I'll drive you back.'

Fuat sold his car in Germany and has a Renault in Turkey now, but he loves to talk about the days when he was still driving a Mercedes. Gül is daunted by the idea of taking the train, so she doesn't think twice before accepting.

Gül's hips hurt as she gets out of the car after the long ride to the clinic. She's surprised by how peaceful this place is, and a little later she's surprised again by how old the people on the streets are, how slow and tranquil things can be in Germany, how small everything is, how clean. There seems to be little connection between the places she's lived and this spa town, except for the language that's spoken here.

Once she's said goodbye to Ferdi, she spends a long while sitting at an ice-cream cafe with Ceyda; they're probably the only non-Germans in the place, aside from the Italian owners. The waiter uses lots of Italian words that Gül doesn't understand, even though he clearly speaks good German. The cafe feels as strange to Gül as the rest of this town, where her daughter has been staying for two weeks now.

Ceyda order two coffees from the waiter with gelled-back hair. She knows her way around here now; she takes charge. The treatment seems to be agreeing with her; she looks well and seems to feel freer. Sitting in this cafe on a dark brown chair with its faux leather seat, Ceyda talks more openly than Gül's ever known her to before.

'You remember,' she says, 'when I was little, Dede had that telephone with the crank. One day when I was on my own in the room, I cranked the handle and then hung up straight away. And then someone from the post office rang and you picked up and they asked you what we wanted. And when you hung up, I lied and said I hadn't cranked it.'

Gül frowns. It's so many years ago now, decades. If Ceyda hadn't mentioned it, she would have forgotten any memory of the crank telephone.

'I remember, yes.'

'And you told me back then that we mustn't lie. That you can never take your words back, and that if I lied, I'd be unhappy and I wouldn't sleep.'

The longer Gül thinks about it, the more clearly she remembers. She remembers seeing the look in Ceyda's eye back then, that look she often had when she was little, a look that said: *How can you tell me what to do? You left me on my own – you left me on my own for eighteen months before I'd even started school. You gave me the wound of my life.* Gül's eyes moisten.

'I did crank it, you know, but I never told you. I did crank it. But I wanted to keep it to myself.'

Gül shakes her head, smiling. *It doesn't matter*, her face says. *None of it matters; what matters is that we can sit together here now.*

They don't speak; they look at the round table with the coffee cups on top and the big ice-cream menu. They don't speak; they don't look each other in the eye – yet they are close to one another, each sensing the other's presence, feeling how their breath moves them, how the past moves them, how the moment moves them.

'I was so young when I got married,' says Gül, 'I was only a child myself. No one talked to us about it, no one explained how it worked, nobody warned us. If I'd known as much as I do today, I'd never have left you on your own in Turkey. It wasn't love I was short of, just sense. But I did leave – I left you. Your dede said to me once, "How should I know if Germany even exists? It's harder to believe in than heaven or hell." The people who went to Germany – for those left behind it was almost as if they'd died – because no one knew what Germany smelt like, what the air felt like on their skin, what it sounded like. These days we have the internet, these days you can picture all sorts of things; back then, though, it was all up to your imagination. That's why I wanted to invite Dede over to Germany, so he could finally see it for himself. But I did leave the two of you behind all those years ago. It was a mistake. For years, I thought my heart bled for eighteen months, but that's not right. It's still bleeding. And it wasn't just my heart. The past isn't over, it's still here with us. It tore a hole and now the blood is trying to seal up the wound. When there's a gash and everything seems to always be falling out of it, it's natural to want to keep something to yourself. But look, here we are, together – we're breathing, we're talking, we've no bad blood. Thanks be to God.'

'Thanks be to God,' says Ceyda, making no effort to keep her grief to herself, a grief which holds as much room for love as for pain.

Ferdi has taken the train to Frankfurt because he wants to buy a used car there, and once Ersin's asleep, Ceren and Gül have some time to themselves. *How wonderful to be able to spend the day with one daughter and the evening with the other*, Gül thinks.

'Do you remember Gesine?' asks Ceren.

'Of course, she was your German friend. She was always in and out of ours, like she was part of the family.'

She thinks about Jochen, the owner of the cleaning company who speaks such good Turkish, and she remembers how Ceren tried in vain to teach Gesine the language.

'I met up with her again.'

'Really?'

'Yes, I found her on Facebook. And last week she came to visit.'

'You didn't tell me anything about this.'

'I wanted to wait until you were here.'

'What's she doing now?'

'She lives in Berlin, in a neighbourhood with lots of Turks and Arabs. She's a social worker at a school. She's interested in everything Turkish: literature, politics, food, the language. Men. She's even had a few Turkish boyfriends, but she's never been married.'

Gül's mind immediately jumps to Fuat's mistress. Was she interested in Turks too? For whatever reason. Perhaps it wasn't that Fuat wanted a German woman; maybe *she* was the one who wanted a Turk. What do people want with Turkish men?

'She's even learnt a bit of Turkish,' Ceren explains. 'She raves about your food, and she's still embarrassed that I was never allowed to eat with her family. Mum?'

Gül tries to push the thought away.

'Do you think that's why she's interested in Turkey; because she knew us back then?'

'That's probably got something to do with it. She's been to Turkey a lot, too — Konya, Diyarbakır, Erzurum, Kars, Doğubeyazit, Trabzon, Rize. She's seen more of Turkey than we have.'

'Did you get on well?'

'It was nice, but it was strange somehow. She used to be more of a dreamer, I think. She had more of an imagination than me – I liked that. Now she talks about how much the Turks have enriched this country, but she's stubborn somehow. Listening to her, you'd think that Germany's on the brink of collapse because its citizens are so hostile and racist, so consumerist, so damaging to the environment, so cold to one another, because they eat so much meat, so much sugar, and so much processed food. Maybe she's only really interested in Turkey because she wants to believe that it's better than here.'

Three weeks after Gül's visit, Ceyda comes back from her cure. She feels relaxed and rested, like her energy's been replenished, and she's still drawing strength from the conversation she had with her mother in the ice-cream cafe. Duygu has said nothing in their daily phone calls, and now Ceyda has to sit down.

'This is Germany,' says Duygu. 'And he's twenty-one. I told him it wasn't a good idea. I told him he should go about it differently, but he didn't listen to me. And I didn't want to tell you while you were away. Mum?'

Ceyda looks at her hands. They look younger now she hasn't picked up a cigarette packet for five weeks, she thinks.

'Mum. Say something, please.'

'What?'

'Anything.'

'We've lived under the same roof for twenty-one years. We're all still alive. For years, I couldn't watch him sleep because I was working nights. But we should be grateful. Those were good times. Now I've got to let go, and he has to build his own life with Jennifer.'

Duygu hears her mother pushing the pain down, holding back her tears, fighting. But she also hears the sincerity in her words. She goes to her room to cry. Out of relief, out of joy, out of compassion for her mother – she can't be sure which.

A few days later, Fuat and Gül decide to give up their flat in Bremen and spend their few weeks in Germany in Timur's now empty room.

It's your own life, but you forget so much. There are some things you don't think about for decades, and it's as if the words, the sounds, the light have disappeared out of time, even though they're there as long as the people who shared them are still living. Perhaps even longer.

Gül was a newlywed and living with her in-laws when she met Suzan, the first friend she'd made since she left her childhood behind her. Suzan, whose husband was in prison on false charges. Suzan, who used to complain that her children needed a father, and who moved to Duisburg with her husband when he was finally released. Suzan was an older friend who always stood by Gül, supporting her and opening her eyes. She lived in Duisburg in an apartment block with Italians and complained that it wasn't worth learning German because the Germans hardly talk. After a while she moved to Naples and stopped coming home even for the summer. They wrote to each other for many years, but at some point, they lost touch. Gül keeps Suzan's letters in her big trunk, along with all the others. This trunk is the only thing she has brought from her flat in Bremen to put in Timur's old room. It's a big wooden chest, filled with letters, keepsakes, her wedding dress and the suit Fuat wore, along with a couple of photo albums and a woollen blanket that belonged to her mother. She can remember some of the letters very well – she spent weeks carrying them around with her and reading them again and again. When she shuts her eyes, she sees the coats and cardigans she'd be wearing when she stuffed the crumpled letters in her pockets.

Some days she spends hours sinking into these old letters, immersing herself in a past that sometimes seems dipped in soft evening light. She hasn't forgotten the pain, the ache of the past, the burdens she had to carry, but they no longer seem as heavy from here, even though she can well remember how it all felt at the time.

I've learned that a lot just passes us by, that it doesn't seem so important from a distance, she says to herself. *And I've grown stronger, I've grown stronger with every load I've had to carry.* But she thinks of the tale of Nasrettin Hoca, when he gave his donkey a little less to eat from one day to the next. In the end, the hoca says: 'Just when the donkey was about get along without any food at all, it died!' Perhaps Gül will collapse right at the moment when she thinks she can shoulder any burden.

Every day, sitting at the kitchen table with the letters in her hands, she travels into the past. She often arranges the letters by person, looking out of the window and holding imaginary conversations with each of them. The sound and the light from those days haven't vanished, all of it is still there and it resonates; it resonates and it binds her to those people.

The friendship request arrives when Gül is sitting in front of her computer, having spent the last two days with Suzan on her mind. Tears prick Gül's eyes. She hasn't seen Suzan for over forty years, and now, just when she's been thinking about her, the world seems to have turned so they can get back in touch. Suzan looks old in her profile picture. Gül thinks for a moment. Suzan must have been in her mid-twenties when she met her, about ten years older than Gül. No wonder she had so much good advice, no wonder she could see so much so clearly and understand things better than her. Ten years older than Gül – that means she must be in her mid-seventies now. She doesn't live in Italy any more; these days, she lives in a small holiday complex on the Aegean, which she moved to five years ago after her husband died. Her children are still in Italy and hardly speak a word of Turkish. Their children have long since grown up, and one of Suzan's granddaughters is married to a German but lives in a village near Rome.

So many years in Germany, Suzan writes, *how did you cope?* She writes that she'd love to see Gül, for as long as God neglects to ask for his servant back. *Who knows how many days each of us is allotted? There is much we've seen and heard and said; our hearts have pumped so much blood, we could give our names to whole oceans.*

Gül suggests they meet up in their hometown in spring.

I haven't been there for such a long time, Suzan replies. *It would be a mistake to go back and see what's become of the place. I turned away from it; I gave up my inheritance. I spent so long there waiting for Murat to get out of prison, I never want to go back.*

Gül is surprised and hesitates before typing out her reply. *These keys*, she thinks, *they keep so much to themselves*. A pen could never hide anger or sadness, haste or even tiredness. The letters on the paper speak of writing, they speak of distance and closeness. A keyboard betrays nothing, it makes you lonely even as it helps you connect to others. It lets you forget the distance, the time it takes to get from here to there; it's faster, but it can't carry the feelings with it.

I'll come, Gül writes. *I'll come to visit you. We'll see one another at last. And until then, we'll see each other on here. Every day.*

Perhaps, like Gül, Suzan finds herself leaning back a little now, to keep her tears from landing on the keys.

Gül's hip is aching. Of course it's aching; it's a long coach ride to Izmir – nine hours through the night. The coaches are more modern than they used to be; the seats are more comfortable and they have clean toilets these days, but Gül is scared of the confined space. The night air, the vibrations of the diesel engine, the smell of the rest stops, the free tea given out by the bus company, the water hoses attached to broom handles to clean the front windows, the puddles in the parking spaces – Gül is used to all of it, but it's the first time she's been on a coach trip alone at night.

Fuat didn't want to come with her; why would he, what would he do with himself while two old girlfriends were busy catching up? Gül had been afraid of taking the long journey all on her own, even though she ends up in a seat next to another woman, as the man assured her she would when she bought the ticket. The woman is a young student who falls asleep early on and doesn't wake up at the rest stops. Gül is scared; the country is so big, so dark, so wide. She's scared she might get left behind at one of the stops – maybe the coach will drive off without her and the woman next to her won't notice she isn't back in her seat. She dashes to the toilet, but only once she's memorised the coach's registration number.

I'm so old now, she thinks, *but that fear of getting lost has never left me. That fear, which always finds me and walks with me, like it did when I didn't know the way to work, or at the job centre, in the corridors of office buildings and factories; and like it does today on my way to embrace someone I've missed for so long. My reasons for going places have changed, but the fear is still the same – even though I've got a mobile phone now and could call someone for help whenever I wanted to.*

Early the next morning in Izmir, Gül has to ask for directions at the coach station before making it onto the minibus that stops where Suzan lives. She's barely slept; she's nervous and excited, becoming more excited with every step she gets closer to Suzan. She tries to remember how Suzan smells, and she wonders how the years will have changed her.

When she reaches the holiday village, she dials Suzan's number; she doesn't have the exact address. Suzan's phone rings and rings, but no one picks up. After the fourth or fifth ring, Gül wonders whether Suzan's still asleep – but it's past ten o'clock. After the sixth or seventh ring, she tells herself Suzan's an old woman – perhaps she's just not very fast on her feet. On the eighth or ninth, she wonders if something might have happened to her. And what she should do next.

'Gül, welcome! How lovely to see you.'

Gül turns, phone in hand, to see Suzan behind her. The two of them hug, Suzan still holding the stick she was leaning on.

They let go, look each other in the face and then hug again. Gül's mouth is dry; she doesn't know what to say, but even if she did know, her tongue would be frozen.

It takes a good minute of hugs, amazement and joy until Gül can say: 'Suzan, wonderful! Did you come here especially to welcome me? You didn't have to.'

Suzan looks older than she does in her profile picture; her cheeks are hollow and wrinkled, her body gaunt, almost threatening to disappear inside Gül's hugs, but her eyes are all aglow.

'Who knows if I'll still be here next time and if I'll be able to pick you up,' she says. 'It's not far from here. Come on, we'll get a taxi to my place.'

'How long were you waiting?'

'Not long. Come on, my lovely.'

Over the next few days, the two women sit on the house's small veranda, drinking espresso made in Suzan's machine, smoking and talking. Forty years is a long time, and twenty years have passed since they last exchanged letters, they realise; a lot has happened. Each of them tries to tell the other what kind of life she has led away from home.

Gül planned to stay five days, but those days turn into two weeks, two weeks that aren't enough because there's no quenching their eyes' and ears' thirst; two weeks in which they feel like long-separated sisters; two weeks in which they sleep well and wake up without a care, in which every word, every gesture, every glance, every cigarette, every espresso seems to express the fullness of life. Two weeks in which they look back – at tears and pain, separation and suffering, at joy and happiness, fights and making up; two weeks in which they get to feel like old people who have found peace, mild as a first summer night but far brighter.

Two weeks in which they eat tiramisu, pasta with chickpeas, stuffed artichokes, and tomato and aubergine dishes Gül has never tried before. Gül understands that Italy was something very different to Suzan than Germany was to her; even the food she eats has changed. Back then, Suzan moved to Naples with the woman next door. She lived among Italians, learned their language, adopted their habits and customs, ate with them, laughed and cried with them, shared table, roof and bread.

Gül can't help remembering the waiter in the Italian ice-cream café, but surely not all Italians are like him.

'I couldn't have done it in Germany,' Suzan says. 'The Germans are different, and anyway there are too many Turks in Germany, so everyone thinks they know right away what you're like. There are hardly any Turks in Italy, and I had Maria as my friend. It would have been much harder without her, I'm sure. People go to Germany without knowing anyone from there.'

'Why did you come back?' Gül wants to know. 'You don't want to go back to your hometown, you didn't visit Turkey for years, your children have built their lives in Italy, your grandchildren are there. So what are you doing here on the Aegean? I don't understand.'

'I wanted to live by the sea.'

'But they've got plenty of sea in Italy. When I listen to you, I can hear how your heart has drifted far away from this country, from the scent of the Anatolian earth, the sound of our songs; you don't feel the need to eat the food of your childhood. I don't understand what wind blew you here.'

'Maria died, Murat died, the children left the house long ago, and I started dreaming every night of speaking Turkish. A whole year, I spoke Turkish in my dreams every night. After that I sold up and moved here. That was three years ago. Then on one single night I dreamed I was speaking Italian, one night, and the next day I looked for you on Facebook and found you. But you're right, I moved away from everything; I'd simply swept this country out of my heart, the place where I spent so much time apart from my husband, and it didn't leave a gap. I didn't nurse any great yearning like you did, and I didn't feel pain at the separation. We didn't get rich like we might have done in Germany, but we had a good life. And then it was the sound of the language that brought me back here, even though I love Italian, even though I like hearing and speaking it. One language, one person, that's what they say. I wanted to come back to the language I heard in my mother's belly.'

'You came here… to die,' Gül says.

Suzan laughs; she laughs often.

'Yes, probably. But I'm not in any rush. The past is over. We're made out of time, and the only time that counts is what we've got ahead of us. Time is a river, and we are that river. If you look around yourself, everything else is dry.'

No one is alone – not ever, no matter what happens, no matter how they feel. There are always others carrying the same burden, or even more. We're not alone. Suzan's brothers and sisters also argued over their inheritance, and it made no difference that she relinquished her share. They took it as arrogance, as a means for stirring the others up against each other, as a lack of sisterly love, as selfishness. We're never alone; there's always someone else whose shoulders feel just the same as ours do. But we still have to carry our cares ourselves.

Three days after returning home, Gül wonders how life could have seemed so easy to her on the Aegean. The past isn't over; she's still bleeding into the river of time, staining it red right up to her feet. All she can do now is look away.

Two years ago, a businessman from Izmir bought the summer house and its orchard at auction. He's never been seen around town, and he's never had any work done on the house. Now Melike is living in the new summer house and the old one is empty. The businessman granted her the right to live there, apparently. She tells anyone willing to listen that she happened to meet him in Izmir, and he was so tickled by the coincidence that he wanted to let her live there until he uses the house himself.

A businessman from Izmir – what would he want in Anatolia? The whole thing stinks, but that doesn't change the fact that Melike is living in the summer house – without the neighbours blanking her, without anyone saying a word against her.

Melike crosses the road when she sees Gül coming. Gül remembers how she used to think she'd always forgive her sister, always do anything to make up with her. She was wrong about that.

Gül rarely speaks to Sibel these days, but she still wonders why she's got their father's tin cup. It's been years since she's seen Nalan, and she only talks to Emin on the phone on religious holidays and his birthday. Melike and Emin are no longer on speaking terms, or that's what she's heard. Nalan and Emin don't speak either, but Sibel and Nalan call each other regularly, whereas Emin hasn't called Sibel for two years. The stories Gül hears sometimes contradict each other; apparently Sibel and Emin see each other often in Istanbul, where Sibel is thinking of exhibiting her paintings after all.

Eventually, Gül calls Emin.

'Remember how little I was when you got married and left the house,' he says. 'Whatever it is you girls can't share, whatever baggage you're carrying around from the past, it has nothing to do with me.'

'But Melike is living–'

'Gül, I don't want to talk about it. Don't be cross with me. How's Ceren? What's Ersin up to?'

'Let's not go digging up old business,' Sibel says when Gül visits her and brings the conversation round to the summer house.

It's not old business, she wants to say. *It's new, it's all still so new. There are fresh wounds in our parents' blood*, she wants to say – but she thinks of Suzan's words and holds her tongue.

'Just forget it,' her friend had told her. 'You'll never come back together, with or without your summer house. Forget it, don't hold onto it, let it go.'

Time doesn't flow like water; it's not a river that we are part of too, Gül thinks now. *Time is like light. As soon as it's here, it's everywhere at once; it's not a river you can step into at one point or another. Everything's here at the same time: the child I was when my father threw the spoon at the wall, the young woman leaving her daughters behind to board a train for Germany, the worker in the wool factory, the patient in a hospital bed while her father's dying. It's all here at the same time; nothing has ever been lost or just flowed past. Perhaps the future is here too, but we can't see it yet because it's shining too brightly. Because at the end of the future the light is waiting, the one we'll all walk into when we step out of time.*

It's all here at the same time – but if Gül doesn't think of the dark places, the shadows, the hidden nooks, the pain that is never lit up, then she feels better. She has to make an effort, but bit by bit she manages to push the bad thoughts away. She thinks of the light in Suzan's laughter, the light of the Aegean, of the moments when her light and the light of another person overlap and shine brighter than that of a single life.

'No wonder people think so badly of the Turks here,' says Ceren.

Gül feels instantly attacked.

'Why? What is it that we do?'

'What *don't* we do? Mum, you must know the stories. People who claim child benefit for kids who live in Turkey and not here, or for kids who aren't theirs but who they just pretend are theirs on paper. People who don't want to send their kids to German schools. People who send their kids to school without breakfast, who force their eight-year-old daughters to wear headscarves, who don't care whether their kids learn German or not. People who use every lie and ruse under the sun to scrounge benefits or to pay a little less, wanting to appear ultra-smart, like they're the slyest foxes in the country, and not just shameless liars.'

'But we're not like that. You know we're not.'

'Yes, we were brought up to be honest. Even though Baba always thinks he's so crafty. But I'm not talking about us, am I?'

'You said, "the Turks here".'

'Yes, we're not all the same. But if someone's lying and cheating and trying to game the system, it always turns out to be a Turk. They're the ones who stand out. They're the reason we've got a bad reputation in this country. It's our own fault.'

'But it's just a few, isn't it? We can't be responsible for them.'

'When I was at uni in Turkey, I used to get people to forge my signature on the register, and I used to do it for others too. I saw corruption, bribery, all sorts of tricks, but I also saw what people were like in the village where Mecnun and I lived. They would share everything they had with us. But here…'

'What?'

'I never saw this much dishonesty in Turkey – it's as if lying is our national sport. It's like we've come here to prove that we're smarter than the Germans; finding loopholes everywhere, ways to cheat people and outsmart the whole country. One of my students' mums complained that she got a flat-rate phone plan in Turkey and now they've told her she can only make four hours of calls a day.'

Gül looks at Ceren, perplexed.

'Four hours per day.'

'But if it's a flat rate, you can use it 24 hours a day, can't you?'

'Four hours, Mum. And that's just one example. We've always got to take advantage of everything here, looking for ways to get the most out of everything. Kids return to school from their summer holidays one week late, and their parents haven't the faintest shred of guilt. "One week," they say, "what's one week in the face of our longing? One week – you're not going to get kept behind for the sake of one week." Or they lie and say, "We broke down in Edirne, just before the border." Or: "The plane was overbooked. We missed the flight because the taxi driver got lost." They've no shame; they're never shy to come up with some excuse or other.'

'But—' Gül starts up, but she doesn't get far. The topic's got Ceren stoked up.

'You must have seen it too, Mum. You know what some people are like. And I can see it now at work, I can see it from the outside – I can't help but judge it. There are children who are the third generation of their family to live in Germany, but they speak worse German than Ersin, even after four years. This is Germany, they have to at least speak the language.'

'It's not like the Germans put any effort into helping those kids' grandparents learn the language,' says Gül now. 'You remember how they wouldn't let me onto the German course.'

'Yes, but that doesn't mean people can just refuse to learn the language.'

'Maybe you're right,' says Gül, 'but don't forget how hard it was for us. It's not like they exactly welcomed us with open arms. I told you about Suzan.'

Ceren thinks for a moment. And then she nods. 'You're right,' she says, 'you can't be one-sided about it. Perhaps it's no one's fault. But even so, the things I see as a teacher… it's unbelievable. Some of us behave poorly here, really poorly.'

A few days after this conversation, two men die in a caravan, and a woman is arrested. The three of them are thought to have been targeting and killing people, almost all of them Turks. Gül thinks about what Serter said all those years ago on Factory Lane: *they're hatching plans; we need to arm ourselves.*

Gül sees the woman's picture. Apparently, she and the two men operated underground for years. Gül thinks: *But her hands and feet look healthy; she's not ugly or disfigured. Why would this woman do such a thing? Who knows what must have happened for her to get to this point? We can never say, 'Oh, I couldn't do that.' It all depends on the circumstances. Perhaps I could have been a murderer, too. Or even a prostitute. Life could have had me wandering alleyways, it could have pushed me into dark corners I felt trapped in. I might have got a divorce like Ceyda. I might never have come to Germany. I might have been born into a family like Can's, into an environment where my idea of right and wrong was completely different. I might have learnt to swim. Or to swindle. I might have grown up with both my mother and my father by my side. I might have chosen a different husband.*

At least one of these thoughts grates in her head; she senses that there's something not right with it and she listens to herself, quietly, to work out what it is. *Might I have become a murderer? Yes. Might I have got a divorce? Yes. Might I have learned to cheat and lie? Yes. Might I have grown up with my mother and my father? No*, she thinks, *that couldn't have happened.* I was born into this blood because something drew me here. Perhaps it was my spirit. I belong to this family, which has broken apart, which has had to bear death and separation; I am part of this melody, the song I must have heard even before I was born.

Her ears aren't what they used to be, her eyesight has deteriorated, and she gets tired quicker; she makes sure to gauge the height of any sofa and avoids sitting down anywhere she knows she'll struggle to get back up. All her energies seem to wane with age, but the ear that hears this melody grows stronger.

People are like raindrops – some fall in the mud, some fall onto rose petals. But Gül thinks she can hear the rain better now, the melody of her blood and the melody of all breath. You might land on a rose petal at first, but eventually you'll drop onto the moist earth and disappear inside it. Everyone is connected, even if we feel like raindrops. And yet each of us has our own song, our own path.

She feels sorry for the woman she sees on the news, whose path looks to have been a hard one. She feels sorry for everyone who has lost a loved one because of these three people. *Lord, is there any creature on this earth, a single one, whose path is easy?*

Fuat opens the door.

Can lives in the countryside now, near Lüneburg. Gül hasn't seen him since the wedding and she's glad; she'd been worried her years of deception might come to light at the wedding reception.

It seems like deception to her, even if she often still tells herself she didn't do anything wrong. She kept it a secret from Fuat. But she also kept her daughters' transgressions from him while they were still small. *That was to protect Ceyda and Ceren, though; I'm kidding myself if I say it was about me*, she thinks.

She doesn't need to tell Fuat that she's recently become friends with Can on Facebook. Nor does she need to tell him that he has invited her to come to visit him and his family. How would he ever find out, anyway? But she can't go; there's no excuse she could use to visit Can, as much as she'd like to see his children. It's one thing to go and sit in a shopping centre café for two hours, but going all the way to Lüneburg is something else altogether. *The bigger the effort, the greater the deceit*, she thinks, *maybe*. She finds herself wondering how much effort Fuat must have put in back then, when he was up to no good. And whether the whole thing might have been that woman's idea in the first place. But does that take away from his betrayal? His denial, his cowardice?

She hasn't had to deny anything, but what would she do if someone found out about her chats with Can and confronted her? *I'd admit it*, she thinks. But she knows no matter how confident she is of that fact, life could find a way to make her deny it. The less she thinks of Can, the quieter her conscience is, but when he suggests they Skype, she still finds a way to pick a time when she won't be disturbed.

'Auntie Gül, it's so lovely to see you. How are you?'

'Oh, don't ask me that, son. So much has happened since we last spoke. How about you?'

'I'm good, really good. Come on, I'll show you our house and the kids.'

Can lives in a large detached house with a huge garden. He has two more sons now, who know no Turkish except for a few swearwords. And he's proud. Gül's never seen him this proud before, even when he used to tell her about the latest deals he'd pulled off. She's happy for him, but once she's done telling him her story, he says: 'Auntie Gül, I feel so sad for you, really I do. But it's like I always told you: money is what counts. Your sister clearly gets that – that's how she came up with the whole businessman excuse. She hasn't tried to take the straight path, that's not how the world turns.'

'My son, look at your children, look at your wife. Do you think they'd sell you for money?'

'No. But they're probably the only four people on this earth who wouldn't. Your daughters and your husband wouldn't sell you either. You can never be sure about anyone else.'

Gül thinks about Öykü's daughter and how great the pain must be when it's your own child who has robbed you. Gül tries to agree with Can, even though there's a voice inside her that knows for certain that it's not money that makes the world turn, it's the love and pain that are handed down from one generation to the next. It's the pain that sometimes chooses money to make itself felt.

Talk. There's always lots of talk in the neighbourhood; it's full of rumours, malicious words, praise, slander and news of deaths. The same goes for Facebook too. Gossip, everywhere. Life and the internet aren't as different as we think.

From the point when Zuhal posts the picture online with an invitation to a class reunion, to the point when Gül hears about it, only twenty-three hours go by. A picture of thirty-six children in school uniforms, all the boys with short crops, all the girls with bows in their hair. Gül sits with this photo of her primary school class for a long time, spending over an hour trying to remember her classmates' names and personalities. She thinks back to the tricks they played, to the times the teacher slapped them with the ruler, to her first two years at school, when they still lived in the village and all five classes were taught in the same room. She remembers how shocked she was by the size of the school in town, how she was scared she might get lost there.

She remembers Zuhal, the woman who posted the picture; she used to sit right in front of her, and Gül admired her long thick plait of black hair. Zuhal was the daughter of Eren the cobbler, who had seven daughters and apparently always complained: *Your cock can be brimming with strength but if you're cursed, your house just fills up with cunts.* Gül remembers being unable to read properly when she joined the new school in the third year. The village teacher had never noticed, because Gül knew the texts in the school book by heart.

She remembers the girl who sat next to her: Özlem, the general's daughter. When Gül's grandmother accused Gül of stealing the köfter, Özlem backed her grandmother up by saying Gül had handed it out to her friends at school. Neither accusation was true. Gül can still remember sitting by the stream back then, alone for the first time. All alone. No one believed her, and there was no one she could tell the truth to. She remembers it took her three days to convince her father, at least, that she hadn't been stealing. But he couldn't accuse his mother of lying. What kind of truth was something that only two people knew? And how often has she told that story since, in how many places, to how many people? Not all that often – when do you find someone you want to talk to about your loneliness? But she has told it, that story, and the light of her words have spread, and the truth expanded, shining brighter now than back then, and the centre of that brightness is the pain of that little girl she once was. Gül finds Özlem in the photo and wonders what has become of her. She wonders whether she'd want to talk to her old classmate, whether she'd confront her. Whether Özlem even remembers what happened. And whether, now, she could explain why she slurred Gül's name back then.

She remembers she liked Özlem at first – but not the girl's mother, because she laughed so often, and her laugh sounded false. She remembers how proud her grandmother was to be friends with Özlem's mother, the general's wife.

In those days, Gül still knew people who happened to be rich. They were neighbours, parents of her classmates, and there was the shopkeeper who drove the only car in town. It was only later, once she'd moved to Germany, that there was suddenly no one else around with a lot of money. It wasn't the brave who left, as Yılmaz said; it was the poor among the brave, and the desperate among the poor.

In Germany we were all the same, Gül thinks. *We came from all over the country, and we had different accents and customs and food, but we all earned the same and had nothing at home. Maybe that meant I learnt less and saw less. Because there was no diversity among the Turks in Germany. Maybe Ceren was right: in a way, we are all the same. Maybe I'd see and learn a lot if I went to this reunion, but I don't know if I want to see Özlem.*

But no – no, that's not it. She doesn't know if she belongs there in the first place. She's in the photo, even though she's never owned a copy and could have sworn no such photo even existed. She's in the photo but she didn't finish the last year of school, she failed her leaving exams, and she doesn't feel like she belongs. She wonders whether anyone would recognise her at all.

You've grown so old, she thinks. *You've seen so much, been through so much, and still there are moments when your feet aren't firmly rooted; still you think you might fall, even though you never have done. You've stumbled, you've lost the ground beneath your feet, your only anchor was anger and pain; but you've never fallen. Only grown tired. Only struggled. Only doubted. But never fallen. What is there to lose? Go. Just go to the reunion.*

Perhaps Melike wasn't lying after all. Perhaps the story about her right to live in the house was really true, including the part about meeting the businessman on the street in Izmir. But perhaps it was a set-up and the two of them fell out later on. That same year, the land with the two summer houses on it is divided into three plots, each of which fetches almost the same price as they got for the whole parcel a few years ago. The summer houses are torn down, to be replaced by new bungalows.

There's plenty of talk about it, but Gül doesn't know whose words she can trust and whose she can't. The house of her childhood is gone, and someone has made a lot of money out of it. The tie to her brother and sisters has broken, and Gül no longer has the strength or the will to change that. It's not just their relationships that have cooled off; her anger has, too.

More than once, Gül has picked up the phone to call Melike, a voice inside her telling her it's the right thing to do. Telling her that now it's all over, they could try to start afresh. But there's also the voice that says there's no point, that siblings can't reconnect once they've reached the place her family at is now.

Aziza recognises Gül before she's all the way through the door and comes straight towards her with open arms.

'Gül, am I right? The blacksmith's daughter. I'm so glad you're here too.'

'Aziza,' Gül says, returning her hug.

'You weren't at our reunion two years ago,' Aziza says.

'No.'

'What luck that we've found you. Come on, you have to tell me how things turned out for you.'

Sitting down, Gül lets her eyes wander while she speaks. She couldn't remember all the names in the photo; in fact, there were some children she couldn't remember at all.

Aziza pumps her with questions, shows her around, introduces her to other people she seems to see more often. Gül doesn't know why Aziza is being so markedly friendly to her. She can't remember them being close friends at school. On top of that, Aziza seems a bit patronising towards the others. What is she up to? How come Gül gets the feeling Aziza is sincere, but at the same time she mistrusts her? Gül isn't used to getting such preferential treatment.

For the first two hours, Aziza barely leaves Gül's side and goes to great lengths to make her feel comfortable. Two hours in which Gül keeps looking around for Özlem, who told her on Facebook that she'd be coming. In the end, Gül finds herself sitting at a table with a piece of dry cake, wondering how much time she'll have to watch the others before someone notices she's on her own and comes to join her. It's not much, but something in her grows soft and warm and radiates to her fingertips, despite the slight sense of discomfort she can't shake off. She feels good in this room full of people she once sat with decades ago. She feels good, even though she doesn't know all their names, and though she detects a hint of competition between some of them. Even though she's still not sure most of them recognise her. Though she thinks she was the only one who didn't pass the exams back then. Though it took her a long time to feel comfortable at school as a child. There's still something here that feels like she's returning to a kind of happiness.

A woman sits down next to her.

'Gül,' she says, 'you're Gül, aren't you? You went to Germany, didn't you?'

'Yes.'

'I'm Bilge,' the woman says.

'Bilge,' Gül repeats slowly. 'Bilge, the one who always came to school without a pencil.'

She instantly regrets saying it, but Bilge smiles. 'Yes, that's me… You and your husband went abroad, you had a cross to bear,' she continues. 'And now you're back, right?'

'We still go to Germany for a month or two in the winter, but most of the time we're here.'

'May God let no one suffer abroad. I'm glad you're back. I wanted to talk to you earlier, but you were so caught up in conversation with Aziza. You two must see each other a lot.'

'No. The last time I saw her was more than fifty years ago. But she lives near our apartment on the coast, so we're going to meet up some time.'

Bilge nods as if she'd expected that answer. 'Aziza doesn't talk to just anyone,' she says. 'When she married a mayor, she started thinking she was better than us. She sticks to the bare basics with most of us; I'm not good enough for her these days. What did you do? Did you get rich in Germany? Decades of working abroad – you and your husband probably have a whole company here somewhere. But you don't boast about it. Some people learn modesty abroad.'

Gül thinks about it. Was Aziza being so friendly because she thinks Gül is rich? Or is Bilge jealous? Or is she just trying to find out what drew Aziza to Gül, like Gül wonders too?

'No,' Gül says. 'We have enough to eat and a little more than that, thank the Lord, but we didn't get rich.'

'We really must meet up when you're back at your summer house,' Aziza says, slightly too loudly, when she says goodbye later. 'You've got my number – call me. I'm afraid I've got to go now.'

Gül notices the sidelong glances she gets from everyone who heard Aziza. She feels flattered, but she knows she won't call Aziza.

She talks to Dursun, Günay, Ramazan, Gaye; she talks, exchanges memories, tells them about her daughters and grandchildren, about Germany, Factory Lane, Herr Bender, about Saniye, about Fuat's weight-loss powder, about their summer house, about Öykü, but she doesn't mention her brother and sisters.

It's well past midnight when the last of the group make their way home. Gül has talked a lot; her head is buzzing pleasantly from the conversations, and she feels light. She's one of the last seven – two men and five women – who squeeze into a car. Men at the front, women at the back. Gül is the fattest, but Leman and Şevval are both very thin, and Leman sits on Şevval's lap.

Gül has learned that Özlem is severely ill and probably doesn't have long to live. She's in hospital in Ankara with liver cirrhosis. She's never drunk alcohol; it's cryptogenic cirrhosis, according to Derman, who became a nurse. Gül has never heard the word and can't keep it in her head long enough to look it up at home. She's impressed that people she went to school with know words like that, even though she understands the job calls for it.

Not until she's outside her own front door does Gül notice her hip didn't hurt at all when she got out of the car. The night air is cool, the stars are sparkling, and Gül thinks about whether to get her keys or her cigarettes out, to smoke before she goes inside. She can't decide, so she stays put on the spot, wondering when she last got home so late on her own. She doesn't know. Perhaps never. She wonders whether Fuat might have been as happy as she is now, back in the day when he used to come home in the early hours. Then again, even if he was happy, he was surely too drunk to notice.

Drunk on words alone, drunk on the past, drunk on having felt at home among so many people she knows and doesn't know at the same time, having felt better than she ever did as a schoolchild, drunk on everyone being so relaxed, drunk on feeling free, she stands outside her house on a July night in her hometown, tired and happy. Not because her daughters are doing well, not because her grandchildren are doing well, not because her work is done; a different kind of happiness.

She stands there, perhaps for three or four minutes, or maybe ten or fifteen; she stands in the velvet-blue night, swaddled in a coat of happiness. The cigarettes remain in her handbag.

Then she wonders what the neighbours would think if they saw her here like this. What they would say. But why would a neighbour look out of the window at this time of night? She takes out a cigarette after all but decides to smoke it at the kitchen table instead. To smoke out of sheer happiness. *Not because of yearning, anger or sleeplessness*, she thinks.

Her pillow is soft. Fuat doesn't smell of alcohol, her hip doesn't hurt. Sleep is like a blanket laid gently over her as her eyes are closing.

'A small wedding, Oma, really small, not like Ceren's,' Timur said on the phone. 'Just a trip to the registry office and then something to eat afterwards. We can't run to twenty people.'

'How many people are coming then?'

'Just Jennifer's two best friends, her mum, her aunt and her nan.'

'Is there something you're not telling me?'

'No, Oma. Why does everyone ask that? We just want to get married.'

At the wedding a few weeks later, Gül is astonished by how plain and understated everything looks. Jennifer doesn't look especially dolled-up; she's wearing a simple white dress that looks nothing like a wedding dress, and Timur has a tight black polo-neck on under his silky grey suit.

'Off to play football afterwards, are you?' Fuat says when he sees him.

'No, what makes you say that?'

'You've got your trainers on.'

'Opa, I'm not buying shoes I'll never wear again after today.'

Fuat shakes his head.

'None of this matters: the trainers, the fact he's not got a tie, the registry office, the signatures, even the vows. The important thing is that they're going to be happy together. There's no need to worry about the rest of it,' says Gül.

She imagined Jennifer's mother would be a slim, severe-looking woman, but Frau Scherzer is slightly plump and has brown hair, not blonde like her daughter. She seems uneasy, perhaps because she's surrounded by so many Turks, but she has given the couple her blessing, as far as Gül knows. Maybe that's because Timur is a police officer now, or perhaps she's changed her mind about Turks. Frau Scherzer's mother is a small woman, her greying hair coiled into a stiff bun. She's got dressed up for the occasion, and she reminds Gül a little of Auntie Tanja. She reaches out to Gül straight away, sitting next to her in the corridor of the registry office, and says: 'I'm happy they're getting married. I liked Timur right from the start. I know there were problems with my daughter, but that's kids for you. My other daughter has always been very trusting. But Marion's never been like that, not even when she was little. She thinks life's a battle and other people are a threat. That's probably why she joined the police. She's my daughter, I love her. What can I say?'

Gül doesn't understand every word, but she gets what the woman wants to say. She nods and says: 'I understand.'

And she understands more than just that. She understands why she sought out Gül and not Ceyda to unburden herself. She understands that what looks like racism might simply just be the fear that others are not like us. Or that they're just as bad as we are, perhaps. She understands that the only thing we can't escape is our own nature; our own melody is the one we're doomed to hear, and when we sing it, it can sound cold if we don't find peace within ourselves. She understands this, but even if Frau Scherzer could speak Turkish, Gül wouldn't find the right words. She simply takes the woman's hand. Frau Scherzer looks surprised at first, but then the two women sit there, hand-in-hand, until it's time for the vows.

Many of Fuat's decisions have proved to be of little benefit to Gül. She considers it an ironic twist of fate that he thinks buying the flat by the sea, which he pushed so hard for, was a mistake, while Gül has come to see it as her home.

'Pff, sun, sea and sand, barbecues, fish and rakı – it beggars belief how soon you get tired of it all,' he says. 'And that's where the boredom starts. What am I supposed to do in a place where they eat goats, and the heat flickers in the air so you can hardly step out the door, a place where no vineyards grow. Nope, I'm for our home province, the place I spent so many years missing.'

He buys grapes and presses his own wine in the cellar in their hometown, forcing one or more bottles on every visitor, every friend, every chance acquaintance he makes – generous as ever and always keen to impress. By the second year, his wine's already good enough for his reputation to spread through the town. Fuat is proud.

'Forty years of my life I gave to Germany,' he says, 'but I learnt more than just how to wash wool and how to stand at an assembly line. I learnt rigour, attention to detail, orderliness. I've not just whipped this up out of nowhere, I read books about winemaking, I educated myself. That's something we lack in this country: education and rigour.'

His wine's not as popular in the tower block by the sea as it is in his hometown; perhaps that's why he tends to get bored there. But perhaps it also has something to do with his new friend Erol, who was a general in the army and who Fuat comes to know because Erol loves his red wine. Erol speculates on the stock market and is quick to get Fuat interested in gambling for riches too. And so they often sit together, buying and selling securities, discussing the economy, risks, stock price developments, returns and funds, but also wine, football and expensive cars.

Following his success with the wine, Fuat hits upon the idea of distilling rakı and buys himself the equipment. He can hardly drink more than a glass of wine himself; his stomach can't take it. He gets all the more joy out of convincing others to drink. When it comes to cigarette smoke, though, he's not averse to complaining, now and then, that it burns his eyes and gives him a headache. He hasn't taken up smoking again, much to Gül's surprise.

Fuat can't stand to stay in the flat by the sea for longer than two weeks at a time. After that he has to get back to his cellar, for a few days at least. Gül, on the other hand, is happy when she's in the flat. She enjoys the air-conditioning, she likes it when her children and grandchildren visit, she always tells them about

Öykü, and she's glad of Öykü's company when her visitors have gone home.

When Gül visits Öykü, she can tell Öykü only turns on the air-conditioning because she's there. Gül never turns up empty-handed; sometimes she brings homemade pastries with her, sometimes cake, or yoghurt, sometimes yarn or wool. When Öykü goes over to Gül's, she often has a bag with the empty plates inside, but she always brings a little crocheted doily, or some lacework, a cardigan or some socks.

Öykü loves to hear the stories from Gül's childhood, about the rings under her mother's eyes before she died, about the many hours she spent with her father. Gül listens intently as her proud friend tells her about her life on the coast. She admires Öykü's strength and independence, but she knows she's not cut out for such things herself. Gül's demanded less space for herself in life than Öykü has, but perhaps that's just because she knew she needed others in order to feel like herself. Öykü doesn't seem troubled by loneliness; it's almost like she comes from another planet where it's possible to live without other people around you, where you can suffer blows without complaining, without licking your wounds and creeping into a corner. Öykü straightens up, opens her arms and surrenders.

It takes all sorts of people to make a world, and the Lord has made everyone different: each blood has its own melody, and every singer in the choir has their own voice. Gül doesn't envy Öykü's energy, and Öykü doesn't envy Gül's ability to make the people around her trust her and fill her house with love, conversation and life. Öykü doesn't envy Gül for the fact that she has enough money and that her hometown hasn't been destroyed beyond recognition. When Gül is with Öykü, she doesn't think about the summer house, her siblings or their disagreement.

Home is not where you're born, it's where you get your fill, so the ancestors say. Gül thinks back to the years in Germany, the years when she couldn't find any aubergines or pepper paste, no lamb, or thyme, no nigella seeds, no fenugreek, no sumac. Though she couldn't cook the way she would at home, she still managed to fill her belly, but she never, never had her fill.

Fuat complains about the locals who eat goat meat, which only ever gives him the runs, but Gül finds her cup is full here. It's not just a question of meals and ingredients; it's a matter for the eyes, and the heart.

Sometimes, when Gül sits on the balcony and lights a cigarette, she can hardly see the lighter flame, it's so bright. And when her daughters and her grandchildren are there, it can hardly get much brighter; she could be anywhere, she thinks, and she'd still call it home.

Gül and Öykü are drinking tea in Gül's flat. Fuat is busy back at home with his wine; the children and grandchildren are in Germany. It's late autumn and there are only a few pensioners left in the hotels a mile or so to the west. Many of the apartments in the blocks are empty because school has started again. Gone are the noise and the children's laughter echoing up from the swimming pool, the air conditioning is off, and Gül sometimes wonders by the by whether she'll survive the winter too. She doesn't like winter – for that reason alone, she'd like to see the light of spring again, stroking her the way waves brush against the sand. She'd like to die in autumn, once her work is done, when hands and feet and tongues have slowed down, when all there is to do is give thanks for the year's gifts and prepare for a time of darkness.

When the doorbell rings, Öykü looks at Gül with a question on her face.

Gül shrugs. 'I don't know who that could be at this time of day.'

She gets up and presses the buzzer. When the lift stops, she stands behind the door and looks through the peephole. Out of the lift comes Aziza. Gül is seized by nerves; she opens the door and sees Aziza beaming at her in high heels.

'Sorry to just drop in like this, I hope I'm not bothering you. I lost your number, but I was in the area, and I asked around a bit – it wasn't hard to find you.'

Gül's not sure what to think of Aziza turning up unannounced, here in the high-rise estate. The woman almost certainly imagined something else when Gül talked about a summer house, but that's just what you say, even if it's only a flat in a tower block. She doesn't know how Öykü will react; she always stays away when Gül has visitors. And she feels bad for not calling Aziza.

'No, no, it's no bother, not at all. How nice that you've found me, without my address. I've got a friend round, but come on in.'

'I don't want to interrupt anything,' Aziza says, but she's already slipped off her shoes.

'This is Aziza, a friend from my school days. This is Öykü, a neighbour,' Gül says, and immediately feels guilty. Öykü is so much more than a neighbour. Before the two of them can shake hands, she adds: 'One of the most precious people I've met over the past few years.'

Then she wonders whether Aziza might take offence to that.

'Aziza's husband used to be mayor of Silifke,' she tries to balance things out, sitting down only to get straight back up again.

'I'll fetch you a tea,' she says to Aziza, and heads for the kitchen. Now she scolds herself for leaving the two of them alone so soon. She knows Öykü won't mince her words if she's ever had an objection to the mayor of Silifke.

'Who's your husband? I probably know his name,' she hears her friend saying.

'Mithat Paraoğlu.'

Gül rushes back to the living room with the tray; Öykü gives her a quick glance and says: 'I do know him, of course. He's done a lot. A great deal.'

'Yes, my husband's a hard worker. How else would he have made it to the mayor's office?'

Gül doesn't know whether she's the only one who hears the undertone in Öykü's voice because she knows her so well, or if Aziza simply isn't sensitive enough to pick up on it.

'Have you known each other long?' Aziza asks.

'A few years,' Öykü answers. 'Four or five, perhaps.'

'Isn't she a wonderful person? I met her as a child, and then I didn't see her for fifty-seven years. But I never forgot her. Thanks to Facebook, we've found each other again now. There's nothing like knowing someone as a child. You see what a person is, in their core. And it's that core that you love. That's what's left when everything else is gone – work, appearances, clothes, all the drama we put on as adults.'

'There was no drama around here, in the old days,' Öykü says. 'We all dressed the same, worked the same, and even if someone had more money, the only thing to buy with it was rice, bulgur and perhaps a few goats. But that didn't mean we were children for all our lives. And then the whole world discovered they liked sweating, lying naked on the beach, drinking beer out of sand-coated bottles, and doing nothing all day except splashing in the sea and then lying back down on the beach.'

Aziza looks at Gül, who's absolutely helpless, and then gives a slightly fake laugh and says: 'Yes, the world has certainly changed. Lots of people come these days to enjoy our beautiful region.'

'Yes,' says Öykü. 'I ought to be grateful, I expect, because that's how I met Gül. But these people who call themselves holidaymakers or tourists – these people who only want to lie around, eat, drink and sleep – they took our village from us, our community, our lives. Yes, they gave us money in return, but it was like a summer rain; we were high and dry again before we could blink. Those people brought me Gül. She tells me her father often used to say: *Profit and loss are like brothers; they keep meeting over and over.* But I think they're more than brothers – they're twins, neither of them bigger or better than the other. Perhaps they're even more than twins; perhaps they're the very same person, but they look one way at times and another at others. I've gained a friend, but how much has been taken from me?'

'Yes,' says Aziza, 'we don't get anything for nothing in life.'

'Apart from the breath God gives us,' Öykü replies.

Gül feels responsible for keeping the peace, but she sees how much divides the two women and that a single conversation will never close that gap.

'If you don't mind,' Öykü says, 'I've got to go home and cook.'

'Oh, I hope I've not bothered you. I didn't mean to. Do stay, I'm leaving in a minute too.'

'No, no, I've got visitors coming. I was just about to go when you rang the doorbell.'

Gül is tempted to confirm that lie, but then she chooses to say nothing.

Aziza shows no sign of leaving and ends up having lunch with Gül, despite emphasising that she doesn't want to be any trouble. By the time she leaves it's early evening. Gül still can't understand why Aziza so obviously wants her company.

'She's lonely,' Öykü says the next day. 'She doesn't want to admit it, of course. And perhaps she feels guilty.'

'Guilty?'

'Her husband is an ox with no honour or shame. Everyone knows how many bribes he took. It's his fault – a good part of it – that everything fell victim to property speculation here. She's your school friend and I'm so old I don't get as angry these days, but otherwise… You know how I shouted at your sister on the street that time. Who'd have thought we'd ever see each other again and become friends? Then again, even back then I could tell something was different about you. Perhaps Aziza saw the same thing when you were children.'

'Don't get me wrong, but I had a nice time with her after you left yesterday.'

'We all want a place to rest from what she calls the drama. The whole world is a stranger; we come here and seek, we curse money and fate, we embroider pictures in the dark of loneliness, pictures no one can make out. We live in fear of missing out on love, comfort, money, we're afraid of loss and separation, we worry about our children – and we call it life. How long does it last? We have a few breaths in this world, and we spend them running around after things. God will take that gift back. You know, people think that they're clever, like that Aziza. They think they're God knows how wise. But they're not. Not even the ones who've read; they're not wise either. The Jews in our village told us how Moses brought ten commandments down from the mountain. That's what it says in our book too, but nowhere does it say what the commandments are. The Jews know the commandments, but they're not commandments at all; they're desires that come over every one of us. Taking the Lord's name in vain, having other gods, lying, killing, stealing, desiring, coveting. Why should Moses have needed forty days and nights to find that out? God forgive me, but I think the truth isn't written in books, and not in ours either. The stories we tell are just a mirror for our hearts. And those who can see straight into our hearts, they're reading the right book.'

'Why don't you write a book, if you're so clever?' Serter's ex-wife Mevlüde said to Gül all those years ago on Factory Lane. Gül has never felt particularly clever. *I crept inside my book and hid myself away, but word by word, they found me*, the old song goes. This winter, Gül has grown used to sitting in the kitchen in the evenings on her own – no cigarettes, no radio, no TV burbling away nearby, as is often the case in the daytime. She abandons this habit during the weeks she spends in Germany at Ceyda's, or when she has a visitor, but most evenings in the year she sits alone in the flat's open-plan kitchen and rarely moves, not troubling to turn on a light, her hands laid out in front of her on the table.

'What are you doing over there?' Fuat has asked a few times, and each time Gül replies: 'Sitting.'

'Sitting? It beggars belief! "Sitting," you say, like that's something a person can spend their time on, as if life was meant for time-wasting. Are you waiting for death already, or what?'

Gül won't be provoked. She doesn't feel any wiser when she sits here like this. Wise isn't the word for it. Clearer, maybe. Brighter, perhaps. Closer. Keener.

She sits and listens to something inside her, when it gets quiet, when, sometimes, the noises outside grow still and the thoughts inside her do the same; there's a silence of will and a silence of desire, and then she sees clearly. She sees which emotions sound right, how some of her thoughts move, break free sometimes, until they have nothing more to do with her, though she still feeds them with her attention.

If she sits quietly for long enough, she understands what it is that's out of tune with her voice and her melody. On these evenings in the kitchen, she finds herself drifting into something, something that might be the mid-point between her two hands.

Her eyes don't always stay dry on these evenings. Sometimes she floats to the source of some great pain. She remembers how it felt to leave her daughters behind with her mother-in-law, how it felt not to see them for a year-and-a-half. She sees now that she did the same as her own mother did. She left her children behind. She feels the anger she felt as a child, when she found out her mother was gone. Grief lies beneath this fury, and beneath that grief is loss. When she lost her mother, she lost that protection, that love, that sense of being safe in the world. Her mother was an orphan, a child who knew fury, grief and loss herself. Pain is passed on, like love, from one generation to the next; it changes its face, but it remains the same pain. Fatma lost her father and now she is alone in Turkey, while the rest of her family lives in Germany. Duygu and Timur grew up without a father, in a sense. Each of them knows the feeling of being left behind, of being alone. And they're not the only ones. This is not one family's pain; it is the pain of many families, perhaps all of them.

She seeks out the pain of knowing the summer house has been destroyed; she follows it into her childhood and sees that her father showed her such great affection because she rarely voiced any desire of her own. When he did scold her, which was rare, it was because she lost track of time or her chores while playing. As a child, she sees, she did everything for her father's love after her mother's love vanished so suddenly. She sees how she denied herself, how life and a desire for love have bent her this way and that. She sees that she still follows this strategy today, decades on from her childhood. How she's always put her own needs last, how she has hardly dared to take up space, to desire things for herself, how she has imposed boundaries on herself.

The more at peace she is in the evenings, the deeper she dips into the pain, and the more clearly she can see what happened. How the little child inside her still believes that all she has to do is take responsibility, be a good girl, and she'll be rewarded with love. How that explains why she has never left Fuat. Why she never could. She's only ever learnt how to make sacrifices.

But when she pursues these images, she sometimes comes to a point where everything softens, where every ache seems to come with its own balm. She sees that many slights have opened old wounds over the course of her life, but these wounds are from the same time the light comes from, the light that has streamed through her life.

Sometimes she follows this light. She sees herself with her daughters, sees the smiles on their faces, the happiness there; she sees how she might help them, how she might reach out a hand to them. She sees herself with her grandchildren, hugging them to her chest; she remembers conversations and how words have bound her to other people. She remembers the trust that people have granted her, the respect they have shown her. She thinks about the night she stood outside the front door after the school reunion, about her stay with Suzan, her conversations with Öykü, and the hours she spent at the restaurant in Malatya with Saniye. She looks at her hands and is glad that the Lord gave her a knack for connecting with people.

She still exists in time, and on these evenings she senses that it's all the same: the past, the future, the pain and the joy; nothing is gone, nothing simply slips by, nothing is forgotten.

She remembers how she prayed she might grow old enough that every belief would fall away, that every illusion and every lie would end. She's not quite there yet, but the shadow that Gül casts on her own life, when she looks around, grows ever smaller on these evenings, which give her strength and sometimes brighten her mornings before she goes to sleep. One day, the shadow will vanish entirely into the light that is waiting for her, at the end of the future.

Thank you:

Seher Özdoğan, Tufan Özdoğan, Gülten Ertekin, Vedat Ertekin, Nermin Turan, Nesrin Demirhan, Maria Steenpass, Markus Martinovic, Tolga Özdoğan, Lutz Freise, Ralf Gerhardi, Christian Asmussen, Georg Hasibeder

Translators' Notes

Dear Gül,

I've known you so long that you feel like part of my family, and now it's time to say goodbye. I first met you in 2005, in *The Blacksmith's Daughter*. To begin with, you weren't even born; that twinkle in Timur's eye, the way he looked at Fatma… And now you're my mother's age, at a guess – I'm never quite sure how old you are, but that's part of your charm.

As a translator, I often feel the process of working on a novel is unbalanced. We immerse ourselves so deeply in our books, revoicing their words, and that gives me a sense of closeness to the writers. Yet often, I meet the writer only once, if at all. And even that is unusual for many translators; it's easier for me because I live in Germany. Our communications are usually brief – I'll send them questions as I'm going along or all in one go at the end.

With Selim, that's always been different. He and I met many years ago at an event and got on really well. We've talked philosophy and politics, he's slept on my sofa and we've exchanged music tips. I love talking to him on the phone, the slow way he speaks; never in a hurry, always happy to veer off the subject, lots to laugh over. I've met his partner, he's met my son; now, via Zoom, I've seen inside his flat and his mother's summer home.

But with you, Gül, it's different again. Ayça and I have spent so much time with you. I often think of that time you first met your stepmother, squabbling with your sister Melike at the top of a ladder while Sibel cried at the bottom. I remember your friendships with other girls and women throughout your life, almost like you told me about them yourself over a glass of tea. Or all the ups and downs with Fuat – how funny that he's now brewing alcohol he can't drink himself.

You don't know me at all but I know you so well, and I remember things from your years in Germany, people and places that seem familiar from my own life here, though you and I have little in common on the surface. The Cans of this world, small-time crooks made good but still sporting that swagger; the greying Yılmazes playing the saz on summer street corners; second-generation daughters proud of what they've achieved. Or the department-store cafeterias unchanged for decades, white coffee cups clattering on saucers; trams and buses and trains full of oblivious strangers, perfect for eavesdropping and people-watching. The unadorned cafés full of smoke and Turkish men, which both of us only know from the outside.

And you introduced me to Turkey, a place I've never been. For me, that was an added bonus. I don't read novels as travel literature; what interests me first and foremost about your life is you, not where it takes place. Still, I'm convinced your story has given me more insight than a short visit ever could. What joy – and sorrow – to know about the cold nights when the water jug froze over, the orchards and streams, the ball games on the street, the rude man running the supermarket, the wedding receptions and school reunions, the fridges with an extra drawer for breakfast bowls.

I'm so glad we don't see you die in this book. That way, like all fictional characters, you will live on in my mind, and I hope in many others.

Thank you for everything,

Katy

Dear Gül,

I saw you at the airport the other day. Fuat was behind you, dragging a little suitcase he'd clearly refused to put in the hold. You've got to be smart, after all. How's the rakı-making business, by the way? I bet it's going from strength to strength, knowing him. Anyway, he looked well. I hope you are too. I hope your hips aren't causing you trouble. Perhaps the two of you were heading to your house by the sea. The summer's come to an end now and I can't bear the thought of the darker months. How did you cope with all those long German winters?

Last month, I went back to Turkey after five long years. On the journey from the airport in the dark, I kept saying to myself: I can't believe we're here, I just can't believe we're here. It was the longest I had ever been away, but the more I thought about it, the more I felt like I must have visited more recently, like I'd been there all along. For three summers, translating your story kept Turkey alive in my mind.

I thought of you again while I was there, sitting under a walnut tree in my auntie's garden. Later, we sat out in the street and drank tea and I thought of you when you were little, those long summer evenings you spent listening to the radio strapped to the roof. At dusk, we walked to the graveyard on the edge of town, but I wasn't scared, because I remembered what your dad said once, that they're the safest of places. No one else is brave enough to venture into a graveyard at night.

I hope I will see you again one day. Maybe if I find myself in the South one summer, I could drop by your flat for tea. I'll make my way up the terrazzo steps with you peering down, your words of welcome echoing in the stairwell. When I get to your door, I'll clumsily try to kiss your hand (you're older than my mum now, after all), but you'll probably laugh and pull me into a hug before I've had a chance to slip off my shoes. Inside, the TV will be on, the aircon will be running, and we'll have tea and kurabiye, maybe börek, maybe fruit. We'll talk and talk and talk, about our lives, about memories from your childhood, and I'll feel that sense of connection that you understand so well. I often think about something you said – or thought – once. You said that when a person can't share things, it makes them lonely. How true. Translating your story over the past three years has reminded me that many of us share the longing that you've felt.

Once evening arrives at your place, I'm sure you'll hurry off to the kitchen and bring out the zeytinyağlı dishes, perhaps some sarma, yoghurt, bread, salad, makarna, and a few dolma just to be on the safe side. Fuat will turn up while we're eating and insist I try his homemade rakı. I'll decide to take my life in my hands – just this once – and give it a try, and he'll reward me with a hearty clap on the back and a resounding 'Bravo!' At least someone's enjoying it, he'll say.

I'm not sure how to end this letter, so I'll just say thank you for everything. Look after yourself, and say hello to your girls from me.

All my love,

Ayça

THE JOY OF SLEEPING ALONE

"A transformative book for women who want to challenge traditional beliefs about nighttime solitude. Cynthia combines scientific, psychological, and spiritual evidence in an enriching guide to transform the act of sleeping alone into an experience of self-discovery and personal well-being. This book will help you find a sacred space for inner growth and connection with your essence."

MARIAM DUM, PH.D., CLINICAL PSYCHOLOGIST,
MENTOR OF THE SELF, AND AUTHOR OF 2050: Yo sí existo

"This book, small on the outside but with immense wisdom on the inside, came into my hands and each night thereafter became an altar. I lit candles, I breathed deeply, I talked to myself quietly. I finally understood: sleeping alone is not emptiness; it is a reunion. Cynthia Zak does not write; she sings. Her voice is a prayer that slips between petals, stars, and warm sheets."

DAHYANA BARRIOS DA CRUZ,
BOOK INFLUENCER @DOPPELBOOKS

"I belong to that ninety percent of women who say they sleep better alone. Yet I never imagined that the bed, the pillow, the silence, the night, and sleep would be so much mine. Thank you, Cynthia, for giving us back this right. I am ecstatic. This is the beauty of research and information—a valuable book with insights that awaken so many dialogues. A beautiful text."

CLAUDIA FRANCO, SEMIOLOGIST, COAUTHOR OF ReCreyendo,
LECTURER, AND WORKSHOP FACILITATOR